By the same author

The Trials of Tiffany Trott
The Making of Minty Malone
Out of the Blue
Rescuing Rose
Behaving Badly
A Question of Love
Forget Me Not

ISABEL WOLFF

A Vintage Affair

Harper Weekend

Published by Harper Weekend, an imprint of
HarperCollins Publishers Ltd

First published in Canada by HarperCollins Publishers Ltd in an original
trade paperback edition: 2009
This Harper Weekend trade paperback edition: 2010

HarperCollins books may be purchased for educational, business,
or sales promotional use through our Special Markets Department.

HarperCollins Publishers Ltd
2 Bloor Street East, 20th Floor
Toronto, Ontario, Canada
M4W 1A8

www.harpercollins.ca

Library and Archives Canada Cataloguing in Publication

Wolff, Isabel
A vintage affair / Isabel Wolff.

ISBN 978-1-55468-765-7

I. Title.
PR6073.O54V55 2010   823'.914   C2010-900430-2

Printed in the United States of America
RRD 9 8 7 6 5 4 3 2

In memory of my father

What a strange power there is in clothing.

Isaac Bashevis Singer

PROLOGUE

Blackheath, 1983

'. . . se*ven*-teen, *eight*-een, *nine*-teen . . . *twenty!* Com-ing!' I yell. 'Ready or *not* . . .' I uncover my eyes and begin the search. I start downstairs, half expecting to find Emma huddled behind the sofa in the sitting room or wrapped, like a sweet, in the crimson curtains, or crouched under the baby grand. I already think of her as my best friend although we've only known each other six weeks. 'You have a new classmate,' Miss Grey had announced on the first day of term. She'd smiled at the girl in the too-stiff blazer standing next to her. 'Her name is Emma Kitts and her family have recently moved to London from South Africa.' Then Miss Grey had led the newcomer to the desk next to mine. The girl was short for nine, and slightly plump with large green eyes, a scattering of freckles, and an uneven fringe above shiny brown plaits. 'Will you look after Emma, Phoebe?' Miss Grey had asked. I'd nodded. Emma had flashed me a grateful smile . . .

1

Now I cross the hall into the dining room and peer under the scratched mahogany table but Emma's not there; nor is she in the kitchen with its old-fashioned dresser with its shelves of mismatched blue-and-white plates. I would have asked her mother which way she'd gone but Mrs Kitts has just 'popped to play tennis' leaving Emma and me on our own.

I walk into the big, cool larder and slide open a low cupboard that looks promisingly large but contains only some old Thermos flasks; then I go down the step into the utility room where the washing machine spasms in its final spin. I even lift the lid of the freezer in case Emma is lying amongst the frozen peas and ice cream. Now I return to the hall, which is oak-panelled and warm, smelling of dust and beeswax. To one side is a huge, ornately carved chair – a throne from Swaziland Emma had said – the wood so dark that it's black. I sit on it for a moment, wondering where precisely Swaziland is, and whether it has anything to do with Switzerland. Then my eyes stray to the hats on the wall opposite; a dozen or so, each hanging from a curving brass peg. There's an African head-dress in a pink and blue fabric and a Cossack hat that could be made of real fur; there's a Panama, a trilby, a turban, a top hat, a riding hat, a cap, a fez, two battered boaters and an emerald green tweed hat with a pheasant feather stuck through it.

I climb the staircase with its wide, shallow treads. At the top is a square landing with four doors leading off it. Emma's bedroom is the first on the left. I turn the handle then hover in the doorway to see if I can hear stifled giggles or tell-tale breathing: I hear nothing, but then Emma's good at holding her breath – she can swim a width underwater. I flip back her shiny blue eiderdown, but she's not in the bed – or under it; all I can see there is her secret box in which I know she keeps her lucky Krugerrand and her diary. I open the big white-painted corner cupboard with its safari stencils, but she's not in there either. Perhaps she's in the room next door. As I enter it I realise, with an uncomfortable feeling, that this is her parents' room. I look for Emma under the wrought-iron bed and behind the dressing table, the mirror of which is cracked in one corner; then I open the wardrobe and catch a scent of orange peel and cloves which makes me think of Christmas. As I stare at Mrs Kitts' brightly printed summer dresses, imagining them under the African sun, I suddenly realise that I am not so much seeking as snooping. I retreat, feeling a vague sense of shame. And now I want to stop playing hide and seek. I want to play rummy, or just watch TV.

'*Bet you can't find me, Phoebe! You'll never, ever find me!*'

Sighing, I cross the landing into the bathroom where I check behind the thick white plastic shower curtain and lift the lid of the laundry basket, which contains nothing but a faded-looking purple towel. Now I go to the window, and lift the semi-closed slats of the Venetian blind. As I peer down into the sun-filled garden a tiny jolt runs the length of my spine. *There's* Emma – behind the huge plane tree at the end of the lawn. She thinks I can't see her, but I can because she's crouching down and one of her feet is sticking out. I dash down the stairs, through the kitchen and into the utility room, then I fling open the back door.

'Found you!' I shout as I run towards the tree. '*Found*

3

you,' I repeat happily, surprised by my euphoria. 'Okay,' I pant, 'my turn to hide. Emma?' I peer at her. She's not crouching down, but lying down, on her left side, perfectly still, eyes closed. 'Get up will you, Em?' She doesn't reply. And now I notice that one leg is folded beneath her at an awkward angle. With a sudden 'thud' in my ribcage I understand. Emma wasn't hiding behind the tree, but *in* it. I glance up through its branches, glimpsing shreds of blue through the green. She was hiding in the tree, but then she fell.

'Em . . .' I murmur, stooping to touch her shoulder. I gently shake her but she doesn't respond, and now I notice that her mouth is slightly agape, a thread of saliva glistening on her lower lip. 'Emma!' I shout. 'Wake *up!*' But she doesn't. I put my hand to her ribs but can't feel them rise and fall. '*Say* something,' I murmur, my heart pounding now. '*Please,* Emma!' I try to lift her up, but I can't. I clap my hands by her ears. '*Emma!*' My throat is aching and tears prick my eyes. I glance back at the house, desperate for Emma's mother to come running over the grass, ready to make everything all right; but Mrs Kitts is still not back from her tennis, which makes me feel angry because we're too young to have been left on our own. Resentment at Mrs Kitts gives way to terror at the thought of what she's likely to say – that Emma's accident was *my* fault because it was my suggestion that we play hide and seek. From inside my head I hear Miss Grey asking me to 'look after' Emma, then her disappointed tut-tutting.

'Wake *up*, Em,' I implore her. '*Please.*' But she just lies there looking . . . crumpled, like a flung-down rag doll. I know I have to run and get help. But first I must

4

cover her as it's turning chilly. I pull off my cardigan and lay it across Emma's upper body, quickly smoothing it over her chest and tucking it under her shoulders.

'I'll be back soon. Don't worry.' I try not to cry.

Suddenly Emma sits bolt upright, grinning like a lunatic, her eyes popping with mischievous delight.

'*Fooled* you!' she sings, clapping her hands together then throwing back her head in glee. 'I *really* fooled you there, didn't I?' she cries as she pushes herself to her feet. 'You were worried, weren't you, Phoebes? Admit it! You thought I was *dead*! I held my breath for *ages*,' she gasps as she brushes down her skirt. 'I'm *right* out of puff . . .' She blows out her cheeks and her fringe lifts a little in the gust, then she smiles at me. 'Okay, Heebee-Phoebee – your turn.' She holds out my cardigan. 'I'll start counting – up to twenty-five, if you like. Here, Phoebes – take your cardi, will you.' Emma stares at me. 'What's up?'

My fists are balled by my sides. My face feels hot. 'Don't *ever* do that again!'

Emma blinks with surprise. 'It was only a joke.'

'It was a *horrible* one!' Tears start from my eyes.

'I'm . . . sorry.'

'Don't *ever* do that again! If you do, I won't talk to you any more – not ever!'

'It was only a *game*,' she protests. 'You don't have to be all . . .' she throws up her hands, 'silly . . . about it. I was only . . . playing.' She shrugs. 'But . . . I won't do it again – if it upsets you. Honestly.'

I snatch my cardigan. 'Promise.' I glare at her. 'You've got to promise.'

'Ok-ay,' she murmurs, then she takes a deep breath.

5

'I, Emma Mandisa Kitts, promise that I won't play that trick on you, Phoebe Jane Swift, ever again. I *promise*,' she repeats then she makes an extravagant slashing gesture. '*Cross* my heart.' Then, with this funny little smile that I have remembered all these years, she adds, 'and hope . . . to . . . *die*!'

ONE

September is at least a good time for a new start, I reflected as I left the house early this morning. I've always felt a greater sense of renewal at the beginning of September than I ever have in January. Perhaps, I thought as I crossed Tranquil Vale, it's because September so often feels fresh and clear after the dankness of August. Or perhaps, I wondered as I passed Blackheath Books, its windows emblazoned with 'Back to School' promotions, it's simply the association with the new academic year.

As I walked up the hill towards the Heath, the freshly painted fascia of Village Vintage came into view and I allowed myself a brief burst of optimism. I unlocked the door, picked the mail off the mat, and began preparing the shop for its official launch.

I worked non-stop until four, selecting the clothes from the stockroom upstairs and putting them out on the rails. As I draped a 1920s tea dress over my arm I ran my hand over its heavy silk satin then fingered its intricate beading and its perfect hand-stitching. This, I told myself, is what I love about vintage clothes. I love their beautiful fabric and their fine finish. I love knowing that so much skill and artistry have gone into their making.

I glanced at my watch. Only two hours to go until the party. I remembered that I'd forgotten to chill the champagne. As I dashed into the little kitchen and ripped open the cases I wondered how many people would come. I'd invited a hundred so I'd need at least seventy glasses at the ready. I stacked the bottles in the fridge, turned it up to 'Frost' then made myself a quick cup of tea. As I sipped my Earl Grey I looked around the shop, allowing myself to savour for a moment the transition from pipe dream to reality.

The interior of Village Vintage looked modern and light. I'd had the wooden floors stripped and limed, the walls painted a dove grey and hung with large silver-framed mirrors; there were glossy pot plants on chrome stands, a spangling of down-lighters on the white-painted ceiling and, next to the fitting room, a large cream-uphol-stered Bergère sofa. Through the windows Blackheath stretched into the far distance, the sky a giddying vault of blue patched with towering white clouds. Beyond the church, two yellow kites danced in the breeze while on the horizon the glass towers of Canary Wharf glinted and flashed in the late afternoon sunlight.

I suddenly realised that the journalist who was supposed to be interviewing me was over an hour late. I didn't even know which paper he was from. All I could remember from yesterday's brief phone conversation with him was that his name was Dan and that he'd said he'd be here at 3.30. My irritation turned to panic that he might not come at all – I needed the publicity. My insides lurched at the thought of my huge loan. As I tied the price tag on an embroidered evening bag I remembered trying to convince the bank that their cash would be safe.

'So you were at Sotheby's?' the lending manager had said as she went through my business plan in a small office every square inch of which, including the ceiling and even the back of the door, seemed to be covered in thick, grey baize.

'I worked in the textiles department,' I'd explained, 'evaluating vintage clothes and conducting auctions.'

'So you must know a lot about it.'

'I do.'

She scribbled something on the form, the nib of her pen squeaking across the glossy paper. 'But it's not as though you've ever worked in retail, is it?'

'No,' I said, my heart sinking. 'That's true. But I've found attractive, accessible premises in a pleasant, busy area where there are no other vintage dress shops.' I handed her the estate agent's brochure for Montpelier Vale.

'It's a nice site,' she said as she studied it. My spirits rose. 'And being on the corner gives it good visibility.' I imagined the windows aglow with glorious dresses. 'But the lease is expensive.' The woman put the brochure down on the grey tabletop and looked at me grimly. 'What makes you think you'll be able to generate enough sales to cover your overheads, let alone make a profit?'

'Because . . .' I suppressed a frustrated sigh. 'I know

that the demand is there. Vintage has now become so fashionable that it's almost mainstream. These days you can even buy vintage clothing in High Street stores like Miss Selfridge and Top Shop.'

There was silence while she scribbled again. 'I know you can.' She looked up again but this time she was smiling. 'I got the most wonderful Biba fake fur in Jigsaw the other day – mint condition and original buttons.' She pushed the form towards me then passed me her pen. 'Could you sign at the bottom there, please?' . . .

Now I arranged the evening gowns on the formal-wear rail and put out the bags, belts and shoes. I positioned the gloves in their basket, the costume jewellery in its velvet trays, then, on a corner shelf, high up, I carefully placed the hat that Emma had given me for my thirtieth birthday.

I stepped back and gazed at the extraordinary sculpture of bronze straw; its crown seeming to sweep upwards into infinity.

'I miss you, Em,' I murmured. 'Wherever you are now . . .' I felt the familiar piercing sensation, as though there was a skewer in my heart.

There was a sharp rapping sound from behind me. On the other side of the glass door was a man of about my age, maybe a little younger. He was tall and well built with large grey eyes and a mop of dark blond curls. He reminded me of someone famous, but I couldn't think who.

'Dan Robinson,' he said with a broad smile as I let him in. 'Sorry to be a bit late.' I resisted the urge to tell him that he was *very* late. He took a notebook out of his battered-looking bag. 'My previous interview overran, then I got caught in traffic, but this should only take twenty minutes or so.' He shovelled his hand into the pocket of his crumpled linen jacket and produced a pencil. 'I just need to get down the basic facts about the business and a bit about your background.' He glanced at the hydra of silk scarves spilling over the counter and the half-dressed mannequin. 'But you're obviously busy, so if you haven't got time I'd quite –'

'Oh, I've got time,' I interrupted. 'Really – as long as you don't mind me working while we chat.' I slipped a sea green chiffon cocktail dress on to its velvet hanger. 'Which paper did you say you were from?' Out of the corner of my eye I registered the fact that his mauve striped shirt didn't go with the sage of his chinos.

'It's a new twice-weekly free-sheet called the *Black & Green* – the *Blackheath and Greenwich Express*. The paper's only been going a couple of months, so we're building our circulation.'

'I'm grateful for any coverage,' I said as I put the dress at the front of the daywear rail.

'The piece should go in on Friday.' Dan glanced round the shop. 'The interior's nice and bright. You wouldn't think it was old stuff that was being sold here – I mean, vintage,' he corrected himself.

'Thank you,' I said wryly, though I was grateful for his observation.

As I quickly scissored the cellophane off some white agapanthus, Dan peered out of the window. 'It's a great location.'

I nodded. 'I love being able to look out over the

11

Heath, plus the shop's very visible from the road so I hope to get passing trade as well as dedicated vintage buyers.'

'That's how I found you,' said Dan as I put the flowers in a tall glass vase. 'I was walking past yesterday and saw you' – he reached into the pocket of his trousers and took out a pencil sharpener – 'were about to open, and I thought it would make a good feature for Friday's paper.' As he sat on the sofa I noticed that he was wearing odd socks – one green and one brown. 'Not that fashion's really my thing.'

'Isn't it?' I said politely as he gave the pencil a few vigorous turns. 'Don't you use a tape-recorder?' I couldn't help asking.

He inspected the newly pointed tip then blew on it. 'I prefer speed writing. Right then.' He pocketed the sharpener. 'Let's start. So . . .' He bounced the pencil against his lower lip. 'What should I ask you first . . .?' I tried not to show my dismay at his lack of preparation. 'I know,' he said. 'Are you local?'

'Yes.' I folded a pale blue cashmere cardigan. 'I grew up in Eliot Hill, closer to Greenwich, but for the past five years I've been living in the centre of Blackheath, near the station.' I thought of my railwayman's cottage with its tiny front garden.

'Station,' Dan repeated slowly. 'Next question . . .' This interview was going to take ages – it was the last thing I needed. 'Do you have a fashion background?' he asked. 'Won't the readers want to know that?'

'Er . . . possibly.' I told him about my History of Fashion degree at St Martin's and my career at Sotheby's.

'So how long were you at Sotheby's?'

12

'Twelve years.' I folded an Yves St Laurent silk scarf and laid it in a tray. 'In fact I'd recently been made head of the costumes and textiles department. But then . . . I decided to leave.'

Dan looked up. 'Even though you'd just been promoted?'

'Yes . . .' My heart turned over. I'd said too much. 'I'd been there almost from the day I'd graduated, you see, and I needed . . .' I glanced out of the window, trying to quell the surge of emotion that was breaking over me. 'I felt I needed . . .'

'A career break?' Dan suggested.

'A . . . change. So I went on a sort of sabbatical in early March.' I draped a string of Chanel paste pearls round the neck of a silver mannequin. 'They said they'd keep my job open until June, but in early May I saw that the lease here had come up for sale, so I decided to take the plunge and sell vintage myself. I'd been toying with the idea for some time,' I added.

'Some . . . time,' Dan repeated quietly. This was hardly 'speed writing'. I stole a glance at his odd squiggles and abbreviations. 'Next question . . .' He chewed the end of his pencil. The man was useless. 'I know: Where do you find the stock?' He looked at me. 'Or is that a trade secret?'

'Not really.' I fastened the hooks on a *café au lait*-coloured silk blouse by Georges Rech. 'I bought quite a bit from some of the smaller auction houses outside London, as well as from specialist dealers and private individuals who I already knew through Sotheby's. I also got things at vintage fairs, on eBay, and I made two or three trips to France.'

13

'Why France?'

'You can find lovely vintage garments in provincial markets there – like these embroidered nightdresses.' I held one up. 'I bought them in Avignon. They weren't too expensive because French women are less keen on vintage than we are in this country.'

'Vintage clothing's become rather desirable here, hasn't it?'

'Very desirable.' I quickly fanned some 1950s copies of *Vogue* on to the glass table by the sofa. 'Women want individuality, not mass production, and that's what vintage gives them. Wearing vintage suggests originality and flair. I mean, a woman can buy an evening dress in the High Street for £200,' I went on, warming to the interview now, 'and the next day it's worth almost nothing. But for the same money she could have bought something made of gorgeous fabric, that no one else would have been wearing and that will, if she doesn't wreck it, actually *increase* in value. Like this –' I pulled out a Hardy Amies petrol blue silk taffeta dinner gown, from 1957.

'It's lovely,' said Dan, looking at its halter neck, slim bodice and gored skirt. 'You'd think it was new.'

'Everything I sell is in perfect condition.'

'Condition . . .' he muttered as he scribbled again.

'Every garment is washed or dry-cleaned,' I went on as I returned the dress to the rail. 'I have a wonderful seamstress who does the big repairs and alterations; the smaller ones I can do here myself – I have a little "den" at the back with a sewing machine.'

'And what do the things sell for?'

'They range from £15 for a hand-rolled silk scarf, to

£75 for a cotton day dress, to £200–300 for an evening dress and up to £1,500 for a couture piece.' I pulled out a Pierre Balmain beaded gold faille evening gown from the early 1960s, embroidered with bugle beads and silver sequins. I lifted its protective cover. 'This is an important dress, made by a major designer at the height of his career. Or there's this –' I took out a pair of silk velvet palazzo pants in a psychedelic pattern of sherbety pinks and greens. 'This outfit's by Emilio Pucci. It'll almost certainly be bought as an investment piece rather than to wear, because Pucci, like Ossie Clark, Biba and Jean Muir, is very collectable.'

'Marilyn Monroe loved Pucci,' Dan said. 'She was buried in her favourite green silk Pucci dress.' I nodded, not liking to admit that I hadn't known that. 'Those are fun.' Dan was nodding at the wall behind me hanging on which, like paintings, were four strapless, ballerina-length evening dresses – one lemon yellow, one candy pink, one turquoise and one lime – each with a satin bodice beneath which foamed a mass of net petticoats, sparkling with crystals.

'I've hung those there because I love them,' I explained. 'They're fifties prom dresses, but I call them "cupcake" dresses because they're so glamorous and frothy. Just looking at them makes me feel happy.' Or as happy as I can be now, I thought bleakly.

Dan stood up. 'And what's that you're putting out there?'

'This is a Vivienne Westwood bustle skirt.' I held it up for him. 'And this –' I pulled out a terracotta silk kaftan, 'is by Thea Porter, and this little suede shift is by Mary Quant.'

'What about this?' Dan had pulled out an oyster pink satin evening dress with a cowl neckline, fine pleating at the sides, and a sweeping fishtail hem. 'It's wonderful – it's like something Katharine Hepburn would have worn, or Greta Garbo – or Veronica Lake,' he added thoughtfully, 'in *The Glass Key*.'

'Oh. I don't know that film.'

'It's very underrated – it was written by Dashiell Hammett in 1942. Howard Hawks borrowed from it for *The Big Sleep*.'

'Did he?'

'But you know what . . .' He held the dress against me in a way that took me aback. 'It would suit you.' He looked at me appraisingly. 'You have that sort of film noir languor.'

'Do I?' Again, he'd taken me aback. 'Actually . . . this dress *was* mine.'

'Really? Don't you want it?' Dan asked almost indignantly. 'It's rather beautiful.'

'It is, but . . . I just . . . went off it.' I returned it to the rail. I didn't have to tell him the truth. That Guy had given it to me just under a year ago. We'd been seeing each other for a month and he'd taken me to Bath one weekend. I'd spotted the dress in a shop window and had gone in to look at it, mostly out of professional interest as it was £500. But later, while I'd been reading in the hotel room, Guy had slipped out and returned with the dress, gift-wrapped in pink tissue. Now I'd decided to sell it because it belonged to a part of my life that I was desperate to forget. I'd give the money to charity.

'And what, for you, is the main appeal of vintage

16

clothing?' I heard Dan ask as I rearranged the shoes inside the illuminated glass cubes that lined the left-hand wall. 'Is it that the things are such good quality compared to clothes made today?'

'That's a big part of it,' I replied as I placed one 1960s green suede pump at an elegant angle to its partner. 'Wearing vintage is a kick against mass production. But the thing I love most about vintage clothes . . .' I looked at him. 'Don't laugh, will you.'

'Of course not . . .'

I stroked the gossamer chiffon of a 1950s *peignoir*. 'What I really love about them . . . is the fact that they contain someone's personal history.' I ran the marabou trim across the back of my hand. 'I find myself wondering about the women who wore them.'

'Really?'

'I find myself wondering about their lives. I can never look at a garment – like this suit . . .' I went over to the daywear rail and pulled out a 1940s fitted jacket and skirt in a dark blue tweed '. . . without thinking about the woman who owned it. How old was she? Did she work? Was she married? Was she happy?' Dan shrugged. 'The suit has a British label from the early forties,' I went on, 'so I wonder what happened to this woman during the war. Did her husband survive? Did she survive?'

I went over to the shoe display and took out a pair of 1930s silk brocade slippers, embroidered with yellow roses. 'I look at these exquisite shoes, and I imagine the woman who owned them rising out of them and walking along, or dancing in them, or kissing someone.' I went over to a pink velvet pillbox hat on its stand.

'I look at a little hat like this,' I lifted up the veil, 'and I try to imagine the face beneath it. Because when you buy a piece of vintage clothing you're not just buying fabric and thread – you're buying a piece of someone's *past*.'

Dan nodded. 'Which you're bringing into the present.'

'Exactly – I'm giving these clothes a new lease of life. And I love the fact that I'm able to restore them,' I went on. 'Where there are so many things in life that can't be restored.' I felt the sudden, familiar pit in my stomach.

'I'd never have thought of vintage clothes like that,' said Dan after a moment. 'I love your passion for what you do.' He peered at his notepad. 'You've given me some great quotes.'

'Good,' I replied quietly. 'I've enjoyed talking to you.' After a hopeless start, I was tempted to add.

Dan smiled. 'Well . . . I'd better let you get on – and I ought to go and write this up, but . . .' His voice trailed away as his eyes strayed to the corner shelf. 'What an amazing hat. What period's that from?'

'It's contemporary. It was made four years ago.'

'It's very original.'

'Yes – it's one of a kind.'

'How much is it?'

'It's not for sale. It was given to me by the designer – a close friend of mine. I just wanted to have it here because . . .' I felt a constriction in my throat.

'Because it's beautiful?' Dan suggested. I nodded. He flipped shut his notebook. 'And will she be coming to the launch?'

I shook my head. 'No.'

'One last thing,' he said, taking a camera out of his bag. 'My editor asked me to get a photo of you to go with the piece.'

I glanced at my watch. 'As long as it won't take long. I've still got to tie balloons to the front, I have to change – and I haven't poured the champagne: that's going to take time and people will be arriving in twenty minutes.'

'Let me do that,' I heard Dan say. 'To make up for being late.' He tucked his pencil behind his ear. 'Where are the glasses?'

'Oh. There are three boxes of them behind the counter, and there are twelve bottles of champagne in the fridge in the little kitchen there. Thanks,' I added, anxiously wondering if Dan would manage to spill it everywhere; but he deftly filled the flutes with the Veuve Clicquot – vintage, of course, because it had to be – while I washed and changed into my outfit, a thirties dove grey satin cocktail dress with silver Ferragamo sling-backs; then I put on a little make-up and ran a brush through my hair. Finally I untied the cluster of pale gold helium balloons which floated from the back of a chair and attached them in twos and threes to the front of the shop where they jerked and bobbed in the stiffening breeze. Then as the church clock struck six I stood in the doorway, with a glass in my hand, while Dan took his photos.

After a minute he lowered the camera and looked at me, clearly puzzled.

'Sorry, Phoebe – could you manage a smile?'

*　　*　　*

19

My mother arrived just as Dan was leaving.

'Who was that?' she asked as she headed straight for the fitting room.

'A journalist called Dan,' I replied. 'He's just interviewed me for a local paper. He's a bit chaotic.'

'He looked rather nice,' she said as she stood in front of the mirror scrutinising her appearance. 'He was hideously dressed, but I like curly hair on a man. It's unusual.' Her reflected face looked at me with anxious disappointment. 'I *wish* you could find someone again, Phoebe – I hate you being on your own. Being on your own is no fun. As I can testify,' she added bitterly.

'I rather enjoy it. I intend to be on my own for a long time, quite possibly forever.'

Mum snapped open her bag. 'That's very likely to be my fate, darling, but I don't want it to be yours.' She took out one of her expensive new lipsticks. It resembled a gold bullet. 'I know you've had a hard year, darling.'

'Yes,' I murmured.

'And I know' – she glanced at Emma's hat – 'that you've been . . . suffering.' My mother could have no idea quite how much. 'But,' she said as she twisted up the colour, 'I still don't understand' – I knew what was coming – '*why* you had to end things with Guy. I know I only met him three times, but I thought he was charming, handsome and nice.'

'He was all those things,' I agreed. 'He was lovely. In fact, he was perfect.'

In the mirror Mum's eyes met mine. 'Then what *happened* between you?'

'Nothing,' I lied. 'My feelings just . . . changed. I told you that.'

'Yes. But you've never said *why*.' Mum drew the colour – a slightly garish coral – across her upper lip. 'The whole thing seemed quite perverse, if you don't mind my saying so. Of course, you were very unhappy at the time.' She lowered her voice. 'But then what happened to Emma . . .' I closed my eyes to try and shut out the images that will haunt me forever. 'Well . . . it was terrible,' she sighed. 'I don't know how she could *do* that . . . And to think what she had going for her . . . so *much*.'

'So much,' I echoed bitterly.

Mum blotted her lower lip with a tissue. 'But what I don't understand is why it *then* followed, sad though you were, that you had to end what appeared to be a happy relationship with a *very* nice man. *I* think you had a sort of nervous breakdown,' she went on. 'It wouldn't be surprising . . .' She smacked her lips together. 'I don't think you knew what you were doing.'

'I knew exactly,' I retorted calmly. 'But you know what, Mum, I don't want to talk ab—'

'How did you meet him?' she suddenly asked. 'You never told me that.'

I felt my face heat up. 'Through Emma.'

'Really?' Mum looked at me. 'How typically sweet of her,' she said as she turned back to the mirror. 'Introducing you to a nice man like that.'

'Yes,' I said uneasily . . .

'I've met someone,' Emma had said excitedly over the phone a year ago. 'My head's in a spin, Phoebe. He's

21

. . . wonderful.' My heart had sunk, not just because Emma was always saying that she'd met someone 'wonderful', but because these men were usually anything but. Emma would be in raptures about them, then a month later she'd be avoiding them, saying they were 'dreadful'. 'I met him at a fund-raising do,' she'd explained. 'He runs an investment fund – but the *good* thing,' she'd added with her usual, endearing artlessness, 'is that it's an ethical one.'

'That sounds interesting. So he must be clever then.'

'He got a first from the LSE. Not that *he* told me that,' she added quickly. 'I got it from Google. We've been on a few dates, but things are moving on so I'd like you to check him out.'

'Emma,' I sighed. 'You are thirty-three years old. You are becoming *very* successful. You now dress the heads of some of the most famous women in the UK. Why do you need *my* approval?'

'Well . . .' I heard her clicking her tongue. 'Because I guess old habits die hard. I've always asked your opinion about men, haven't I?' she mused. 'Right from when we were teenagers.'

'Yes – but we're not teenagers now. You've got to have confidence in your *own* judgement, Em.'

'I hear what you say. But I still want you to meet Guy. I'll have a little dinner party next week and sit you next to him, okay?'

'Okay,' I sighed . . .

I wish I didn't have to be involved, I thought as I helped Emma in the kitchen of her rented house in Marylebone the following Thursday evening. From the sitting room came the sound of nine people laughing and talking. Emma's idea of a 'little' dinner party was a five-course meal for twelve. As I got down the plates I thought of the men Emma had been 'madly in love with' over the past couple of years: Arnie the fashion photographer who'd two-timed her with a hand-model; Finian the garden designer who spent every weekend with his six-year-old daughter – and her mum. Then there'd been Julian, a bespectacled stockbroker with an interest in philosophy but precious little else. Emma's latest attachment had been to Peter, a violinist with the London Philharmonic. That had looked promising – he was very nice and she could talk to him about music; but then he'd gone on a three-month world tour with the orchestra and had come back engaged to the second flute.

Maybe this chap Guy would be a better bet, I thought as I rummaged in a drawer for Emma's napkins.

'Guy is *perfect*,' she said as she opened the oven, releasing a burst of steam and an aroma of roasting lamb. 'He's the one, Phoebe,' she said happily.

'That's what you always say.' I began folding the napkins.

'Well, *this* time it's true. I'm going to kill myself if it doesn't work out,' she added gaily.

I stopped mid-fold. 'Don't be so *silly*, Em. It's not even as though you've known him that long.'

'True – though I know what I feel. But he's *late*,' she wailed as she took the lamb out to rest it. She thumped the Le Creuset meat dish down on to the table, her face a mask of anxiety. 'Do you think he's going to turn up?'

23

'Of course he is,' I said. 'It's only eight forty-five – he's probably just been held up at work.'

Emma kicked shut the oven door. 'Then why didn't he phone?'

'Maybe he's stuck on the tube . . .' Anxiety contorted her features again. 'Em – don't *worry* . . .'

She began basting the meat. 'I can't help it. I'd love to be calm and collected like you usually are, but I've never had your poise.' She straightened up. 'How do I look?'

'Beautiful.'

She smiled with relief. 'Thanks – not that I believe you, as you always say that.'

'Because it's always true,' I said firmly.

Emma was dressed in her characteristically eclectic way, in a Betsey Johnson floral silk dress, with canary yellow fishnets and black ankle boots. Her wavy auburn hair was held off her face by a silver band.

'And does this dress *definitely* suit me?' she asked.

'Definitely. I like the sweetheart neckline, and the silhouette's flattering,' I added, then instantly regretted it.

'Are you saying I'm fat?' Emma's face fell. 'Please don't say that, Phoebe – not today of all days. I know I could do with losing a few pounds, but –'

'No, *no* – I didn't mean that. Of course you're not fat, Em, you're lovely, I just meant –'

'Oh God!' She clapped her hand to her mouth. 'I haven't done the blinis!'

'*I'll* do them.' I opened the fridge and got out the smoked salmon and the tub of crème fraîche.

'You're a fabulous friend, Phoebe,' I heard Emma say.

'What would I do without you,' she added as she began sticking bits of rosemary into the lamb. 'Do you know' – she waved a sprig at me – 'we've now known each other for a quarter of a century.'

'Is it that long?' I murmured as I began to chop the smoked salmon.

'It is. And we'll probably know each other for, what, another fifty years?'

'If we drink the right brand of coffee.'

'We'll have to go into the same old people's home!' Emma giggled.

'Where you'll *still* be getting me to check out your boyfriends. "Oh, Phoebe,"' I said in a crotchety voice, '"he's ninety-three – do you think he's a bit old for me?"'

Emma snorted with laughter then chucked the bunch of rosemary at me.

Now I began grilling the blinis, trying not to burn my fingers as I quickly turned them over. Emma's friends were talking so loudly – and someone was playing the piano – that I'd only dimly registered the ring of the door bell, but the sound electrified Emma.

'He's here!' She checked her appearance in a small mirror, adjusting her hair-band; then she ran down the narrow staircase. 'Hi! Oh, thanks,' I heard her squeal. 'They're *gorgeous*. Come on up – you know the way.' I'd registered the fact that Guy had been to the house before – that was a good sign. 'Everyone's here,' I heard Emma say as they came up the stairs. 'Were you stuck on the tube?' By now I'd assembled the first batch of blinis. Then I reached for the peppermill and vigorously turned the top. Nothing. Damn. Where did Em keep the peppercorns? I began to look, opening a couple of cupboards before spotting a new tub of them on top of her spice rack.

'Let me get you a drink, Guy,' I heard Emma say. 'Phoebe.' I had taken the seal off the peppercorns and was trying to prise off the lid, but it was stuck. 'Phoebe,' Emma repeated. I turned round. She was standing in the kitchen, smiling radiantly, clutching a posy of white roses: just behind her, framed in the doorway, was Guy.

I looked at him in dismay. Emma had said that he was 'gorgeous', but it had meant nothing to me as she always said that, even if the man was hideous. But Guy was heart-stoppingly handsome. He was tall and broad shouldered, with an open face and fine, evenly spaced features, dark brown hair that was cut endearingly short and dark blue eyes that had an amused expression in them.

'Phoebe,' Emma said, 'this is Guy.' He smiled at me and I felt a little 'thud' in my ribcage. 'Guy, this is my best friend, Phoebe.'

'Hi!' I said, smiling at him like a lunatic as I wrestled with the peppercorns. *Why* did he have to be so attractive? '*God!*' The lid suddenly came off the peppercorns and they shot out in a black arc then scattered like gunshot across the worktops and floor. 'Sorry, Em,' I breathed. I grabbed a brush and began vigorously sweeping, if only to disguise my turmoil. 'I'm sorry!' I laughed. 'What a twit!'

'It doesn't matter,' Emma said. She quickly put the roses into a jug then grabbed the plate of blinis. 'I'll take these in. Thanks, Phoebes – they look lovely.'

I'd expected Guy to follow her, instead of which he went to the sink, opened the cupboard underneath and got out the dustpan and brush. I registered with a pang the fact that he knew his way round Emma's kitchen.

'Don't worry,' I protested.

'It's okay – let me help you.' Guy hitched up the knees of his City trousers then stooped down and began to sweep up the peppercorns.

'They get everywhere,' I wittered. 'So silly of me.'

'Do you know where pepper comes from?' he suddenly asked.

'No idea,' I replied as I stooped to pick up a few in my fingertips. 'South America?'

'Kerala. Until the fifteenth century, pepper was so valuable that it could be used in lieu of money, hence "peppercorn rent".'

'Really?' I said politely. Then I pondered the weirdness of finding myself crouched on the floor with a man I'd met a minute earlier, discussing the finer points of black pepper.

'Anyway,' Guy straightened up then emptied the dustpan into the pedal bin. 'I guess I'd better go in.'

'Yes . . .' I smiled. 'Emma will be wondering. But . . . thanks.'

The rest of the dinner party passed in a blur. As promised, Emma had put me next to Guy, and I struggled to control my emotions as I politely chatted to him. I kept praying that he'd say something off-putting – that he'd just come out of re-hab, for example, or that he had two ex-wives and five kids. I'd hoped that I'd find his conversation dull, but he only said things that increased

27

his appeal. He talked interestingly about his work, and of his responsibility to invest his clients' money in ways that not only were not injurious, they could even be positive in their effect on the environment and on human health and welfare. He spoke of his association with a charity that was working to end child labour. He talked affectionately about his parents and his brother, whom he played squash with at the Chelsea Harbour Club once a week. Lucky Emma, I thought. Guy seemed to be everything she'd claimed him to be. As the meal progressed she frequently glanced at him or made passing references to him.

'We went to the opening of the Goya exhibition the other night, didn't we, Guy?' Guy nodded. 'And we're trying to get tickets for *Tosca* at the Opera House next week, aren't we?'

'Yes . . . that's right.'

'It's been sold out for months,' she explained, 'but I'm hoping to get returns online.'

Emma's friends were gradually picking up on the connection. 'So how long have you two known each other?' Charlie asked Guy with a sly smile. The words 'you two', which had produced in me a stab of envy, made Emma blush with pleasure.

'Oh, not that long,' Guy replied quietly, his reticence seeming only to confirm his interest in her . . .

'So what did you *think*?' Emma asked me over the phone the morning after her party.

I fiddled with my Rotadex. 'What did I think of what?'

'Of *Guy*, of course! Don't you think he's gorgeous?'

'Oh . . . yes. He is . . . gorgeous.'

'Beautiful blue eyes – especially with his dark hair. It's a devastating combination.'

I glanced out of the window into New Bond Street. 'Devastating.'

'And he's a good conversationalist. Don't you agree?'

I could hear the hum of the traffic. 'I . . . do.'

'Plus he's got such a nice sense of humour.'

'Hmm.'

'He's so nice and *normal* compared to the other men I've dated.'

'That's certainly true.'

'He's a *good* person. Best of all,' she concluded, 'he's keen!'

I couldn't bring myself to tell her that Guy had phoned me an hour earlier to ask me out to dinner.

I hadn't known what to do. Guy had tracked me down easily enough through Sotheby's switchboard. I was elated, then horrified. I'd thanked him but said that I wouldn't be able to come. He'd phoned me another three times just that day but I'd been unable to speak to him as I was frantically preparing for an auction of Twentieth-Century Fashion and Accessories. The fourth time Guy had phoned I'd spoken to him briefly, being careful to lower my voice in the open-plan office. 'You're very persistent, Guy.'

'I am, but that's because I . . . like you, Phoebe, and I think – if I don't flatter myself – that you like me.' I'd tied the lot number to a Pierre Cardin flecked green wool trouser suit from the mid seventies. 'Why don't you say yes?' he pleaded.

'Well . . . because . . . it's a bit tricky, isn't it?'

There was an awkward silence. 'Look, Phoebe . . . Emma and I are just friends.'

'Really?' I inspected what looked suspiciously like a moth-hole on one leg. 'You seem to have seen quite a bit of her.'

'Well . . . that's largely because Emma rings me and gets tickets for things, like the Goya opening. We've hung out together and had a few laughs, but I've *never* given her the impression that I'm . . .' His voice trailed away.

'But it was clear that you'd been to her flat before. You knew *exactly* where she kept her dustpan and brush,' I whispered accusingly.

'Yes – because last week she asked me to mend a leak under her sink and I had to take everything out of the cupboard.'

'Oh.' Relief swept through me. 'I see. But . . .'

Guy emitted a sigh. 'Look, Phoebe, I like Emma – she's very talented and she's fun.'

'Oh, she is – she's lovely.'

'I find her a bit intense, though,' he went on. 'If not slightly bonkers,' he confided with a nervous laugh. 'But she and I aren't . . . *dating*. She can't really think that.' I didn't reply. 'So will you *please* have dinner with me?' I felt my resolve weaken. 'How about next Tuesday?' I heard him say. 'At the Wolseley? I'll book a table for seven thirty. Will you come, Phoebe?'

If I'd had any idea then where it would lead, I'd have said, 'No. I won't. Absolutely not. Never.'

'Yes,' I heard myself say . . .

I considered not telling Emma, but couldn't bring myself to keep it from her, not least because it would be awful if she somehow found out. So I told her on the Saturday when we met at Amici's, our favourite coffee shop in Marylebone High Street.

'Guy's asked you out?' she repeated faintly. Her pupils seemed to retract with disappointment. '*Oh.*' Her hand had trembled as she lowered her cup.

'I haven't . . . encouraged him,' I explained gently. 'I didn't . . . flirt with him at your dinner party, and if you'd rather I didn't go, then I won't, but I couldn't not tell you. Em?' I reached for her hand, noticing how red her fingertips were from all the stitching and gluing and straw-stretching that she did. 'Emma – are you okay?' She stirred her cappuccino then stared out of the window. 'Because I wouldn't see him, even once, if you didn't want me to.'

Emma didn't reply at first. Her large green eyes strayed to a young couple walking hand in hand on the other side of the street. 'It's okay,' she said after a moment. 'After all . . . I hadn't known him that long, as you pointed out – although he *didn't* discourage me from thinking . . .' Her eyes suddenly filled. 'And those roses he brought me. I thought . . .' She pressed a paper napkin to her eyes. It had 'Amici's' printed on it. 'Well,' she croaked. 'It doesn't look as though I'll be going to *Tosca* with him after all. Maybe *you* could take him, Phoebe. He said he was looking forward to it . . .'

I sighed with frustration. 'Look, Em, I'm going to say no. If it's going to make you miserable, then I'm not interested.'

'No,' Emma murmured after a moment. She shook her head. 'You should go – if you like him, which I assume you do, otherwise we'd hardly be having this conversation. Anyway . . .' She picked up her bag. 'I'd

31

better be off. I've got a bonnet to be getting on with – for Princess Eugenie, no less.' She gave me a cheery wave. 'I'll speak to you soon.'

But she didn't return my calls for six weeks . . .

'I wish you'd ring Guy,' I heard Mum say. 'I think you meant a lot to him. In fact, Phoebe, there's something I need to tell you . . .'

I looked at her. 'What?'

'Well . . . Guy phoned me last week.' I felt a falling sensation, as though I were sliding down a steep incline. 'He said he'd like to see you, just to talk to you – now *don't* shake your head, darling. He feels you've been "unfair" – that was the word he used, though he wouldn't say why. But I suspect you *have* been unfair, darling – unfair and, quite frankly, idiotic.' Mum took a comb out of her bag. 'It's not as though it's easy, finding a nice man. I think you're lucky that he still holds a candle for you after the way you threw him over.'

'I want nothing to do with him,' I insisted. 'I just don't . . . feel the same about him.' Guy knew why.

Mum ran the comb through her wavy blonde hair. 'I just hope you won't come to regret it. And I hope you won't also come to regret leaving Sotheby's. I still think it's a shame. You had prestige there, and stability – the excitement of conducting auctions.'

'The stress of it, you mean.'

'You had the company of your colleagues,' she added, ignoring me.

'And now I'll have the company of my customers – and of my part-time assistant, when I can find myself one.' This was something I needed to pursue – there was

32

a fashion auction coming up at Christie's that I wanted to go to.

'You had a regular income,' Mum went on, swapping her comb for a powder compact. 'And now here you are, opening this . . . *shop*.' She managed to make the word sound like 'bordello'. 'What if it doesn't work out? You've borrowed a small fortune, darling . . .'

'Thanks for reminding me.'

She dabbed powder on her nose. 'And it's going to be *such* hard work.'

'Hard work will suit me just fine,' I said evenly. Because then I'd have less time to think.

'Anyway, I've said my piece,' she concluded unctuously. She snapped shut her compact and returned it to her bag.

'And how's work going?'

Mum grimaced. 'Not well. There've been problems with that huge house on Ladbroke Grove – John's going insane, which makes it hard for me.' Mum works as PA to a successful architect, John Cranfield, a job she's been doing for twenty-two years. 'It's not easy,' she said, 'but then I'm very lucky to have a job at my age.' She peered at herself in the mirror. 'Just look at my face,' she moaned.

'It's a lovely face, Mum.'

She sighed. 'More furrows than Gordon Ramsay in a fury. None of those new creams seem to have made the slightest difference.'

I thought of Mum's dressing table. It used to have a single bottle of Oil of Olay on it – now it resembles the unguents counter of a department store with its tubes of Retin A and Vitamin C, its pots of Derma Genesis and Moisture Boost, its pseudo-scientific capsules of

33

slow-release Ceramides and Hyaluronic Acid with Cellular-Nurturing, Epoxy-Restoring this, that and the other.

'Just dreams in a jar, Mum.'

She prodded her cheeks. 'Perhaps a little Botox might help . . . I've been toying with the idea.' She stretched up her brow with the index and middle fingers of her left hand. 'Sod's law, it would go wrong and I'd end up with my eyelids round my nostrils. But I do so loathe all these lines.'

'Then learn to love them. It's normal to have lines when you're fifty-nine.'

Mum flinched, as though I'd slapped her. '*Don't*. I'm dreading getting the bus pass. Why can't they give us a "taxi pass" when we hit sixty? Then I wouldn't mind so much.'

'Anyway, lines don't make beautiful women less beautiful,' I went on as I put a stack of Village Vintage carriers behind the till. 'Just more interesting.'

'Not to your father.' I didn't reply. 'Mind you, I thought he liked old ruins,' Mum added dryly. 'He is an archaeologist, after all. But now here he is with a girl barely older than you are. It's grotesque,' she muttered bitterly.

'It was certainly surprising.'

Mum brushed an imaginary speck off her skirt. 'You didn't invite him tonight? *Did* you?' In her hazel eyes I saw a heart-rending combination of panic and hope.

'No I didn't,' I replied softly. Not least because *she* might have come. I wouldn't have put it past Ruth. Or rather Ruthless.

'Thirty-*six*,' Mum said bitterly, as though it was the 'six' that offended her.

'She must be thirty-eight now,' I pointed out.

'Yes – and he's sixty-two! I wish he'd never *done* that wretched TV series,' she wailed.

I took a forest green Hermès Kelly out of its dust bag and put it in a glass display case. 'You couldn't have known what would happen, Mum.'

'And to think I persuaded him – at *her* behest!' She picked up a glass of champagne and her wedding ring, which she continues to wear in defiance of my father's desertion, gleamed in a beam of sunlight. 'I thought it would help his career,' she went on miserably. She sipped her fizz. 'I thought that it would lift his profile and that he'd make more money which would come in handy in our retirement. Then off he goes to film *The Big Dig* – but the main thing he seems to have been digging' – Mum grimaced – 'was *her*.' She sipped her champagne again. 'It was just . . . ghastly.'

I had to agree. It was one thing for my father to have his first affair in thirty-eight years of marriage; it was quite another for my mother to find out about it in the diary section of the *Daily Express*. I shuddered as I remembered reading the caption beneath the photo of my dad, looking uncharacteristically shifty, with Ruth, outside her Notting Hill flat:

TELLY PROF DUMPS WIFE AMIDST BABY RUMOURS.

'Do you see much of him, darling?' I heard Mum ask with forced casualness. 'Of course, I can't stop you,' she went on. 'And I wouldn't want to – he's your father; but, to be honest, the thought of you spending time with him, and *her* . . . and . . . and . . .' Mum can't bring herself to mention the baby.

'I haven't seen him for ages,' I said truthfully.

Mum knocked back her champagne, then carried the

glass out to the kitchen. 'I'd better not drink any more. It'll only make me cry. Right,' she said briskly as she came back, 'let's change the subject.'

'Okay – tell me what you think of the shop. You haven't seen it for weeks.'

Mum walked round, her elegant little heels tapping over the wooden floor. 'I like it. It's not remotely like being in a second-hand shop – it's more like being somewhere *nice*, like Phase Eight.'

'That's good to hear.' I lined up the flutes of champagne gently fizzing on the counter.

'I like the stylish silver mannequins, and there's a pleasantly uncluttered feel.'

'That's because vintage shops can be chaotic – the rails so crammed that you give yourself an upper-body workout just going through them. Here there's enough light and air between the garments so that browsing will be a pleasure. If an item doesn't sell, I'll simply bring out something else. But aren't the clothes lovely?'

'Ye-es,' Mum replied. 'In a way.' She nodded at the cupcake dresses. 'Those are fun.'

'I know – I adore them.' I idly wondered who would buy them. 'And look at this kimono. It's from 1912. Have you seen the embroidery?'

'Very pretty . . .'

'*Pretty?* It's a work of art. And this Balenciaga opera coat. Look at the cut – it's made in just two pieces, including the sleeves. The construction is amazing.'

'Hmm . . .'

'And this coatdress – it's by Jacques Fath. Look at the brocade with its pattern of little palm trees. Where could you find something like that today?'

'That's all very well, but –'

'And this Givenchy suit: now this would look great on *you*, Mum. You can wear a knee-length skirt because you've got great legs.'

She shook her head. 'I'd never *wear* vintage clothes.'

'Why not?'

She shrugged. 'I've always preferred *new* things.'

'I don't know why.'

'I've told you before, darling – it's because I grew up in the era of *rationing*. I had nothing but hideous hand-me-downs – scratchy Shetland jumpers and grey serge skirts and coarse woollen pinafores that smelled like a damp dog when it rained. I used to long for things that *no one else* had owned, Phoebe. I still do – I can't help it. Added to which I have a distaste for wearing things that other people have worn.'

'But everything's been washed and dry-cleaned. This isn't a charity shop, Mum,' I added as I gave the counter a quick wipe. 'These clothes are in pristine condition.'

'I know. And it all smells delightfully fresh – I detect no mustiness whatsoever.' She sniffed the air. 'Not the faintest whiff of a mothball.'

I plumped up the cushions on the sofa where Dan had been sitting. 'Then what's the problem?'

'It's the thought of wearing something that belonged to someone who's probably . . .' – she gave a little shudder – '*died*. I have a thing about it,' she added. 'I always have had. You and I are different in that way. You're like your father. You both like old things . . . piecing them together. I suppose what you're doing is a kind of archaeology, too,' she went on. 'Sartorial archaeology. Ooh, look, someone's arriving.'

37

I picked up two glasses of champagne, then, with adrenaline coursing through my veins and a welcoming smile on my face, I stepped forward to greet the people walking through the door. Village Vintage was open for business . . .

TWO

I always wake in the early hours. I don't need to look at the clock to know what time it is – it's ten to four. I've been waking at ten to four every night for six months. My GP said it's stress-induced insomnia, but I know it's not stress. It's guilt.

I avoid sleeping pills, so sometimes I'll try to make the time pass by getting up and working. I might put on a wash – the machine's always on the go; I might iron a few things, or do a repair. But I know it's better to try and sleep so I usually lie there, attempting to lull myself back to oblivion with the World Service or some late-night phone-in. But last night I didn't do that – I just lay there thinking about Emma. Whenever I'm not busy she goes round and round my mind, on a loop.

I see her at our little primary school in her stripy green summer dress; I see her diving into the swimming pool like a seal; I see her kissing her lucky Krugerrand before a tennis match. I see her at the Royal College of Art with her milliner's blocks. I see her at Ascot, photographed in *Vogue*, beaming beneath one of her fantastic hats.

Then, as my bedroom began to fill with the grey light of dawn I saw Emma as I saw her for the very last time.

'Sorry,' I whispered.

You're a fabulous friend.

'I'm sorry, Em.'

What would I do without you . . .?

As I stood under the shower I forced my thoughts back to work and to the party. About eighty people had come including three former colleagues from Sotheby's as well as one or two of my neighbours from here in Bennett Street and a few local shop-owners. Ted from the estate agent's just along from the shop had popped in – he'd bought a silk waistcoat from the menswear rail; then Rupert who owns the florist's had turned up and Pippa who runs the Moon Daisy Café dropped in with her sister.

One or two of the fashion journalists I'd invited were there. I hoped that they'd become good contacts, borrowing my clothes for shoots in return for publicity.

'It's very elegant,' Mimi Long from *Woman & Home* said to me as I circulated with the champagne. She tipped her glass towards me for a refill. 'I adore vintage. It's like being in Aladdin's cave – one has this wonderful sense of *discovery*. Will you be running the place on your own?'

'No – I'll need someone to help out part time so that I can be out and about buying stock, and taking things to be cleaned and repaired. So if you hear of anyone . . . They'll need to have an interest in vintage,' I added.

'I'll keep my ear to the ground,' Mimi promised. 'Ooh – is that real Fortuny I can see over there . . .?'

I'll have to advertise for an assistant, I thought now as I dried myself and combed my wet hair. I could place an ad in a local paper – perhaps the one Dan worked for, whatever it was called.

As I dressed – in wide linen trousers and a short-sleeved fitted shirt with a Peter Pan collar – I realised that Dan had correctly identified my style. I do like the bias-cut dresses and wide-leg trousers of the late thirties and early forties; I like my hair shoulder length and falling over one eye. I like swing coats, clutch bags, peep toes and seamed stockings. I like fabric that drapes like oil.

I heard the clatter of the letter box and went downstairs where there were three letters on the mat. Recognising Guy's handwriting on the first I tore it in half and dropped the pieces in the bin. I knew from his others what this one would say.

In the next envelope was a card from Dad. *Good luck with your new venture,* he'd written. *I'll be thinking of you, Phoebe. But please come and see me soon. It's been too long.*

That was true. I'd been so preoccupied that I hadn't seen him since early February. We'd met at a café in Notting Hill for a conciliatory lunch. I hadn't been prepared for him bringing the baby. The sight of my sixty-two-year-old father with a two-month-old clamped to his chest was, to put it mildly, a shock.

'This is . . . Louis,' he'd said awkwardly as he fumbled with the baby-sling. 'How *do* you undo this thing?' he muttered. 'These damn clips . . . I can never . . . ah,

41

got it.' He sighed with relief then lifted the baby out and cradled him with a tender but somehow puzzled expression. 'Ruth's away filming so I had to bring him. Oh . . .' Dad peered at Louis anxiously. 'Do you think he's hungry?'

I looked at Dad, appalled. 'How on earth should *I* know?'

As Dad rummaged in the changing bag for a bottle I stared at Louis, his chin shining with dribble, not knowing what to think, let alone say. He was my baby brother. How could I not love him? At the same time, how *could* I love him, I wondered, when his conception was the cause of my mother's distress?

Meanwhile Louis, unfazed by the complexities of the situation, had grasped my finger in his tiny hand and was smiling at me gummily.

'Pleased to meet you,' I'd said . . .

The third envelope was from Emma's mother. I recognised her writing. My thumb trembled as I ran it under the flap.

I just wanted to wish you every success with your new venture, she'd written. *Emma would have been so thrilled. I hope you're all right,* she'd gone on. *Derek and I are still taking things one day at a time. For us the hardest part remains the fact that we were away when it happened – you can't imagine our regret.* 'Oh yes, I can,' I murmured. *We still haven't gone through Emma's things . . .* I felt my insides coil. Emma had kept a diary. *But when we do, we'd like to give you some small thing of hers as a keepsake. I also wanted to let you know that there'll be a little ceremony for Emma on the first anniversary – February 15th.* I needed no reminder – the date would remain seared on my memory for the rest of my life. *I'll be in touch nearer the time but, until then, God bless you, Phoebe. Daphne.*

She wouldn't be blessing me if she knew the truth, I thought bleakly.

I collected myself, took some French embroidered nightdresses out of the washing machine, hung them to dry, then locked the house and walked to the shop.

There was still some clearing up to be done and as I opened the door I detected the sour scent of last night's champagne. I returned the glasses to Oddbins in a cab, put the empty bottles out for recycling, swept the floor and squished Febreze on the sofa. Then as the church clock struck nine I turned over the 'Closed' sign.

'This is it,' I said to myself. 'Day one.'

I sat behind the counter for a while repairing the lining of a Jean Muir jacket. By ten o'clock I was dismally wondering whether my mother might not be right. Perhaps I *had* made a huge mistake, I thought as I saw people pass by with no more than a glance. Perhaps I'd find sitting in a shop dull after the busyness of Sotheby's. But then I reminded myself that I wouldn't simply be sitting in a shop – I'd be going to auctions and seeing dealers and visiting private individuals to evaluate their clothes. I'd be talking to Hollywood stylists about sourcing dresses for their famous clients and I'd be making the odd trip to France. I'd also be running the Village Vintage website, as I'd be selling clothes directly from that. There'd be more than enough to do, I told myself as I re-threaded my

43

needle. Then I reminded myself of how pressured my previous life had been.

At Sotheby's I'd constantly been under the cosh. There was the continual pressure to put on successful auctions, and to conduct them competently; there was the fear of not having enough for the next sale. If I did manage to get enough then there was the worry that the clothes wouldn't sell, or wouldn't sell for a high enough price, or that the buyers wouldn't pay their bills. There was the constant anxiety that things would get stolen or damaged. Worst of all was the habitual, gnawing fear that an important collection would go to a rival auction house – my directors would always want to know why.

Then February 15th happened and I couldn't cope. I knew I had to get out.

Suddenly I heard the click of the door. I looked up expecting to see my first customer; instead it was Dan, in salmon-coloured cords and a lavender checked shirt. The man had zero colour sense. But there was something about him that was attractive; perhaps it was his build – he was comfortingly solid, like a bear, I now realised. Or perhaps it was his curly hair.

'I don't suppose I left my pencil sharpener here yesterday, did I?'

'Er, no. I haven't seen it.'

'Damn,' he muttered.

'Is it . . . a special one?'

'Yes. It's silver. Solid,' he added.

'Really? Well . . . I'll keep a look out for it.'

'If you would. And how was the party?'

'Good, thanks.'

'Anyway . . .' He held up a newspaper. 'I just wanted to bring you this.' It was the *Black & Green* and on the masthead was Dan's photo of me, captioned PASSION FOR VINTAGE FASHION.

I looked at him. 'I thought you said the article was for Friday's paper.'

'It was to have been, but then today's lead feature had to be held back for various reasons, so Matt, my editor, put yours in instead. Luckily we go to press late.' He handed it to me. 'I think it's come out quite well.'

I quickly glanced through the piece. 'It's great,' I said trying to keep the surprise out of my voice. 'Thanks for putting the website at the end and – *oh*.' I felt my jaw slacken. '*Why* does it say that there's a five per cent discount on everything for the first week?'

A red stain had crept up Dan's neck. 'I just thought an introductory offer might be . . . you know . . . good for business what with the credit crunch.'

'I see. But, that's a bit of a . . . cheek, to put it mildly.'

Dan grimaced. 'I know . . . but I was busy writing it up and I suddenly thought of it, and I knew your party was going on so I didn't want to phone you, and then Matt said he wanted to run the piece straight away and so . . . well . . .' He shrugged. 'I'm sorry.'

'It's okay,' I said grudgingly. 'I must say, you took me aback, but five per cent is . . . fine.' In fact it *would* be good for business, I reflected, not that I was prepared to concede that. 'Anyway,' I sighed, 'I was a little distracted when we were talking yesterday – who did you say gets this paper?'

'It's handed out at all the stations in this area on Tuesday and Friday mornings. It also goes through the doors of selected businesses and homes, so potentially it reaches a wide local audience.'

'That's wonderful.' I smiled at Dan, genuinely appreciative now. 'And have you worked for the paper long?'

He seemed to hesitate. 'Two months.'

'From the start then?'

'More or less.'

'And are you from round here?'

'Just down the road in Hither Green.' There was an odd little pause, and I was just waiting for him to say that he ought to be on his way when he said, 'You must come Hither.'

I looked at him. 'I'm sorry?'

He smiled. 'All I mean is you must come round sometime.'

'Oh.'

'For a drink. I'd love you to see my . . .' *What?* I wondered. Etchings?

'Shed.'

'Your shed?'

'Yes. I've got a fantastic shed,' he said evenly.

'Really?' I imagined a jumble of rusty gardening tools, cobwebbed bicycles and broken flowerpots.

'Or it will be when I've finished.'

'Thanks,' I said. 'I'll bear that in mind.'

'Well . . .' Dan tucked the pencil behind his ear. 'I guess I'd better find my sharpener.'

'Good luck.' I smiled. 'See you around.' He left the shop, then gave me a little wave through the window. I waved back. 'What an oddball,' I said under my breath.

Within ten minutes of Dan's departure a trickle of people began to arrive, at least two of them holding

46

copies of the *Black & Green*. I tried not to annoy them with offers of help or to watch them too obviously. The Hermès bags and the more expensive jewellery were in lockable glass cases, but I hadn't put electronic tags on the clothes for fear of damaging the fabric.

By twelve, I'd had about ten people through the door and had made my first sale – a 1950s seersucker sundress with a pattern of violets. I felt like framing the receipt.

At a quarter past one a petite red-haired girl in her early twenties came in with a well-dressed man in his mid to late thirties. While she looked through the clothes he sat on the sofa, one silk-socked ankle resting on his knee, thumbing his BlackBerry. The girl went through the evening-wear rail, finding nothing; then her eye was drawn to the cupcake dresses hanging on the wall. She pointed to the lime green one – the smallest of the four.

'How much is that?' she asked me.

'It's £275.' She nodded thoughtfully. 'It's silk,' I explained, 'with hand-sewn crystals. Would you like to try it on? It's a size eight.'

'Well . . .' She glanced anxiously at her boyfriend. 'What do you think, Keith?' He looked up from his BlackBerry and the girl nodded to the dress, which I was now taking off the wall.

'That won't do,' he said bluntly.

'Why not?'

'Too colourful.'

'I like bright colours,' the girl protested meekly.

He turned back to his BlackBerry. 'It's not appropriate for the occasion.'

'But it's a dance.'

'It's too colourful,' he insisted. 'Plus it's not smart enough.' My dislike of the man turned to detestation.

'Let me try it.' She smiled pleadingly. 'Go on.'

He looked at her. 'Ok-*ay*.' He sighed extravagantly. '*If* you must . . .'

I showed the girl into the changing room and drew the curtain round the rail. A minute later she emerged. The dress fitted her perfectly and showed off her small waist, lovely shoulders and slim arms. The vibrant lime complimented her red-blonde hair and creamy skin, while the corseting flattered her bust. The green tulle petticoats floated in layers around her, the crystals winking in the sunlight.

'It's . . . gorgeous,' I murmured. I couldn't imagine any woman looking more beautiful in it. 'Would you like to try a pair of shoes on with it?' I added. 'Just to see how it would look with heels?'

'Oh, I won't need to,' she said as she stared at herself, on tiptoe, in a side mirror. She shook her head. 'It's . . . fantastic.' She seemed overwhelmed, as though she'd just discovered some wonderful secret about herself.

Behind her another customer had come in – a slim, dark-haired woman of about thirty in a leopard-print shirtdress with a gold chain belt worn low on the hips and gladiator sandals. She stopped in her tracks, gazing at the girl. 'You look *glorious*,' she exclaimed. 'Like a young Julianne Moore.'

The girl smiled delightedly. 'Thanks.' She stared at herself in the mirror again. 'This dress makes me feel . . . as though I'm in . . .' She hesitated. 'A fairytale.' She glanced nervously at her boyfriend. 'What do you think, Keith?'

He looked at her, shook his head then returned to his BlackBerry. 'Like I say – much too bright. Plus it makes you look like you're going to hop about in the ballet, not go to a sophisticated dinner dance at the Dorchester. Here –' He stood up, went over to the evening rail and pulled out a Norman Hartnell black crepe cocktail dress and held it up to her. 'Try this.'

The girl's face fell, but she retreated into the fitting room, emerging in the dress a minute later. The style was far too old for her and the colour drained her complexion. She looked as though she was going to a funeral. I saw the woman in the leopard-print dress glance at her then discreetly shake her head before turning back to the rails.

'*That's* more like it,' Keith said. He made a circulating gesture with his index finger and with a sigh the girl slowly spun round, her eyes upturned. At that I saw the other customer purse her lips. 'Perfect,' said Keith. He thrust his hand into his jacket. 'How much?' I glanced at the girl. Her mouth was quivering. 'How much?' he repeated as he opened his wallet.

'But it's the green one I like,' she murmured.

'How *much*?' he repeated.

'It's £150.' I felt my face flush.

'I don't *want* it,' the girl pleaded. 'I like the *green* one, Keith. It makes me feel . . . happy.'

'Then you'll just have to buy it yourself. If you can afford it,' he added pleasantly. He looked at me again. 'So that's £150?' He tapped the newspaper. 'And it says here that there's a five per cent discount, which makes it £142.50, by my reckoning.'

'That's right,' I said, impressed by the speed of his

49

calculation and wishing that I could charge him twice the amount and *give* the girl the cupcake dress.

'Keith. Please,' she moaned. Her eyes were shining with tears.

'C'mon, Kelly,' he groaned. 'Give me a break. That little black number's just the ticket and I've got some top people coming so I don't want you looking like bloody Tinker Bell do I?' He glanced at his expensive-looking watch. 'We've got to get back – I've got that conference call about the Kilburn site at two thirty, remember. Now – am I buying the black dress or not? Because if I'm not, then you won't be coming to the Dorchester on Saturday, I can tell you.'

She looked out of the window then nodded mutely.

As I tore the receipt off the terminal the man held his hand out for the bag then slotted his card back in his wallet. 'Thanks,' he said briskly. Then, with the girl trailing disconsolately behind him, he left.

As the door clicked shut the woman in the leopard-print dress caught my eye.

'I wish she'd had the fairytale dress,' she said. 'With a "prince" like that, she needs it.' Not sure that I should be seen to be knocking my customers, I smiled a rueful smile of agreement then put the green cupcake dress back on the wall. 'She isn't just his girlfriend – she works for him,' the woman went on as she inspected a Thierry Mugler hot pink leather jacket from the mid eighties.

I looked at her. 'How do you know?'

'Because he's so much older than her, because of his power over her and her fear of offending him . . . her knowledge of his diary. I like people-watching,' she added.

'Are you a writer?'

'No. I love writing, but I'm an actor.'

'Are you in anything at the moment?'

She shook her head. 'I'm "resting", as they say – in fact, I've had more rest than Sleeping Beauty lately, *but*' – she heaved a theatrical sigh – 'I refuse to give up.' She looked at the prom dresses again. 'They really *are* lovely. I don't have the curves for them, sadly, even if I had the cash. They're American, aren't they?'

I nodded. 'Early fifties. They're a bit too frothy for post-war Britain.'

'Gorgeous fabric,' the woman said, squinting at them. 'Dresses like that are usually made of acetate with nylon petticoats, but these ones are all silk.' So she had knowledge and a good eye.

'Do you buy much vintage?' I asked as I re-folded a lavender cashmere cardigan and put it on the knitwear stand.

'I buy as much as I can afford – and if I get bored of anything I can always sell – not that I do, because in the main I've always bought well. I've never forgotten the thrill of my first find,' she went on as she put the Thierry Mugler back on the rail. 'It was a Ted Lapidus leather coat bought in Oxfam in '92 – it still looks good.'

I thought about *my* first vintage find. A Nina Ricci guipure lace shirt bought in Greenwich Market when I was fourteen. Emma had pounced on it for me on one of our Saturday foraging trips.

'Your dress is Cerutti, isn't it?' I said to the girl. 'But it's been altered. It should be ankle length.'

She smiled. 'Spot on. I got it in a jumble sale ten

51

years ago, but the hem was ripped so I shortened it.'
She brushed an imaginary speck off the front. 'Best
fifty pence I ever spent.' She went over to the daywear
rail and picked out a turquoise crepe de Chine tiered
dress from the early seventies. 'This is Alice Pollock,
isn't it?'

I nodded. 'For Quorum.'

'I thought so.' She glanced at the price. 'Out of my
reach, but I can never resist looking, and when I read
in the local paper that you'd opened I just had to come
and see what you had. Oh well,' she sighed. 'I can
dream.' She gave me a friendly smile. 'I'm Annie, by
the way.'

'I'm Phoebe. Phoebe Swift.' I stared at her. 'I'm just
wondering . . . are you working at the moment?'

'I'm temping,' she replied. 'Just doing whatever comes
along.'

'And are you local?'

'Yes.' Annie looked at me curiously. 'I live in
Dartmouth Hill.'

'The reason I'm asking . . . Look, I don't suppose you'd
be interested in working for me, would you? I need a
part-time assistant.' I explained why.

'Two days a week?' Annie echoed. 'That might suit
me very well – I could do with some regular work – as
long as I could go to auditions. Not that I have many
to go to,' she added ruefully.

'I'd be flexible about the hours – and there'd be some
weeks when I'd need you for more than two days – and
did you say you can sew?'

'I'm fairly nifty with a needle.'

'Because it would be helpful if you could do a few

small repairs in the quiet times, or a bit of ironing. And if you could help me dress the windows – I'm not much good with mannequins.'

'I'd enjoy all that.'

'And you wouldn't have to worry about whether or not you and I would get on, because when you were here I'd mostly be out, which would be the whole point of it. But here's my number.' I handed Annie a Village Vintage postcard. 'Have a think.'

'Well . . . actually . . .' She laughed. 'I don't have to. It would be right up my street. But you ought to get a reference for me,' she added, 'if only to make sure I'm not going to run off with the stock, because it would be *extremely* tempting.' She smiled. 'But apart from that, when would I start?'

So this morning, Monday, Annie began work, having provided letters from two previous employers extolling her honesty and industry. I'd asked her to come early so that I could show her how everything worked before I left for Christie's.

'Spend some time familiarising yourself with the clothes,' I advised her. 'Evening wear is here. This is lingerie . . . there's some menswear here . . . shoes and bags are on this stand. Knitwear on this table . . . Let me open the till.' I fiddled with the electronic key. 'And if you could do a little mending . . .'

'Sure.' I went into the 'den' to pick up a Murray Arbeid skirt that needed a small repair. 'That's an Emma Kitts, isn't it?' I heard Annie say. I came back into the shop. She was gazing up at the hat. 'That was so sad. I read about it in the papers.' She turned to me. 'But why do you have it here, given that it's not vintage and it says it's not for sale?'

For a split second I fantasised about confessing to Annie that looking at the hat every day was a form of penance.

'I knew her,' I explained as I put the skirt on the counter with the sewing box. 'We were friends.'

'That's hard,' said Annie softly. 'You must miss her.'

'Yes . . .' I coughed to cover the sob that I could feel rising in my throat. 'Anyway . . . this seam here – there's a little split.' I breathed deeply. 'I'd better get going.'

Annie took the lid off the sewing box and selected a reel of thread. 'What time does the auction start?'

'At ten. I went to the preview last night.' I picked up the catalogue. 'The lots I'm interested in won't come up until after eleven, but I want to get there in good time so that I can see what's selling well.'

'What are you going to bid for?'

'A Balenciaga evening gown.' I turned to the photo of Lot 110.

Annie peered at it. 'How *elegant*.'

The long sleeveless indigo silk dress was cut very simply, its scooped neckline and gently raised hem encrusted in a wide band of fringed silver glass beading.

'I want to buy it for a private client,' I explained. 'She's a Beverly Hills stylist. I know exactly what her customers want, so I'm sure she'll take it. Then there's this dress by Madame Grès that I'm dying to get for my own collection.' I turned to the photo of Lot 112, a Neo-classical sheath of cream silk jersey falling in dozens of fine pleats from an empire-line bust with crossover straps and a chiffon train floating from each shoulder. I emitted a wistful sigh.

'It's magnificent,' Annie murmured. 'It would make a fabulous wedding dress,' she added teasingly.

I smiled. 'That's *not* why I want it. I simply love the incomparable draping of Madame Grès' gowns.' I picked up my bag. 'Now I really *must* go – oh, one other thing –' and I was just about to tell Annie what to do if anyone brought clothes in to sell when the phone rang.

I picked up. 'Village Vintage . . .' The novelty of saying it still gave me a thrill.

'Good morning,' said a female voice. 'My name is Mrs Bell.' The woman was clearly elderly and her accent was French, though almost imperceptibly so. 'I saw from the local newspaper that you have just opened your shop.'

'That's right.' So Dan's article was still having an effect. I felt a rush of good will towards him.

'Well . . . I have a selection of clothes I no longer want – some quite lovely things that I am never going to wear again. There are also some bags and shoes. But I am elderly. I cannot bring them . . .'

'No, of course not,' I interjected. 'I'd be happy to come over to you, if you'd like to give me your address.' I reached for my diary. 'The Paragon?' I repeated. 'That's very near. I could walk up. When shall I come?'

'Is there any chance that you could come today? I am in the mood to dispose of my things sooner rather than later. I have an appointment this morning, but would three o'clock be possible?'

I'd be back from the auction by then, and I had Annie to mind the shop. 'Three o'clock would be fine,' I said as I scribbled down the house number.

As I walked down the hill to Blackheath station I reflected on the art of evaluating a collection of clothes in someone's home. The usual scenario is that a woman has died and you're dealing with her relatives. They can be very emotional, so you have to be tactful. They're often offended if you leave some garments out; then they can be upset if you offer less than they'd hoped for those things you do choose. 'Only £40?' they'll say. 'But it's by Hardy Amies.' And I'll gently point out that the lining's ripped, that three buttons are missing, and that it'll have to go to the specialist dry cleaners for the stains on the cuff.

Sometimes the family can find it hard to part with the garments at all and resent your presence, especially if the estate is being sold to pay tax. In those cases, I reflected as I waited on the station platform, you're made to feel like an intruder. Quite often, when I've gone to do a valuation of this kind in a grand country house, I've had the maid or valet standing there weeping, or telling me – and this is very annoying – not to touch the clothes. If I'm with a widower he'll often go into minute detail about everything that his wife wore, and how much he paid for it in Dickins & Jones in 1965 and how beautiful she looked in it on the QE2.

The easiest scenario by far, I thought as the train pulled in, is where a woman is getting divorced and wants to be shot of everything that her husband ever bought her. In those cases I can justifiably be brisk. But when it comes to seeing elderly women who are selling their entire wardrobe it can be emotionally draining. As I say, these are more than clothes – they're the fabric, almost literally, of someone's life. But however much I like to hear the stories I have to remind myself that my time is limited. I therefore try to keep my visits to no more than an hour, which is what I resolved to do with Mrs Bell.

As I came out of the underground at South Kensington I called Annie. She sounded upbeat, having already sold a Vivienne Westwood bustier and two French night-dresses. She also told me that Mimi Long from *Woman & Home* had asked if she could borrow some clothes for one of her shoots. Cheered by this, I walked down the Brompton Road to Christie's then turned into the foyer, which was crowded as the fashion sales are popular. I queued to register then picked up my bidding 'paddle'.

The Long Gallery was about two-thirds full. I sat at the end of an empty row halfway down on the right, then looked around for my competitors, which is always the first thing I do when I go to an auction. I saw a couple of dealers I know and a woman who runs a vintage dress shop in Islington. I recognised the fashion editor of *Elle* sitting in the fourth row and to my right I spotted Nicole Farhi. The air seemed clogged with expensive scent.

'Lot number 102,' announced the auctioneer. I sat bolt upright. Lot 102? But it was only ten thirty. When I was conducting auctions I never messed about, but this man had *torn* through the list. Pulse racing, I looked at the Balenciaga gown in the catalogue then flicked forward to the Madame Grès. It had a reserve of £1,000 but was likely to go for more. I knew I shouldn't be buying anything I wasn't planning to sell, but told myself that this was an important piece that would only appre-ciate in value. If I could get it for £1,500 or less, I would.

'Lot 105 now,' said the auctioneer. 'An Elsa Schiaparelli

"shocking pink" silk jacket from her "Circus" collection of 1938. Note the original metallic buttons in the shape of acrobats. Bidding for this item starts at £300. Thank you. And £320, and £340 . . . £360, thank you, madam . . . Do I hear £380?' The auctioneer peered over his glasses then nodded at a blonde woman in the front row. 'So, for £360 . . .' The gavel came down with a 'crack'. '*Sold*. To . . .?' The woman held up her bidding paddle. 'Buyer number 24. Thank you, madam. On now to Lot 106 . . .'

Despite my years as an auctioneer my heart was pounding as 'my' first lot approached. I glanced anxiously round the room, wondering who my rivals for it might be. Most of the buyers were women, but at the very end of my row was a distinguished-looking man in his mid forties. He was flicking through the catalogue, marking it here and there with a gold fountain pen. I idly wondered what he was going to bid for.

The next three lots were each despatched in less than a minute with telephone bids. The Balenciaga was about to come up. I felt my fingers tighten around my bidding paddle.

'Lot number 110,' announced the auctioneer. 'An elegant Cristóbal Balenciaga evening gown of dark blue silk, made in 1960.' An image of the dress was projected on to the two huge flat screens on either side of the podium. 'Note the typical simplicity of the cut and the slightly raised hem, to reveal shoes. I'm going to start the bidding at £500.' The auctioneer looked around the room. 'Do I hear £500?' As there were no bids, I waited. 'Who'll offer me £450?' He peered at us all over his glasses. To my surprise there were no raised hands. 'Do

I hear £400 then?' A woman in the front row nodded so I nodded too. 'I have £420 . . . £440 . . . £460. Do I hear £480?' The auctioneer looked at me. 'Thank you, madam – the bid is yours, at £480. Any advance above £480?' He looked at the other bidder but she was shaking her head. 'Then £480 it is.' Down came the gavel. 'Sold for £480 to buyer number . . .' he peered at me over his glasses and I held up my paddle '. . . 220. Thank you, madam.'

My euphoria at having got the Balenciaga at such a good price was swiftly replaced by stomach-churning anxiety as bidding for the Madame Grès approached. I shifted on my seat.

'Lot number 112,' I heard the auctioneer say. 'An evening gown, circa 1936, by the great Madame Grès, famed for her masterful pleating and draping.' An aproned porter carried the dress, which had been put on to a mannequin, up to the podium. I cast a nervous glance around the room. 'I'm going to start at £1,000,' the auctioneer announced. 'Do I hear £1,000?' To my relief only one other hand went up with my own. 'And £1,100. And £1,150.' I bid again. 'And £1,200. Thank you – and £1,250?' The auctioneer looked at us in turn – the other bidder was shaking her head – then returned his gaze to me. 'Still at £1,250. The bid is with you, madam.' I held my breath – £1,250 would be a great price. 'Last call. Last call then,' the auctioneer repeated. *Thank* you, God. I closed my eyes with relief. *'Thank* you, sir.' Confounded, I looked to my left. To my irritation the man at the end of my row was now bidding. 'Do I hear £1,300?' enquired the auctioneer. He glanced at me and I nodded. 'And £1,350? Thank you, sir.' I felt my pulse race. 'And £1,400? Thank you, madam. Do I hear £1,500 now?' The man nodded. *Damn.* 'And £1,600?' I raised my hand. 'And will you give me £1,700, sir? Thank you.' I threw another glance at my rival, noting his calm expression as he drove up the price. 'Do I hear £1,750?' This suave-looking creep wasn't going to stop me from getting the dress. I raised my hand again. 'At £1,750 – still with the lady at the end of the row there. *Thank* you, sir – with you now at £1,800. And £1,900? Are you still in, madam?' I nodded, but beneath my excitement I was seething. 'And £2,000 . . .? Will you bid, sir?' The man nodded again. 'Who'll give me £2,100?' I raised my hand. 'And £2,200? *Thank* you, sir. Still with you, sir, at £2,200 now . . .' The man gave me a sideways glance. I raised my hand again. 'I have £2,*300* now,' said the auctioneer happily. 'Thank you, madam. And £2,400 . . .?' The auctioneer stared fixedly at me, whilst extending his right hand to my rival as though to keep us locked in competition – a familiar trick. '£2,400?' he repeated. 'It's the gentleman against you, madam.' I nodded now, adrenaline scorching my veins. '£2,600?' said the auctioneer. I could hear people shift on their seats as the tension mounted. 'Thank you, sir. Do I hear £2,800? Madam – will you bid £2,800?' I nodded, as if in a dream. 'And £2,900, sir? Thank you.' There were whispers from behind. 'Do I hear £3,000 . . . £3,000?' The auctioneer peered at me as I raised my hand. 'Thank you very much, madam – £3,000 then.' What was I *doing*? 'At £3,000 . . .' I didn't *have* £3,000 – I'd have to let the dress go. 'Any advance on £3,000?' It was sad, but there it was. '£3,100?' I heard the auctioneer repeat. 'No, sir? You're out?' I looked at my rival. To my horror he was shaking his head. Now the auctioneer turned to me. 'So the bid is still with you then, madam, at £3,000 . . .' Oh my God. 'Going once . . .' The auctioneer raised his gavel. '*Twice* . . .' He flicked his wrist, and with a strange mix of euphoria and dismay I watched the gavel come down. 'Sold then for £3,000 to buyer – what was the number again, please? –' I held up my paddle with a shaking hand '– 220. *Thank* you everyone. Terrific bidding there. Now on to lot 113.'

I stood up, feeling sick. With the buyer's premium, the total cost of the dress would be £3,600. How, with all my experience, not to mention my supposed *sangfroid,* could I have got so carried away?

As I looked at the man who'd bid against me an irrational hatred overwhelmed me. He was a City slicker, polished in his Savile Row pin-stripe and his hand-made shoes. No doubt he'd wanted the dress for his wife – his trophy wife, in all probability. Irrationally, I conjured her, a vision of blonde perfection in this season's Chanel.

I left the saleroom, my heart still thudding. I couldn't possibly keep the dress. I could offer it to Cindi, my Hollywood stylist – it would be a perfect red-carpet gown for one of her clients. For a moment I imagined Cate Blanchett wearing it to the Oscars – she'd do it justice. But I didn't *want* to sell it, I told myself as I headed downstairs to the cashier. It was sublimely beautiful and I had battled to get it.

As I queued to pay I nervously wondered whether my Mastercard would combust on contact with the machine. I calculated that there was just enough credit on it to make the transaction possible.

As I waited my turn I looked up and saw Mr Pin-
Stripe coming down the stairs, his phone pressed to his
ear.

'No, I didn't,' I heard him say. He had a very pleasant
voice, I noticed, with a slight huskiness to it. 'I just
didn't,' he repeated wearily. 'I'm sorry about that,
darling.' Trophy Wife – or possibly Mistress – was clearly
furious with him for not getting the Madame Grès.
'Bidding was intense,' I heard him explain. He glanced
at me. 'I had stiff competition.' At that, to my astonishment, he threw me a wink. 'Yes, I know it's disappointing, but there'll be lots of other lovely dresses,
sweetie.' He was obviously getting it right in the neck.
'But I did get the Prada bag that you liked. Yes, of course,
darling. Look, I have to go and pay now. I'll call you
later, okay?'

He snapped shut his phone with a slightly conspic-
uous air of relief then came and stood behind me. I
pretended not to know he was there.

'Congratulations,' I heard him say.

I turned around. 'I'm sorry?'

'Congratulations,' he repeated. 'You've got the lot,'
he added jovially. 'The wonderful white dress by . . . who
was it again?' He opened the catalogue. 'Madame Grès
– whoever she was.' I was outraged. He didn't even know
what it was that he'd been bidding for. 'You must be
pleased,' he added.

'Yes.' I resisted the temptation to tell him that I was
far from pleased with the price.

He tucked the catalogue under his arm. 'To be honest,
I could have gone on bidding.'

I stared at him. 'Really?'

'But then I looked at your face, and when I saw how *intensely* you seemed to want it, I decided to let you have it.'

'Oh.' I nodded politely. Was the wretch expecting me to *thank* him? If he'd quit the race earlier, he'd have saved me two grand.

'Are you going to wear it to some special occasion?' he asked.

'No,' I replied frigidly. 'I just . . . adore Madame Grès. I collect her gowns.'

'Then I'm delighted that you got this one – anyway.' He adjusted the knot of his Hermès silk tie. 'That's me done for the day.' He glanced at his watch and I caught a glint of antique Rolex. 'Will you be bidding for anything else?'

'Good God, no – I've blown the budget.'

'Oh dear – so it was a case of hammer horror, was it?'

'It was rather.'

'Well . . . I guess that's my fault.' He gave me an apologetic smile and I noticed that his eyes were large and deep brown with hooded lids that gave him a slightly sleepy expression.

'Of course it's not your fault.' I shrugged. 'That's how auctions work.' As I knew only too well.

'Yes please, madam?' I heard the cashier say.

I turned round and handed her my credit card. As I did so I asked her to make out the invoice to Village Vintage, then I sat on the blue leather bench and waited for my lots to be brought out.

Mr Pin-Stripe completed his payment then came and sat next to me while he waited for his purchases.

As we sat there, side by side, not talking now because he was reading his BlackBerry – with a slightly intense air I couldn't help noticing – I found myself wondering how old he was. I stole a glance at his profile. His face was quite lined. Whatever his age, he was attractive with his iron filings hair and aquiline nose. He was forty-three-ish, I decided as a porter handed us our respective carrier bags. I felt a thrill of ownership as my bag was handed to me. I quickly checked the contents then gave Mr Pin-Stripe a valedictory smile.

He stood up. 'Do you know . . .?' he glanced at his watch '. . . all that bidding has made me hungry. I'm going to pop into the café over the road. I don't suppose you'd feel like joining me, would you? Having bid so vigorously against you, the least I can do is to buy you a sandwich.' He extended his hand. 'My name's Miles, by the way. Miles Archant.'

'Oh. I'm Phoebe. Swift. Hi,' I added impotently as I shook his hand.

'So?' He was looking at me enquiringly. 'Can I interest you in an early lunch?'

I was amazed at the man's audacity. He a) didn't know me from Eve and b) clearly had a wife or girlfriend – a fact he knew that *I* knew because I'd overheard him on his mobile.

'Or just a cup of coffee?'

'No, thank you,' I said calmly. I presumed he made a habit of picking up women in auction houses. 'I have to . . . get back now.'

'To . . . work?' he enquired pleasantly.

'Yes.' I didn't have to say where.

'Well, enjoy the dress. You'll look stunning in it,' he added as I turned to leave.

Unsure whether to be indignant or delighted I gave him an uncertain smile. 'Thanks.'

THREE

On my return I showed Annie the two dresses. I told her that I'd had to fight for the Madame Grès, though I didn't go into details about Mr Pin-Stripe.

'I wouldn't worry about the cost,' she said as she gazed at the gown. 'Something as magnificent as this should transcend such . . . petty considerations.'

'If only,' I said wistfully. 'I still can't believe how much I spent.'

'Couldn't you say it's part of your pension?' Annie suggested as she re-stitched the hem of a Georges Rech skirt. She shifted on her stool. 'Perhaps the Inland Revenue would knock the cost of it off your tax bill.'

'I doubt it as I'm not selling it, although I rather like the idea of a pension-à-porter. Oh,' I added. 'You've put those up there.' While I'd been out, Annie had hung some hand-embroidered evening bags on a bare patch of wall by the door.

'I hope you don't mind,' she said. 'I thought they'd look good there.'

'They do. You can see the detail on them so much better.' I zipped the two dresses I'd bought into new protective covers. 'I'd better put these in the stockroom.'

'Can I ask you something?' Annie said as I turned to go upstairs.

I looked at her. 'Yes?'

'You collect Madame Grès?'

'That's right.'

'But you have a lovely gown by Madame Grès right here.' She went over to the evening rail and pulled out the dress that Guy had given me. 'Someone tried it on this morning and I saw the label. The woman was too short for it – but it would look great on you. Don't you want it for your own collection?'

I shook my head. 'I'm . . . not mad about that particular gown.'

'Oh.' Annie looked at it. 'I see. But –'

To my relief the bell above the door began to tinkle. A couple in their late twenties had walked in. I asked Annie to look after them while I went up to the stockroom. Then I nipped back down to the office to check the Village Vintage website.

'I need an evening dress,' I heard the girl say as I opened the e-mail enquiries. 'It's for our engagement party,' she added with a giggle.

'Carla thought she'd get something a bit more original in a shop like this,' her boyfriend explained.

'You will,' I heard Annie say. 'The evening-wear rail is over here – you're a size 12, aren't you?'

'Gosh no.' The girl snorted. 'I'm a 16. I should go on a diet.'

'*Don't*,' said her boyfriend. 'You're lovely as you are.'

'You're a lucky woman,' I heard Annie chuckle. 'You've got the perfect husband-to-be there.'

'I know I have,' the girl said fondly. 'What are you looking at there, Pete? Ooh – what lovely cufflinks.'

Envious of the couple's evident happiness together, I turned to the e-mail orders. Someone wanted to buy five of my French nightdresses. Another customer was interested in a Dior long-sleeved dress with a bamboo pattern, and was asking about the sizing.

When I say that the garment is a 12, I e-mailed back, *that really means it's a 10 because women today are bigger than the women of fifty years ago. Here are the dimensions that you requested, including the circumference of the sleeve at the wrist. Please let me know if you'd like me to keep it for you.*

'When is your party?' I heard Annie ask.

'It's this Saturday,' the girl replied. 'So I haven't given myself much time to find something. These aren't quite what I'm looking for,' I heard her add after a few moments.

'You could always accessorise a dress you already have with something vintage,' I heard Annie suggest. 'You might add a silk jacket – we've got some lovely ones over there – or a pretty shrug. If you brought something in, I could help you give it a new look.'

'*Those* are wonderful,' the girl suddenly said. 'They're so . . . *joyous.*' I knew that she could only be talking about the cupcake dresses.

'Which colour do you like best?' I heard her boyfriend ask her.

'The . . . turquoise one, I think.'

'It'd go with your eyes,' I heard him say.

'Would you like me to get it down for you?' Annie said.

I glanced at my watch. It was time to go and meet Mrs Bell.

'How much is it?' the girl asked. Annie told her. 'Ah. I see. Well, in that case . . .'

'At least try it on,' I heard her boyfriend say.

'Well . . . okay,' she replied. 'But it's way over budget.'

I put on my jacket and prepared to leave.

As I went out into the shop a minute later the girl emerged from the dressing room in the turquoise cupcake. She wasn't in the least bit fat, she just had a lovely voluptuousness. Her fiancé had been right about the blue-green complimenting her eyes.

'You look wonderful in it,' Annie said. 'You need an hourglass figure for these dresses, and you've got one.'

'Thank you.' She tucked a hank of glossy brown hair behind one ear. 'I must say, it really is . . .' She sighed with a mixture of happiness and frustration '. . . *gorgeous*. I love the tutu skirts and the sequins. It makes me feel . . . happy,' she said wonderingly. 'Not that I'm not happy,' she added with a warm smile at her fiancé. She looked at Annie. 'And it's £275?'

'That's right. It's all silk,' Annie added, 'including the lace banding round the bodice.'

'And there's five per cent off everything at the moment,' I said as I picked up my bag. I'd decided to extend the offer. 'And we can keep things for up to a week.'

The girl sighed again. 'It's okay. Thanks.' She gazed at herself in the mirror, the tulle petticoats whispering as she moved. 'It's lovely,' she said, 'but . . . I don't know . . . Perhaps . . . it's not really . . . quite me.' She retreated

into the changing room and drew the curtain. 'I'll just
. . . keep looking,' I heard her say as I left for The
Paragon.

I know The Paragon well – I used to go there for piano
lessons. My teacher was called Mr Long, which used to
make my mother laugh as Mr Long was very short. He
was also blind, and his brown eyes, magnified behind
the thick lenses of his NHS specs, used to roll inces-
santly from side to side. When I was playing he would
pace up and down behind me in his worn Hush Puppies.
If I fumbled something he'd smack the fingers of my
right hand with a ruler. I wasn't so much offended as
impressed by his aim.

I went to Mr Long every Tuesday after school for five
years until one June day his wife phoned my mother to
say that Mr Long had collapsed and died while walking
in the Lake District. Despite the hand smacking, I was
very upset.

I haven't set foot in The Paragon since then, although
I've often passed by it. There's something about the
imposing Georgian crescent, with its seven massive
houses, each linked by a low colonnade, that still makes
me catch my breath. In The Paragon's heyday the houses
each had their own stables, carriage rooms, fishponds
and dairies, but during the war the terrace was bombed.
When it was restored in the late 1950s it was carved
into flats.

Now I walked up Morden Road past the Clarendon
Hotel, skirting the Heath with its trail of traffic trundling
around the perimeter; then I passed the Princess of Wales
pub, and the nearby pond, its surface rippling in the

breeze, then I turned into The Paragon. As I walked down the terrace I admired the horse chestnut trees on the huge front lawn, their leaves already flecked with gold. I climbed the stone steps of number 8 and pressed the buzzer for flat 6. I looked at my watch. It was five to three. I'd aim to be out by four.

I heard the intercom crackle, then Mrs Bell's voice. 'I am just coming down. Kindly wait a little moment.'

It was a good five minutes until she appeared.

'Excuse me.' She lifted her hand to her chest as she caught her breath. 'It always takes me some time . . .'

'Please don't worry,' I said as I held the heavy black door open for her. 'But couldn't you have let me in from upstairs?'

'The automatic catch is broken – somewhat to my regret,' she added with elegant understatement. 'Anyway, thank you so much for coming, Miss Swift . . .'

'Please, call me Phoebe.'

As I stepped over the threshold Mrs Bell extended a thin hand, the skin on which was translucent with age, the veins standing out like blue wires. As she smiled at me her still-attractive face folded into a myriad creases which here and there had trapped particles of pink powder. Her periwinkle eyes were patched with pale grey.

'You must wish there was a lift,' I said as we began to climb the wide stone staircase to the third floor. My voice echoed up the stairwell.

'A lift would be extremely desirable,' said Mrs Bell as she gripped the iron handrail. She paused for a moment to hitch up the waist of her caramel wool skirt. 'But it's only lately that the stairs have bothered me.' We stopped again on the first landing so that she could rest. 'However,

71

I may be going elsewhere quite soon, so I will no longer have to climb this mountain – which would be a distinct advantage,' she added as we carried on upwards.

'Will you be going far?' Mrs Bell didn't seem to hear so I concluded that in addition to her general frailty she must be hard of hearing.

She pushed on her door. '*Et voilà . . .*'

The interior of her flat, like its owner, was attractive but faded. There were pretty pictures on the walls, including a luminous little oil painting of a lavender field; there were Aubusson rugs on the parquet floor and fringed silk lampshades hanging from the ceiling of the corridor along which I now followed Mrs Bell. She stopped halfway and stepped down into the kitchen. It was small, square and time-warped, with its red Formica-topped table and its hooded gas stove upon which stood an aluminium kettle and a single white-enamelled saucepan. On the laminate worktop was a tea tray set out with a blue china teapot, two matching cups and saucers, and a little white milk jug over which she'd put a dainty white muslin cover fringed with blue beads.

'Can I offer you a cup of tea, Phoebe?'

'No thank you – really.'

'But I have everything ready, and though I may be French I know how to make a nice cup of English Darjeeling,' Mrs Bell added wryly.

'Well . . .' I smiled. 'If it's no trouble.'

'None at all. I have only to re-heat the water.' She took a box of matches off the shelf, struck one then held it to the gas ring with a shaky hand. As she did so I noticed that her waistband was secured with a large safety pin. 'Please, take a seat in the sitting room,' she said. 'It's just there – on the left.'

The room was large, with a big bow window, and was papered in a light green slubbed silk which was curling at the seams in places. A small gas fire was alight despite the warmth of the day. On the mantelshelf above it a silver carriage clock was flanked by a pair of snooty-looking Staffordshire spaniels.

As I heard the kettle begin to whistle I went over to the window and looked down on to the communal garden. As a child I'd been unable to appreciate its size. The lawn swept the entire length of the crescent, like a river of grass, and was fringed by a screen of magnificent trees. There was a huge cedar that cascaded to the ground in tiers, like a green crinoline: there were two or three enormous oaks. There were three copper beeches and a sweet chestnut in the throes of a half-hearted second flowering. To the right, two young girls were running through the skirts of a weeping willow, shrieking and laughing. I stood there for a few moments, watching them . . .

'Here we are . . .' I heard Mrs Bell say. I went to help her with the tray.

'No – thank you,' she said, almost fiercely, as I tried to take it from her. 'I may be somewhat *antique*, but I can still manage quite well. Now, how do you take your tea?' I told her. 'Black with no sugar?' She picked up the silver tea strainer. 'That's easy then . . .'

She handed me my tea then lowered herself on to a little brocade chair by the fire while I sat on the sofa opposite her.

'Have you lived here long, Mrs Bell?'

'Long enough.' She sighed. 'Eighteen years.'

'So are you hoping to move to ground-floor accommodation?' It had crossed my mind that she might be moving to one of the sheltered housing flats just down the road.

'I'm not sure where I'm going,' she replied after a moment. 'I will have a clearer idea next week. But whatever happens, I am . . . how can I put it . . .?'

'Downsizing?' I suggested after a moment.

'Downsizing?' She smiled ruefully. 'Yes.' There was an odd little silence, which I filled by telling Mrs Bell about my piano lessons, though I decided not to mention the ruler.

'And were you a good pianist?'

I shook my head. 'I only got up to Grade 3. I didn't practise enough, and then after Mr Long died I didn't want to continue with it. My mother wanted me to, but I guess I wasn't that interested . . .' From outside came the silvery laughter of the two girls. 'Unlike my best friend Emma,' I heard myself say. 'She was brilliant at the piano.' I picked up my teaspoon. 'She got Grade 8 when she was only fourteen – with Distinction. It was announced in school at assembly.'

'Really?'

I began stirring my tea. 'The headmistress asked Emma to come up on stage and play something, so she played this lovely piece from Schumann's *Scenes from Childhood*. It was called "Träumerei" – Dreaming . . .'

'What a gifted girl,' said Mrs Bell with a faintly puzzled expression. 'And are you still friends with this . . . paragon?' she added wryly.

'No.' I noticed a solitary tea leaf at the bottom of the

cup. 'She's dead. She died earlier this year, on the fifteenth of February, at about ten to four in the morning. At least, that's when they think it happened, although they couldn't be sure; but I suppose they have to put something down, don't they . . .'

'How terrible,' Mrs Bell murmured after a moment. 'What age was she?'

'Thirty-three.' I continued to stir my tea, gazing into its topaz depths. 'She would have been thirty-four today.' The spoon gently chinked against the cup. I looked at Mrs Bell. 'Emma was very talented in other ways, too. She was a wonderful tennis player – although . . .' I felt myself smile. 'She had this peculiar serve. She looked as though she was tossing pancakes. It worked, mind you – they were un-returnable.'

'Really . . .'

'She was a terrific swimmer – and a brilliant artist.'

'What an accomplished young woman.'

'Oh yes. But she wasn't in the least bit conceited – quite the opposite, actually. She was full of self-doubt.'

I suddenly realised that my tea, being black and sugarless, didn't need stirring. I laid my spoon in the saucer.

'And she was your best friend?'

I nodded. 'She was. But I wasn't really a "best" friend to her or even a good friend, come to that.' The cup had blurred. 'In fact, when the chips were down, I was a terrible friend.' I was aware of the steady sound of the gas fire, like an unending exhalation. 'I'm sorry,' I said quietly. I put down my cup. 'I came here to look at your clothes. I think I'll get on with that now, if you don't mind. But thank you for the tea – it was just the ticket.'

Mrs Bell hesitated for a moment, then she stood up

and I followed her across the corridor into the bedroom. Like the rest of the flat it seemed not to have been touched for years. It was decorated in yellow and white, with a glossy yellow eiderdown on the small double bed, and yellow Provençal curtains and matching panels set into the doors of the white built-in cupboards that lined the far wall. There was a cream alabaster lamp on the bedside table and next to it a black-and-white photo of a handsome, dark-haired man in his mid forties. On the dressing table was a studio portrait of Mrs Bell as a young woman. She had been striking rather than beautiful, with her high forehead, Roman nose and wide mouth.

Ranged against the nearest wall were four cardboard boxes, all spilling over with gloves, bags and scarves. While Mrs Bell sat on the bed, I knelt on the floor and quickly went through them.

'These are all lovely,' I said. 'Especially these silk squares here – I adore this Liberty one with the fuchsia pattern. This is smart . . .' I pulled out a boxy little Gucci handbag with bamboo handles. 'And I like these two hats. What a pretty hatbox,' I added, looking at the hexagonal box the hats were stored in, with its pattern of spring flowers on a black background. 'What I'll do today,' I went on as Mrs Bell walked, with visible effort, towards the wardrobe, 'is to offer you a price for those clothes I'd like to buy. If you're happy with it, I'll write you a cheque now, but I won't take anything until it's cleared. Does that sound all right?'

'It sounds *fine*,' Mrs Bell replied. 'So . . .' She opened the wardrobe and I caught the scent of Ma Griffe. 'Please go ahead. The clothes for consideration are in the left-hand section here, but please don't touch anything beyond this yellow evening dress.'

I nodded then began to pull out the clothes on their pretty satin hangers, laying them in 'yes' and 'no' piles on the bed. For the most part, the things were in very good condition. There were nipped-in suits from the fifties, geometric coats and shifts from the sixties – including a Thea Porter orange velvet tunic and a wonderful candy pink raw silk Guy Laroche 'cocoon' coat with elbow-length sleeves. There were romantic smocked dresses from the seventies and a number of shoulder-padded suits from the 1980s. There were some labels – Norman Hartnell, Jean Muir, Pierre Cardin, Missoni and Hardy Amies 'Boutique'.

'You have some lovely evening wear,' I remarked as I looked at a Chanel sapphire blue silk faille evening coat from the mid sixties. 'This is wonderful.'

'I wore that to the premiere of *You Only Live Twice*,' said Mrs Bell. 'Alastair's agency had done some of the advertising for the film.'

'Did you meet Sean Connery?'

Mrs Bell's face lit up. 'Not only did I meet him – I *danced* with him at the after-film party.'

'Wow . . . And this is gorgeous.' I pulled out an Ossie Clark chiffon maxi dress with a pattern of cream-and-pink florets.

'I adore that dress,' Mrs Bell said dreamily. 'I have many happy memories of it.'

I felt in the left-hand seam. 'And here's the tiny trademark pocket that Ossie Clark put in each one. Just big enough for a five-pound note –'

'– and a key,' Mrs Bell concluded. 'A charming idea.'

There was also quite a bit of Jaeger, which I told her I wouldn't be taking.

'I've hardly worn it.'

'It's not that – it's because it's not old enough to qualify as vintage. I don't have anything in the shop that's later than the early eighties.'

Mrs Bell fingered the sleeve of an aquamarine wool suit. 'I don't know what I'll do with it, then.'

'They're lovely things – surely you could still wear them?'

She gave a little shrug. 'I rather doubt it.'

I looked at the labels – size 14 – and realised that Mrs Bell was at least two sizes smaller than when she'd bought these clothes, but then people often shrink in old age.

'If you'd like any of them altered, I could take them to my seamstress for you,' I suggested. 'She's very good, and her charges are fair. In fact, I have to go there tomorrow, so –'

'Thank you,' Mrs Bell interjected, shaking her head, 'but I have enough to wear. I no longer need very much. They can go to the charity shop.'

Now I pulled out a chocolate brown crepe de Chine evening dress with shoe-string straps, edged in copper sequins. 'This is by Ted Lapidus, isn't it?'

'That's right. My husband bought it for me in Paris.'

I looked at her. 'Is that where you're from?'

She shook her head. 'I grew up in Avignon.' So that explained the lavender field painting and the Provençal curtains. 'It said in that newspaper interview that you go to Avignon sometimes.'

'I do. I buy things from the weekend markets in the area.'

'I think that's why I decided to phone you,' said Mrs

Bell. 'I was somehow drawn to that connection. What sort of things do you buy?'

'Old French linen, cotton dresses and nighties, broderie anglaise vests – they're popular with young women here. I love going to Avignon – in fact, I'll need to go again soon.' I pulled out a black-and-gold silk moiré evening gown by Janice Wainwright. 'And how long have you lived in London?'

'Almost sixty-one years.'

I looked at Mrs Bell. 'You must have been so young when you came here.'

She nodded wistfully. 'I was nineteen. And now I am seventy-nine. *How* did that happen . . .?' She looked at me as though she genuinely thought I might know, then shook her head and sighed.

'And what brought you to the UK?' I asked as I began looking through a box of Mrs Bell's shoes. She had neat little feet, and the shoes, mostly by Rayne and Gina Fratini, were in excellent condition.

'What brought me to the UK?' Mrs Bell smiled wistfully. 'A man – or more precisely an Englishman.'

'And how did you meet him?'

'In Avignon – not quite "*sur le pont*", but close by. I had just left school and was working as a waitress in a smart café on the Place Crillon. And this attractive man a few years older than me called me over to his table and said, in atrocious French, that he was *desperate* for a *proper* cup of English tea and could I *please* make him one? So I did – to his satisfaction, evidently, because three months later we were engaged.' She nodded at the photo on the bedside table. 'That's Alastair. He was a lovely man.'

79

'He was very good looking.'

'Thank you.' She smiled. 'He was *un bel homme.*'

'But didn't you mind leaving your home?'

There was a little pause. 'Not really,' Mrs Bell replied. 'Nothing felt the same after the war. Avignon had suffered occupation and bombing – I had lost . . .' She fiddled with her gold watch. 'Friends. I was in need of a new start – and then I met Alistair . . .' She ran her hand over the skirt of a damson-coloured gabardine two-piece. 'I adore this suit,' she murmured. 'It reminds me so much of my early life with him.'

'How long were you married?'

'Forty-two years. But that is why I moved to this flat. We'd had a very nice house on the other side of the Heath, but I couldn't bear to stay there after he . . .' Mrs Bell paused for a moment to collect herself.

'And what did he do?'

'Alastair started his own advertising agency – one of the first. It was an exciting time; he did a lot of business entertaining, so I had to look . . . presentable.'

'You must have looked fantastic.' She smiled. 'And did you – do you – have a family?'

'Children?' Mrs Bell fiddled with her wedding ring, which was loose on her finger. 'We were rather unfortunate.'

As the subject was clearly painful, I steered the conversation back to her clothes, indicating the ones I wished to buy. 'But you must only sell them if you're truly happy to do so,' I added. 'I don't want you to have any regrets.'

'Regrets?' Mrs Bell echoed. She placed her hands on her knees. 'I have many. But I will *not* regret parting with these garments. I would like them to go on and –

how did you put it in that newspaper article – have a new life . . .'

Now I began to go through my suggested prices for each piece.

'Excuse me,' Mrs Bell suddenly said, and from her hesitant demeanour I thought she was about to query one of my valuations. 'Please forgive me for asking,' she said, 'but . . .' I looked at her enquiringly. 'Your friend . . . Emma. I hope you don't mind . . .'

'No,' I murmured, aware that, for some reason, I didn't mind.

'What happened to her?' Mrs Bell asked. 'Why did she . . .?' Her voice trailed away.

I lowered the dress I was holding, my heart thudding, as it always does when I recall the events of that night. 'She'd become ill,' I replied carefully. 'No one realised quite how ill she was, and by the time any of us did realise, it was too late.' I looked out of the window. 'So I spend a large part of each day wishing that I could turn back the clock.' Mrs Bell was shaking her head with an expression of intense sympathy, as though she was somehow involved in my sadness. 'As I can't do that,' I went on, 'I have to find a way of living with what happened. But it's hard.' I stood up. 'I've seen all the clothes now, Mrs Bell – there's just that one last dress there.'

From down the corridor I could hear the telephone ringing. 'Please excuse me,' she said.

As I heard her retreating footsteps I went to the wardrobe and took out the final garment – the yellow evening dress. The sleeveless bodice was of a lemon-coloured raw silk and the skirt was of knife-pleated

81

chiffon. But as I pulled it out I found my eye drawn to the garment hanging alongside it – a blue woollen coat. As I peered at it through its protective cover, I saw that it wasn't an adult's coat but a child's. It would have fitted a girl of about twelve.

'Thank you for letting me know,' I heard Mrs Bell say as she concluded her phone call. 'I wasn't expecting to hear from you until next week . . . I saw Mr Tate this morning . . . Yes – that remains my decision . . . I do understand, perfectly . . . Thank you for calling . . .'

As Mrs Bell's voice carried down the hall, I wondered why she would have a girl's coat hanging in her wardrobe. It had clearly been cherished. A tragic explanation flashed into my mind. Mrs Bell *had* had a child – a girl, and this coat had been hers; something awful had happened to her and Mrs Bell couldn't bear to part with it. She hadn't said that she hadn't *had* any children – only that she and her husband had been 'rather unfortunate' – very likely an understatement. I felt a wave of sympathy for Mrs Bell. But then, as I furtively unzipped the clear plastic cover to look at the coat more closely, I realised that it was much too old to fit my scenario. As I pulled it out, I could see that it was from the 1940s and was of woollen worsted with a re-used silk lining. It had been hand made with considerable skill.

I heard Mrs Bell's returning steps and quickly zipped up the cover, but too late: she saw me holding the coat and flinched.

'I am not disposing of that particular garment. Kindly put it back.' Taken aback by her tone, I did. 'I did ask you not to look at anything beyond the yellow evening dress,' she added as she stood in the doorway.

82

'I'm sorry.' My face went hot with shame. 'Was the coat yours?' I added quietly.

Mrs Bell hesitated for a moment, then came back into the room. I heard her sigh. 'My mother made it for me. It was in February 1943. I was thirteen. She had queued for five hours to buy the fabric and it took her two weeks to make. She was rather proud of it,' Mrs Bell added as she sat on the bed again.

'I'm not surprised – it's beautifully made. But you've kept it for . . . sixty-five years?' What had motivated her to do so? I wondered – pure sentimentality, because it had been made by her mother?

'I have kept it for sixty-five years,' Mrs Bell reiterated quietly. 'And I will keep it until I die.'

I glanced at it again. 'It's in amazing condition – it looks almost unworn.'

'That's because it *is* almost unworn. I told my mother that I had lost it. But I hadn't – I had only hidden it.'

I looked at her. 'You hid your winter coat? During the war? But . . . why?'

Mrs Bell looked out of the window. 'Because there was someone who needed it far more than I did. I kept it for that person, and I have been keeping it for her ever since.' She heaved another profound sigh; it seemed to come from her very depths. 'It's a story I have never told anyone – not even my husband.' She glanced at me. 'But lately I *have* felt the need to tell it . . . just to one person. If just *one* person in this world could hear my story, and tell me that they understand – then I would feel . . . But now . . .' Mrs Bell lifted her hand to her temple, pressed it, then closed her eyes. 'I am tired.'

'Of course.' I stood up. 'I'll go.' I heard the carriage

clock chime five thirty. 'I didn't mean to stay for so long
– I've enjoyed talking to you. I'll just put everything
back in the wardrobe.'

I hung up on the left side the clothes that I intended
to buy, then I wrote Mrs Bell a cheque for £800. As I
gave it to her, she shrugged as though it were of no
interest.

'Thank you for letting me see your things, Mrs Bell.'
I picked up my bag. 'They're lovely. I'll phone you next
Monday, to arrange a time for me to collect everything.'
She nodded. 'And can I do anything for you before I
go?'

'No. Thank you, my dear. But I would be grateful if
you could let yourself out.'

'Of course. So . . .' I held out my hand. 'I'll see you
next week then, Mrs Bell.'

'Next week,' she echoed. She looked at me then
suddenly clasped my hand in both hers. 'I already look
forward to it – *very* much.'

FOUR

This morning as I drove to see my seamstress, Val, in unexpected drizzle my mind kept returning to the little blue coat. It was sky blue – the blue of freedom – yet it had been hidden away. As I crawled up Shooter's Hill Road in nose-to-tail traffic I tried to imagine what the reason might be. Sometimes – and now I remembered my mother's remark about sartorial archaeology – I can work out a garment's history from the way it's been worn. When I was at Sotheby's, for example, someone brought me three dresses by Mary Quant. They were all in good condition, except that each had a threadbare patch on the right sleeve. The woman who'd brought them in told me that they had belonged to her aunt, a novelist, who wrote all her books in longhand. A pair of Margaret Howell linen trousers with a worn left hip had been owned by a model who'd had three babies in the space of four years. But now, as I flicked on the windscreen wipers, I could come up with no theory for Mrs Bell's coat. Who, in 1943, had needed it more than she did? And why had Mrs Bell never told anyone the story – not even her adored husband?

I hadn't mentioned it to Annie when she'd arrived for work this morning. I'd simply said that I'd be buying quite a few things from Mrs Bell.

'Is that why you're going to your seamstress?' she asked as she re-folded the knitwear. 'To have some of them altered?'

'No. I've got some repairs to collect. Val phoned me last night.' I picked up my car keys. 'She doesn't like things hanging around once they're done.'

Val, who'd been recommended to me by Pippa at the Moon Daisy Café, is extremely quick and very reasonable. She is also a dressmaking genius and can restore even a wrecked garment to its former glory.

By the time I parked outside her house in Granby Road at the nicer end of Kidbrooke the drizzle had become pelting rain. I peered through the misted windscreen and watched the raindrops bounce off the bonnet like ball bearings. I'd need my umbrella just to get to Val's porch.

She opened the door – a tape measure slung round her neck – and her pointy little face folded into a smile. Then she noticed my umbrella and looked at it suspiciously. 'You won't put that up in here, will you?'

'Of course not,' I replied as I lowered it. I gave it a good shake. 'I know you think it would be . . .'

'Unlucky.' Val shook her head. 'It *would* be – especially as it's black.'

'Is that worse then?' I stepped inside.

'Much worse. And you won't drop it on the floor, will you?' she added anxiously.

'No – but why not?'

'Because if you drop a brolly it means there'll be a murder in the house in the near future, and I'd rather avoid it, especially as my husband's been driving me up the wall lately. I don't want to . . .'

'Push your luck?' I suggested as I placed the umbrella in her stand.

'Exactly.' I followed her down the passage.

Val is short, sharp and thin – like a pin. She is also superstitious to the point of it being a compulsion. It isn't just that she – by her own admission – salutes solitary magpies left, right and centre, bows to the full moon and strenuously avoids greeting black cats. She has an encyclopaedic knowledge of superstition and folklore. In the four months that I've known her I have discovered that it's unlucky to eat a fish from the tail towards the head, to try and count the stars, or to wear pearls on your wedding day. It's unlucky to drop your comb while doing your hair – it portends disappointment – or to stick knitting needles through balls of yarn.

On the other hand it's *lucky* to find a nail, eat an apple on Christmas Eve, and to accidentally put a garment on inside out.

'Right then,' Val said as we went into her sewing room, every surface of which was stacked up with shoe boxes brimming with cotton reels and zips, sewing patterns, cards of ribbon, swatches of fabric and spools of bias binding. She reached under the table and produced a large carrier bag. 'I think these have come up quite nicely,' she said as she handed it to me.

I looked inside it. They had. A maxi-length Halston coat with a ripped hémline had been shortened to mid-calf; a fifties cocktail dress with perspiration stains had had the arms cut out so that it was now elegantly sleeve-less; and an Yves St Laurent silk jacket, which had been sprayed with champagne, had been speckled with sequins to cover the stains. I'd have to point out these alter-ations to prospective buyers, but at least the clothes had been saved. They were much too beautiful and good just to be thrown away.

'They've come up brilliantly, Val,' I said as I reached for my bag to pay her. 'You're so clever.'

'Well, my gran taught me to sew; and she always said that if there's a fault on a garment then don't just mend it – make a *virtue* of it. I can still hear her saying it to me now: "Make a *virtue* of it, Valerie." *Oh.*' She'd dropped her scissors and was staring at them with a look of insane happiness. '*That's* great.'

'What is?'

'They've landed with both points sticking into the floor.' She stooped to pick them up. 'That's *really* good luck,' she explained, waving them at me. 'It usually means that more work's coming into the household.'

'It is.' I told her that I was buying a collection of clothes and that about eight of the garments would need minor repairs.

'Bring them in,' Val said as I handed her the money I owed her. 'Thanking you. Ooh . . .' She peered at the coat. 'That bottom button's a bit loose – let me do it before you go.'

Suddenly the door bell rang three times in quick succes-sion.

'Val?' called a gravelly voice. 'You there?'

'That's my neighbour, Maggie,' Val explained as she threaded her needle. 'She always rings three times to let me know it's her. I leave the door on the latch as we're forever popping in and out of each other's houses. We're in the sewing room, Mags!'

'Thought you would be! Hiya!' Maggie was standing in the doorway, almost filling it. She was the physical opposite of Val, being big, blonde and spready. She was wearing tight black leather trousers, gold stilettos, the sides of which struggled to contain her plump feet, and a low-cut red top which displayed a massive, if somewhat crepey, cleavage. She was also wearing tawny-toned foundation, bright blue eye-liner and false lashes. As for her age, she could have been anywhere between thirty-eight and fifty. She exuded the scent of Magie Noire mingled with cigarettes.

'Hi, Mags,' said Val. 'This is Hoebe,' she added through gritted teeth as she bit the end of the cotton. 'Phoebe's just opened a vintage dress shop over in Blackheath – haven't you, Phoebe. By the way,' she added to me, 'I hope you put salt on the doorstep like I told you to. It helps protect against misfortune.'

I'd had so much misfortune it would have made no difference, I reflected. 'I can't say I did do that, no.'

Val shrugged as she put a rubber thimble on her middle finger. 'Don't say I didn't warn you.' She began to re-stitch the button. 'So how's it going then, Mags?'

Mags sank into a chair, evidently exhausted. 'I've just had *the* most difficult client. For ages he refused to get started – he just wanted to talk; then he took forever about it, and afterwards he was tricky about paying because he wanted to pay by cheque and I said it's cash or nothing, as I had made *quite* clear beforehand.' She rearranged her breasts in an indignant manner. 'When I said I'd call the Bill he produced the notes sharp enough. I couldn't half do with a cup of something though, Val – I'm all in and it's only half eleven.'

'Put the kettle on then,' said Val.

Mags disappeared into the kitchen, her nicotine rasp carrying down the passageway. 'Then I had this other customer – he had this weird obsession with his mother – he'd even brought one of her dresses with him. *Very* demanding, he was. I did what I could for him, but he then had the cheek to say that he was "dissatisfied" with my "services". Imagine!'

The probable nature of Maggie's business was by now clear.

'You poor sweetheart,' said Val warmly as Mags reappeared with a packet of digestives. 'Those punters of yours don't half take it out of you.'

Mags gave a long-suffering sigh. 'You can say that again.' She took out a biscuit, and bit on it. 'Then to cap it all, I had that woman at number 29 – Sheila Whatsit.' My eyes started from my head. 'She was a right nuisance. Wanted to get in touch with her ex-husband. He'd dropped dead on the golf course last month. She said she felt so bad about how she'd treated him when they were married that she couldn't sleep. So I get through to him, right . . .' Mags sank into the chair. 'And I begin passing on his messages to her, but within two minutes she's furious with him about something and starts screaming and shrieking at him like a bagful of cats –'

'I think I heard her through the wall,' Val said evenly as she pulled the thread taut. 'Sounded like quite a carry-on.'

'You're telling me,' agreed Mags as she flicked crumbs off her lap. 'So I said, "Look, sweetheart, you really shouldn't *talk* to dead people like that. It's disrespectful."'

'So . . . you're a medium?' I said shyly.

'A medium?' Maggie looked at me so seriously that I thought I'd offended her. 'No – I'm *not* a medium,' she said. 'I'm a *large*!' At that she and Val hooted with laughter. 'Sorry,' Maggie snorted. 'I can never resist that one.' She wiped away a tear with a scarlet talon. 'But to answer your question . . .' She patted her banana yellow hair. 'I *am* a medium – or clairvoyant – *yes*.'

My pulse was racing. 'I've never met a medium before.'

'Never?'

'No. But . . .'

'*There* you are, Phoebe – all done!' Val snipped the end of the thread, deftly wound it round the shank five or six times, and quickly folded the coat back into the bag. 'So when do you want to bring the other things over?'

'Well – probably a week today as I have help in the shop on Mondays and Tuesdays. Will you be here if I come at the same time?'

'I'm always here,' Val replied wearily. 'No rest for the wicked.'

I looked at Maggie. 'So . . . I'm . . . just wondering . . .' I felt a sudden rush of adrenaline. 'Someone very close to me died recently. I was very fond of . . . this person.

I miss them . . .' Maggie nodded sympathetically. 'And
. . . I've never ever done this before and in fact I've always
been sceptical – but if I could just talk to them, if only
for a few seconds, or *hear* something from them,' I went
on anxiously. 'I've even looked up a few psychics in
Yellow Pages – there's this thing called "Dial-a-Medium";
and I actually selected one of them and called their
number but then I couldn't bring myself to speak
because I felt so embarrassed but now that I've met *you*
I feel I –'

'Do you want a reading?' Maggie interjected patiently.
'Is that what you're trying to tell me, sweetheart?'

I sighed with relief. 'It is.'

She reached into her cleavage and pulled out first a
packet of Silk Cut, then a little black diary. She slid
the tiny pen out of its spine, licked her index finger
and flicked over the pages. 'So when shall I put you in
for?'

'Well . . . after I've dropped off the things I'm bringing
Val?'

'This time next week then?' I nodded. 'My terms are
fifty quid cash, no refunds for a bad connection – and
no dissing the deceased,' Mags added as she scribbled
away. 'That's my new rule. So . . .' She tucked the diary
back into her bosom then opened the pack of cigarettes.
'That's a private sitting at eleven a.m. next Tuesday. See
you then, sweetheart,' she said as I left.

As I drove back to Blackheath I tried to analyse my
motives for going to a medium. I'd always regarded such
activities with distaste. My grandparents had all died,
but I'd never felt the slightest urge to try and contact

any of them on 'the other side'. But since Emma's death I'd increasingly been aware of the desire, somehow, to reach her. Meeting Mags had made me feel that I could at least try.

But what did I hope to get out of the experience? I wondered as I approached Montpelier Vale. A message from Emma, presumably. Saying what? That she was . . . okay? How *could* she be? I reflected as I pulled up outside the shop. She's probably floating around in the ether, bitterly pondering the fact that thanks to her so-called 'best friend' she was now never going to get married, have children, turn forty, go to Peru like she'd always wanted to do, let alone get the OBE for services to the fashion industry as we'd often drunkenly predicted. She would now never get to enjoy the prime of her life, or the peaceful retirement that should have followed it, surrounded by her children and grandchildren. That Emma had been deprived of all this was, I reflected bleakly, thanks to me – and to Guy. If only Emma had never *met* Guy, I wished as I parked . . .

'It's been an amazing morning,' Annie said as I pushed on the door.

'Has it?'

'The Pierre Balmain evening gown has sold – subject to the cheque clearing, but I doubt there'll be a problem.'

'Fabulous,' I breathed. That would help the cash flow.

'And I've sold two of those fifties circle skirts. Plus you know the pale pink Madame Grès – the one you don't want?'

'Yes.'

'Well, that woman who tried it on the other day came back –'

'*And?*'

'Bought it.'

'*Great.*' I clapped my hand to my chest in relief.

Annie looked at me with puzzlement. 'Well, yes, it means you've taken over £2,000 and it's still only lunchtime.' I couldn't tell Annie that my reaction to the sale of the dress had nothing to do with the money. 'The woman's completely the wrong shape for it,' Annie went on as I went through to the office, 'but she said she *had* to have it. The card payment was fine, so she took it away.'

For a split second I wrestled with my conscience – the £500 from the sale of the gown would be so useful. But I had vowed to give the money to charity and that's what I'd do.

Suddenly the bell over the door tinkled and in came the girl who'd tried on the turquoise cupcake dress.

'I'm back,' she announced happily.

Annie's face lit up. 'I'm delighted,' she said with a smile. 'The prom dress looked lovely on you.' She went to get it down.

'Oh, I haven't come for that,' the girl explained, although she threw the dress a glance that was tinged with regret. 'I've come to buy something for my fiancé.' She went over to the jewellery display and pointed to the 18-carat-gold art deco octagonal cufflinks with abalone insets. 'I saw Pete looking at these when we were here the other day and thought they'd make a perfect wedding present for him.' She opened her bag. 'How much are they?'

'They're £100,' I replied, 'but with the five per cent discount that's £95, and there's an additional five per

cent off as I'm having a good day, so that makes them
£90.'

'Thank you.' The girl smiled. 'Done.'

As Annie had now done her two days I manned the
shop for the rest of the week. In between helping
customers I was assessing clothes that people brought
in, photographing stock for the website and processing
online orders, doing small repairs, talking to dealers,
and trying to keep on top of my accounts. I posted the
cheque for Guy's dress to Unicef, relieved to have no
reminders left of our few months together. Gone were
the photos, the letters, the e-mails – all deleted – the
books, and the most hated reminder of all, the engagement ring. And now, with the dress sold, I breathed a
sigh of relief. Guy was finally out of my life.

On the Friday morning my father phoned, imploring me
to visit him.

'It's been such a long time, Phoebe,' he said sadly.

'I'm sorry, Dad. I've had so much on my mind these
past few months.'

'I know you have, darling, but I'd love to see you;
and I'd love you to see Louis again. He's so sweet, Phoebe.
He's just . . .' I heard Dad's voice catch. He gets a bit
emotional sometimes, but then he's been through a lot,
even if it is of his own making. 'How about Sunday?'
he tried again. 'After lunch.'

I looked out of the window. 'I *could* come then, Dad
– but I'd rather not see Ruth – if you'll forgive my
candour.'

'I understand,' he replied softly. 'I know the situation
has been hard for you, Phoebe. It's been hard for me too.'

'I hope you're not appealing for sympathy, Dad.'

I heard him sigh. 'I don't really deserve it, do I?' I didn't reply. 'Anyway,' he went on, 'Ruth's flying to Libya on Sunday morning for a week's filming, so I thought that might be a good time for you to come over.'

'In that case, yes, I will.'

On Friday afternoon Mimi Long's fashion editor came in and chose some clothes for their shoot – a seventies-style spread for their January edition to be called RING IN THE OLD. I had just given them the receipt for the things they'd chosen, and was about to cash up, when I looked up and saw Pete the fiancé tearing over the road towards Village Vintage, his tie flapping over his shoulder.

He pushed on the door. 'I've just dashed here from work,' he panted. He nodded at the turquoise cupcake dress. 'I'll take it.' He reached for his wallet. 'Carla still hasn't found anything to wear for the party tomorrow and she's in a panic about it and I know that the reason *why* she still hasn't found anything is because she really liked *this* dress and okay it is a bit pricey but I want her to have it and to hell with the money.' He put six £50 notes on the counter.

'My assistant was right,' I said as I folded the dress into a large carrier. 'You *are* the perfect husband-to-be.'

As Pete waited for his receipt I saw him idly looking at the tray of cufflinks. 'Those gold and abalone cufflinks,' he said, 'the ones you had the other day – I don't suppose . . .'

'Oh, I'm sorry,' I said. 'But they've gone.'

As Pete left, I wondered who would buy the other

cupcake dresses. I thought of the sad girl who'd looked so lovely in the lime one. I'd seen her on the other side of the road once or twice, looking preoccupied, but she hadn't come in. I'd also seen a photo of her boyfriend in the *South London Times*. He'd been the guest speaker at a Business Network Dinner at Blackheath Golf Club. It seemed he owned a successful property company, Phoenix Land.

Saturday started badly and got worse. Firstly the shop was very busy and, although I was happy about this, it was as much as I could do to keep an eye on the stock. Then someone came in eating a sandwich so I had to ask them to leave, which I disliked having to do, especially in front of other customers. Then Mum phoned up and needed a bit of a cheer-up as she's often down at weekends.

'I've decided not to have Botox,' she said.

'That's great, Mum. You don't need it.'

'That's not the point – the clinic I went to said I've left it too late for Botox to make any difference.'

'Then . . . never mind.'

'So I'm going to have gold threads in my face instead.'

'You're what?'

'Basically they insert these gold threads under your skin, and on the ends of them are these tiny hooks which they catch up so that the thread pulls taut – and up comes your face with it! The trouble is, it costs £4,000. But then it is 24 carat,' she mused.

'Don't even *think* about it,' I said. 'You're still very attractive, Mum.'

'Am I?' she said mournfully. 'Ever since your father left me, I've felt like a gargoyle.'

97

'Nothing could be further from the truth.' In fact, like many dumped wives, Mum had never looked better. She'd lost weight, bought some new clothes and was now far better groomed than when she was with Dad.

Then at lunchtime the woman who'd bought Guy's dress came back with it.

At first I didn't know who she was.

'I'm *so* sorry,' this woman began as she lifted a Village Vintage carrier on to the counter. I looked inside it and my spirits sank. 'I don't think the dress is right after all.' How could she ever have thought that it was? As Annie had said, the woman was completely the wrong shape, being short and broad – like a milk loaf. 'I'm *so* sorry,' she repeated as I took the dress out of the bag.

'Don't worry, it's not a problem,' I lied. As I refunded her the money, I wished I hadn't been quite so quick in sending the £500 to Unicef. It was now a donation that I couldn't afford.

'I guess I got carried away with the romance of it,' the woman explained as I waited to tear off the receipt. 'But this morning I put on the dress, looked at myself in the mirror and realised that I'd been, well . . .' She turned up her palms as if to say, *I'm not exactly Keira Knightley, am I!* 'I don't have the height,' she went on. 'But do you know what?' She cocked her head to one side. 'I can't help thinking that it would suit *you*.'

After the woman had left, a succession of customers came in, including one fifty-something man who showed an unhealthy interest in the corsets: he even wanted to

98

try one on, but I wouldn't let him. Then this woman phoned up offering me some furs that had belonged to her aunt, including – and this was meant to be the clincher – a hat made out of a leopard cub. I explained that I don't sell fur, but the woman insisted that as these particular furs were vintage there shouldn't be a problem. So I told her that I can't bring myself to touch let alone deal in bits of dead baby leopard, however long it might have been since the poor creature had been murdered. Then a little later my patience was tested again when a woman came in with a Dior coat that she wanted to sell me. I could see at a glance that it was fake.

'It *is* by Dior,' she protested after I'd pointed this out to her. 'And I'd call £100 a *very* reasonable price for a genuine Christian Dior coat of this quality.'

'I'm sorry,' I said. 'But I've worked in vintage fashion for twelve years and I can assure you that this coat is not by Dior.'

'But the label –'

'The label *is* original. But it's been sewn into a non-Dior garment. The interior construction of the coat is all wrong, the seams aren't finished properly, and the lining, if you look a little more closely, is by Burberry.' I pointed to the logo.

The woman went the colour of a Victoria plum. '*I* know what you're trying to do,' she sniffed. 'You're trying to get it at a knock-down price, so that you can sell it for £500 like that one you've got over there.' She nodded at a mannequin on which I'd put a Dior dove grey grosgrain New Look winter coat from 1955 in pristine condition.

'I'm not trying to "get" it at all,' I explained pleasantly. 'I don't want it.'

The woman folded the coat back into the carrier bag, radioactive with affected indignation. 'Then I shall have to take it elsewhere.'

'That's a good idea,' I replied calmly, resisting the temptation to suggest Oxfam.

The woman turned on her heel, and as she stomped out, another customer, on his way in, politely held the door open for her. He was elegantly dressed in pale chinos and a navy blazer and was in his mid forties. I felt my heart lurch.

'Good God!' Mr Pin-Stripe's face had lit up. 'If it isn't my bidding rival – Phoebe!' So he'd remembered my name. 'Don't tell me – is this *your* shop?'

'Yes.' The euphoria I'd felt on seeing him suddenly evaporated as the door opened again and in came Mrs Pin-Stripe on a cloud of perfume. As I'd imagined she was tall and blonde – but so young that I had to fight the urge to call the police. She *couldn't* be his wife I decided as she pushed her sunglasses on top of her head. She was his twenty-five-year-old mistress and he was her sugar daddy – the man was brazen. Her scent – J'adore – made me feel sick.

'I'm Miles,' he reminded me. 'Miles Archant.'

'I remember,' I said pleasantly. 'And what brings you here?' I added, trying not to look askance at his companion, who was now riffling through the evening wear. He nodded at the girl. 'Roxy . . .' Of course. A suitably sexy name for a mistress. Foxy Roxy. 'My daughter.'

'Ah.' The wave of relief I felt took me aback.

100

'Roxanne's looking for a special dress to wear for a teenagers' charity ball at the National History Museum, aren't you, Rox?' She nodded. 'This is Phoebe,' he added. As the girl gave me a tepid smile I could now see how young she was. 'We met at Christie's,' her father explained. 'Phoebe bought that white dress you liked.'

'Oh,' she said resentfully.

I looked at Miles. 'You were bidding for the Madame Grès for . . .?' I indicated Roxy.

'Yes. She saw it on the Christie's website and fell in love with it – didn't you, darling? She couldn't come to the auction because she was at school.'

'What a shame.'

'Yeah,' said Roxy. 'It clashed with double English.'

So it was *Roxy* who'd been giving Miles such a hard time at the auction. And now I marvelled why anyone would be prepared to spend nearly £4,000 on a dress for a teenager.

'Roxanne wants to work in fashion,' he said. 'She's very interested in vintage clothing – aren't you, darling?'

Roxanne nodded again. As she carried on looking through the rails I wondered where her mother was and what *she* looked like. The same, I imagined, but in her mid forties.

'Anyway, we're still looking,' Miles said. 'That's why we've come here. The ball isn't until November, but we happened to be in Blackheath, and we saw this shop had opened . . .' I saw Roxy give her father a quizzical glance. 'So we thought we'd take a look and we find – *you*! An unexpected bonus,' he added.

101

'Thank you,' I said, wondering what his wife would think if she could see him chatting to me in such a blatantly friendly fashion.

'An amazing coincidence,' he concluded.

I turned to Roxanne. 'So what sort of things do you like?' I asked, trying to keep things professional.

'Well . . .' She pushed her Ray-Bans a little higher on her head. 'I thought something a bit *Atonement*y or – what was that other film? – *Gosford Park*y.'

'I see . . . So that's mid to late thirties then. Bias cut. In the style of Madeleine Vionnet . . .' I mused as I went up to the evening-wear rail.

Roxy shrugged her slim shoulders. 'S'pose . . .' It cynically occurred to me that there might be an opportunity here to get rid of Guy's dress. Then I realised that Roxy was too slim for it – it would hang off her.

'See anything you like, darling?' her father asked.

She shook her head, and her hair, a hank of blonde silk, swished around her slim shoulders. Suddenly her mobile phone rang – what was that ringtone? Oh yes. It was 'The Most Beautiful Girl in the World'.

'Hi there,' Roxy drawled. 'No. With my dad. In some vintage dress shop . . . Last night? Yeah . . . Mahiki's. It was cool. Yeah. Cool . . . Then it got hot . . . *Really* hot. Yeah. Cool . . .' I felt like checking the thermostat.

'Do take that call outside, darling,' her father said. Roxy shouldered her Prada bag and pushed on the door, then she stood outside, leaning against the glass, one coltish leg crossed in front of the other. Her 'conversation' was clearly not going to be brief.

Miles rolled his eyes in mock despair. 'Teenagers . . .'

He smiled indulgently then he began to look round the shop. 'What lovely things you have here.'

'Thanks.' I noticed again how attractive his voice was – it had this slight break in it which I found somehow touching. 'Do you know, I might buy a pair of those braces.'

I opened the counter and took out the tray. 'They're from the 1950s,' I explained. 'They're unsold stock, so they've never been worn. They're by Albert Thurston, who made top-quality English braces.' I pointed to the straps. 'You can see that the leather is hand stitched.'

Miles peered at them. 'I'll have these ones,' he said, picking out a green-and-white striped pair. 'How much are they?'

'Fifteen pounds.'

He looked at me. 'I'll give you twenty.'

'I'm sorry?'

'Twenty-five then.'

I laughed. 'You *what*?'

'Okay, I'm prepared to go up to thirty pounds, if you're going to be hard-nosed about it, but that's *it*.'

I smiled. 'It's not an auction – I'm afraid you'll just have to pay the asking price.'

'You drive a hard bargain,' Miles muttered. 'In that case, I'll have the navy pair too.' As I put them both in a bag I was aware that Miles was scrutinising me and I felt my face go warm. I was surprised to find myself wishing that he wasn't married. 'I enjoyed bidding against you the other day,' I heard him say as I opened the till. 'I don't suppose you felt the same, though.'

'No, I didn't,' I replied pleasantly. 'In fact, I was rather furious. But as you were prepared to pay so much for the dress I assumed that you were trying to get it for your wife.'

Miles shook his head. 'I don't have one.' Ah. So he lived with someone – or maybe he was an unmarried father or a divorced dad. 'My wife died.'

'Oh.' My euphoria returned, to my shame. 'I'm sorry.'

Miles shrugged. 'It's all right – in the sense that it happened ten years ago,' he added quickly. 'So I've had plenty of time to get used to it.'

'Ten years?' I echoed wonderingly. Here was a man who hadn't married again in a whole *decade*? Let alone the week after his wife's funeral, as so many widowers do. I felt my frostiness thaw.

'At home it's just Roxy and me. She's just started at Bellingham College in Portland Place.' I'd heard of it – an upmarket crammer. 'Can I ask you something?' Miles added.

I handed him his receipt. 'Of course.'

'I just wondered . . .' He cast an anxious glance at Roxanne, but she was still chatting away, winding a white-blonde tendril around her finger as she did so. 'I just wondered whether you'd . . . have dinner with me sometime . . .'

'Oh . . .'

'I'm sure you think I'm too old,' he went on quickly. 'But I'd love to see you again, Phoebe. In fact – can I confess something?'

'What?' I said, intrigued.

'It isn't *entirely* due to coincidence that I'm here. In fact, to be perfectly honest, coincidence has nothing to do with it.'

I stared at him. 'But . . . how did you know where I was?'

'Because as you were paying for the dress at Christie's I heard you say "Village Vintage". So I Googled you there and then, and up came your website.' So *that's* what he was looking at so intently on his BlackBerry as he sat next to me! 'As I don't live far away – in Camberwell – I thought I'd just drop in and say . . . "Hi".' So his honesty had triumphed over his cunning. I smiled to myself. 'Now . . .' He shrugged in a good-natured way. 'You didn't want to have lunch with me the other day – or even a coffee. You probably thought I was married.'

'I did think that. Yes.'

'But now that you know that I'm not, I wonder whether you might like to have dinner with me?'

'I . . . don't know.' I felt my face flush.

Miles glanced at his daughter, still talking on her mobile. 'You don't have to say now. Here . . .' He opened his wallet and took out his business card. I glanced at it. *Miles Archant LLB, Senior Partner, Archant, Brewer & Clark, Solicitors*. 'Just let me know if you're tempted.'

I suddenly realised that I *was*. Miles was very attractive, and he had this lovely husky voice – and he was a real grown-up, I reflected, unlike so many men of my own age. Like Dan, I suddenly found myself thinking, with his unruly hair and his ill-matching clothes, and his pencil sharpener and his . . . *shed*. Why would I want to go and see Dan's *shed*? I looked at Miles. He was a man, not an overgrown boy. But on the other hand, I now reflected as reality took hold, he was a virtual stranger and, yes, he was much older than me – forty-three or -four.

'I'm forty-eight,' he said. 'Don't look so shocked!'

'Oh, sorry, I'm not, it's just that . . . you don't look that . . .'

'Old?' he finished wryly.

'That's not what I meant. It's really nice of you to ask me, but to be honest I *am* pretty busy at the moment.' I began rearranging the scarves. 'And I have to focus on my business,' I floundered on. Nearly *fifty* . . . 'And the thing is – oh.' The phone was ringing. 'Excuse me.' I picked up the handset, grateful for the interruption. 'Village Vintage.'

'Phoebe?' My heart was suddenly pounding in my chest. 'Please speak to me, Phoebe,' said Guy. 'I must speak to you,' I heard him insist. 'You've ignored all my letters and –'

'That's . . . right,' I said quietly, struggling to control my emotions in front of Miles, who was now sitting on the sofa, gazing out at the Blackheath cloudscape. I closed my eyes and took a deep breath.

'I need to *talk* to you,' I heard Guy say. 'I refuse to let things be left like this, and I'm not going to give up until I've got you to –'

'I'm sorry, I can't help you,' I said with a calmness I did not feel. 'But thank you for calling.' I put down the phone without a scintilla of guilt. Guy knew what he'd done.

You know how Emma exaggerates, Phoebe.

I switched the phone over to 'answer' mode. 'I'm sorry,' I said to Miles. 'What were you saying?'

'Well . . .' He stood up. 'I was just telling you that I'm

106

. . . forty-eight, and that, if you were prepared to over-
look that handicap, I'd be delighted if you'd have dinner
with me sometime. But it doesn't sound as though you'd
want to.' He gave me an anxious smile.

'Actually, Miles . . . I *would*.'

FIVE

On Sunday afternoon I made my way over to Dad's – or, more accurately, to Ruth's. Although I'd met her – once – for about ten seconds – it would be the first time I'd set foot in her flat. I'd asked Dad if we could meet on neutral territory, but he said that because of Louis it would be easier if I could come and see him 'at home'.

'At home . . .' I reflected wonderingly as I walked down Portobello. All my life 'home' had been the Edwardian villa in which I'd grown up and in which my mother, for the time being, still lives. The idea that 'home', for Dad, was now a smart duplex in Notting Hill with the hatchet-faced Ruth and their baby son was still impossible to grasp. Going there would make it all depressingly real.

Dad simply wasn't a Notting Hill kind of person, I thought as I passed the fashionable boutiques of Westbourne Grove. What did L.K. Bennett or Ralph Lauren mean to my father? He belonged in friendly, old-fashioned Blackheath.

Ever since the separation, Dad's had this slightly stunned expression on his face, as though he's just been slapped by a stranger. That was how he looked now, as he opened the door of number 88 Lancaster Road.

'Phoebe!' Dad bent to hug me, but it was hard to do with Louis in his arms and the baby got squished between us and squawked. 'It's so lovely to see you.' Dad ushered me inside. 'Oh, would you mind taking your shoes off – it's the rule here.' No doubt one of many, I thought as I removed my sling-backs and tucked them under a chair. 'I've missed you, Phoebe,' Dad said as I followed him down the limestone-tiled hallway into the kitchen.

'I've missed you too, Dad.' I stroked Louis' blond head as he sat in Dad's arms at the brushed stainless-steel table. '*You've* changed, sweetie.'

Louis had morphed from a wrinkled, liver-coloured scrap of flesh into the sweet-faced infant who was waving his bendy little limbs at me like a baby octopus.

I glanced at all the gleaming metal surfaces. Ruth's kitchen struck me as far too hygienic an environment for a man who'd spent most of his professional life grubbing around in the dirt. It didn't even look like a kitchen – it resembled a morgue. I thought of the old scrubbed pine table at *real* home, and the stacks of Portmeirion 'Botanical Garden' crockery. What the hell was my dad doing *here*?

I smiled at him. 'Louis looks like you.'

'Do you think so?' said Dad happily.

I didn't, but I didn't want Louis to look like Ruth. I opened the Hamley's bag I'd been carrying and handed Dad a big white bear with a blue ribbon round its neck.

'*Thank* you.' He jiggled the teddy in front of Louis. 'Isn't this lovely, baby? Oh look, Phoebe, he's smiling at it.'

I stroked the baby's plump little legs. 'Don't you think Louis should be wearing more than just a nappy, Dad?'

'Oh yes,' he said vaguely. 'I was just changing him when you arrived. Now *where* did I put his clothes? Ah. Here we go.' I watched, appalled, as Dad clamped a surprised-looking Louis to his chest with his left arm then somehow slotted his limbs into a stripy blue sleep-suit. Having done that, he then wrestled him into his stainless-steel high chair, getting two legs jammed down one hole so that Louis was stuck, rigid, in a bob-sleighing position. Dad then went to the gleaming American fridge and took out an assortment of small jars.

'Let's see . . .' he said, unscrewing the first. 'I'm getting him on to solids,' he explained over his shoulder. 'We'll try this one, shall we, Louis?' Louis opened his mouth wide, like a baby bird, and Dad began to spoon the contents of the jar into it. '*What* a good boy. Well *done*, my little boy. *Oh* . . .' Louis had pebble-dashed Dad with beige mush.

'I don't think he likes it,' I said as Dad wiped what I now knew to be organic chicken and lentil casserole off his glasses.

'Sometimes he does.' Dad grabbed a J-cloth and wiped Louis' chin. 'He's in a funny mood today – probably because his mum's away again. We'll try this one now, shall we, Louis?'

'Aren't you supposed to heat it up, Dad?'

'Oh, he doesn't mind it straight from the fridge.' Dad

opened the second jar. 'Moroccan lamb with apricots and couscous – yum.' Louis opened his tiny mouth again and Dad posted a few teaspoons into it. 'Oh, he likes *this*,' Dad said triumphantly. 'Definitely.'

Suddenly Louis extruded his tongue, like a Maori, expelling the Moroccan lamb in an orange slick that now flowed down his front like lava.

'You should have put a bib on him,' I pointed out as Dad scraped the *ejecta* off Louis' chest. 'No, Dad. Don't put it back in.' On the table was a leaflet called 'Weaning Success'.

'I'm not much good at this,' Dad said miserably. He scraped the rejected jar into the gleaming chrome bin. 'It was so much easier when I could just give him a bottle.'

'I'd help you, Dad, but I'm clueless myself – for obvious reasons. But why do *you* have to do so much childcare?'

'Well . . . because Ruth's away again,' he said wearily. 'She's very busy at the moment, and the thing is, I *want* to do it. Firstly, there's no point paying a nanny now that' – Dad flinched – 'I'm not working. Plus, when *you* were a baby I was away so much that I missed out on fatherhood.'

'You *were* away a lot,' I agreed. 'All those field-trips and excavations. I always seemed to be waving goodbye to you,' I added ruefully.

'I know, darling,' he sighed. 'And I'm very sorry for it. So now, with this little chap' – he stroked Louis' head – 'I feel I've been given the chance to be more of a hands-on father.' Louis looked as though he'd prefer Dad to be hands off.

Suddenly the telephone rang. 'Sorry, darling,' Dad said. 'That'll be Radio Lincoln. I'm doing a telephone interview with them.'

'Radio Lincoln?'

Dad shrugged. 'It's better than Radio Silence.'

As Dad did the interview, the phone clamped to his ear with his right hand while he posted more goo into Louis with his left, I reflected on his calamitous professional fall. Only a year ago Dad was still the widely respected Professor of Comparative Archaeology at Queen Mary's College, London. Then came *The Big Dig*, and in the wake of the humiliating media coverage – the *Daily Mail* dubbed him 'The Big Pig' – Dad was asked to take early retirement with immediate effect. He'd had five years lopped off his career, had taken a big cut in his pension, and, despite six weeks of prime-time exposure on Sunday night, his burgeoning TV career had ground to a halt.

'Well, when we ask what archaeology *is*,' Dad said as he shovelled mango and lychee purée into Louis, 'we might say that it's the study of artefacts and habitation – the discovery of "lost" civilisations even, using the increasingly sophisticated means that we now have of interpreting past societies, the most important of which is of course carbon dating. *However*, when we say "civilisation" we should be aware that that is of course a modern definition imposed upon the past from a Western intellectual perspective . . .' He grabbed a grubby muslin. 'Sorry, should I take that again? You did say it's pre-recorded, didn't you? Oh, I'm so sorry . . .'

On TV Dad had come across very well, largely because he'd had a scriptwriter to render his more erudite phrases into homely ones. If it hadn't been for the media fuss about Ruth's pregnancy, perhaps he'd have got more presenting work, but all he'd been offered since the series ended was *Ready, Steady, Cook!* Ruth's career, on the other hand, had flourished. She'd been promoted to executive producer and was producing a major profile of Colonel Gaddafi, for which she was even now flying to Tripoli.

Suddenly we heard the front door fly open.

'Can you *believe* it?' I heard Ruth yell. 'Effing terrorists closing down Heathrow *again*! Except that it *wasn't* terrorists, was it? No! Of *course* not' – she sounded almost disappointed. 'Just some loony trying to thumb a lift to Tenerife on the tarmac. Terminal Three's been shut down – it took two hours for me and the crew to get out. I'm going to try and get us all on a flight tomorrow – Christ, what a mess you've made in here, darling. And *don't* put carrier bags on the table' – she removed the Hamley's bag – 'they carry bacteria, and *no* toys in here, please, it's a kitchen not a playroom – and do *please* keep the cupboard doors shut as I can't *stand* seeing them open like that – oh.' She'd suddenly noticed me, sitting behind the door.

'Hello, Ruth,' I said calmly. 'I've come to see my father.' I looked at Dad. He was frantically tidying up. 'I hope you don't mind.'

'Not in the least,' she replied airily. 'Make yourself at home.' That would be hard here, I was tempted to say.

'Phoebe brought Louis that lovely teddy bear,' Dad said.

'Thank you,' said Ruth. 'That's very kind.' She kissed

Louis on the head, ignoring his outstretched arms, then went upstairs. Louis threw back his head and started wailing.

'Sorry, Phoebe.' Dad gave me a baleful smile. 'Could we make another date soon?'

The next morning, as I walked up to Village Vintage, I thought about Dad and about how he seemed to have stumbled into an affair with no idea of the turmoil that might follow. It was Mum's belief that he'd never strayed before, despite the opportunities he must have had over the years with attractive archaeology students hanging on his every word as they'd huddled over the dust together, delightedly scraping up bits of the Phoenicians or the Mesopotamians or the Mayans or whoever it was. The ineptitude with which Dad had handled his relationship with Ruth suggested that he was hardly an experienced adulterer.

After he'd left home, Dad had written to me. In his letter he'd said that he still loved Mum, but that once Ruth was pregnant he'd felt he had to stay with her. Then he'd added that he was genuinely fond of Ruth and that I needed to understand that. I couldn't understand it. I still can't.

I could perfectly well see why Ruth would be attracted to my father, despite the twenty-four-year age gap. Dad was one of those tall, handsome, craggy-looking men who'd somehow grown into their faces, added to which he was intelligent, easy-going and kind. But what did he see in Ruth? She wasn't soft or pretty like my mother had been. She was as hard as a plank – with about as much sensitivity. The trauma of seeing Dad move his

114

things out of the marital home had been made infinitely worse by the fact that a heavily pregnant Ruth was seen waiting for him, outside, in her car.

Mum and I had sat there that night, trying not to look at the yawning spaces on the shelves where Dad's books and treasures had been. His most prized artefact, a small bronze of an Aztec woman giving birth – presented to him by the Mexican government – was no longer on the kitchen mantelpiece. Given the circumstances, Mum said she wouldn't miss it.

'If only it wasn't for the *baby*,' she'd wept. 'I don't want to be mean about a poor little baby that hasn't even been born yet – but I can't help wishing that this *particular* baby had never happened, because if it *hadn't* then I could have forgiven and forgotten – instead of which I'm now going to be spending the rest of my life on my *own*!'

With a sinking heart I'd realised that I was going to be spending the rest of her life cheering her up.

I'd tried to persuade Dad not to leave Mum. I'd pointed out that at her age it wasn't fair.

'I feel awful about it,' he'd said over the phone. 'But I've got myself into this . . . situation, Phoebe, and I feel I have to do the right thing.'

'Why is leaving your wife of thirty-eight years the right thing?'

'Why is not being there for my child the right thing?'

'You weren't there for me, Dad.'

'I know – and that has a bearing on my decision now.' I heard him sigh. 'Perhaps it's because I've spent my whole life poring over the distant past, and now, with this baby, I'm being offered a piece of the *future* – at my age, that's cheering. Plus I do *want* to be with Ruth. I know that's hard for you to hear, Phoebe, but it's true. Your mother will get the house and half my pension. She has her job and her bridge circle and her friends. *I'd* like to stay friends with her,' he'd added. 'How can we *not* be friends after such a long marriage?'

'How *can* we be, when he's deserted me?' Mum had wailed when I'd repeated this to her. I could perfectly well see her point . . .

I made my way up Tranquil Vale wishing that I could feel more tranquil myself. Annie wouldn't be coming until mid-morning as she'd gone to an audition. As I unlocked the door I found myself guiltily hoping that she wouldn't get the job, as it was for a two-month regional tour. I liked having Annie around. She was always punctual and smiling, she was great with the customers and she took initiative in rearranging the stock to keep everything looking fresh. She was an asset to Village Vintage.

I'd started the day with a sale, I realised happily as I read my e-mails. Cindi had messaged me from Beverly Hills to say that she definitely wanted the Balenciaga gown for one of her A-Listers to wear to the Emmys and that she'd phone me with payment at the end of the day.

At nine I turned the sign to 'Open' then I phoned Mrs Bell to ask her when I could come and collect the clothes I was buying.

'Can you come this morning?' she asked. 'Say at eleven?'

'Could we make it eleven thirty? My assistant will be here by then. I'll bring my car.'

'Very well, I'll expect you then.'

Suddenly the doorbell jangled and a slim blonde woman in her mid thirties walked in. She spent a few moments looking through the rails with a slightly intense, distracted air.

'Are you looking for anything in particular?' I asked after a minute.

'Yes,' she replied. 'I'm looking for something . . . *happy*. A happy dress.'

'Right . . . and is that for day or evening?'

She shrugged. 'Doesn't matter. It just has to be very bright and cheerful.'

I showed her a Horrocks polished cotton sundress from the mid fifties with a pattern of cornflowers. She fingered the skirt. 'It's lovely.'

'Horrocks made gorgeous cotton dresses – they used to cost a week's wages. And have you seen those?' I nodded at the cupcakes.

'*Oh*.' The woman's eyes widened. 'Those are *fabulous*. Can I try on the pink one?' she asked, like a child, almost. 'I'd like to try the pink one!'

'Of course.' I took it down. 'It's a 12.'

'It's wonderful,' she enthused as I hung it in the changing room. She went inside and pulled round the linen curtain. I heard her unzipping her skirt, then the soft rustle of the net petticoats as she stepped into the dress. 'It looks so . . . joyful,' I heard her say. 'I adore the tutu skirts – I feel like a flower fairy.' She poked her head through the curtain. 'Could you pull up the zip for me? I can't quite manage . . . Thanks.'

'You look gorgeous,' I said. 'It's a perfect fit.'

'It really is.' She gazed at herself in the mirror. 'It's just what I had in mind – a lovely, *happy* dress.'

117

'Are you celebrating something?' I asked.

'Well . . .' She fluffed up the *mille-feuille* of stiffened tulle. 'I've been trying for a baby.' I nodded politely, unsure what to say. 'And I wasn't getting pregnant naturally so after two and a half years we went for IVF – a ghastly business,' she added over her shoulder.

'You don't have to tell me this,' I protested. 'Really . . .'

The woman stepped back and appraised her reflection. 'Anyway, I took my temperature ten times a day and I sniffed all these chemicals, and I injected myself until my hip was like a pin cushion. And I went through this hell *five times* – bankrupting myself in the process, incidentally: and then a fortnight ago it came to the sixth cycle, which was to be the last ever attempt because my husband had told me that he wasn't prepared to go through it again.' She paused for breath. 'So it was the very last throw of the dice . . .' She stepped out of the cubicle and gazed at herself in the side mirror. 'And I got the results this morning. My gynaecologist phoned me to tell me that . . .' She patted her tummy. 'It hadn't worked.'

'*Oh*,' I murmured. 'I'm sorry.' Of course. Why would she be buying a prom dress if she were pregnant?

'So just for today I've pulled a sickie and I'm looking for ways to cheer myself up.' She smiled at her reflection. 'And this dress is the perfect start. It's wonderful,' she enthused as she turned to face me. 'I mean, how could anyone feel sad in a dress like this? It would be impossible, wouldn't it?' Her eyes were shimmering. 'Quite impossible . . .' The girl sank on to the changing-room chair, her features distorted with distress.

I ran to the door and turned over the sign.

'I'm sorry . . .' the woman wept. 'I shouldn't have come in. I'm feeling . . . fragile.'

'It's totally understandable,' I said quietly. I handed her some tissues.

She looked up at me. 'I'm thirty-seven.' A fat tear rolled down her cheek. 'Women a lot older than me have babies, don't they, so why can't *I* have one? Just *one*,' she sobbed. 'Is that too greedy?'

I pulled the curtain round her so that she could change.

A couple of minutes later the woman brought the dress to the counter. She was calm now, though her eyes were red veined.

'You don't have to buy it,' I said.

'I want to,' she protested gently. 'Then whenever I'm feeling down, I'll just put it on, or I could hang it on the wall like you've done here, and just looking at it will make me feel positive again.'

'Well, I hope it has the desired effect, but if you change your mind just bring it back. You need to be sure.'

'I *am* sure,' she protested. 'But thanks.'

'Well . . .' I smiled at her impotently. 'I wish you the very best.' Then I handed her the 'happy' dress in its bag.

Annie came back from her audition at eleven. 'The director was vile,' she exclaimed. 'He actually asked me to turn round – like a piece of meat!'

I remembered the ghastly Keith making his girlfriend turn round for him. 'I hope you didn't.'

'Of course I didn't – I walked out! I should report him to Equity,' she muttered as she took off her jacket. 'Anyway, after that experience it's very nice to be back in your shop.'

Feeling guiltily happy that Annie's audition hadn't been a success, I told her about the girl who'd bought the pink cupcake.

'Poor kid,' she murmured, calm again now. 'Do *you* want children?' she added as she quickly glossed her lips.

'No,' I replied. 'Babies are not on my radar.' Except for my father's baby, I thought wryly.

'Do you have a boyfriend?' Annie asked as she zipped up her bag. 'Not that it's any of my business.'

'No. I'm single – bar the odd date.' I thought of my forthcoming dinner with Miles. 'My priority now is my work. How about you?'

'I've been seeing this chap Tim for a few months,' Annie replied. 'He's a painter – he lives down in Brighton. But I'm still too focused on my career to want to settle down, plus I'm only thirty-two – I've got time.' She shrugged. 'You've got time.'

I looked at my watch. 'No, I haven't – I'm going to be late. I'm collecting the clothes I've bought from Mrs Bell.' Leaving Annie in charge, I walked home then got two suitcases and drove up to The Paragon.

In the week since I'd last been there the catch on the front door of number 8 had been mended, so Mrs Bell didn't have to come down; which just as well I thought when she opened her own door, since she seemed a little frailer even than when I'd last seen her.

She greeted me warmly as I stepped inside, laying her thin, freckled hand on my arm. 'Now go and collect the clothes together – and I do hope you'll stay and have a cup of coffee with me?'

'Thank you – I'd love to.'

I went into the bedroom with the cases and put the bags, shoes and gloves in one of them, then I opened the wardrobe to take out the garments. As I did so, I caught a glimpse of the little blue coat and wondered again about its history.

I heard Mrs Bell's footsteps behind me. 'Are you all done now, Phoebe?' She fiddled with the waistband of her green-and-red plaid skirt, which was slipping a little.

'Almost,' I replied. I put the two hats into the lovely old hatbox that Mrs Bell was including; then I folded the Ossie Clark maxi dress into the second suitcase.

'The Jaeger . . .' said Mrs Bell as I snapped shut the clasps. 'I would like to give it all to a charity shop as I want to get rid of as much as I can while I'm in the mood to do so. I would ask my home-help, Paola, but she is away. Is there any chance that you could do it for me, Phoebe?'

'Of course.' I put the clothes in a large carrier bag. 'There's the Oxfam shop – shall I take them there?'

'Please,' said Mrs Bell. 'Thank you. Now, go and make yourself comfortable while I make the coffee.'

In the sitting room, the gas fire emitted its low hiss. The sun shone through the small square panes of the bow window, casting a grid of shadows across the room like the bars of a cage.

Mrs Bell came in with the tray and with a shaking hand poured us both a cup of coffee from the silver pot. As we drank it she asked me about the shop, and about how I'd started it. I told her some more about myself and my background. I then discovered that she had a nephew by marriage who lived in Dorset who sometimes visited her, and a niece in Lyon who didn't.

'But it's difficult for her as she has to look after her two young grandchildren, but she phones me from time to time. She is my closest relative – the daughter of my late brother, Marcel.'

We chatted for a few more minutes, then the carriage clock chimed half past twelve.

I put down my cup. 'I ought to get going. But thank you for the coffee, Mrs Bell. It's been lovely to see you again.'

A look of regret crossed her face. 'I have so enjoyed seeing you, Phoebe. I am rather hoping you will stay in touch,' she added. 'But you are a very busy young woman. Why ever would you want to bother . . .?'

'I'd love to stay in touch,' I interjected. 'But for now I should get back to the shop – plus I don't want to tire you.'

'I am not tired,' Mrs Bell said. 'For once I have a strange kind of energy.'

'Well . . . can I do anything for you before I go?'

'No,' she replied. 'But thank you.'

'I'll say goodbye then – for now.' I stood up.

Mrs Bell was staring at me, as though weighing something in her mind. 'Stay a little longer,' she said suddenly. 'Please.' My heart filled with pity. The poor woman was lonely and needed company. And I was about to tell her that I could stay for another twenty minutes or so when Mrs Bell disappeared, crossing the corridor into the bedroom, where I heard the wardrobe door being opened. When she returned she was holding the blue coat.

She looked at me, her eyes shining with a strange intensity. 'You wanted to know about this . . .'

'No.' I shook my head. 'It's . . . none of my business.'

'You were curious.'

I stared at her, aghast. 'A . . . little,' I conceded. 'But it's not my concern, Mrs Bell. I shouldn't have touched it.'

'But I *want* to tell you about it,' she said. 'I *want* to tell you about this little coat, and why I hid it. More than anything else, Phoebe, I want to tell you why I have kept it for so long.'

'You don't have to tell me anything,' I protested weakly. 'You barely know me.'

Mrs Bell sighed. 'That's true. But, lately, I have felt a great need to tell someone the story – the story that I have kept inside all these years – here – right *here*.' She jabbed at her chest, hard, with the fingers of her left hand. 'And for some reason I feel that if I were to tell anyone – it would be *you*.'

I stared at her. 'Why?'

'I'm not sure,' she replied carefully. 'I only know that I feel some . . . affinity with you, Phoebe – some connection that I can't explain.'

'Oh. But . . . in any case, why would you want to talk about it *now*?' I asked weakly. 'After so long?'

'Because . . .' Mrs Bell sank on to the sofa, anxiety etched on her face. 'Last week – in fact, while you were here – I received the results of some medical tests. They do not exactly augur well for my future,' she went on calmly. 'I had already guessed that the news would not be positive from the way my weight has been falling lately.' Now I understood Mrs Bell's odd reaction when I'd suggested that she was 'downsizing'. 'I have been offered treatment, but have declined. It would be very unpleasant, it would only buy me a little extra time, and at my age . . .' She held up her hands, as if in surrender. 'I am almost eighty years old, Phoebe. That is a longer life than many – as you know only too well.' I thought of Emma. 'But now, with this acute sense I have of life retreating, the anguish I've felt for so long has only got worse.' She looked imploringly at me. 'I *need* to tell just one person about this coat, now, while I am still clear in my mind. I need that one person just to listen, and perhaps to understand what I did, and why.' She looked towards the garden, the shadows from the window frames bisecting her face. 'I suppose the truth is I need to confess. If I believed in God I would go to a priest.' She turned her gaze back to me. 'Could I tell *you*, Phoebe? Please? It will not take long, I promise – no more than a few minutes.'

I nodded, bemused, then sat down. Mrs Bell leaned forward on her chair, fingering the coat, which was laid across her lap, lifelessly. She took a deep breath, her eyes narrowing as she now looked past me, through the window, as though it were a portal to the past.

'I come from Avignon,' she began. 'You know that.' I nodded. 'I grew up in a large village about three miles from the city centre. It was a sleepy sort of place, with narrow streets leading on to a large square which was shaded by plane trees, with a few shops and a pleasant bar. On the north side of the square was the church, over the door of which was carved, in huge Roman letters, *Liberté, Égalité et Fraternité*.' At that a sardonic smile flickered across Mrs Bell's face. 'The village bordered open countryside,' she went on, 'and was skirted by a railway line. My father worked in the centre of Avignon, where he managed a hardware store. He also had a little vineyard not far from the house. My mother was *maîtresse de maison*, looking after my father, me, and my younger brother, Marcel. To make a little extra money she took in sewing.'

Mrs Bell tucked a stray wisp of white hair behind her ear. 'Marcel and I went to the local school. It was very small – there were no more than a hundred children, many of them descended from families who had lived in the village for generations – the same names would come up again and again – Caron, Paget, Marigny – and Aumage.' It was clear that this last name was to be of particular significance. Mrs Bell shifted a little on her seat. 'In September 1940, when I was eleven, a new girl joined my class. I had seen her once or twice over the summer, but I hadn't known who she was. My mother said that she'd heard that the girl and her family had moved to our village from Paris. My mother had added that, after the Occupation, many such families had fled to the south.' Mrs Bell looked at me. 'I could not know it at the time, but that little word "such" was to prove of immense significance. Anyway, this girl's name was . . .' Mrs Bell's voice caught '. . . Monique,' she whispered after a moment. 'Her name was Monique . . . Richelieu – and I was assigned to look after her.' At this Mrs Bell began to stroke the coat, consolingly almost, then she looked through the window again.

'Monique was a sweet, friendly girl. She was clever and hard-working; she was also very pretty with lovely cheekbones, a quick expression in her dark eyes, and hair so black that in certain lights it looked blue. And, however much she tried to disguise it, she had a foreign inflexion to her voice that stood out all the more amongst the Provençal accents that were spoken around her.' Mrs Bell looked at me. 'Whenever Monique was teased about this at school, she would say that her accent was Parisian. But my parents said that it wasn't Parisian – it was German.'

Mrs Bell clasped her hands together, the enamelled bangle she was wearing clinking gently against the gold bracelet of her watch. 'Monique started coming over to my house to play, and we would roam the fields and hillsides together, picking wild flowers, chatting about girlish things. I sometimes asked her about Paris, which I had only ever seen in photographs. Monique told me about her life in the city, although she was always vague about where precisely her family had lived. But she often talked about her best friend, Miriam. Miriam' – Mrs Bell's face suddenly lit up – '*Lipietzka*. The name has *just* come back to me – after all these years.' She looked at me, shaking her head in wonderment. 'This is what happens, Phoebe, when you are old. Things *long* buried suddenly surface with startling clarity. Lipietzka,' she murmured. 'Of course . . . I think she said that they were originally from the Ukraine. But Monique told me that she very much missed Miriam, of whom she was terribly proud, not least because

126

Miriam was a wonderful violinist. I remember feeling quite a pang as Monique talked about Miriam, and I secretly hoped that in time *I* might become Monique's best friend – even though I had no musical ability at all. I remember I enjoyed going to Monique's house, which was some way away, on the other side of the village, near the railway line. It had a pretty front garden with lots of flowers, and a well, and above the front door was a plaque with the head of a lion carved on to it.'

Mrs Bell put down her cup. 'Monique's father was a dreamy, rather impractical sort of man. Each day he cycled into Avignon, where he worked as a book-keeper for a firm of accountants. Her mother stayed at home looking after Monique's twin brothers, Olivier and Christophe, who were then three. I remember once when I was there Monique cooked the entire evening meal, despite being only ten at the time. She told me that she'd had to learn how to cook because her mother had been bedridden for two months after the twins were born. Monique was a very good cook, though I remember not liking the bread very much.

'Anyway . . . on went the war. We children were aware of it, but we knew little about it because of course there were no televisions, few radios, and the adults sheltered us from it as far as they could. In fact, they hardly spoke of it in our hearing, except to complain about rationing – my father's main complaint was that it was hard to get beer.' Mrs Bell paused again, her lips pursing slightly. 'One day, in the summer of 1941, by which time we had become close friends, Monique and I went for a walk. After about two miles or so along one of the little back

127

roads that criss-cross the area we came upon a ramshackle old barn. As we went inside it to explore we happened to be talking about names. I said that I didn't like my name – Thérèse. I felt it was too ordinary. I wished that my parents had called me Chantal. Then I asked Monique if she liked hers. To my surprise she went very red – then she suddenly blurted out that Monique wasn't her real name. Her real name was Monika – Monika Richter. I was . . .' Mrs Bell shook her head in wonderment. '*Amazed*. Then Monique said that her family had moved to Paris from Mannheim, five years earlier, and that her father had changed their name to make them fit in. He'd decided on Richelieu, she told me, because of the famous Cardinal.'

Mrs Bell looked out of the window again. 'When I asked Monique why they'd left Germany, she replied that it was because they didn't feel safe. At first she refused to say why, but when I pressed her she told me that it was because her family were Jewish. She told me that they never spoke of this to anyone, and that they hid all outward signs of it. Then she made me swear never to reveal what she had said to a living soul, otherwise we could no longer be friends. I agreed, of course, although I couldn't understand why being Jewish had to be a secret – I knew that Jewish people had lived in Avignon for hundreds of years; there was an old synagogue in the city centre. But if that was how Monique felt, I would respect it.'

Mrs Bell began to finger the coat again, stroking the sleeves. 'Then I felt I should offer Monique a secret of my own. So I confided that I had recently fallen in love with a boy in our school – Jean-Luc Aumage.' Mrs Bell's lips were pressed into a thin line. 'I remember, when I told Monique about Jean-Luc, that she looked a little uncomfortable. Then she said that he did seem to be a nice boy and that he was certainly good looking.'

Mrs Bell's eyes strayed to the window again. 'Time went by, and we did our best to ignore the war, thankful to be living in the southern "free" zone. But one morning – it was in late June '42, I could see that Monique was very upset. She told me that she had just received a letter from Miriam in which Miriam had told her that she was now required, as were all Jewish people in the Occupied Zone, to wear a yellow star. This six-pointed star, which had to be sewn on to the left side of her jacket, had in the centre one word – "*Juive*". Mrs Bell rearranged the coat on her lap, repeatedly smoothing the blue fabric. 'From that time on I opened my ears to the war. At night I would sit on the landing, outside my parents' room, straining to hear the broadcasts from BBC London, which they covertly tuned in to; like many people, my father had bought our first wireless just for that purpose. I remember that when they were listening to these bulletins I would hear my father exclaim in disgust or despair. From one of these programmes I learned that there were now special laws for Jewish people in both zones. They were not allowed to join the army, or to hold important jobs in government any more or to buy property. They had to observe a curfew and in Paris they were obliged to travel in the last carriage on the Metro.

'The next day I asked my mother why these things were happening, but she would only say that we were living in difficult times and that it was best for me not

129

to think about this dreadful war which would soon be over – *grace à Dieu.*

'So we tried to carry on with our lives as "normal". But in November 1942 that pretence of normality came to an abrupt end. On November 12th my father came home early, all out of breath, to say that he had seen two German soldiers, with machine guns attached to the sidecars of their motorbikes, stationed at the main road leading from our village to the city centre.

'The next morning, along with many others, my parents, my brother and I walked into Avignon and were horrified to see German soldiers standing beside their official, shiny black Citroëns which were parked in rows outside the Palais des Papes. We saw other German troops stationed outside the town hall, or riding down our historic streets in armoured vehicles, wearing helmets and goggles. To us children they looked funny – like aliens – and I remember my parents being angry with Marcel and me for pointing at them and laughing. They told us to look through them as though they weren't there. They said that if all the people of Avignon did that, then the Germans' presence wouldn't affect us. But Marcel and I knew that this was just bravado – we understood perfectly well that the "free zone" no longer existed and that now we were *all "sous la botte"*!'

Mrs Bell paused, and tucked another wisp of hair behind her ear.

'From then on Monique became distant and watchful. At the end of school each day she would go straight home. She was no longer free to play on Sundays, and I was no longer invited to her house. I was hurt by this, but when I tried to talk to her about it, she just said that she had less time now because her mother needed her to help at home more.

'A month later, I was queuing to buy flour when I overheard the man in front of me complaining that from now on all Jewish people in our area had to have their identity and ration cards stamped with the word "Jew". The man, who I realised must himself be Jewish, said it was a dreadful affront. His family had lived in France for three generations – had he not fought for France during the Great War?' Mrs Bell narrowed her pale blue eyes. 'I remember he shook his fist at the church and said where now was the notion of *Liberté, Égalité et Fraternité*? I just thought to myself, naïvely, 'At least he's not being made to wear the star, like Miriam has to – that would be . . . awful.' She looked at me, then shook her head. 'Little did I know that wearing the yellow star would have been *infinitely* preferable to the stamping of official papers.'

Mrs Bell closed her eyes for a moment, as if exhausted by her memories. Then she opened them again, staring ahead. 'In early 1943, around the middle of February, I saw Monique standing by the school gate, deep in conversation with Jean-Luc, who by now was a very handsome young man of fifteen. I could see from the way he wrapped her scarf a little closer round her neck – it was bitterly cold – that he was very attracted to Monique. I could also see that she liked *him*, because of the way she was smiling up at him, not encouragingly exactly, but sweetly and . . . a little anxiously I suppose.' Mrs Bell sighed then shook her head. 'I was still infatuated with Jean-Luc, even though he'd never so much as looked at me. What a fool I was,' she added bleakly. 'What a *fool.*' She tapped her chest again, as though striking herself. Then she went on, her voice shaking: 'The next day I asked Monique if she liked Jean-Luc. She just looked at me very intently, almost sadly, and said, "Thérèse, you don't understand," which only seemed to confirm that she *did* like him. Then I remembered how she'd reacted when I'd first told her about my crush. She'd seemed uncomfortable, and now I knew why.' Mrs Bell was tapping her chest again. 'But Monique was right – I *didn't* understand. If only I had,' she croaked. She shook her head. 'If only I *had* . . .'

Mrs Bell paused for a moment to collect herself, then carried on. 'After school I ran home in tears. My mother asked me why I was crying, but I was too embarrassed to tell her. Then she put her arms round me and told me to dry my eyes because she had a surprise for me. She went to her sewing corner and brought out a bag. Inside was a lovely little coat of wool as blue as the sky on a clear June morning. As I tried it on, she told me that she had queued for five hours to buy the material and that she had sewed it for me at night, while I was asleep. I hugged my mother and said that I loved the coat *so* much that I would keep it forever. She laughed and said, "No you won't, silly."' Mrs Bell gave me a bleak smile. 'But I *have.*'

She stroked the lapels again, the lines on her brow scored a little deeper now. 'Then, one day in April, Monique didn't come to school. She didn't come the next day either, or the day after that. When I asked our teacher where Monique was she said she didn't know but that she was sure she'd be back before long. Then the Easter holidays started, and still I didn't see Monique, and I kept asking my parents where she might be, but they told me that it would be better to forget her – I would make new friends. I said I didn't *want* new friends – I wanted Monique. So the next morning I ran to her house. I knocked on the door, but no one came. I peered through a gap in the shutters and saw the remains of a meal on the table. There was a broken plate on the floor. Seeing that they had left in a dreadful rush, I resolved to write to Monique at once. I sat down by the well, and I'd started to compose a letter to her in my head when I realised that of course I *couldn't* write to her because I hadn't the faintest idea where she was. I felt just terrible . . .' I heard Mrs Bell swallow.

'At that time,' she went on, 'the weather was still cold.' She shivered, involuntarily. 'Although it was late spring I was still wearing my blue coat. And all the time I was wondering where Monique could have gone, and why she and her family had left so suddenly. But my parents wouldn't discuss it with me. Then, in my selfish child's way, I realised that there was a silver lining to the situation. No doubt Monique would return, if not now then when the war was over – but in her absence maybe Jean-Luc might notice *me*. I remember doing what I could to try and make him. I had just turned fourteen and I began to steal a little of my mother's lipstick; I'd put curling papers in my hair at night, like she did, and I'd darken my pale lashes with a little boot polish – sometimes with comical results: I'd pinch my cheeks to make them rosy. Marcel, who was two years younger than me, began to notice these things and would tease me mercilessly.

'Then one warm Saturday morning I had a row with Marcel – he was goading me so much, I couldn't stand it. I ran out of the house, slamming the door. And I'd walked for perhaps an hour or so when I came to the old broken-down barn. I went inside, and sat down on the floor in a patch of sunlight with my back to a hay bale, listening to the swifts chattering in the eaves above me, and the distant rumble of trains. Suddenly I felt overwhelmed with sadness. I started crying and couldn't stop. And as I sat there, my face bathed in tears, I heard a faint rustling sound from behind. I thought it might be a rat; I was scared. But then curiosity overwhelmed me. I got up and went to the back of the barn, and there, behind a stack of hay bales, lying on the ground beneath a coarse grey blanket was . . . *Monique.*' Mrs Bell looked at me, bewildered. 'I was *astounded.* I couldn't understand *why* she was there. I gently called her name, but she didn't respond. I began to panic. I clapped my hands by her ear, then I knelt down and gently shook her . . .'

'Did she wake up?' I asked. My heart was pounding. 'Did she wake *up?*'

Mrs Bell looked at me curiously. 'She did wake up – thank God. But I will never forget her expression when she did so. Because even as she recognised me, her eyes were straying over my shoulder: her look of terror then changed to one of *relief* mingled with bewilderment. Then she told me, in this tiny whisper, that she had not heard me come in because she had been asleep, because she found it so hard to sleep at night and was exhausted. Then she got up, very stiffly, and stood there just looking

134

at me; she put her arms round me and clung to me, gripping me so tightly while I tried to comfort her . . .' Mrs Bell paused, her eyes shimmering with tears. 'We sat down together on a bale of hay. Monique told me that she had been in the barn for eight days. In fact it was ten. I knew this because she said that on April 19th the Gestapo had come to her house while she was out getting bread, and that they had taken her parents and her brothers, but that their neighbours, the Antignacs, had seen her returning and had headed her off. They'd kept her in their attic, then at nightfall they'd brought her here to this disused barn – by chance the barn where Monique had first revealed to me her true identity. She said that Monsieur Antignac had told her to stay there until it was safe. He'd said that he had no idea how long that would be and that she would have to be patient and brave. He'd told her not to make a sound, and never to leave the barn, except to creep the few metres to the stream when it was dark to collect water in the pitcher that he'd given her.'

Mrs Bell's mouth was trembling. 'My heart broke for Monique, that she was all alone, separated from her family, with no idea where they were, and with the terrible thought of their abduction tormenting her every waking moment. I tried to imagine how I would cope in such a horrible situation. Now I *truly* understood the dreadfulness of this war.' Mrs Bell looked at me, her eyes ablaze. 'How *could* it be that people guilty of *no* crime, men and women – and children,' she added vehemently. '*Children* . . .' Her pale blue eyes were shining with tears. 'How could it *be*,' she went on, 'that they could just be taken from their homes – like *that* – and bundled on to trains bound for . . . "New horizons",' she enunciated scornfully. 'That was the euphemism we learned afterwards – and "work camps in the east".' Her voice had caught. '"Destinations unknown",' she croaked. 'That was another . . .' Her hands sprang to her face.

I could hear the ticking of the clock. 'Are you sure you want to go on?' I asked her gently.

Mrs Bell nodded. 'I do want to.' She reached into the sleeve of her blouse and pulled out a hanky. 'I *need* to . . .' She pressed the hanky to her eyes, blinked a few times, then continued, her voice fracturing now with effort and emotion. 'Monique already looked gaunt and thin. Her hair was tangled and her clothes and face were dirty. But round her neck was a beautiful Venetian glass necklace that her mother had given her for her thirteenth birthday. The beads were large and rectangular, with a swirling pattern of pink and bronze. Monique fingered it constantly as she spoke, as though it consoled her just to touch it. She told me that she was desperate to find her family but she understood that for now she had to stay where she was. She said that the Antignacs were very kind, but that they weren't able to bring her food every day.

'So then I said that *I* would. Monique said that I mustn't, because I would be putting myself in danger. "No one will see me," I protested. "I'll pretend that I'm picking wild strawberries – who's going to care what *I* do?" For the second time in that place, Monique swore me to secrecy. She told me to tell *no one* that I had seen her – not even my parents or brother. I vowed to say nothing, then I ran home, my head spinning. I went into the kitchen and took some bread from my ration and put a little butter on it, then I cut a piece of cheese from my meagre allowance: I found an apple and I put all this, such as it was, into a basket. Then I told my mother that I was going out again because I wanted to pick some irises that grow wild at that time of year. She made some comment about my having lots of energy and told me not to go too far. Then I ran to the barn, slipped in very quietly, and gave Monique the food. She ate half of it, ravenously, saying that she would have to make the other half last for the next two days. She said that she was worried about rats, so she put the rest of the provisions under an old pot. I told her that I would come again, soon, with more. I asked her if there was anything else that she needed. She replied that although she was warm enough in the day, she was cold at night – so cold that she couldn't sleep. All she had was the cotton dress and the cardigan she was wearing, and that thin grey blanket. 'You need a coat,' I said. 'A really warm coat – you need . . .' And then I knew. 'I will bring you mine,' I promised, 'tomorrow, in the late afternoon. But I'd better go now or my parents will miss me.' I kissed her on the cheek and left.

'That night I could hardly sleep. I was tortured by thoughts of Monique, all alone in the barn, starting at the sound of rats and mice and the hooting of owls, and having to endure cold so biting that she would wake in the morning aching from the physical exertion of shivering. Then I thought about the coat, and how warm it would make her, and I felt elated at the thought of giving it to her. Monique was my friend' – Mrs Bell's mouth was quivering – 'and I was going to look after her.'

I looked away, almost unable to bear this story with its painful echoes of my own.

Mrs Bell was stroking the coat again now, as if to soothe it. 'I planned all the wonderful things I would take to Monique – this coat; some pencils and paper to pass the time; a few books, a bar of soap and some toothpaste. And of course food – lots of it . . .' From somewhere far away I thought I could hear ringing. 'I went to sleep dreaming of the feast that I would lay before Monique.' Mrs Bell tapped her chest again. 'But I didn't do that. Instead, I let her down – terribly. In fact, catastrophically –'

Drrrrrrring.

Mrs Bell looked up, startled, as the front door bell registered now. Then she got to her feet, carefully laid the coat over the back of her chair, and left the room, smoothing down her hair as she went. I heard her steps in the hallway, then a woman's voice.

'Mrs Bell? . . . district nurse . . . just a chat . . . sorry, didn't your surgery tell you? . . . about half an hour . . . sure it's convenient?'

'No, it's *not*,' I whispered. As Mrs Bell came back into the sitting room, followed by the nurse, a fair-haired woman in her fifties, she quickly swept up the coat and took it back into the bedroom.

The nurse smiled at me. 'I hope I'm not interrupting.' I fought the urge to tell her that she was. 'Are you a friend of Mrs Bell's?'

'Yes. We were just having a . . . chat.' I stood up and looked at Mrs Bell, who had now returned. The emotion of the story was still etched on her face. 'I'll go now, Mrs Bell – but I'll ring you soon.'

She laid her hand on my arm, gazing at me intently. 'Yes, Phoebe,' she said quietly. 'Please do.'

I walked down the stairs feeling weighed down, though not by the two suitcases, which I barely noticed. As I drove the short distance back home I thought about Mrs Bell's story and felt sad for her that she was still so distressed about events that had happened such a long time ago.

At home I separated those clothes of hers that would go to Val – I thought with a shiver of my private sitting; then I put the others ready to be washed or dry-cleaned.

On the way back to the shop I called in at Oxfam. I handed the bag of Mrs Bell's things to the volunteer, a woman in her early seventies who I've often seen in there. She can be a bit grumpy. 'These are all Jaeger and in excellent condition,' I explained. Out of the corner of my eye I noticed the calico curtain that was pulled across the changing cubicle twitch. I took out the aquamarine suit. 'This would have cost £250 new – it's only two years old.'

'It's quite a nice colour,' said the woman.

'Yes – it's subtle, isn't it?'

Now the curtain was drawn back and there was Dan, in a bright turquoise corduroy jacket and crimson trousers. I felt like reaching for my sunglasses.

'Hi, Phoebe. I thought it was you.' He looked at himself in the mirror. 'What do you think of the jacket?'

'What do I think of the jacket?' What could I say? 'The cut's okay, but the colour's . . . ghastly.' His face fell. 'Sorry, but you did ask.'

'I like this colour,' Dan protested. 'It's . . . well . . . how would you describe it?'

'Peacock blue,' I suggested. 'No – "cyan".'

'Oh.' He squinted at himself. 'As in cyanide?'

'Exactly. And it is a bit . . . toxic.' I grimaced at the volunteer. 'Sorry.'

She shrugged. 'Don't worry – I think it's vile too. Mind you, he can *almost* carry it off.' She nodded at him. 'He's got a lovely face under all that hair.' I looked at Dan, who was smiling gratefully at the woman. He did have a lovely face, I realised; a strong straight nose, nice lips that dimpled slightly at the corners; a clear, grey-eyed gaze. Who *was* it he reminded me of? 'But what will that jacket *go* with?' the volunteer demanded. 'You've got to think about that. As you're a valued customer, I feel I should give you that advice.'

'Ooh, it'll go with lots of things,' Dan replied amiably. 'These trousers for a start.'

'I'm not sure that they *do* go,' I said. Dan's approach to clothes seemed to be mix'n'don't match.

He took the jacket off. 'I'll take it,' he said happily. 'And the books.' He nodded at the pile of hardbacks on the counter. The top one was a biography of Greta Garbo. Dan tapped it, then looked at me. 'Did you know that Louis B. Mayer wanted her to drop the name Garbo because he thought it sounded too much like "garbage"?'

'Erm . . . no, I didn't.' I gazed at the beautiful face on the cover. 'I love Garbo's films. Not that I've seen one for ages,' I added as Dan handed the volunteer the cash.

Dan looked at me. 'Then you're in luck. The Greenwich Picturehouse is doing a "Mother Russia" season later this month and they're showing *Anna Karenina*.' He accepted his change. 'We'll go.'

I stared at Dan. 'I'm not . . . sure.'

'Why not?' He slotted the coins into the collection tin by the till. 'Don't tell me – you *vont* to be alone.'

'No – it's just that . . . I'd like to think about it.'

'I don't know *why*,' the volunteer said as she tore off Dan's receipt. 'It sounds marvellous to me – going to see a Greta Garbo film with a nice young man.'

'Yes – but . . .' I didn't want to say that, apart from objecting to the presumptuous way in which I'd been invited, I'd only ever met Dan twice. 'I don't know whether I . . . can.'

'Don't worry.' Dan had opened his bag. 'I've got the Picturehouse leaflet right here.' He took it out and looked at it. 'The screening's on . . . Wednesday 24th at seven thirty. Is that okay for you?' He was looking at me expectantly.

'Well . . .'

The volunteer heaved a sigh. 'If you don't go with him, *I* will. I haven't been to the pictures for five years,' she added. 'Not since my husband died – we used to go *every* Friday; there's no one to go with now; I'd give anything for an invitation like that.' She shook her head as if disbelieving of my churlishness, then handed Dan his bags with a consoling smile. 'Here you go, sweetheart. See you again soon.'

'You will,' said Dan. Then he and I left the shop together. 'Where are you going?' he asked as we strolled down Tranquil Vale.

'I've got to go up to the bank – I meant to do it earlier.'

'I'm going that way too – I'll walk with you. And how's Village Vintage doing?'

141

'It's . . . good,' I replied. 'Thanks, largely, to your article,' I added, feeling a little guilty now at my irritability: but as usual Dan had thrown me off balance with his . . . spontaneity. 'And what about the paper?'

'It's going okay,' he replied judiciously. 'The circulation's gone up to eleven thousand, from ten thousand at launch, which is good. But we could do with more advertising – a lot of the local advertisers still aren't aware of us.'

We went down the hill then crossed over at the junction. Suddenly Dan stopped outside the Age Exchange Reminiscence Centre. 'Well I'm going in here.'

I looked at its maroon-painted shop front. 'Why?'

'I'm planning a feature on it, so I need to do a recce.'

'I haven't been in here for years,' I mused as I gazed into the window.

'Come in with me now then,' I heard Dan say.

'Well . . . I'm not sure I've got time, so I don't think I will, Dan. I'll just . . .' Why was I refusing, I wondered? Annie was minding the shop – there was no particular time pressure on me. 'All right, then. Just for a minute.'

Going into the Age Exchange was like stepping back in time. The interior was done in the style of an old-fashioned general store, the shelves stocked with pre-war packaging for Sunlight soap, Brown & Polson custard, Eggo dried egg and Player's Senior Service cigarettes. There was an ornate brass till like an old typewriter, a Bakelite wireless and some Brownie box cameras; there was also a wooden chest, the little drawers of which had been left open to reveal an assortment of old medals, crochet hooks, knitted dolls and cotton reels – the bric-à-brac of times gone by.

Dan and I walked through to the gallery at the back of the centre where there were some black-and-white photos forming part of an exhibition about life in the East End in the 1930s and 40s. One of the figures, a little girl playing in a bombed-out street in Stepney, was circled because, now in her eighties, she lived in Blackheath.

'So this place is a kind of museum,' I said.

'It's more of a community centre,' Dan replied, 'where the elderly can reminisce about their lives. There's a theatre at the back and a café. In fact . . .' He nodded at the kitchen counter. 'I'm in need of a coffee – will you have one?'

As we sat at a table Dan got out his pad and pencil, which he began to sharpen.

'So you found it then.' I nodded at the sharpener.

'Yes – thank goodness.'

'Is it special?'

Dan put it on the table. 'My grandmother left it to me. She died three years ago.'

'She left you a pencil sharpener?' He nodded. 'Is that all she left you?' I couldn't help asking.

'No.' Dan blew on the sharpened tip. 'She also left me a rather hideous painting. I did feel a tad . . . disappointed,' he concluded delicately. 'But I like the sharpener.'

As Dan began to scribble a few notes on his pad in his odd shorthand, I asked him how long he'd been a journalist.

'Only a few months,' he replied. 'I'm a novice.' So that explained his inept interviewing technique.

'What did you do before?'

143

'I worked for a marketing agency, designing product promotions – mostly tailor-made rewards schemes, voucher giveaways, loyalty cards, cashback incentives, buy-one-get-one-free offers –'

'Five per cent off everything for the first week?' I interjected wryly.

'Yes.' Dan had blushed. 'That sort of thing.'

'So why did you give it up?'

He hesitated. 'I'd been doing the same thing for ten years and was looking for a change. And my old school friend Matt had just left the *Guardian*, where he'd been business editor, to set up his own paper – a long-held dream; and he said he needed . . . help,' Dan went on. 'So I had a little think then decided to go for it.'

'So he asked you to come and write for his newspaper?'

'No, he'd already hired two full-time reporters; I do the marketing, but I have carte blanche to write about anything that interests me.'

'So I should feel flattered then.'

Dan was staring at me. 'I saw you,' he said. 'The day before you opened – I think I told you; I was walking past on the other side of the road, and you were in the window, dressing a dummy –'

'Mannequin, please.'

'– and you were having trouble – one of its arms kept falling off.'

I rolled my eyes. 'I hate wrestling with those things.'

'And you were *so* determined to remain composed – and I thought, I'd love to talk to that woman – so I did. That's the good thing about journalism,' he added with a smile.

'Two coffees!' said the volunteer, putting them on the

counter. I went and got them then held them out to Dan. 'Which do you want? The red or the green?'

'The . . .' He hesitated. 'Red.' He put out his hand.

'But that's the green one you've taken.'

Dan squinted at it. 'So it is.'

The penny dropped with a clatter. 'Dan – are you colour-blind?' He pursed his lips, then nodded. How slow I'd been. 'Is that . . . tricky?'

'Not really.' He gave a philosophical shrug. 'It just means that I was unable to become an electrician –'

'Oh, all those coloured wires.'

'Or an air-traffic controller – or a pilot, for that matter. Being colour "deficient" as they say, also means that tabby cats have green stripes, that I'm useless at picking strawberries and that I often mis-match my clothes – as you've clearly noticed.'

I felt my face heat up. 'If I'd known there was a reason for it, I'd have been more tactful.'

'People do sometimes make rude remarks about what I'm wearing – I never explain unless I have to.'

'And when did you find out?'

'On my first day at primary school. We were asked to paint a tree – mine had bright red leaves and a green trunk. My teacher advised my parents to get my vision tested.'

'So your trousers don't look crimson to you then?'

Dan looked down at them. 'I don't know what "crimson" is – to me it's an abstract concept, like the sound of a bell to a deaf person: but these trousers look olive green.'

I sipped my coffee. 'So what colours can you see well?'

'Pastels – pale blue, mauve – and of course black and

white. I do like looking at things in black and white,' he added with a nod at the exhibition. 'There's something about monochrome that just . . .'

From somewhere I could hear 'As Time Goes By'; for a moment I thought it was coming over a sound system, then I realised that it was Dan's ringtone.

He threw me an apologetic glance then took the call. 'Hi, Matt,' he said quietly. 'I'm round the corner at the Age Exchange . . . Yes, I can talk – just for a minute. *Sorry*,' he mouthed at me. 'Oh . . . right . . .' Dan stood up, his expression serious now. 'Well, if she'll stand by the story,' he added as he walked away. 'Hard evidence,' I heard him say as he stepped into the courtyard garden; '. . . have to be libel-proof . . . I'll be back in two minutes . . .'

'Sorry about that,' Dan said to me as he returned to the table. He looked distracted. 'Matt needs to discuss something with me – I'd better go.'

'And I've got things to do.' I picked up my bag. 'But I'm glad I came in here – thanks for the coffee.'

We left the Centre then stood on the pavement for a moment. 'Well, I'm going this way.' Dan nodded to the right. 'The *Black & Green* is just up there, next to the Post Office, and you're going that way. But . . . we'll go and see *Anna Karenina*.'

'Well . . . why don't you let me think about it?'

Dan shrugged. 'Why don't you just say "yes"?' Then, as if it were perfectly normal for him to do so, he kissed me on the cheek and left.

As I pushed on the door of Village Vintage five minutes later, I saw Annie putting down the phone. 'That was Mrs Bell,' she said. 'Apparently you forgot the hatbox when you left this morning.'

146

'I forgot the hatbox?' I hadn't even noticed.

'She suggested that you collect it tomorrow at four. She said to ring her back only if you can't make it. But I could run up and get it for you . . .'

'No, no, I'll do it myself – thanks. Tomorrow at four would be good. Very good . . .'

Annie gave me a puzzled glance. 'So how *was* Mrs Bell?' she asked as she picked up a satin evening dress that had slipped off its hanger.

'She's . . . lovely: an interesting person.'

'I imagine some of the older people chat to you sometimes.'

'They do.'

'I bet some of them have incredible stories to tell. I'd find that part of the job fascinating,' Annie went on. 'I love hearing the elderly talk about their lives – I think we should listen to old people more.' And I was just telling Annie about the Age Exchange, which she said she'd never been into, when the phone rang. It was a producer from Radio London saying that he'd seen the interview with me in the *Black & Green*, and would I come in on the following Monday to talk about vintage clothing. I said I'd be happy to. Then Miles texted me to say that he'd booked a table at the Oxo Tower for Thursday at eight. Then I had a number of website orders to deal with, five of which were for French nightdresses. Seeing how low my stock was getting, I booked a Eurostar ticket to Avignon for the last weekend in September. The rest of the afternoon was taken up with talking to people who'd brought in clothes for me to buy.

'I won't be in until lunchtime tomorrow,' I said to Annie as I closed the shop for the day. 'I'm going to see

147

Val, my seamstress.' I didn't add that I was also going to see a medium. I suddenly found the thought terrifying. I resolved that in the afternoon I'd go back to Mrs Bell.

SIX

The next morning I posted the Balenciaga gown to Cindi in Beverly Hills, idly wondering which of her A-Listers it was destined for, then, with butterflies in my stomach I drove to Kidbrooke. In my handbag I'd put three photos of Emma and me. The first was taken when we were ten – on the beach in Lyme Regis where Dad had taken us for a day's fossil-hunting. In the photo Emma was holding up a large ammonite that she'd found and which I knew she'd always kept. I remember both of us flatly refusing to believe my dad when he said that it was about 200 million years old. The second photo was taken at Emma's graduation show at the Royal College of Art. The third was a snap of us together on what was to be her last birthday. On her head was a hat she'd made for herself, unusually – a green straw cloche with a starched silk pink rose 'growing' out of it. 'I *like* this,' she'd said, with mock surprise as she'd looked at herself in a hand mirror. 'This is the hat I'm going to be buried in!'

Now I lifted my hand to Val's bell. When she opened the door she said she was feeling upset because she'd just spilled a tub of peppercorns.

'What a nuisance,' I said, recalling, with a sharp pang, Emma's dinner party. 'They get everywhere, don't they?'

'Oh, I'm not upset because it's a nuisance,' Val said. 'I'm upset because spilling peppercorns is terribly unlucky.'

I stared at her. 'Why?'

'Because it usually portends the end of a close friendship.' I felt a shiver run the length of my spine. 'So I'll have to mind my P's and Q's with Mags for a while, won't I?' she added. 'Now . . .' Val nodded at my suitcase. 'What have you brought me?' Feeling shaken from what she'd just said, I showed Val the six dresses and three suits of Mrs Bell's. 'Just small repairs then,' she commented as she appraised them. 'Ooh, I love this Ossie Clark dress. I can just imagine it strolling down the King's Road in 1965.' She turned it inside out. 'Torn lining? Leave it to me, Phoebe. I'll call you when they're done.'

'Thanks. Right then,' I added with false brightness. 'I'll just . . . pop next door.'

Val gave me an encouraging smile. 'Good luck.'

As I rang Maggie's bell I realised that my heart was pounding like a tom-tom.

'Come in, sweetheart,' Mags yelled. 'I'm in the living room.' I followed the trail of Magie Noire mingled with stale cigarette smoke down the corridor and found Mags sitting behind a small square table. She nodded for me to sit in the chair opposite her. As I did so I glanced around. There was nothing to indicate the activity that regularly took place here. There were no fringed lamp-shades or crystal balls. No decks of Tarot cards waiting to be dealt. There was simply a three-piece suite, a huge plasma TV, a carved oak sideboard and an inglenook shelf on which was an enormous china doll with glossy brown ringlets and a vacant expression.

'If you were expecting a Ouija board, you're going to be disappointed,' Mags said flatly. It was as though she'd read my mind – I found this encouraging. 'I don't go in for that "holding hands and waiting for the lights to go out" nonsense. No. All I'll be doing is linking you to your loved one. Just think of me as your switchboard operator, putting you through.'

'Mags . . .' I was suddenly filled with apprehension. 'Now that I'm here, I'm feeling a little . . . worried. I mean, don't you think it's a bit profane to, well . . . call up the dead?' Especially in the 'living' room, it suddenly occurred to me.

'No – it's not,' Mags replied. 'Because the point *is* they're not really dead, are they? They've just gone some-where else, *but'* – she held up her finger – 'they can be contacted. Right then, Phoebe. Let's start.' Mags was looking at me expectantly. 'Let's start then.' She nodded at my handbag.

'Oh. Sorry.' I reached for my purse.

'Business before pleasure,' Mags said. 'Thanking you.' She took the £50 from me, then tucked it into her cleavage. I imagined the notes becoming warm. Then I wondered what else she kept down there. A hole punch? Her address book? A small dog?

Now that Mags was ready, she placed her hands, palms down, on the table, pressing her fingers against the

151

tabletop as if to steady herself for the psychic journey. Her vermillion nails were so long that they curved at the ends, like little scimitars. 'So . . . you lost someone,' she began.

'Yes.' I'd already decided that I wasn't going to show Mags the photos, or give her any clues about Emma.

'You lost someone,' she repeated. 'Someone you loved.'

'Yes.' I could feel the familiar constriction in my throat.

'Very much.'

'Yes,' I repeated.

'A close friend. Someone who meant the world to you.' I nodded, struggling not to cry.

Mags closed her eyes then breathed in deeply through her nose with a soughing sound. 'And what would you like to say to this friend . . .?'

I was taken aback as I hadn't expected to say anything at first. I closed my eyes for a moment and I thought that most of all I'd like to tell Emma that I'm sorry; then I'd like to tell her how much I miss her – it's like this constant ache at the heart. Lastly I'd like to tell Emma that I'm angry with her for doing what she did.

I looked at Mags and was suddenly overcome with anxiety. 'I . . . can't think of anything right now.'

'All right, sweetheart – but . . .' She paused theatrically. 'Your friend wants to say something to *you*.'

'What?' I said weakly.

'It's very important.'

'Tell me what it *is* . . .' My heart was beating wildly. 'Please.'

'Well . . .'

'*Tell* me.'

She took a deep breath. 'He *says* –'

I blinked. 'It isn't a "*he*".'

Mags opened her eyes and looked at me, dumb-founded. 'Not a "he"?'

'No.'

'Are you sure?'

'Of course I'm sure.'

'That's odd – because I'm getting the name Robert.' She peered at me. 'It's coming through very strongly.'

'But I don't know anyone called Robert.'

'How about Rob?' I shook my head. Mags cocked her head to one side. 'Bob?'

'*No*.'

'Does David ring any bells?'

'Maggie – my friend was a *woman*.'

She narrowed her eyes, peering at me through her false lashes. 'Of course she was,' she said reasonably. 'I *thought* so . . .' She closed her eyes again, inhaling noisily. 'Okay. I've got her. She's coming through . . . I'll be connecting you in just a moment now.' I half expected to hear a call-waiting beep, or a tinny recording of the *Four Seasons*.

'So what name are you getting?' I asked.

Mags pressed her forefingers to her temples. 'I can't answer that yet – but I *can* tell you that I'm getting a strong connection with overseas.'

'Overseas?' I said happily. 'That's *right*. And what *is* the connection?'

Maggie stared at me. 'Well, that your friend enjoyed . . . going overseas. Didn't she?'

'Ye-es.' Along with nearly everyone else. 'Mags, just to make sure that you're getting the right person, can you tell me which country my friend had a particular connection with – a country that in fact she'd visited just three weeks before she . . .'

'Passed over? I *can* tell you that.' Mags closed her eyes again. Her lids were rimmed with electric blue eyeliner that flicked up at the corners. 'I'm getting it now – loud and clear.' She clapped her hands to her ears then looked crossly at the ceiling. 'I *heard* you, sweetie! No need to shout!' Mags calmly turned her gaze back to me. 'The country your friend had a particular connection with *is* . . . South . . .' I held my breath '. . . America.'

A groan escaped me. 'No. She'd never even *been* there. She'd always wanted to,' I added.

Mags stared at me blankly. 'Well . . . that's . . . *why* I'm getting it. Because your friend wanted to go there, and she never did . . . and now it's bugging her.' Mags scratched the side of her nose. 'Now, this friend of yours . . . whose name was . . .' She closed her eyes, inhaling noisily. 'Nadine.' She opened one eye and peered at me. 'Lisa?'

'Emma,' I said wearily.

'*Emma.*' Mags tutted. 'Of course. Now . . . Emma was a very sensible, no-nonsense sort of person, wasn't she?'

'No,' I replied. This was hopeless. 'Emma wasn't like that at all. She was intense and slightly naïve – a bit . . . neurotic, even. Although she could be a lot of fun, she was prone to black moods. She was also unpredictable – she could do . . . reckless things.' I thought, bitterly, of the final reckless thing that Emma had done. 'But could you tell me about her career? Just to make sure you get the right Emma?'

Mags closed her eyes again then opened them, wide.

'I'm seeing a hat . . .' I felt a burst of euphoria mingled with terror. 'It's a black hat,' Maggie went on.

'What shape is it?' I asked, my heart banging like a kettle drum.

Mags narrowed her eyes. 'It's flat, and . . . it's got four corners and . . . a long black tassel.'

My spirits sank. 'You're describing a mortarboard.'

Mags smiled. 'That's right – because Emma was a teacher, wasn't she?'

'*No.*'

'Well . . . did she wear a mortarboard for her graduation? Maybe *that's* what I'm seeing.' Mags narrowed her eyes again, lifting her head slightly, as though trying to focus on something that was just disappearing over the horizon.

'No.' I sighed with exasperation. 'Emma went to the Royal College of Art.'

'I *thought* she was artistic,' Mags said happily. 'Got that right then.' She wriggled her shoulders then closed her eyes again as if in prayer. From somewhere I could hear a ringtone. What was the tune? Oh yes – 'Spirit in the Sky'. I realised that it was coming from Mags' chest. 'Do excuse me,' she said as she pulled out of her cleavage first a packet of Silk Cut, then her mobile phone. 'Hi there,' she said into it. 'I see . . . You can't . . . That's quite all right. Thanks for letting me know.' She snapped shut the phone and tucked it back into her bosom, daintily pushing it down with her middle finger. 'You're in luck,' she said. 'My twelve o'clock's just cancelled – we can carry on.'

I stood up. 'Thanks, Mags, but no.'

* * *

Serves me right for doing something so dodgy, I reflected as I drove back to Blackheath. I was mad even to have contemplated it. What if Mags *had* made a connection with Emma? The shock might have given me a nervous breakdown. I was *glad* that Mags was a charlatan. My indignation subsided and was replaced by relief.

I parked in my usual place outside the house, went inside just to empty the washing machine and put on another load, then I walked up to the shop. Realising that I was hungry I stopped at the Moon Daisy Café for a quick lunch. As I sat at a table outside, Pippa, who runs the café and who first told me about Val, brought me a copy of *The Times*. I idly looked at the home news, then the foreign pages and then I read a piece about London Fashion Week, which had just started. Then, as I turned to the business pages, I found myself staring, shocked, at a photo of Guy. It was captioned GOOD GUY FLIES HIGH. As I read the article beneath it my mouth dried to the texture of felt. *Guy Harrap . . . 36 . . . Friends Provident . . . went on to found Ethix . . . investing in companies that have no negative environmental impact . . . clean-tech . . . that do not use child labour . . . animal welfare . . . companies committed to enhancing human health and safety.*

I felt sick. Guy hadn't exactly enhanced Emma's human health or safety, had he! *You know how she exaggerates everything, Phoebe. It's probably attention seeking.* He wasn't such a 'good Guy' as he liked to think.

I surveyed the omelette Pippa had brought me with a sudden lack of interest. My mobile phone rang. It was Mum.

'How are you, Phoebe?'

'I'm fine,' I lied. With a trembling hand I closed the newspaper so that I didn't have to look at Guy. 'What about you?'

'I'm fine too,' she replied airily. 'I'm fine, fine, I'm absolutely . . . miserable, actually, darling.' I could hear her struggling not to cry.

'What's happened, Mum?'

'Well, I'm on site today, at Ladbroke Grove. I had to bring John some drawings that he needed, and . . .' I heard her gulp. 'It's upset me, knowing that I'm so close to where your father lives now with . . . *her* . . . and . . . *and* . . .'

'Poor Mum. Just . . . try not to think about it. Look to the future.'

'Yes, you're right, darling.' She sniffed. 'I will. And actually to that end I've just found a wonderful new . . .' – *man,* I was hoping she'd say – 'treatment.' My heart sank. 'It's called Fractional Resurfacing or "Fraxel". It's done with this laser thingy – it's very scientific. It actually *reverses* the ageing process.'

'Really?'

'What it does – I've got the leaflet here' – I heard the squeak of glossy paper – 'is to "eliminate old epidermal pigmented cells. It restores the patient's face one piece at a time, just as a fine painting is restored one piece at a time." The only downside,' Mum added, 'is that it causes "vigorous exfoliation".'

'Then keep the Hoover handy.'

'And you need a minimum of six sessions.'

'At a cost of . . .?'

I heard her draw in her breath. 'Three thousand

pounds. But the difference between the "before" and "after" photos is amazing.'

'That's because in the "after" photos the women are smiling and wearing make-up.'

'Wait until *you're* sixty.' Mum groaned. 'You'll be having all these things plus whatever else they'll have thought of by then.'

'I won't be having anything,' I protested. 'I don't shun the past, Mum – I value it. That's why I do what I do.'

'No need to be all pious about it,' she said huffily. 'Now do tell me – what's been happening with you?'

I decided not to tell Mum that I'd just been to a medium. I told her that I'd be going to France at the end of the month; then, on an impulse, I mentioned Miles. I hadn't meant to, but I thought it might cheer her up a little.

'That sounds promising,' she said as I began to describe him. 'A daughter of sixteen?' she interjected. 'Well, you'd make a lovely stepmother and you can still have a few of your own. So he's divorced is he? . . . A widower? Oh – *perfect* . . . And how old is Miles? . . . Ah. I *see*. On the *other* hand,' she added, her tone brightening as she seemed to glimpse the possibilities of the situation, 'that means he's not young and hard up. Oh gosh – John's waving at me. I'd better go, darling.'

'Chin up, Mum. No – on second thoughts leave your chin where it is.'

I spent the two hours after lunch stock-taking, phoning dealers and looking at the auction house websites, noting any upcoming sales that I'd want to go to. Then at ten to four I put on my jacket and headed for The Paragon.

Mrs Bell let me in from upstairs and I climbed the three flights, my feet ringing against the stone steps.

'Ah, Phoebe. I'm so glad to see you again. Come in.'

'I'm sorry I forgot the hats, Mrs Bell.' On the hall table I saw a booklet about Macmillan cancer nurses.

'It doesn't matter a bit. I'll make some tea – go and sit down.'

I went into the sitting room and stood at the window, looking down on to the garden, which was deserted, except for a small boy in grey shorts and shirt, kicking through the leaves, looking for conkers.

Mrs Bell appeared with the tray, but this time, when I offered to carry it, she let me. 'My arms are not as strong as they were. My body is going over to the enemy. I will feel reasonably well this first month, apparently, and then . . . not so good.'

'I'm . . . sorry,' I said impotently.

'There it is.' She shrugged. 'Nothing to be done – except to appreciate every moment of the short time I have left while I am still able to do so.' She lifted the pot, though she had to use both hands.

'And how was the nurse?'

Mrs Bell sighed. 'As pleasant and well organised as one would expect. She said I may be able to stay here until . . .' Her voice faltered. 'I wish to avoid hospital.'

'Of course.'

We sat in silence, drinking our tea. By now it was clear that Mrs Bell was not going to resume her story. For whatever reason, she'd decided against it. Perhaps she regretted telling me what she *had* told me. She put down her cup, then brushed away a stray wisp of hair. 'The hatbox is still in the bedroom, Phoebe. Do go in

159

and get it.' I did so, and as I picked it up I heard her call out, 'And would you be very kind and bring the blue coat?'

My pulse began to race as I went to the wardrobe, took the coat out of its cover, then carried it in to the sitting room where I handed it to Mrs Bell.

She laid it across her knee, her hand stroking the lapel. 'So,' she said quietly as I sat down again. 'Where was I?'

'Well . . .' I put the hatbox down by my feet. 'You . . . told me that you had found your friend – Monique – in the barn, and that she'd been there for ten days.' Mrs Bell nodded slowly. 'You took her some food . . .'

'Yes,' she murmured. 'I took her some food, didn't I – then I promised to take her this coat.'

'That's right.' It was as though Mrs Bell was involving me in her story.

She looked through the window again as her memories flooded back. 'I remember how happy I was to think that I was going to help Monique. But I didn't help her,' she added quietly. 'I betrayed her . . .' She pressed her lips together for a moment then I heard her inhale. 'I was due to go back to Monique in the late afternoon. I kept thinking of all that I would do for my friend . . .' Mrs Bell paused.

'After lunch I went to the *boulangerie* to get my ration of bread. I had to queue for an hour, enduring the mutterings of my fellow customers about this person or that, supposedly buying things on the *marché noir*. At last I got the half-baguette I was entitled to and then, as I was walking back across the square, I saw Jean-Luc sitting outside the Bar Mistral, on his own. To my astonishment, he didn't look past me as he usually did – he looked *at* me. Then, to my further amazement, he beckoned to me to join him. I was so thrilled I could barely speak. He bought me a glass of apple juice, which I sipped while he had his beer. I felt intoxicated with joy and excitement, suddenly finding myself sitting there in the April sunshine with this divinely handsome boy who I had hankered after for so long.

'Over the bar radio I could hear Frank Sinatra, singing "Night and Day", which was a popular song at that time. I suddenly thought of Monique being in that barn night and day, and I realised that I had to leave – *now*. But then the waiter brought another beer for Jean-Luc, and Jean-Luc asked me if I'd ever tried beer so I said no, of course not, I was only fourteen. He laughed and said that it was high time I did. He offered me a taste of his Kronenbourg and again this felt so romantic to me, not least because beer was strictly rationed. So I had a little sip, then another, and another – even though I didn't like it at all – but I wanted Jean-Luc to think that I did. Daylight was fading. I knew I *had* to go – *now*. But by then my head was whirling, and it was almost dark and I realised, to my shame, that there was no way that I'd be walking to the barn that night. So I resolved to go at dawn, consoling myself with the thought that it would be a delay of only a few hours.'

Mrs Bell was still stroking the coat, as if to soothe it. 'Jean-Luc said that he would take me home. It felt so romantic to be walking across the square in the dusk, past the church, with the first stars shining in the evening sky. I realised that it was going to be a clear night – and a cold one.' Mrs Bell's thin fingers absently sought the coat's buttons. 'I felt racked with guilt now about Monique – and my head felt light and strange. And it suddenly occurred to me that maybe Jean-Luc could help her. His father was a gendarme, after all – the authorities must have made some mistake. And so . . . just before we reached my house . . .' Mrs Bell's hands clutched at the coat. Her knuckles were white. 'I told Jean-Luc about Monique . . . I told him that I had found her in the old barn. I explained that I was only telling him this in case he could possibly help her. Jean-Luc looked very concerned, so much so that I remember even feeling a little stab of jealousy, and then I recalled that affectionate gesture of his with Monique's scarf. Anyway . . .' Mrs Bell swallowed '. . . he asked me where the barn was, so I described the location.' She shook her head. 'For a moment Jean-Luc didn't speak, then he said that he'd heard of other children hiding in similar places, and even being hidden in people's homes. He added that it was a tough situation for all concerned. Then we came to my house, so we said goodbye.

'My parents were listening to a music programme on the wireless so they didn't hear me creep in and go up the stairs. I drank a lot of water because I felt thirsty, then got into bed. On my chair, visible in the moonlight, was the blue coat . . .' Mrs Bell lifted it now, hugging it to her. 'The next morning I awoke – not at first light, as I'd intended, but two hours later. I felt terrible that I'd failed to keep my word to Monique. But I consoled myself with the thought that I would soon be at the barn and that I would be giving her my lovely coat – a significant sacrifice, I reminded myself. Monique would be able to sleep at night and everything would be okay – and maybe Jean-Luc might really be able to help her.' At that Mrs Bell smiled grimly.

'Because I felt so guilty about not meeting her the night before, I packed as much food as I thought my mother wouldn't miss into the basket, then set off for the barn. When I got there I went inside. "Monique," I whispered as I took off the coat. There was no answer. Then I saw her blanket in a heap to one side. I called her name again but there was no reply – just the sound of the swifts darting about in the eaves. By now I had this pit in my stomach – except that it was like having a pit in my whole body. I walked round to the back of the barn, behind the hay bales, and on the patch of floor where Monique had been sleeping I saw her glass beads scattered amongst the straw.'

Mrs Bell gripped one of the sleeves. 'I could not imagine where Monique had gone. I went out to the stream, but she wasn't there. I kept hoping that she would suddenly come back so that I could give her the coat – she *needed* it.' Involuntarily, Mrs Bell offered the coat to *me*, then, realising what she'd done, she let it fall back on to her lap. 'I waited there for about two hours, then I guessed that it must be lunchtime and that my parents would be wondering about me, so I left. When I got home they saw that I was distressed and asked why. I lied and said that it was because there was this boy I liked – Jean-Luc Aumage – but that I didn't think he liked me. 'Jean-Luc Aumage!' my father exclaimed. 'René Aumage's boy? That no-good chip off a nasty old block. Don't waste your time, my girl – there'll be better men for you than that!'

'Well . . .' Mrs Bell's eyes were shining with indignation.

'I wanted to slap my father for his nasty remarks. He didn't know what *I* knew – that Jean-Luc had agreed to help Monique. Then I wondered whether he had already helped her. Perhaps *that* was why she wasn't in the barn, because even now Jean-Luc was taking her to find her parents and brothers. I felt confident that he would do everything he could. So with hope in my heart I ran to his house; but Jean-Luc's mother said that he had gone to Marseille and would not be back until the following afternoon.

'That evening I went to the barn again, but Monique still wasn't there. Even though it was getting cold I couldn't bring myself to put on the coat, because by now I saw it as *hers*. So when I got home I went up to my room, and under my bed was a loose floorboard beneath which I kept a few of my secret things. I decided to store the coat there until I could give it to Monique. But first I needed to wrap it in newspaper to protect it. So I found the copy of the *Gazette Provençal* that my father had been reading, but as I separated the pages an article caught my eye. It was all about the "successful arrest" of "aliens" and other "stateless persons" in Avignon, Carpentras, Orange and Nîmes on April 19th and 20th. The "success" of this round-up, it went on, had been directly due to the policy of stamping the ration cards of Jewish people with their ethnic identity.' Mrs Bell looked at me. '*Now* I knew what had happened to Monique's family. The article talked of trains heading north, "loaded" with "foreign Jews" and "other aliens". Having hidden the coat, I went downstairs, my head reeling.

'The next afternoon I ran to Jean-Luc's house and

knocked on the door. To my joy he opened and, my heart pounding, I asked him, in a whisper, if he had been able to help Monique. He laughed and said he'd "helped her, all right". With this sick feeling, I asked him what he meant. He didn't reply, so I told him that Monique needed to be looked after. Jean-Luc replied that she *would* be looked after – along with "others of her kind". I demanded to know where she was, and he replied that he had helped his father escort her to St Pierre Prison in Marseille, from where she would be put on a train to Drancy as soon as possible. I knew what Drancy was – an internment camp on the outskirts of Paris. What I didn't know,' Mrs Bell added, 'was that Drancy was the place from which Jewish people were being sent further east – to Auschwitz, Buchenwald and Dachau.' Her eyes were shimmering. 'Then, as Jean-Luc shut the door, the enormity of the situation hit me.

'I sank on to a wall, and whispered to myself, "What have I *done?*" I had tried to help my friend, but instead my utter naïvety and *stupidity* had led to her being discovered, and sent to . . .' Mrs Bell's mouth quivered, then I saw two tears fall on to the coat, darkening the fabric. 'I heard the whistle of a train in the distance, and I thought Monique could be on *that* train, *now* – I wanted to run down to the track and make it *stop* . . .' She reached for the tissue that I held out to her, and pressed it to her eyes. 'Then, after the war, when we all learned what the true fate of the Jews had been, then I was . . .' Mrs Bell's voice caught '. . . distraught. Every day, without cease, I imagined the ordeal that my friend, Monique Richelieu – born Monika Richter – must have suffered. I was in torment, knowing that she had certainly

165

died, in God knows what hellish place – and in what terror – because of *me*.' Mrs Bell struck her sternum again with a little 'thud'. 'I have never forgiven myself, and I never will.' My throat was aching – as much for myself now as for Mrs Bell. 'As for the coat . . .' She clenched the tissue. 'I kept it hidden under the floor, despite my mother's angry protestations that I must find it. But I didn't care – it was Monique's. I longed to be able to give it to her – I longed to be able to help her into it, and to do up the buttons.' She fingered one of the buttons now. 'I also longed to give Monique this –' She slipped her hand into the nearest pocket and pulled out a necklace. The pink and bronze glass shimmered in the sunlight. Mrs Bell laced the beads through her fingers then held it to her cheek. 'It was my fantasy that I would one day give Monique the coat and this neck-lace and, can you believe . . .?' She looked at me. 'It still *is*.' She smiled, bleakly. 'You probably find that very strange, Phoebe.'

I shook my head. 'No.'

'But I kept the coat in its hiding place until 1948, when, as I told you, I left Avignon for a new life here in London – a life far from the arena in which these events had happened; a life in which I would not be bumping into Jean-Luc Aumage or his father in the street, or passing the house where Monique and her family had lived: I could not bear to see it again, knowing that they had never returned to it. And I never did see it again.' Mrs Bell heaved a deep sigh. 'But even then, when I moved to London, I took the coat with me, still hoping to have the chance some day to keep my promise to my friend – which yes, really *was* insane, because by then I

166

had learned that the last known sighting of Monique was on August 5th, 1943, when she arrived at Auschwitz.' Mrs Bell blinked. 'But I have kept the coat, nonetheless, all these years. It is my . . . my . . .' She looked at me. 'What is the word I am searching for?'

'It's "penance",' I replied quietly.

'Penance.' Mrs Bell nodded. 'Of course.' Then she slipped the necklace back into the pocket from which she'd taken it. 'And that,' she concluded, 'is the story of this small blue coat.' She stood up. 'I am going to put it back now. Thank you for listening, Phoebe. You have no idea what you have just done for me. All these years I have longed for one person to hear my story, and if not to condemn me then at least to . . . understand.' She looked at me. '*Do* you understand, Phoebe? Do you understand why I did what I did? Why I still feel what I feel?'

'Yes, I do, Mrs Bell,' I said quietly. 'More than you know.'

Mrs Bell went into the bedroom, and I heard the wardrobe door being shut, then she came back and sat down, her face drained of emotion.

'But . . .' I shifted on my seat. 'Why didn't you tell your husband? From all you've said about him, you obviously loved him.'

Mrs Bell nodded. 'Very much. But it's *because* I loved him that I didn't dare tell him. I was terrified that if he knew what I'd done he might regard me differently, or even condemn me.'

'For what? Being a young girl who tried to do the right thing but ended up doing . . .'

167

'The wrong thing,' Mrs Bell concluded. 'The worst thing I *could* have done. Of course it wasn't a deliberate betrayal,' she went on. 'As Monique had said, I didn't understand. I *was* very young, and I've often tried to console myself with the thought that Monique might have been discovered anyway, who knows . . .'

'Yes,' I said quickly. 'She might. She might have died anyway, and it might have had nothing to do with you, Mrs Bell – nothing at all, absolutely nothing.' Mrs Bell was staring at me curiously. 'What you did was just an error of judgement,' I added quietly.

'But that's made it no easier to live with, because it was an error of judgement that led to the death of my friend.' She drew in her breath then slowly released it. 'And that's been *so* hard to bear.'

I picked up the hatbox and held it on my lap. 'I do . . . understand that – only too well. It's as though you're staggering around with this huge rock in your arms, and no one but you can carry it and you can't see anywhere to put it down . . .' A sudden silence enveloped us. I was aware of the soft gasp of the fire.

'Phoebe,' Mrs Bell murmured. 'What really happened to your friend? To Emma?' I stared at the little bouquets of flowers on the hatbox; the design was semi-abstract but I could see tulips and bluebells.

'You said she was ill . . .'

I nodded, aware now of the light tick of the carriage clock. 'It started almost a year ago, in early October.'

'Emma's illness?'

I shook my head. 'The events that led up to it – that, in a way, caused it.' Now I told Mrs Bell about Guy.

'So Emma must have been hurt by that.'

I nodded. 'I didn't realise quite how much. She insisted that she'd be okay about it, but it became clear that she wasn't okay – she was suffering.'

'And you feel you're to blame?'

My mouth had dried. 'Yes. Emma and I had been close friends for almost twenty-five years. But after I started seeing Guy her almost daily phone calls just . . . stopped: when I tried to phone her she either didn't call me back or was distant with me. She simply withdrew from my life.'

'But your relationship with Guy went on?'

'Yes, you see, we couldn't help it – we'd fallen in love. Guy's view was that we'd done nothing wrong. It wasn't our fault, he said, if Emma had read too much into his friendship with her. He said that she'd come round in time. He added that if she were a real friend she'd have accepted the situation and tried to be happy for me.'

Mrs Bell nodded. 'Do you think there's some truth in that?'

'Yes – of course. But it's easier said than done when your feelings have been hurt. And I knew, from what Emma did next, how badly hers had been.'

'What did she do?'

'After Christmas Guy and I went skiing. On New Year's Eve we went out to dinner, and to start with we had a glass of champagne. And as Guy handed my glass to me I could see that there was something in it.'

'*Ah*,' said Mrs Bell. 'A ring.'

I nodded. 'A beautiful solitaire. I was elated – and also amazed because we'd only known each other three months. But even as I accepted, and we kissed, I was already in knots about how Emma would take it. I was to find out soon enough, because the next morning, to my surprise, she phoned to wish me a Happy New Year. We chatted for a while and she asked me where I was. So I told her that I was in Val d'Isère. She asked me if I was there with Guy, so I said yes. Then I blurted out that we'd just got engaged. There was this . . . stunned silence.'

'*La pauvre fille*,' Mrs Bell murmured.

'Then, in this thin, shaky voice Emma said she hoped we'd be very happy. I told her that I'd love to see her and that I'd phone her on my return.'

'So you were trying to keep your relationship with her going?'

'Yes – I thought that if she could just get used to seeing Guy with me then she'd come to view him in a different way. I also believed that she'd soon fall in love with someone else and that our friendship would return to normal.'

'But that's not what happened.'

'No.' I threaded the string of the hatbox through my fingers. 'She'd clearly had very intense feelings for Guy and had convinced herself that their friendship would have developed into something more, if only . . . he . . .'

'Hadn't fallen for you.'

I nodded. 'Anyway when I got back to London on January 6th I phoned Emma, but she didn't pick up. I rang her mobile but she didn't answer. I sent her texts and e-mails but she didn't reply. Her assistant, Sian, was away so I couldn't find out from her where Emma was, so then I rang Emma's mother, Daphne. She told me that Emma had decided, just three days before, to go to South

170

Africa to visit old friends and that where she was, in Transvaal, the phone signal was poor. Then Daphne asked me if I thought that Emma was okay because she'd seemed upset recently but had refused to say why. I pretended not to know what the problem might be. Daphne added that Emma could be moody at times and one just had to let it pass. Feeling an utter hypocrite, I agreed.'

'Did you hear from Emma while she was in South Africa?'

'No. But by the third week of January I knew she was back because I got her written RSVP to the engagement party that Guy and I were having on the following Saturday. She sent her regrets.'

'That must have hurt you.'

'Yes,' I murmured. 'I can't tell you how much. Then came Valentine's Day . . .' I hesitated. 'Guy had booked a table at the Bluebird Café in Chelsea, not far from his flat. And we were just getting ready to leave when, to my surprise, Emma phoned me – it was the first time she'd called me since New Year's Day. I thought her voice sounded a bit strange – as though she was short of breath – so I asked her if she was okay. She said that she was feeling "dreadful". She sounded weak and shivery, as though she had 'flu. I asked her if she'd taken anything, and she said she'd had some paracetamol. She added that she felt "so bad" that she "wanted to die". That set alarm bells ringing, so I said that I wanted to come round. And I heard Emma whisper, "*Will* you? Will you come, Phoebe? Please come." So I said I'd be there in half an hour.

'As I shut my phone I could see that Guy was very

upset. He said he'd booked a nice Valentine's Day dinner for us and wanted to enjoy it – plus he didn't believe that Emma *was* in such a bad way. "You know how she exaggerates things," he said. "It's probably attention seeking." I insisted that Emma had sounded ill, and pointed out that a lot of people had 'flu. Guy said that, knowing Emma, it was probably just a bad cold. He added that I was over-reacting out of misplaced guilt, when it was Emma who should feel guilty. She'd sulked for three months and had even shunned my engagement party. Now here I was proposing to rush round the second she deigned to call. I told Guy that Emma was a slightly fragile person who needed careful handling. He said he'd had enough of the "mad milliner", as he'd taken to calling her. We were going to have dinner. He put on his coat.

'Every instinct told me that I should go and see Emma, but I couldn't bear the thought of conflict with Guy. I remember standing there, twisting my engagement ring back and forth, saying, "I just don't know what to *do* . . ." Then . . . as a compromise . . .' I cast my mind back '. . . Guy suggested that we have dinner and that I ring Emma when we got back. As we wouldn't be out for very long, I agreed. So we went to the Bluebird. I remember we discussed our wedding, which was to have been this month. It's weird to think of it now,' I added.

'Do you feel sad about it?'

I looked at Mrs Bell. 'It's strange, but I feel . . . almost *nothing*. Anyway . . . when we got back to Guy's flat at ten thirty I phoned Emma again. At the sound of my voice she started crying. She said she was sorry that she hadn't been nicer about Guy and me. She said she'd been

172

a poor friend. I told her that it didn't matter and she wasn't to worry about anything because I was going to look after her.' I felt tears prickle my lower lashes. 'Then I heard her mumble, "Tonight, Phoebe?" "Tonight," I repeated. I looked at Guy, but he was shaking his head and making drink-driving gestures, and I realised I probably was over the limit, so I told her . . .' I tried to swallow but it was as though my throat was crammed with rags. 'I told her . . . that I'd be there in the morning.' I paused. 'At first Emma didn't respond, then I heard her whisper, ". . . sleep now." So I said, "Yes, you go to sleep now – I'll see you first thing. Have a lovely sleep, Em."' I looked at the hatbox. The tulips and bluebells had blurred.

'I woke at six with a churning feeling in my stomach. I wondered about phoning Emma but I didn't want to wake her. So I drove to Marylebone and parked close to the house she rented on Nottingham Street. I knew where she kept her spare key, so I discreetly fished it out of its hiding place and let myself in. The house looked very unkempt. There was loads of mail on the mat. The kitchen sink was piled high with unwashed plates.

'It was the first time I'd been to Emma's house since the fateful dinner party. As I stood there I remembered the dismay I'd felt when Emma had first introduced me to Guy, then my euphoria when he'd phoned me. Our friendship had been tested to destruction, I reflected, but now everything was going to be all right. Then I went into the sitting room and that was a mess too, with towels on the sofa and the wastepaper basket overflowing with used tissues and empty water bottles. Emma had obviously been in a bad way. Then I went up the narrow stairs, past photos of models wearing her lovely hats, and stood outside her bedroom door. There was silence from the other side, and I remember feeling relieved, because it meant that Emma was in a deep sleep which would be the best thing for her.

'I pushed on the door and crept in. As I went a little closer to the bed I realised that Emma was sleeping so deeply that I couldn't hear her breathing. Then I remembered that she'd always been good at holding her breath, because she was a strong swimmer. When we were children she used to scare me by falling down and holding it for ages. Then I thought, But why would Emma be doing that *now*, when we're both thirty-three? As I stood there, I could suddenly hear in my head that piano piece she played when we were at school – "*Träumerei*". She's dreaming, I thought to myself.

'"Emma," I said gently. "It's me." There was no movement. "Emma," I whispered, "wake up." She didn't stir. "Wake *up*, Emma," I said, my heart pounding now. "Please. I need to see how you are. Come on, Em." She didn't reply. "Emma, would you please wake *up*," I said, panicking now. I clapped my hands, twice, by her head. And this brought back to me how once, when we were playing hide and seek she'd played dead so convincingly that I'd thought she *was* dead and I'd been distraught; but then she'd suddenly jumped to her feet, roaring with laughter. I was so upset and angry I'd cried.

'I half expected Emma to jump up now, laughing and shouting, "*Fooled you, Phoebe! You thought I was dead, didn't you!*" until I remembered that she'd sworn never to do that again. But still she wasn't moving. "Don't *do* this to me, Em," I moaned. "*Please.*" I put out my hand and touched her . . .' I stared at the hatbox, and now I could see lupins – or were they foxgloves? 'I pulled back the duvet. Emma was lying on her side, in jeans and a tee-shirt, her eyes half open, just staring ahead. Her skin was grey. Her fingers were curled round the phone.

'I remember letting out a cry, then fumbling for my mobile. My hand was shaking so much that I kept missing the "9" button and had to try three or four times. I saw a bottle of paracetamol on the floor and picked it up – it was empty. Now I could hear the 999 woman asking me what emergency service I required. I was hyper-ventilating and could hardly speak, but I managed to say that my friend needed an ambulance straight away, this very minute, so would they please send one *now,* right now . . .' I tried to swallow. 'But even as I said it, I knew that it was . . . that Em . . . that Emma had . . .'

A tear fell on to the hatbox with a tiny 'splash'.

'Oh, Phoebe,' I heard Mrs Bell whisper.

I lifted my head and looked out of the window. 'They told me afterwards that she'd died about three hours before I got there.'

I sat in silence for a few moments, still cradling the hatbox, running the pale green string back and forth through my fingers.

'But how terrible to do that,' said Mrs Bell quietly. 'Whatever her sadness . . . to commit . . .'

I looked at her. 'But that's not what it was – although that's how it seemed at first. For a while there was confu-sion about what had actually happened to Emma . . .

175

about what had caused her . . .' Mrs Bell's face had blurred. I felt my head drop.

'I'm sorry, Phoebe. It's too upsetting for you to talk about.'

'Yes – it is. Because I feel to blame.'

'But it wasn't your fault that Guy fell in love with you, rather than Emma.'

'But I knew how much she liked him. Some people would say I shouldn't have pursued the relationship, knowing that.'

'But it might have been your one chance in life at love.'

'That's what I told myself. I told myself that I might never feel this way about anyone ever again. And I consoled myself that Emma would get over Guy, and fall in love with someone else, because that's what she'd always done with men before. But this time she didn't.' I heaved a sigh. 'And I can understand her *hating* the thought of having to see him with me when she'd so hoped to be with him herself.'

'You can't blame *your*self that that hope of hers was misguided, Phoebe.'

'No. But I can and do blame myself for not going to see her that night, when every instinct told me I should.'

'Well . . .' Mrs Bell shook her head. 'Perhaps it might have made no difference.'

'That's what my GP said. She said that by then Emma would have been slipping into the coma from which she would never . . .' I drew in my breath in a juddery gasp. 'I'll never know. But I believe that if I had gone when she'd first called me, rather than twelve hours later, then Emma would still be alive.'

I put down the hatbox then went to the window. I gazed down at the deserted garden.

'So that's why you've felt an affinity with me, Mrs Bell. We both had friends who waited for us to come.'

SEVEN

On my way to meet Miles for dinner I thought about how there are some people who say they're able to 'compartmentalise' things, as though it's possible to put negative or distressing thoughts into neat mental drawers to be taken out only at a psychologically convenient time. It's a beguiling idea, but I've never bought it. In my experience sadness and regret seep into one's consciousness willy-nilly, or they suddenly leap out at you with a cosh. The only real remedy is time, though even the best part of a lifetime, as Mrs Bell's story proved, may still not be time enough. Work is also an antidote to unhappiness of course, as is distraction. Miles was a welcome distraction, I decided as I went to meet him on Thursday, just after eight.

I'd dressed up a little, in a sixties cocktail dress in pale pink sari silk. Over it I'd put an antique gold pashmina.

'Mr Archant is already here,' said the maître d' of the Oxo Tower restaurant. As I followed him across the floor, I saw Miles sitting at a table by the vast window, studying the menu. With a sinking heart I registered his grey hair and his half-moon reading glasses. Then as he looked up and saw me his face broke into a delighted but anxious smile that dispelled my disappointment. He got to his feet, slotting his spectacles back into his top pocket and holding his yellow silk tie to stop it from flapping. It was endearing to see such a sophisticated man behaving so awkwardly.

'Phoebe.' He kissed me on both cheeks, placing his hand on my shoulder, as though to draw me towards him. Seeing now how attractive Miles was I felt a sudden surge of interest in him that took me aback.

'Would you like a glass of champagne?' he asked.

'That would be lovely.'

'Is Dom Pérignon okay?'

'If there's nothing better,' I joked.

'They're out of Vintage Krug – I did ask.' I laughed, then realised that Miles hadn't been joking.

As we chatted, enjoying the views across the sunlit river to the Temple and St Paul's, I was touched by how much Miles was trying to impress me, and by how happy he seemed to be in my company. I asked him about his work, and he explained that he was the founder partner of the law firm that he now consulted for three days a week.

'I'm semi-retired now.' He sipped his champagne. 'But I like to keep my hand in, and I help get in new business by entertaining clients. Now tell me about your shop, Phoebe – what made you decide to open it?' I briefly told Miles about my time at Sotheby's. His eyes widened. 'So I was up against a professional then.'

'You were,' I said as he handed the wine list back to the waiter. 'But I behaved like a rank amateur. I got all emotional about it.'

'I must say, you *were* rather intense. But what's so wonderful about – sorry, what was the name of that designer again?'

'Madame Grès,' I said patiently. 'She was the greatest couturière in the world. She draped and pleated vast amounts of cloth, pinning it directly on to the body to form an amazing gown that turned the woman into a beautiful statue almost – like the Spirit of Ecstasy on a Rolls Royce. Madame Grès was a sculptor, who carved in cloth. She was also very brave.'

Miles folded his hands. 'In what way?'

'When she opened the House of Grès in Paris in 1942 she hung a huge French flag out of her windows in defiance of the Occupation. Each time the Germans ripped it down she'd put out another one. They knew she was Jewish, but left her alone because they hoped she'd dress their officers' wives. When she refused to do so, they shut her down. She died in obscurity and poverty sadly, but she was a genius.'

'And what will you do with the dress?'

I gave a little shrug. 'I don't know.'

He smiled. 'Keep it for your wedding.'

'That *has* been suggested to me, but I doubt it will ever be worn for that purpose.'

'*Have* you been married?' I shook my head. 'Ever come close?' I nodded. 'Were you engaged?' I nodded again.

'Am I allowed to ask you about it?'

'Sorry – I'd rather not talk about it.' I pushed Guy from my thoughts. 'What about you?' I asked as our starters arrived. 'You've been on your own for ten years – why haven't you . . .?'

'Married again?' Miles shrugged. 'There've been a few girlfriends.' He picked up his soup spoon. 'They were all very nice, but . . . it just hasn't happened.' Now the conversation naturally turned to Miles' wife. 'Ellen was a lovely person. In fact I adored her,' he added. She was American – a successful portrait painter, of children mostly. She died ten years ago, in June.' He drew in his breath then held it as though he were considering a difficult question. 'She just collapsed one afternoon.'

'Why . . .?'

He lowered his spoon. 'It was a brain haemorrhage. She'd had a terrible headache all that day, but as she got migraines it didn't register with her that it wasn't a normal sort of headache.' Miles shook his head. 'You can imagine the shock . . .'

'Yes,' I said quietly.

'But I could at least console myself that it was no one's fault.' I felt a stab of envy. 'It had been simply one of those dreadful, unavoidable things – the finger of God, or however one wants to put it.'

'And how terrible for Roxanne.'

He nodded. 'She was only six. I just sat her on my lap and tried to explain that Mummy . . .' His voice caught. 'I'll never forget the expression on her face as she struggled to understand the incomprehensible – that half her universe had simply . . . *vanished*.' Miles sighed. 'I know that it's always there with Roxy – just beneath the surface. She has this acute sense of not *having* . . . a sense of . . . of . . .'

'Deprivation?' I suggested gently.

Miles looked at me. 'Deprivation. Yes. That's it.'

Suddenly his BlackBerry rang. He took his glasses out of his top pocket and placed them on the end of his nose as he peered at the screen. 'That's Roxy now. Oh dear – would you excuse me, Phoebe?' He removed his glasses again then went out of the restaurant on to a corner of the terrace where I saw him leaning against the balcony, his tie flapping a little in the breeze, evidently having a serious chat with Roxanne about something. Then I saw him pocket the phone.

'I'm sorry about that,' he said as he returned to the table. 'It must have seemed rude, but when it's your child . . .'

'I understand,' I said.

'She's stuck on her ancient history essay,' he explained as the waiter brought our main courses. 'It's on Boadicea.'

'Isn't she called Boudica these days?'

Miles nodded. 'I always forget. I still have to remind myself that Bombay has become "Mumbai".'

'And how about the Dome being "O2"?'

'*Is* it?' he said, then smiled. 'Anyway, Roxy has to hand this essay in tomorrow and she's hardly started. She's a bit disorganised about her work sometimes.' He gave an exasperated sigh.

I picked up my fork. 'And does she like her school?'

Miles narrowed his eyes. 'She seems to, though it's very early days – she's only been there two weeks.'

'Where was she before?'

'At St Mary's – a girls' school in Dorking. But . . .' I looked at him. 'It didn't really work out.'

'Didn't she like boarding?'

'She didn't mind it, but there was . . .' Miles hesitated

182

'. . . a misunderstanding – a few weeks before her GCSEs. It was all . . . cleared up,' he went on. 'But after that I felt it would be better for her to have a fresh start. So now she's at Bellingham. She seems to like it there, so my fingers are crossed that she'll get good A-levels.' He sipped his wine.

'Then go to university?'

Miles shook his head. 'Roxy says it's a waste of time.'

'Really?' I put down my fork. 'Well . . . it *isn't*. Didn't you say she wants to work in the fashion business?'

'Yes, though doing what I don't know. She talks about working for a glossy magazine, like *Vogue* or *Tatler*.'

'But it's an extremely competitive world – if she's serious, she'd be much better off with a degree.'

'I've told her that,' Miles said wearily. 'But she's very headstrong.'

The waiter came to take our plates, so I took the chance to change the subject. 'Your surname's unusual,' I pointed out. 'I once met a Sebastian Archant who owns Fenley Castle. I had to go there to evaluate a collection of eighteenth-century textiles.' I remembered a velvet tailcoat and breeches from the 1780s, beautifully embroidered with anemones and forget-me-nots. 'Most of them went to museums.'

'Sebby's my second cousin,' Miles explained, slightly wearily. 'Now – don't tell me: he tried to ravish you behind the pergola.'

'Not exactly.' I rolled my eyes. 'But I had to stay at the castle for three nights because it was a very big job and there were no hotels nearby and . . .' I cringed at the memory. 'He tried to come into my room. I had to push a trunk against the door – it was ghastly.'

'That's Sebby all over, I'm afraid – not that I blame him for trying.' Miles held his gaze in mine for a moment. 'You're lovely, Phoebe.' The directness of his compliment made me catch my breath. I felt a little wave of desire ripple through me. 'I'm closer to the French side of the family,' I heard Miles say. 'They're wine-growers.'

'Where?'

'In Châteauneuf-du-Pape, a few miles to the north of –'

'Avignon,' I interjected.

He looked at me. 'Do you know it well?'

'I go to Avignon from time to time to buy stock; in fact, I'll be there next weekend.'

Miles lowered his glass of red wine. 'Where are you staying?'

'At the Hôtel d'Europe.'

He was shaking his head in delighted wonderment. 'Well, Miss Swift, if you're agreeable to a second date with me, I'll take you out to dinner again as I'm going to be in the area too.'

'You are?' Miles nodded happily. 'Why?'

'Because this other cousin of mine, Pascal, owns the vineyard. We've always been close, and I go down every September to help with the harvest. It's just started and I'll be there for the last three days. When will you be arriving?' I told him. 'So we'll overlap then,' he said with a delight that tugged at my heartstrings. 'You know,' he added as our coffee arrived, 'I can't help feeling that this must be Fate.' He suddenly winced, then reached for his phone. 'Not again – I'm so sorry, Phoebe.' He put on his glasses and stared at the screen, a frown corrugating his brow. 'Roxy's still in a state about her essay. She says she's "desperate" – in capitals with several exclamation marks.' He sighed. 'I'd better get back. Will you forgive me?'

'Of course.' We'd almost come to the end of the evening, and I found his attachment to his child touching.

Miles signalled to the waiter then looked at me. 'I've enjoyed this evening so much.'

'So have I,' I said truthfully.

Miles smiled at me. 'Good.'

He paid the bill then we went downstairs in the lift. As we stepped on to the pavement I prepared to say goodbye to Miles and walk the five minutes to London Bridge station, but a taxi was pulling up beside us.

The driver pulled down the window. 'Mr Archant?'

Miles nodded then turned to me. 'I've booked the cab to take me to Camberwell then to go on to Blackheath to drop you.'

'Oh. I was going to get the train.'

'I wouldn't hear of it.'

I glanced at my watch. 'It's only ten fifteen,' I protested. 'It's fine.'

'But if I give you a lift – then I get to spend a bit more time with you.'

'In that case . . .' I smiled at him. 'Thanks.'

As we drove through South London, Miles and I tried to remember what we knew about Boudica. We could remember only that she was an Iron Age queen who rebelled against the Romans. Dad would know, I thought, but it was too late to ring him as he has to get up in the night to Louis.

'Didn't she raze Ipswich?' I said as we drove down Walworth Road.

Miles was surfing the net on his BlackBerry. 'It was Colchester,' he said, peering at the screen through his half-moon glasses. 'It's all here on Britannica dotcom. When I get back I'll just lift chunks straight off it and rewrite it.' It occurred to me that at sixteen this was surely something Roxy could have done for herself.

Now we were crossing Camberwell Green, then we turned into Camberwell Grove and stopped halfway down on the left. So this was where Miles lived. As I looked at his elegant Georgian house set a little way back from the road, I saw a downstairs curtain being drawn aside and there was Roxy's pale face.

Miles turned to me. 'It's been lovely to see you, Phoebe.' He leaned forward and kissed me, holding his cheek against mine for a moment. 'So . . . see you in France then.' His anxious expression told me that that had been a question, not a statement.

'I'll see you in France,' I said.

I was delighted to have been asked to take part in Radio London's discussion about vintage clothes until I remembered that their studio was in Marylebone High Street. I braced myself for the walk down Marylebone Lane on Monday morning. As I passed the ribbon shop where Emma used to buy trimmings for her hats, I tried to imagine her house, just a few streets away, no doubt with other occupants now. I tried to imagine her things, all packed into trunks in her parents' garage. Then I thought with dismay of her diary, which Emma wrote in every day. Her mother would surely read it before long.

As I approached Amici's, the cafe Emma and I always

went to, I suddenly fancied that I could see her, sitting in the window, looking out at me with a hurt, puzzled expression. But of course it wasn't Emma – just someone who looked a little like her.

I pushed on the glass doors of Radio London. The commissionaire wrote out a name badge for me then asked me to wait. As I sat in reception I listened to the output blaring. *Travel news now ... South Circular ... incident at Highbury Corner ... 94.9 FM ... And the weather for London ... highs of 22 ... with me, Ginny Jones ... and in a few minutes I'll be talking old hat – or rather old clothes – with vintage dress shop owner, Phoebe Swift.* I felt a cloud of butterflies take flight in my stomach. The producer, Mike, appeared, clipboard in hand.

'It's just a friendly five-minute chat,' he explained, as he led me down the brightly lit corridor. He put his shoulder to the heavy studio door and it opened with a muffled 'swish'. 'We've got a pre-record on, so it's okay to talk,' he explained as we went in. 'Ginny – meet Phoebe.'

'Hi, Phoebe,' said Ginny as I sat down. She nodded at the headphones lying in front of me. I slipped them on and heard the pre-record finishing. Then there was a bit of banter with the sports reporter – something to do with the London Olympics – and a trail for Danny Baker. 'Now,' Ginny said, smiling at me. 'From rags to riches, that's what Phoebe Swift is hoping for. She's just opened a vintage dress shop down in Blackheath – Village Vintage – and she joins me now. Phoebe, London Fashion Week has just finished – this year vintage was quite a big theme, wasn't it?'

'It was. Several of the major houses had a vintage feel to their new collections.'

'And why *does* vintage seem to be the flavour *de nos jours?*'

'I think the fact that a style icon like Kate Moss chooses to wear it has had a big impact on the market.'

'She wore that gold satin thirties dress that got ripped to shreds, didn't she?'

'She did – but that was a case of riches to *rags,* because it was said to have cost £2,000. There are lots of Hollywood stars wearing vintage now on the red carpet – one thinks of Julia Roberts at the Oscars in vintage Valentino, or Renée Zellweger in that 1950s canary yellow gown by Jean Desses. All this has changed the perception of vintage, which used to be seen as something Bohemian and quirky, rather than the highly sophisticated choice that it is now.'

Ginny scribbled on her script. 'So what does vintage *do* for a girl?'

'The fact that you know you're wearing something that is both highly individual and beautifully made is itself uplifting. And you're aware that the garment has a history – a heritage, if you like – which gives it a kind of backbone. No contemporary piece of clothing can offer this added dimension.'

'So what tips do you have when buying vintage?'

'Be prepared to spend time looking, and know what *suits* you. If you're curvy, then don't go for the twenties or sixties as the boxy style won't flatter you; go for the more fitted silhouette of the forties and fifties. If you like the thirties, be aware that those figure-skimming designs are unforgiving on a round tummy or large bust.

I'd also say be realistic. Don't go into a vintage shop and ask to be turned into, say, Audrey Hepburn in *Breakfast at Tiffany's* because that style may well not do anything for you and you might miss something that would.'

'What are *you* wearing then, Phoebe?'

I glanced at my dress. 'A non-label floral chiffon tea dress from the late 1930s – *my* favourite era – with a vintage cashmere cardigan.'

'Very nice too. You strike me as quite a cool lady.' I smiled. 'And do you always wear vintage?'

'I do – if not a whole outfit, then vintage accessories; the days when I wear nothing that's vintage are rare.'

'But' – Ginny pulled a face – 'I don't think I'd want to wear anyone else's old clothes.'

'Some people do feel like that.' I thought of Mum. 'But we vintage lovers are born, not made, so we're not squeamish about it. We feel that a tiny stain or mark is a small price to pay for owning something that's not just original, it may even bear an iconic name.'

Ginny held up her pen, 'so what are the main issues with vintage then? The prices?'

'No, for the quality, the prices remain reasonable – another plus point in these credit-crunched times. It's the sizing: vintage clothes tend to run small. Waists were fashionably tiny from the forties through to the sixties, dresses and jackets were very fitted, and women wore corsets and girdles to be able to squeeze into them. Added to which women today are simply bigger. My advice when buying vintage is simply to ignore the number on the label and try it on.'

'What about the care of these old clothes?' Ginny

asked. 'Could you tell us how to keep our vintage mintage?'

I smiled. 'There are some basic rules. Hand wash knitwear using baby shampoo and don't soak it, as that could stretch the fibres; then dry it inside out and flat.'

'What about mothballs?' said Ginny, holding her nose.

'They do smell foul and the more fragrant alternatives don't seem to work. The best thing is to keep anything moth-prone in polythene bags; and a squish of perfume in the wardrobe can work wonders – anything strong and sweet like Fendi will deter moths.'

'It certainly deters me,' Ginny laughed.

'With silk,' I went on, 'store it on padded hangers, away from direct sunlight as it fades easily. When it comes to satin, *don't* let water near it – it'll wrinkle – and never buy satin that's brittle or frayed as it won't stand up to wear.'

'As Kate Moss discovered.'

'Indeed. I'd also advise your listeners to avoid anything that desperately needs cleaning, as it may prove impossible. Gelatine sequins melt under modern cleaning techniques. Bakelite or glass beads can crack.'

'Now there's a vintage word – "Bakelite",' said Ginny with an amused expression. 'But where do we buy vintage clothes? Apart from at shops like yours, obviously . . .'

'At auctions,' I replied, 'and at vintage fairs – they take place a few times a year in the bigger cities. Then there's eBay, of course, though make sure you ask the vendor for every single measurement.'

'What about charity shops?'

'You will find vintage in them, but not at bargain

prices as the charities have become more clued up about its worth.'

'Presumably you have a steady stream of people bringing in clothes they want to sell or asking you to look through their wardrobes and attics?'

'I do – and I love it, because I never know what I'll find; and when I see something I like, I get this wonderful feeling – *here*.' I laid my hand on my chest. 'It's like . . . falling in love.'

'So it's a vintage *affair*.'

I smiled. 'You could put it like that.'

'Do you have any other advice?'

'Yes. If you're selling – check the pockets.'

'Do things get left in them?'

I nodded. 'All sorts – keys, pens and pencils.'

'Ever found hard cash?' Ginny joked.

'Sadly not – though I did find a postal order once – for two shillings and sixpence.'

'So check your pockets then, everyone,' said Ginny, 'and check out Phoebe Swift's shop, Village Vintage, in Blackheath, if you want to know' – she leaned into the mic – 'the way we *wore*.' Ginny gave me a warm smile. 'Phoebe Swift – thanks.'

Mum phoned me as I was walking towards the tube. She'd been listening at work. 'You were terrific,' she enthused. 'I was gripped. So how did that come about?'

'Through that newspaper interview. The one that chap Dan did on the day of the party. Do you remember him? He was leaving just as you arrived.'

'I know – the badly dressed man with the curly hair. I like curly hair on a man,' Mum added, 'it's unusual.'

'Yes, Mum; anyway, the radio producer happened to read it, and as he was planning to do something on vintage for Fashion Week he phoned me.'

I suddenly realised that nearly all of the helpful things that had happened lately had come about through Dan's piece. It had brought Annie into the shop, and it had led me to Mrs Bell, and now to this radio opportunity, quite apart from all the customers who'd come in because they'd read it. I felt a sudden rush of warmth towards him.

'I'm not going to have Fraxel,' I heard Mum say.

'Thank goodness.'

'I'm going to have "Radiofrequency Rejuvenation" instead.'

'What's that?'

'They heat up the deeper layer of your skin with lasers, and that shrinks everything so that it doesn't sag so much. Basically, they cook your face. Betty from my bridge circle's had it. She's thrilled – except that she said it was like having cigarettes stubbed out on her cheeks for an hour and a half.'

'What torture. And how does Betty look now?'

'To be honest, exactly the same; but *she's* convinced she looks younger, so it was obviously worth it.' I considered the logic of this. 'Oh, I'd better go, Phoebe – John's waving at me . . .'

I pushed on the door of the shop. Annie looked up from her repair.

'I only heard half the programme, I'm afraid, because I had a brush with a shoplifter.'

My heart skipped a beat. 'What happened?'

'As I was fiddling with the radio this man tried to slip

one of the crocodile-skin wallets into his pocket.' Annie nodded at the basket of wallets and purses I keep on the counter. 'Luckily I glanced into the mirror at the critical moment, so at least I didn't have to chase after him down the street.'

'Did you call the police?'

She shook her head. 'He begged me not to, but I told him that if I ever saw him in here again I would. Then I had this woman . . .' Annie rolled her eyes. 'She picked up the Bill Gibb silver lace mini-dress, slapped it on the counter and said she'd give me twenty quid for it.'

'Damn cheek!'

'So I explained that at £80 the dress was already very reasonable, and that if she wanted to haggle she should go to the souk.' I snorted with laughter. 'Then I had a bit of a thrill – Chloë Sevigny came in. She's filming in South London – we had a nice chat about acting.'

'She wears a lot of vintage, doesn't she – and did she buy anything?'

'One of the Jean-Paul Gaultier Body Map tops. Now I've got some messages for you.' Annie picked up a piece of paper. 'Dan phoned – he's got the tickets for *Anna Karenina* next Wednesday and says he'll meet you outside the Greenwich Picturehouse at seven.'

'*Will* he now . . .?'

Annie glanced at me. 'Aren't you going?'

'I wasn't sure . . . but . . . well, it seems I am, doesn't it?' I added irritably.

Annie gave me a puzzled look. 'Then Val rang – she's finished your repairs and says please can you collect them. And there was a message on the answerphone from a Rick Diaz in New York.'

193

'He's my American dealer.'

'He's got some more prom dresses for you.'

'Great – we need them for the party season.'

'We do. He added that he's got some bags he'd like you to take.'

I groaned. 'I've got *hundreds* of bags.'

'I know – but he says please can you e-mail him. Then, last but not least – *these* arrived.' Annie disappeared into the kitchen and came out carrying a bouquet of red roses so huge it obscured her top half.

I stared at them.

'Three dozen,' I heard her say from behind the flowers. 'Are they from this chap Dan?' she asked as I unpinned the envelope and took out the card. 'Not that your personal life is any of my business,' she added as she put the roses on the counter.

Love Miles. Was that a salutation or a command? I wondered.

'They're from someone I've met quite recently,' I said to Annie. 'In fact, I met him at the Christie's auction.'

'Really?'

'He's called Miles.'

'Is he nice?'

'Seems to be.'

'And what does he do?'

'He's a solicitor.'

'A successful one, judging by the flowers he sends. And how old is he?'

'Forty-eight.'

'*Ah.*' Annie raised an eyebrow. 'So he's vintage, too.'

I nodded. 'Circa 1960. A bit of wear and tear . . . a few creases . . .'

'But plenty of character?'

'I think so . . . I've only met him three times.'

'Well, he's clearly smitten so I hope you're going to see him again.'

'Perhaps.' I didn't want to admit that I'd be seeing Miles this very weekend, in Provence.

'Would you like me to put them in a vase for you?'

'Yes, please.'

She cut the ribbon. 'In fact, I'll need two vases.'

I took off my coat. 'By the way, you're still okay to work on Friday and Saturday, aren't you?'

'I am,' Annie replied as she removed the cellophane. 'But you will definitely be back by Tuesday?'

'I'm returning on Monday evening. Why?'

Annie was stripping off the lower leaves with a pair of scissors. 'I've got another audition on Tuesday morning, so I won't be able to get here until after lunch. I'll make up the time on the Friday, if that's okay?'

'That would be fine. What's the audition for?' I asked with a sinking heart.

'Regional rep,' she replied wearily. 'Three months in Stoke-on-Trent.'

'Well . . . fingers crossed,' I said disingenuously, then I felt guilty about hoping that Annie would fail. But it would only be a matter of time before she did get a job and then . . .

My train of thought was interrupted by the bell. And I was just going to leave Annie to it when I saw who the customer was.

'Hi,' said the red-haired girl who'd tried on the lime green cupcake dress nearly three weeks ago.

'Hi,' Annie replied warmly as she put half the roses

195

in a vase. The girl stood staring at the green cupcake dress, then she slowly closed her eyes. 'Thank God,' she breathed. 'It's still here.'

'It's still here,' Annie echoed cheerfully as she put the first vase on the centre table.

'I was convinced it wouldn't be,' the girl said, turning to me now. 'I almost couldn't bear to come in, in case it had sold.'

'We have sold two of those prom dresses recently, but not your one – I mean that one,' I corrected myself. 'The green one.'

'I'll have it,' she said happily.

'Really?' As I unhooked it from the wall I noticed how much more self-confident the girl seemed than when she'd come in with . . . what was his name?

'Keith didn't like it.' The girl opened her bag. 'But I loved it.' She looked at me. 'And he knew that. I don't need to try it on again,' she added as I hung the dress in the changing room. 'It's perfect.'

'It is perfect,' I said. 'On you. I'm thrilled you've come back for it,' I confided as I took it to the till. 'When a garment suits a customer as well as this suited you, then I really want them to have it. Have you got some glamorous party to wear it to?' I thought of her looking dismal in black at the Dorchester with the vile Keith and his 'top people'.

'I've no idea when I'm going to wear it,' the girl replied calmly. 'I only knew that I *had* to have it. Once I'd tried it on, well . . .' She shrugged. 'The dress *claimed* me.'

I folded it, pressing down its voluminous underskirts so that it wouldn't burst out of the carrier.

The girl took a pink envelope out of her bag and

handed it to me. It was a Disney Princess one, with a picture of Cinderella in the corner. I opened it. Inside was £275 in cash.

'I'm happy to give you the five per cent discount,' I said.

The girl hesitated for a second. 'No. Thank you.'

'I really don't mind . . .'

'It's £275,' she insisted. 'That was the price,' she added firmly, almost aggressively. 'Let's stick to it.'

'Well . . . okay.' I shrugged, slightly taken aback. As I handed her the dress, she emitted a little sigh, of ecstasy almost. Then, her head held high, she left the shop.

'So she got her fairytale dress after all,' Annie said as I watched the girl cross the road. She was arranging the rest of the roses. 'I just wish she had a fairytale man. But she seemed quite different today, didn't she?' Annie added as she put the vase on the counter. She went to the window and looked out. 'She's even walking taller – look.' Her eyes narrowed as they tracked her down the street. 'Vintage clothes can do that,' she added after a moment. 'They can be subtly . . . transforming.'

'That's true. But how weird that she refused the discount.'

'I guess it was important to her that she'd paid for the dress herself, every penny. But I wonder what's happened that she was able to buy it,' Annie mused.

I shrugged. 'Maybe Keith relented and gave her the cash.'

Annie shook her head. 'He'd never have done that. Perhaps she stole the money from him,' she suggested. I had a sudden vision of the girl wearing the dress behind bars. 'Perhaps a friend lent it to her.'

'Who knows?' I said as I went back to the counter. 'I'm just glad she's got it, even if we'll never know how she came by it.'

Annie was still staring out of the window. 'Maybe we will.'

I told Dan about the incident when I met him at the cinema on Wednesday. I'd decided that it would be a good talking point in case conversation flagged.

'She was buying one of those fifties prom dresses,' I explained as we sat in the bar before the film started.

'I know the ones – you called them "cupcake" dresses.'

'That's right. And I offered her the five per cent discount but she said she didn't want it.'

Dan sipped his Peroni. 'How weird.'

'It was more than weird – it was mad. How many women would turn down the chance to have £15 knocked off the price of something? But this girl insisted on paying the full £275.'

'Did you say £275?' Dan echoed. As I explained the background to the purchase, something seemed to be puzzling Dan.

'Are you okay?' I said.

'What? Oh yes, sorry . . .' He snapped out of it. 'I'm just a bit distracted at the moment – I've got a lot on at work. Anyway.' He stood up. 'The film's about to begin. Would you like another drink? We can take them in.'

'Another glass of red wine would be great.'

As Dan went up to the bar I reflected on the start to the evening. As I'd arrived at the cinema at seven Dan had phoned me to say that he'd be a bit late; so I'd sat upstairs on one of the sofas enjoying the view of Greenwich through the panoramic windows. Then I'd glanced at a newspaper that someone had left behind. At the back was a full-page ad for World of Sheds. As I'd looked at it, I'd idly wondered what Dan's fabled shed was like. Was it a 'Tiger Shiplap Apex', I wondered, or a 'Walton's Premium Overlap' with double doors, or a 'Norfolk Apex Xtra' or a 'Tiger Mini-barn'? And I was just wondering if it might be a 'Titanium Wonder' metal-sided shed offering 'excellent functionality' when Dan had arrived, at a run.

He'd sunk down next to me, then picked up my left hand and swiftly lifted it to his lips before returning it to my lap.

I looked at him. 'Do you usually do that to women you've only met twice?'

'No,' he replied. 'Just to you. Sorry I'm a bit late,' he went on as I struggled to recover my composure. 'But I was busy on a story . . .'

'The one about the Age Exchange?'

'No, that's all done. This was a . . . business piece,' he explained, slightly evasively. 'Matt's writing it, but I'm . . . involved. There were a few difficulties which we had to get sorted out – and now we have done. Right.' He clapped his hands. 'Let me get you a drink. What's it going to be? Don't tell me – "Gimme a visky,"' he said huskily. '"Ginger ale on the side – and don't be stinchy, baby."'

'Sorry?'

'Garbo's first ever on-screen words. Until then all her films had been silent. Luckily her voice matched her face – but what would you like?'

'Definitely *not* "visky" – but a glass of red wine would be nice.'

Dan picked up the bar card. 'The choice is Merlot – the Le Carredon from the Pays d'Oc, which is apparently "soft, rounded and easy drinking with a full body" – or the Châteauneuf-du-Pape, Chante le Merle, which has a "terrific nose of red berries and a seductive bouquet . . ." So what's it to be?'

I thought of my trip to Provence. 'The Châteauneuf-du-Pape, please – I like the name.'

Now, half an hour on – the conversation having flowed – Dan was buying me another glass of the Chante le Merle, then we went downstairs to the screen, sank into the black leather chairs and gave ourselves up to *Anna Karenina* and to Garbo's luminous beauty.

'With Garbo it's all about the face,' Dan said afterwards as we walked out of the cinema. 'Her body's irrelevant – so is her acting, even though she was a great actress. People only talk about Garbo's face – that alabaster perfection.'

'Her beauty's almost a mask,' I said. 'She's like a Sphinx.'

'She is. She projects this remote, rather melancholy self-containment. You do that, too,' he added casually. Once again Dan had taken me aback, but perhaps because of the wine, or the fact that I'd been enjoying his company and didn't want to spoil the evening, I decided to let the remark go. 'Let's get something to eat,' he was saying now. Without waiting for a reply he tucked his arm through mine. I didn't mind his physical warmth. In fact I liked it, I realised. It made things . . . easy. 'Is Café Rouge okay?' I heard him ask. 'I'm afraid it's not quite the Rivington Grill.'

'Café Rouge is *fine* . . .' We went inside and found a corner table. 'Why did Garbo retire so young?' I asked him now as we waited for the waiter to take our order.

'The story is that she was so upset by a bad review for her latest film, *Two-Faced Woman*, that she threw in the towel on the spot. The likelier explanation is that she knew that her beauty was at its peak and she didn't want her image to be tarnished by time. Marilyn Monroe died at thirty-six,' Dan went on. 'Would we feel the same about her if she'd died at seventy-six? Garbo wanted to live – but not in public.'

'You're very knowledgeable.'

Dan unfurled his napkin. 'I love film – especially black-and-white film.'

'Is that because you have difficulty seeing colour?'

The waiter offered him a piece of bread. 'No. It's because there's an essential mundanity to colour on screen because we see things in colour every day: with black and white there's the inherent suggestion that it's "art".'

'You've got paint on your hands,' I said. 'Have you been DIY-ing?'

Dan examined his fingers. 'I did a bit more to the shed late last night – it's just finishing touches now.'

'But what's *in* this mysterious shed of yours?'

'You'll see on October 11th when I have the official gala opening – invitations to follow shortly. You will come, won't you?'

I thought of how much I'd enjoyed the evening. 'Yes – I will. And what will the dress code be? Gardening clothes? Wellies?'

Dan looked affronted. 'Smart casual.'

'Not black tie then?'

'That would be a *bit* OTT, though you can wear one of your grand vintage frocks if you like – in fact, you should wear that pale pink dress – the one that you said had belonged to you.'

I shook my head. 'I definitely won't be wearing that.'

'I wonder why not?' Dan mused.

'I just . . . don't like it.'

'You know, *you're* a bit of a Sphinx,' Dan said. 'An enigma, at least. And I think you're struggling with something.' He'd taken me aback again.

'Yes,' I said quietly. 'I am. I'm struggling with the fact that you're so . . . cheeky.'

'Cheeky?'

I nodded. 'You make very direct, if not downright personal remarks. You keep saying and doing things that completely . . . throw me. You're always . . . what's the word I'm looking for here?'

'Spontaneous? I'm always spontaneous?'

'No. You're always discomfiting me . . . discon*cert*ing me . . . Dis*combobulating* me! *That's* it – you're always discombobulating me, Dan.'

He smiled. 'I love the way you say "discombobulated" – could you say it again? It's rather a wonderful word,' he went on. 'We don't hear it often enough. Dis-com-bob-u-late,' he added happily.

I rolled my eyes. 'Now you're trying to . . . annoy me.'

'Sorry. Perhaps it's because you're so cool and restrained. I really like you, Phoebe, but occasionally I get the urge to . . . I don't know . . . wreck your poise a little.'

'Oh. I see. Well, you haven't wrecked it. I'm still very . . . poised. So, what about you, Dan?' I went on, determined to wrest control of the conversation. 'You know quite a bit about me – you've interviewed me, after all. But I know very little about you –'

'Except that I'm cheeky.'

'Extremely.' I smiled then felt myself relax again. 'So why don't you tell me something about yourself.'

Dan shrugged. 'Okay – well, I grew up in Kent, near Ashford. My father was a GP; my mother was a teacher – now both retired. I think the most interesting thing about us as a family was that we had a Jack Russell, Percy, who lived to eighteen, which in human years was one hundred and twenty-six. I went to the local boys' grammar, then to York to read history. Then followed my glorious decade in direct marketing, and now my work with the *Black & Green*. No marriages, no children, a few relationships, the last of which ended three months ago without acrimony. Bingo – my potted history.'

'And are you enjoying working for the paper?' I asked him, calm again now.

'It's an adventure; but it's not what I want to do long term.' And before I could ask Dan what he did want to do long term, he'd already moved the conversation on. 'Okay, so we've just seen *Anna Karenina*. On Friday, as part of the same season, they're showing a new print of *Dr Zhivago* – would you like to come?'

I looked at Dan. 'I would have done actually – but I can't.'

'Oh,' Dan said. 'Why not?'

'Why not?' I repeated. 'Dan – you're doing it again.'

'Discombobulating you?'

'Yes. Because . . . Look . . . I don't have to tell you why I can't come.'

'No, you don't,' he said. 'I've already guessed. It's because you've got some boyfriend who, if he saw us now, would tear me limb from limb. Is that the reason?'

'No,' I said wearily. Dan smiled. 'It's because I'm going to France – to buy stock.'

'Ah.' He nodded. 'I remember. You go to Provence. In that case, we'll see something when you get back. No, sorry, you need six weeks to think about it, don't you – shall I phone you in mid November? Don't worry – I'll e-mail you first to say that I'm going to phone – and perhaps I should write to you the week before that to let you know that I'll be e-mailing so that you don't think I'm being cheeky.'

I looked at Dan. 'I think it'd be a lot easier if I just said "yes".'

EIGHT

Early this morning I boarded the Eurostar at St Pancras for my trip to Avignon. I decided to give myself up to the pleasure of the journey which would take about six hours with a change in Lille. As the train waited to depart I skimmed through my *Guardian*. In the City section I was surprised to see a photo of Keith. The piece that accompanied it was about his property company, Phoenix Land, which specialised in buying up brownfield sites for redevelopment. It had recently been valued at £20 million and was about to be floated on the Alternative Investment Market. The piece explained that Keith had started out selling self-assembly kitchens by mail order, but in 2002 his warehouse had been destroyed in an arson attack by a disgruntled employee. There was a quote from Keith: *That was the worst night of my life. But as I watched the building burn I vowed to make something worthwhile rise out of the ashes.* Hence the name of his new company, I thought as the train pulled away from the platform.

Now I turned to the copy of the *Black & Green* that I'd picked up at Blackheath station. I'd been too tired to read it before. There were the expected local news stories about spiralling commercial rents, the threat to independent shops from the High Street chains, and problems with parking and traffic. There was a weekend curtain-raiser including a page detailing what was going to be on at the O2. There was a 'Social Whirl' section, with snaps of well-known visitors to the area, including a shot of Chloë Sevigny looking in the window of Village Vintage. There were also photos of famous residents out and about – there was one of Jools Holland buying flowers, and another of Glenda Jackson at a fund-raising concert at Blackheath Halls.

Filling the centre pages was Dan's piece about the Age Exchange, which was headed À LA RECHERCHE DU TEMPS: *The Age Exchange is a place where the past is treasured,* he'd written. *It's a place where the elderly can come to share their memories with each other and with younger generations . . . the importance of story-telling,* he'd gone on. *Oral history . . . Carefully selected memorabilia help to trigger recollection . . . The centre helps improve the quality of life for older people by emphasising the value of their reminiscences to old and young . . .*

It was a sympathetic, well-written piece.

Now, as the train gathered pace, I closed the paper and gazed out at the Kent countryside. The harvest was recently over, the pale fields blackened here and there from stubble burning, the still-smouldering ground wafting drifts of alabaster smoke into the late summer air. As we went through Ashford I suddenly imagined Dan, standing on the platform in his mis-matched clothes, waving at me as I sped by. Then the train soon plunged under the Channel, emerging into Belgian flatness, the featureless fields bestridden by gigantic pylons.

At Lille I changed trains, boarding the TGV which would take me to Avignon. Leaning my head against the window I fell asleep and dreamed of Miles and Annie and the girl who came back for the green cupcake dress and the girl who couldn't have a baby who'd bought the pink one. Then I dreamed of Mrs Bell as a young girl, walking through the fields with her blue coat, desperately searching for the friend that she would never find. Then I opened my eyes and to my surprise the Provençal countryside was already flashing past, with its terracotta houses, and its silvery soil, and its green-black cypress trees standing up against the landscape like exclamation marks.

In all directions were vines, planted in such straight lines that it looked as though the fields had been combed. Agricultural workers in bright colours were following grape-picking machines as they trundled down the rows, driving up the dust. The *vendanges* was clearly still in full swing.

Avignon TGV, I heard over the tannoy. *Descendez ici pour Avignon – Gare TGV.*

I made my way out of the station, blinking into the sharp sunlight; then I picked up my hire car and drove into the city, following the road around its medieval walls then negotiating the narrow streets to my hotel.

Once I'd checked in I washed and changed then strolled down Avignon's main drag, the Rue de la République, where the shops and cafés hummed with early evening trade. I stopped for a few minutes in the Place de l'Horloge.

There, in front of the imposing town hall, a fairground carousel whirled gently around. As I looked at the children rising and falling on the gold-and-cream-painted horses, I imagined Avignon in a less innocent time. I imagined German soldiers standing where I was now standing, their machine guns by their sides. I imagined Mrs Bell and her brother laughing and pointing at them, and being hushed by their anxious parents. Then I walked on to the Palais des Papes and sat at a café in front of the medieval fortress as the sun sank in an almost turquoise sky. Mrs Bell had told me that towards the end of the war the palace cellars had been used as air-raid shelters. As I looked at the huge building I imagined the crowds running towards it as the sirens sounded.

Now I turned my thoughts back to the present time and planned the trips I'd need to make over the next couple of days. As I was looking at the map my phone rang. I peered at the screen then pressed 'answer'.

'Miles,' I said happily.

'Phoebe – are you in Avignon yet?'

'I'm sitting in front of the Palais des Papes. Where are you?'

'We've just got to my cousin's.' I registered the fact that Miles had said 'we', meaning that Roxy must be with him. Although I could hardly be surprised, my heart sank a little. 'What are you doing tomorrow?' I heard Miles ask.

'In the morning I'll go to the market at Villeneuve lez Avignon, then after that to the one at Pujaut.'

'Well, Pujaut's halfway to Châteauneuf-du-Pape. Why don't you just come on here after you've finished, and I'll take you out to dinner locally?'

'I'd like that, Miles; but where's "here"?'

'It's called Château de Bosquet. It's easy to find. You drive straight through Châteauneuf-du-Pape then as you leave the village take the road to Orange and it's a large square house about a mile on the right. Come as early as you can.'

'Okay – I will.'

So this morning I drove across the Rhône to Villeneuve lez Avignon. I parked at the top of the village, then walked back down the narrow main street to the market place where traders had laid out their *antiquités* on cloths on the ground. There were old bicycles and faded deckchairs, chipped porcelain and scratched-looking cut glass; there were antique bird cages, rusty old tools and balding teddy bears with creased leather paws. There were stalls selling old oil paintings and faded Provençal quilts, and strung between the plane trees were washing lines hung with old clothes which flapped and twisted in the breeze.

'*Ce sont que des* vrais *antiquités, madame,*' said one vendor reassuringly, as I looked through her garments. '*Tous en* très *bon état.*'

There was so much to look through. I spent a couple of hours selecting simple printed dresses from the 1940s and 50s, and white nightgowns, from the 20s and 30s. Some of these were made of chambre – a coarse rustic linen, others of metisse – a linen and cotton mix, and some of Valencienne, a gossamer-light cotton voile that floated in the wind. Many of the nightgowns were beautifully embroidered. I wondered whose hands had stitched the perfect little flowers and leaves that I now touched, and if it had given them pleasure to do such fine work,

and if it had ever occurred to them that later generations would appreciate it and wonder about them.

When I'd bought all I wanted, I sat at a café, having
an early lunch. Now I allowed myself to think about the
date. I'd thought I'd feel upset, but I didn't, though I
was glad to be away. I briefly wondered what Guy was
doing, and how he would be feeling. Then I phoned
Annie.

'The shop's been very busy,' she said. 'I've already
sold the Vivienne Westwood bustle skirt and the Dior
grosgrain coat.'

'That's good going.'

'But you know what you were saying on the radio
about Audrey Hepburn?'

'Yes.'

'Well, I had a woman in here this morning who asked
me to turn her into Grace Kelly. It was rather tricky.'

'Not attractive enough?'

'Oh, she was gorgeous. It's just that it would have
been easier to turn her into Grace Jones.'

'Ah.'

'And your mother dropped in to see if you wanted to
have lunch with her – she'd forgotten that you were in
France.'

'I'll call her.' So I did, straight away, but she began
going on about some new treatment she'd just been to
see someone about – Plasma Regeneration. 'I took
yesterday morning off to go to this clinic about it,' she
said as I sipped my coffee. 'It's good for deep wrinkles,'
I heard her explain. 'They use nitrogen plasma to stim-
ulate the skin's natural regenerative processes – they inject
it under your skin and that gets the fibroblasts going.

210

The result, believe it or not, is a brand-new epidermis.'
I rolled my eyes. 'Phoebe? Are you still there?'

'Yes, but I've got to go now.'

'If I don't have the Plasma Regeneration,' Mum went
on, 'I may try one of the fillers – they said there's
Restylane, Perlane or Sculptra – and they talked about
autologous fat transfer, where they extract the fat from
your behind and stick it in your face – cheek to cheek,
as it were, but the thing about *that* is . . .'

'Sorry, Mum – I'm going *now*.' I felt sick.

I got back in the car, forcing from my mind thoughts
of the grotesque procedures my mother had just
described, then set off for Pujaut.

As I saw the sign for Châteauneuf-du-Pape I began to
feel pleasantly apprehensive about seeing Miles again.
I'd brought a dress to change into before I got there
as I'd been in the same things all day.

The market at Pujaut was small, but I bought six
more nightgowns and some broderie anglaise vests with
scalloped necks, as girls like to wear them with jeans.
By now it was half past three. I found a café and changed
into my dress, a navy-and-white striped St Michael cotton
pinafore from the early sixties.

As I left Pujaut I could see agricultural workers toiling
in the vineyards that stretched away in all directions.
Signs along the roadside invited me to stop at this
domaine or that *château* for wine tasting.

Ahead of me now, perched on a hill, was Châteauneuf-
du-Pape, its cream-coloured buildings huddled together
beneath a medieval tower. I drove through the village
then turned right towards Orange. About a mile or so
on I saw the sign for Château de Bosquet.

I turned off the road on to the cypress-tree-lined drive at the end of which I could see a large, square castel-lated house. In the vineyards on either side of the drive men and women were stooped over the vines, their faces obscured by hats. At the sound of my wheels, a grey-haired figure straightened up, shielded his eyes against the sun, then waved. I waved back.

As I parked I saw Miles striding through the vines towards me. As I lowered the window he smiled; his face was so streaked with dust that the lines round his eyes stood out like little spokes.

'Phoebe!' He opened my car door. 'Welcome to Château de Bosquet.' As I stood up, he kissed me. 'You'll meet Pascal and Cecile a bit later – for now everyone's working flat out.' He nodded at the vine-yard. 'Tomorrow's our last day, so we're pushed for time.'

'Can I help?'

Miles looked at me. 'Would you? It's dusty work though.'

I shrugged. 'It doesn't matter.' I gazed at the workers, with their black buckets and secateurs. 'Don't you use a grape-cutting machine?'

He shook his head. 'In Châteauneuf-du-Pape the grapes have to be hand-picked to conform to the laws of "appel-lation" – that's why we need this small army.' He glanced at my lace-up pumps. 'Your footwear's fine, but you'll need an apron. Wait here.' As Miles walked towards the house I suddenly noticed Roxy sitting on a bench by a huge fig tree reading a magazine.

'Hi, Roxy,' I called out. I took a few steps towards her. 'Hi there, Roxy!' Roxanne looked up, and without

212

lifting her sunglasses gave me a thin smile then returned to her reading. I felt rebuffed, until I remembered that most sixteen-year-olds have poor social skills, added to which she'd only met me once, so why should she be friendly?

Miles came out of the house holding a blue sunhat. 'You'll need this.' He plonked it on my head. 'You'll also need this . . .' He handed me a bottle of water. 'And this apron will protect your dress. It belonged to Pascal's mother: she was a sweet lady, wasn't she, Roxy – but somewhat on the large side.'

Roxy sipped her Coke. 'You mean fat.'

Miles unfolded the voluminous apron and put it over my head, then reached behind me to pass back the ties, brushing my ear with his breath as he did so. Now he was pulling the ties around to the front. 'There,' he said, fastening them in a bow. He took a step back and appraised me. 'You look lovely.' I was suddenly uncomfortably aware of Roxy focusing on me from behind her Ray-Bans. Miles picked up two empty buckets and walked towards the vineyard, swinging them from either hand. 'Come on then, Phoebe.'

'Is much skill needed?' I asked as I caught up with him.

'Practically none,' he replied as we stepped in among the gnarled vines. Here and there a sparrow flew up as we walked down the rows, or a grasshopper glided away at our approach. Miles picked a small bunch of grapes then passed it to me.

I burst one against my tongue. 'Delicious. What sort are they?'

'These are Grenache – the vines are quite old. They

213

were planted in 1960, like me. But they're still fairly vigorous,' he added slyly. He squinted at the sky, shielding his eyes with his hand. 'Thank God the weather's been good. In '02 we had catastrophic floods and the grapes rotted – we produced five thousand bottles that year instead of one hundred thousand – it was a disaster. The village priest always blesses the harvest; he seems to have done a good job this year, because it's a bumper crop.'

Scattered all around us were huge round pebbles: inside the cracked ones I glimpsed the occasional sparkle of white quartz. 'These big stones are a nuisance,' I said as I picked my way through them.

'They are a pain,' Miles agreed. 'They were deposited here by the Rhône aeons ago. But we need them because the heat they store during the day is released at night, which is one of the reasons why this is such good wine-growing country. Now, could you start here?' Miles stooped to a vine, and pulled back the red-gold foliage to reveal a huge cluster of black grapes. 'Hold them underneath.' They felt warm in my hand. 'Now cut the stem – no leaves, please – then place it in the first pail, with the minimum of handling.'

'What goes in the second pail?'

'The ones we reject – we discard twenty per cent of what we pick, and they go to make table wine.'

Around us a party atmosphere prevailed – the dozen or so workers were laughing and talking – some were listening to Walkmans and iPods. One girl was singing – it was an aria from *The Magic Flute*, the one about husbands and wives. Her clear, sweet soprano rang across the vineyard.

Mann und Weib, und Weib und Mann . . .

How strange to be hearing that today of all days, I thought.

reichen an die Gottheit an.

'Who are the grape pickers?' I asked Miles.

'A few local people who help us every year, plus some students and a few foreign workers. On this estate the *vendanges* takes about ten days, then Pascal throws a big party to thank everyone.'

I put the secateurs to the stem. 'Should I cut here?'

Miles bent down and put his hand over mine. 'It's better there,' he said. 'Like that.' I felt a current of desire crackle through me. 'Now snip – but they're heavy, so don't let them fall.' I placed the bunch carefully in the first pail. 'I'll be over here,' Miles said as he went back to his own pails a few yards away.

It was hot, hard work. I was glad of the water – and I was especially glad of the apron, which was already floured with pale dust. I straightened up to relieve my back. As I did so, I glanced at Roxy, sitting in the shade with her copy of *Heat* and her cold drink.

'I ought to make Roxy help,' I heard Miles say, as though he'd read my mind. 'But with teenagers it's counterproductive to push things.'

I felt a bead of sweat trickle between my shoulder blades. 'And how did her ancient history project go?'

'In the end it was fine. I'm hoping to get an A star,' he added dryly. 'I deserve one, as I was up all night writing it.'

'Then you're an A-star dad. My bucket's full – now what?' Miles came and sorted the less good grapes into the second bucket then he picked up both pails. 'We'll

215

take them to the pressing machine.' He nodded at the big concrete sheds to the right of the house.

As we entered the first shed the sweet yeasty scent was overpowering, as was the noise from the huge white cylinder juddering in front of us. Beside it was a tall stepladder from the top of which a thick-set man in blue overalls was tipping in the grapes that were being passed up to him by a petite blonde woman in a yellow dress.

'That's Pascal,' Miles said, 'and that's Cecile.' He waved at them both. 'Pascal! Cecile! This is Phoebe!'

Pascal gave me a friendly nod, then he took the pail that Cecile passed up to him and tumbled the grapes into the cylinder. She turned and gave me a warm smile.

Miles indicated the four vast red tanks that lined the far wall. 'Those are the fermentation vats. The grape juice is pumped straight into them from the cylinder with that hose there. Now we go through here . . .' I followed him into the next shed, which was cooler, and where there were a number of steel containers with dates chalked on them. 'This is where the fermented grape juice is aged. We also age it in these oak casks over here, then, after a year or so, it's ready to be bottled.'

'And when can it be drunk?'

'The table wine after eighteen months, the decent stuff after two to three years, and the vintage wines are kept for up to fifteen years. Most of what's produced here is red.'

To one side was a table with some half-empty bottles, sealed with grey stoppers; there were also glasses, a couple of corkscrews and a number of wine reference books. The walls were studded with various framed

216

diplômes d'honneur that Château de Bosquet wines had garnered at international wine festivals.

I noticed that one bottle had a pretty label, with a blackbird on it holding a bunch of grapes in its beak. I looked at it more closely. 'Chante le Merle,' I said. I turned to Miles. 'I had this wine only last week – at the Greenwich Picturehouse.'

'The Picturehouse chain do buy our wines. Did you like it?'

'It was delicious. It had a . . . seductive bouquet, I seem to remember.'

'And what film were you seeing?'

'*Anna Karenina.*'

'With . . . ?'

'Greta Garbo.'

'No – I mean . . . who did you see the film with? I . . . was just wondering,' he added, diffidently.

I found Miles' insecurity touching – especially as he'd seemed so smooth and suave when I'd first met him. 'I went with this friend of mine, Dan. He's a bit of a film buff.'

Miles nodded. 'Well . . .' He glanced at his watch. 'It's almost six. We'd better get ready. We'll have dinner in the village. Roxy will probably stay with Pascal and Cecile. She can practise her French,' he added. 'Now, I imagine you'd like to wash . . .'

I held up my purple-stained hands.

As we walked round to the house I saw that Roxy had vacated her seat, leaving her empty Coke bottle, the neck of which was being probed by wasps. Miles pushed on the enormous front door and we stepped into the cool interior. The hall was huge with vaulted ceilings, exposed beams and a cavernous fireplace with a stack of logs to one side. Against one wall was a long settle made of old casks. At the foot of the staircase a stuffed bear stood guard, its teeth and claws bared.

'Don't worry about him,' Miles said as we passed it. 'He's never bitten anyone. Up we go. Now . . .' We crossed the landing and Miles pushed on a panelled door revealing a vast limestone bath, shaped like a sarcophagus. He took a towel from the rail. 'I'm going to have a soak.'

'Elsewhere presumably,' I joked, wondering if Miles was going to strip off in front of me. I suddenly realised that I wouldn't mind if he did.

'I've got an en-suite,' I heard him explain as he left the room. 'I'm at the end of the landing there. I'll see you downstairs in what . . . twenty minutes? Roxy . . .' he called as he went out, shutting the door. *'Ro-xy* – I need to *speak* to you . . .'

I untied the apron, which had protected my dress perfectly, and wiped the dust off my shoes. I showered with the ancient-looking brass attachment, twisting my wet hair into a knot, then I dressed again and put on a little make-up.

As I stepped out on to the landing I could hear Miles' whispered voice floating up, then Roxy's plaintive tones.
– 'I won't be out for long, sweetie . . .'
– '*Why's* she *here?*'
– 'She has work to do in the area . . .'
– '. . . *don't* want *you* to go out . . .'
– 'Then come with us.'
– '*Don't* feel *like it* . . .'
The top step creaked beneath my feet.

Miles seemed slightly startled as he looked up. 'There you are, Phoebe,' he said. 'So you're ready to go then?' I nodded. 'I was just seeing if Roxy wanted to come,' he added as I came down the stairs.

'I hope you will,' I said to Roxy, determined to try and charm her. 'We could talk about clothes: your dad says you're interested in a career in fashion.'

She gave me a sullen glance. 'That's what I'm going to do, yeah.'

'Why *don't* you join us then?' her dad asked warmly.

'I don't *want* to go out.'

'In that case, have supper with the grape-pickers.'

She gave a moue of distaste. 'No *thanks*.'

Miles shook his head. 'Roxy – there are some lovely young people here. That Polish girl Beata is training to be an opera singer. She speaks wonderful English, you could chat to her.' Roxy shrugged her slender shoulders. 'Then eat with Pascal and Cecile.' The girl groaned then folded her arms. 'Don't be awkward,' said her father. 'Please, Roxanne, I'd just like you to –' But she was already halfway across the hall.

Miles turned to me. 'I'm sorry, Phoebe.' He sighed. 'Roxy's at that difficult age.' I nodded politely then suddenly remembered the French expression for the teenage years – *l'âge ingrat*. 'She'll be fine here for a couple of hours. Now . . .' He jingled his car keys. 'Let's go.'

Miles drove down to the village then parked his hired Renault in the main street. As we got out, he nodded at a restaurant with tables outside, the white cloths flapping in the breeze. We crossed over to it, then Miles pushed on the door.

219

'Ah . . . Monsieur Archant,' said an unctuous-looking maître d' as he held open the door. *'C'est un plaisir de vous revoir. Un* grand *plaisir.'* Suddenly the man's face cracked into a smile and the two men slapped each other on the back, laughing uproariously.

'Good to see you, Pierre,' said Miles. 'I'd like to introduce you to the fair Phoebe.'

Pierre lifted my hand to his lips. *'Enchanté.'*

'Pierre and Pascal were at school together,' Miles explained as Pierre showed us to a corner table. 'We all used to hang out together in the summer holidays, what, thirty-five years ago, Pierre?'

Pierre blew out his lips. *'Oui – il y a trente cinq ans.* Before you were born,' he added to me with a chuckle. I had a sudden vision of a fifteen-year-old Miles holding me, as a baby.

'Would you like a glass of wine?' Miles asked me as he opened the *carte des vin.*

'I would,' I replied carefully. 'But I probably shouldn't as I'll be driving back to Avignon.'

'It's up to you,' Miles said as he put on his reading glasses. He peered at the list. 'You're having dinner, after all.'

'I'll just have one then – but no more.'

'And if you decide to get hammered, you can always stay at the house,' he added casually. 'There's a spare room – with a big trunk!'

'Oh, I won't be needing that – I mean the room,' I corrected myself, blushing. 'I mean, I won't be staying, thanks.' Miles was smiling at my embarrassment. 'So . . . you said you help with the harvest every year?'

He nodded. 'I do it to keep the family connection alive

– the estate was founded by my great-grandfather, Philippe, who was also Pascal's great-grandfather. And I come because I was left a small share in the business so I like to feel involved.'

'So Château de Bosquet is *your* "village vintage".'

'I suppose it is.' Miles smiled. 'But I love the whole wine-making process. I love the machinery and the noise and the scent of the grapes and the connection with the land. I love the fact that viticulture involves so many things – geography, chemistry, meteorology – and history. I love the fact that wine is one of those few things that time improves.'

'Like you?' I suggested playfully.

He smiled. 'Now what are you going to drink?' I chose the Châteauneuf-du-Pape Fines Roches. 'And I'll have a glass of the Cuvée Reine,' Miles said to Pierre. 'I drink non-Bosquet wines when I'm out,' he told me as I picked up the menu. 'It's good to know what the competition's like.'

Pierre placed our glasses of wine in front of us with a plate of fat green olives. Miles raised his glass. 'How lovely to see you again, Phoebe. When I was having dinner with you last week I hoped to see you again, but I *never* imagined that we'd be . . . oh.' He reached into his pocket for his BlackBerry. 'Look, Roxy,' he whispered as I studied the menu, 'I did tell you where I was going – I did – we're at the Mirabelle.' He stood up. 'You *were* invited.' I heard him sigh as he headed for the door. 'You *know* you were, darling. What's the point of saying that *now*?'

Miles stood outside chatting to Roxy then he returned, looking exasperated. 'Sorry about that,' he sighed as he pocketed his phone. 'Now she's cross because she didn't come! I have to say, Roxy can be rather awkward sometimes – but at heart she's a very good girl.'

'Of course,' I murmured.

'She would never do anything . . .' Miles hesitated '. . . wrong.' Pierre came to the table again and we placed our orders. 'But I'd like to talk about you, Phoebe,' Miles went on. 'When we had dinner last week you fended off all my questions – I'd love to know a bit more.'

I shrugged. 'About what?'

'Well . . . personal things. Tell me about your family.' So I told Miles about my parents, and about Louis.

Miles shook his head. 'That's a tough one. And it must give you a conflict,' he added as Pierre brought our starters.

I spread my napkin on my lap. 'It does. I wish I'd seen more of Louis, but it was all so awkward. I've decided I'm going to visit him more often and just say nothing to my mother. In the normal way, she adores babies,' I added, 'but how could she ever adore this one?'

'Well . . .' Miles shook his head. 'I don't know.'

'She feels very vulnerable now,' I went on as I broke a bread roll in half. 'She says she never thought my father would leave her; but if I think about it they didn't really *do* anything together – or hadn't done for years; not that I can remember, anyway.'

'It must still be hard for her though.'

'It is – but at least she has her work.' Now I told Miles about Mum's job.

He picked up his soup spoon. 'So she's worked for this chap for twenty-two years?'

I nodded. 'It's like a professional marriage. When John

retires, she will too – but as he says he wants to work until he's seventy, that's some way off, thankfully. She needs the distraction of work and the money's useful, especially as my dad's having a . . . career break,' I concluded carefully.

'And there's no chance that your mum and her boss . . .?'

'Oh no.' I laughed. 'John adores her, but he's not really into women.'

'I see.'

I sipped my wine. 'Did your parents stay together?'

'For fifty-three years – 'til death did them part – they died within a few months of each other. Has what happened to your parents shaken your belief in marriage?'

I lowered my fork. 'You're assuming that I have one.'

'As you told me that you'd been engaged, I am.' Miles sipped his wine then he nodded at my right hand. 'Was that your engagement ring?'

'Oh. No.' I glanced at the lozenge-cut emerald flanked by two little diamonds. 'This belonged to my grand-mother. I'm very fond it, not least because I have so many memories of her wearing it.'

'So was your engagement long ago?'

I shook my head. 'It was earlier this year.' Surprise flickered across Miles' face. 'In fact . . .' I looked out of the window. 'I was due to get married today.'

'Today?' Miles lowered his glass.

'Yes. I was due to get married today at Greenwich Register Office at 3 p.m. followed by a sit-down dinner and dance for eighty people at the Clarendon Hotel in Blackheath. Instead of which I've been grape-picking in Provence with a man I hardly know.'

223

Miles looked bemused. 'You don't seem . . . too upset about it.'

I shrugged. 'It's odd, but I feel almost . . . nothing.'

'Which means that you must have been the one to end it.'

'Yes.'

'But . . . why did you?'

'Because . . . I had to. That had become clear.'

'Didn't you love your fiancé?'

I sipped my wine. 'I did. Or rather I *had* loved him – very much. But then something happened that profoundly changed the way I felt about him, so I called it off.' I looked at Miles. 'Does that make me seem callous?'

'A . . . little,' he said, frowning slightly. 'But without knowing anything about it I'm not going to judge. I'm assuming that he was unfaithful to you, or that there was a betrayal of that kind.'

'No. He just did something that I couldn't forgive.' I looked at Miles' puzzled face. 'I'll tell you – if you like. Or we could change the subject.'

Miles hesitated. 'Okay,' he said after a moment. 'I can't deny that I'm curious now.' So I briefly told him about Emma, and about Guy. Miles snapped a bread-stick in half. 'That must have been awkward.'

'It was.' I sipped my wine again. 'I wish I'd *never* met Guy.'

'But . . . what did the poor man *do*?'

I drained my glass, and as I felt the warmth of the wine seep through my veins I told Miles about my engage-ment, then about Valentine's Day and Emma's phone call. Then I told him about going to her house.

Miles was shaking his head. 'What a trauma, Phoebe.'

'Trauma?' I echoed. *Träumerei*. 'Yes. It comes back to me all the time. I often dream that I'm in Emma's room, pulling back the duvet . . .'

Miles' face was clouded with sadness. 'So she'd taken all the paracetamol?'

'She had, but according to the pathologist she'd only had four – the last four evidently, because the bottle was empty.'

Miles looked bewildered. 'Then why did she . . .?'

'We didn't at first realise what had happened to Emma. It looked like an overdose.' I clenched my napkin. 'But ironically it was an *under*dose that caused her to . . .'

Miles was staring at me. 'You said that you thought she had 'flu.'

'Yes – that's what it seemed to be when she first phoned me.'

'And she'd recently been to South Africa?'

I nodded. 'She'd been back for three weeks.'

'Was it malaria?' he asked gently. 'Undiagnosed malaria?'

I felt the familiar sliding sensation, as though I was hurtling downhill. 'Yes,' I murmured. 'It was.' I closed my eyes. 'If only I'd been as quick off the mark as you've just been.'

'My sister Trish got malaria some years ago,' Miles said quietly. 'It was after a trip to Ghana. She was lucky to survive, because it was the deadly kind –'

'Plasmodium falciparum,' I interjected. 'Transmitted by an infected anopheles mosquito – but only the female. I'm an expert on it now – sadly.'

225

'Trish hadn't finished her anti-malarial pills. Is that what happened with Emma? I assume that's what you meant when you used the word "underdose"?'

I nodded. 'A few days after she'd died, her mother found the anti-malarial medication in Emma's washbag. From the blister packs, she could see that Emma had taken them for only ten days instead of eight weeks. Plus she started the course too late – she should have been taking them from a week before she travelled.'

'Had she been to South Africa before?'

'Many times – she used to live there.'

'So she'd have known the score.'

'Oh yes.' I paused as Pierre took away our plates. 'And even though the risk of malaria is low there, Emma always gave me the impression that she'd been careful to take the pills. But this time she seems to have been reckless.'

'Why do you think that was?'

I fiddled with the stem of my wine glass. 'There's a part of me that thinks it could have been deliberate . . .'

'You mean – self-inflicted?'

'Perhaps. She was feeling very low – I think that's why she'd suddenly decided to go there. Or perhaps she simply forgot to take them, or was happy to play Russian roulette with her health. I only know that I should have gone to see her when she first phoned me.' I looked away.

Miles reached for my hand. 'You had no idea how ill she was.'

'No,' I said bleakly. 'It simply didn't occur to me that she might have . . .' I shook my head. 'Emma's parents would have realised, but they were on a walking holiday in Spain and couldn't be reached – she'd tried to call her mother twice, apparently.'

'So that's a regret *they* have to live with.'

'Yes. Plus the way it happened . . . the fact that Emma was alone . . . It's very hard for them – and for me. I had to tell them . . .' I felt my eyes fill. 'I had to tell them . . .'

Miles reached for my hand. 'What an ordeal.'

My throat ached with a suppressed sob. 'Yes. But her parents still don't know that Emma was upset with me in the weeks before she died. And if she hadn't been so upset then perhaps she wouldn't have gone to South Africa and wouldn't have fallen ill.' My heart lurched as I thought of Emma's diary. 'I hope they never find out . . . Miles, could I have another glass of wine?'

'Of course.' He waved at Pierre. 'But if you have any more, I think it might be better if you stayed at the house – okay?'

'Yes – but that won't happen.'

Miles looked at me. 'I *still* don't understand why you felt you had to end your engagement.'

I fiddled with the stem of my wine glass. 'I couldn't cope with the fact that Guy had persuaded me not to go and see Emma. He said that she was attention seeking.' I felt a sudden rush of anger at the memory. 'He said that it was probably just a bad cold.'

'But . . . do you actually blame him for her death?'

I waited while Pierre poured my wine. 'I blame myself, first and foremost, because I was the one person who might have prevented it. I blame Emma, for not taking her pills. But yes, I blame Guy too, because if it weren't for him . . . I'd have gone round to her house straight away . . . if it weren't for him I would have seen how ill she was, and I'd have called the ambulance and she might have survived. Instead of which Guy persuaded me to wait, so I didn't go until the next morning, by which time . . .' I closed my eyes.

'Did you tell Guy this?'

I had another sip of wine. 'Not at first. I was still in shock, trying to take it all in. But on the morning of Emma's funeral . . .' I paused as I remembered her coffin, on top of it her favourite green hat in a sea of pink roses. '. . . I took off my engagement ring. When Guy drove me home afterwards he asked me where it was, so I said that I'd felt unable to wear it in front of Emma's parents. Then there was this awful scene. Guy insisted that I had nothing to feel guilty about. He said that it was Emma's own fault that she'd died, and that her neglect of her health had not only cost her her life, it had brought misery to her parents and friends. I told Guy that I did feel guilty and always would. I told him that I was tormented by the thought that while he and I were sitting in the Bluebird, eating and drinking, Emma was dying. Then I said what I'd been burning to say for two weeks – that if he hadn't intervened she might be alive.

'Guy looked at me as though I'd hit him. He was outraged at the accusation, but I said it was true. Then I went upstairs, got the ring and gave it back to him – and that was the last time I saw him. So that's why I didn't get married today,' I concluded quietly.

I heaved a sigh. 'You said you didn't know anything personal about me – and now you do. But that was probably more personal than you would have liked.'

'Well . . .' Miles reached for my hand. 'I'm sorry that

you've been through something so . . . harrowing. But I'm glad you told me.'

'I'm surprised I have. I hardly know you.'

'No – you don't know me. At least not yet,' he added gently. He stroked my fingers and I felt a sudden charge go through me, like static.

'Miles . . .' I looked at him, 'I think I *would* like that third glass of wine.'

We didn't stay at the restaurant very much longer, not least because Roxy began phoning again. Miles told her he'd be back by ten. Then as our desserts arrived she called once more. I had to bite my tongue. Roxy had refused to come out with her father but seemed determined that he shouldn't enjoy himself.

'Couldn't she read a book?' I suggested. Or perhaps a few more copies of *Heat* I thought dismissively.

Miles fiddled with his wine glass. 'Roxy's an intelligent girl, but she's not as . . . resourceful as I'd like,' he added carefully. 'No doubt because I've danced too much attendance on her over the years.' He put up his hands as if to say, It's a fair cop. 'But when you're a lone parent to an only child, it's almost inevitable – plus I'm trying to compensate her for what happened, I'm aware of that.'

'But ten years is a long time. You're a very attractive man, Miles.' He fiddled with his fork. 'I'm amazed you've never found anyone to be a mother figure to Roxy, as well as to fulfil your own needs and emotions.'

Miles sighed. 'Nothing would have made me happier – *would* make me happier. There *was* someone a few years ago who I was very fond of, but it didn't work out. But maybe, now, things will come right . . .' He smiled briefly and the delta of lines beneath his eyes deepened. 'Anyway . . .' He pushed back his chair. 'We'd better get back.'

At the house Pascal told Miles that Roxy had just gone to bed. Having made her father come back from the restaurant early, I reflected. Miles explained that I needed to stay the night.

'*Mais bien sûr,*' said Pascal, clasping his hands together. He smiled at me. '*Vous êtes bienvenue.*'

'Thank you.'

'I'll make up the spare bed,' said Miles. 'Will you give me a hand, Phoebe?'

'Sure.' I followed him, a little unsteady from the wine, up the stairs. At the top he opened a huge airing cupboard that smelt deliciously of warm cotton, then he took some bedding off the slatted shelves.

'My room's at the end,' he explained as I followed him down the long landing. 'Roxy's is opposite. You'll be in here.' He pushed on the door and we went into the large bedroom, the walls of which were hung with dark pink Toile de Jouy depicting a pastoral scene of boys and girls apple-picking.

It felt strange to be making up the bed with Miles; I found the intimacy of it both discomfiting and exciting as we wrestled with the plump duvet. As we smoothed the sheet our fingertips collided and I felt a sudden voltage go through me. Miles dragged the linen sleeve over the bolster. 'There . . .' He gave me a diffident smile. 'Can I lend you a shirt to sleep in?' I nodded. 'Stripey or plain?'

'Tee please.'

He headed for the door. 'Tee for one, coming up.'

Miles quickly returned with a grey Calvin Klein tee-shirt and handed it to me. 'Well . . . I suppose I ought to get to bed.' He kissed me on the cheek. 'I've got another long day in the vines tomorrow.' He kissed me on the other cheek, then held me for a few seconds. 'Goodnight, sweet Phoebe,' he murmured. I closed my eyes, enjoying the feeling of being encircled by his arms. 'I'm so glad you're here,' he whispered. His breath was warm in my ear. 'But how strange to think that this would have been your wedding night.'

'It is strange.'

'And now here you are, in a bedroom in Provence with a virtual stranger. But . . . I've got a problem.' I looked at Miles – his face was suddenly filled with anxiety.

'What?'

'I want to kiss you.'

'Oh.'

'I mean, really kiss you.'

'I see.' He ran his finger down my cheek. 'Well . . .' I murmured. 'You can.'

'Kiss you?' he whispered.

'Kiss me,' I whispered back.

Miles cupped my face in his hands, then he leaned down and touched his upper lip to mine – it felt cool and dry – and we stood like that for a few moments. Now we were kissing more intensely, then with a gathering urgency, and now I felt Miles reach to the back of my dress to unzip it; but he couldn't.

'Sorry,' he said with a laugh. 'I haven't done this for a while.' He fumbled with it a bit more. 'Ah . . . there.'

Now he was pushing the straps down over my shoulders and the dress was falling to the floor and I was stepping out of it, and Miles was leading me towards the bed. As he unbuttoned his shirt I unzipped his jeans, releasing his erection, then I lay back on the bed and looked at him as he undressed. He might be nearly fifty, but his body was slim and hard, and he was indeed, like the vines planted in the year of his birth, still 'vigorous'.

'Do you want this, Phoebe?' he whispered as he lay next to me, stroking my face. 'Because that trunk I told you about is just over there.' He kissed me. 'You just have to push it against the door.'

'To keep you out?'

'Yes.' He kissed me again. 'To keep me out.'

'But I don't want to.' I kissed him back, more urgently now, and then, with a shudder of desire I pulled him to me. 'I want you in.'

NINE

Mann und Weib, und Weib und Mann ...

I awoke to the sound of the Polish girl singing in the vineyards below me.

Reichen an die Gottheit an ...

Miles had gone, leaving only an indentation on the bolster and his masculine scent on the sheets. I sat up then hooped my arms round my knees, pondering the turn my life had taken. The room was still in darkness except for some slivers of light on the floor where the sun had sliced through the shutters. From outside I could hear the cooing of doves, and from further off the rumble and whirr of the pressing machine.

I opened the windows and looked out at the pale red landscape with its viridian cypresses and billowy pines. In the distance I could see Miles loading some pails on to a trailer. I stood there for a few moments, watching him, thinking of the intense, almost reverential way he'd made love to me, the delight he'd taken in my body. Below my window was the fig tree, in which two white doves were pecking at the over-ripe purple-brown fruit.

I washed and dressed, stripped the bed, and went downstairs. In the morning light the stuffed bear seemed to be grinning, not growling.

I crossed the hall to the kitchen. At one end of an enormously long table Roxy was having breakfast with Cecile.

'*Bonjour,* Phoebe,' Cecile said warmly.

'*Bonjour*, Cecile. Hi, Roxanne.'

Roxy raised a salon-plucked eyebrow. 'You're still here?'

'Yes,' I replied evenly. 'I didn't want to drive back to Avignon in the dark.'

'*Et vous avez bien dormi?*' Cecile asked with the faintest hint of a knowing smile.

'*Très bien. Merci.*'

She indicated the pile of croissants and biscottes then passed me a plate. 'And you would like a cup of coffee?'

'Please.' As Cecile poured me a cup from the percolator gasping away on the range I glanced round the huge kitchen with its terracotta floor tiles, its garlands of garlic and chillies, and its old copper pans aglow on their racks. 'This is lovely – it's a wonderful house, Cecile.'

'Thank you.' She offered me a piece of brioche. 'I hope that you visit us again.'

'So are you going now?' Roxanne asked as she spread butter thickly on her bread. Her tone of voice had been neutral, but her hostility was clear.

'I'll be leaving after breakfast.' I turned to Cecile. 'I have to go to Île sur la Sorgue.'

'*C'est pas trop loin,*' she said as I sipped my coffee. 'Perhaps one hour only.'

I nodded. I'd been to Île sur la Sorgue before, but not from this direction. I'd need to work out the route.

As Cecile and I chatted in 'Franglais' a pretty little black cat sauntered in, its tail at ninety degrees. I made kissing noises at it, and to my surprise it jumped up and curled itself into my lap, purring happily.

'That is Minou,' said Cecile as I stroked its head. 'I think she like you.' I noticed that Cecile was peering at my right hand. '*Quelle jolie bague,*' she said admiringly. 'Your ring – it is beautiful.'

'Thank you.' I glanced at it. 'It was my grandmother's.' Suddenly Roxanne pushed back her chair and stood up. Then she took a peach from the bowl of fruit and threw it up with her right hand then deftly caught it.

'Have you had enough *petit déjeuner,* Roxanne?' Cecile asked her.

'Yes,' Roxy replied casually. 'I'll see you later.'

'You won't see me,' I said. 'But I hope to meet you again, Roxy.'

She didn't answer, and as she left the room an awkward silence descended as Cecile registered the slight.

'*Roxanne est très belle,*' she said as she cleared away Roxy's breakfast things.

'She is beautiful, yes.'

'*Miles l'adore.*'

'Of course,' I agreed. I shrugged. '*Elle est sa fille.*'

'*Oui.*' Cecile sighed. '*Mais elle est aussi . . . comment dire? Son talon d'Achille.*'

I feigned a renewed interest in the cat, which had suddenly twisted itself on to its back to have its tummy

235

stroked. I drank my coffee then glanced at my watch. 'I ought to get going now, Cecile. *Mais merci bien pour votre hospitalité.*' I tipped the cat off my lap then made to put my breakfast plate and cup in the dishwasher, but Cecile took them from me, tut-tutting. She walked with me to the front door.

'*Au revoir, Phoebe,*' she said as we stepped outside into the sunshine. 'I wish you a nice stay in Provence.' She kissed me on each cheek. 'And I wish you . . .' she glanced at Roxanne sitting in the sunshine ' . . . good luck.'

As I walked to the car I wished Cecile hadn't said what she had done. Roxy might be bolshie, selfish and demanding, but weren't lots of teenagers like that? In any case I'd only just met Miles so good luck didn't come into it. But I did like him, I realised . . . I liked him very much.

Shielding my eyes against the sunlight, I now scanned the vineyard for Miles and saw him walking towards me with that slightly anxious air he always has, as though he's worried that I'm going to run off. I found his blend of polish and vulnerability endearing.

'You're not going, are you?' he said as he drew close.

'I am, yes. But, well . . . thank you for . . . everything.'

Miles smiled then lifted my hand to his lips in a way that made my heart turn over. He nodded at my map, lying on the bonnet. 'Have you worked out how to get to Isle sur la Sorgue?'

'I have. It's quite straightforward. So . . .'

I got behind the wheel. As I did so I heard the silvery arpeggios of a blackbird. 'Chante le Merle,' I said.

'That's right.' Miles bent down and kissed me through

the open window. 'I'll see you in London. At least, I hope I will.'

I laid my hand on his, then kissed him again. 'You'll see me in London,' I said . . .

I enjoyed the drive to Île sur la Sorgue, along pristine roads in the bright sunshine, past neat cherry orchards and newly harvested vineyards, the golden verges splashed crimson with poppies. I thought about Miles and about how attractive I found him. My lips still felt bruised from his mouth.

I parked at one end of the pretty riverside town then strolled among the milling crowds through the first part of the market. Here were stalls selling lavender soap, flagons of olive oil, piles of pungent salamis, Provençal quilts, and straw baskets in earthy shades of terracotta, yellow and green. The atmosphere in this part of the market was commercial and noisy.

– 'Vingt euros!'
– 'Merci, monsieur.'
– 'Les prix sont bas, non?'
– 'Je vous enprie.'

Then I walked over the little wooden bridge that spanned the narrow river. Here, in the upper part of the town the atmosphere was calm as shoppers quietly contemplated the *antiquités* and bric-à-brac stalls. I paused at one on which was an old saddle, a pair of red boxing gloves, a large ship in a bottle, several stamp albums and a pile of *L'illustration* news magazines from the 1940s. I glanced through them: there were covers variously featuring Magnum photos of the Normandy Landings, Resistance fighters alongside Allied troops, and the celebrations in Provence when the Occupation ended. *L'ENTRÉE DES TROUPES ALLIÉES,* the cover was captioned. *LA PROVENCE LIBÉRÉE DU JOUG ALLEMAND.*

Now I did what I'd come to do and looked through the vintage clothing, selecting white percale shirts and printed dresses and shifts and broderie anglaise vests, all in pristine condition. Then I heard the church clock strike three. It was time to head back. I imagined Miles, still toiling in the vineyard, helping to gather in the last of the harvest, then this evening there'd be the party for the grape-pickers.

I put the bags in the boot and got into the car, opening all the windows to let out the heat. The route to Avignon seemed straightforward, but as I got closer to it I realised that I'd lost the sign: I wasn't heading south as I should have been but due north. The frustration of knowing that I was going 180 degrees in the wrong direction was compounded by the fact that there was nowhere to turn. Worse, a long queue of cars had built up behind me. Now I was driving into a place called Rochemare.

I glanced in my mirror. The car behind was so close that I could practically see the driver's eyeballs. I flinched at his irritable beeps. Desperate to rid myself of him, I suddenly turned right up a narrow street, as I did so breathing a sigh of relief. I followed it for about half a mile until it suddenly came out on to a large, pleasant square. On one side were a few small shops and a bar with tables outside, shaded by gnarled plane trees, where an old man was having a beer. On the opposite side of the square was an impressive-looking church. As I drove by it I glanced at the door and a jolt ran through me.

From somewhere I could hear Mrs Bell's voice.

I grew up in a large village about three miles from the city centre. It was a sleepy sort of place, with a few narrow little streets leading on to a large square which was shaded by plane trees with a few shops and a pleasant bar . . .

I pulled into the nearest space, outside a *boulangerie*, then I got out and walked back to the church, Mrs Bell's voice still sounding in my ears.

On the north side of the square was the church, over the door of which was carved, in huge letters, Liberté, Égalité, Fraternité . . .

My heart pounding, I studied the famous inscription, cut into the stone in emphatic Roman letters, then I turned round and looked at the square. This was where Mrs Bell had grown up. There could be no doubt. This was the church. There was the bar, Bar Mistral – I could see the name now – where she'd sat that night. It suddenly occurred to me that that old man sitting there now could even be Jean-Luc Aumage. The man was probably in his mid eighties, so it was possible. As I stood there he drained his glass, got up, pulled down his beret and walked slowly through the square, leaning heavily on a stick.

I went back to the car and drove on again. Already the houses were thinning out, and I could see pockety vineyards and little orchards and, in the middle distance, a railway crossing.

The village bordered open countryside and was skirted by a railway line. My father had a small vineyard not far from the house . . .

I pulled into a lay-by, and as I sat in the car I imagined

Thérèse and Monique walking across these fields, through these vineyards and orchards. I imagined Monique hiding to survive, in the barn. Now the dark cypress trees seemed to me like accusing fingers, pointing skywards. I reached for the ignition and drove on again. Here, at the furthest edge of the village were a number of newish houses; but there was a row of four that were much older. I drew up just beyond the last of these and got out.

In front was a pretty garden, with pots of pink-and-white pelargoniums. There was also an old well and, above the door, an oval plaque on which was carved the head of a lion. As I stood there I imagined the house seven decades earlier, being abandoned to the sound of protesting, frightened voices.

Suddenly I saw a movement behind the shutters – just a fleeting shadow, nothing more, but for some reason I felt the hairs on my neck raise themselves up. I hesitated for a moment then returned to the car, my pulse racing.

I sat in the driver's seat, looking back at the house in the driving mirror; then, hands trembling, I drove away.

Now, as I found the village centre again, I felt my heartbeat slow. I was glad that Chance had brought me to Rochemare, but it was time to leave. As I tried to find the road out I turned left down a narrow little street. At the end of it I stopped, then lowered the window. Placed there with an almost casual lack of ceremony was a war memorial. *Aux Morts Glorieux* it affirmed in black lettering on the slender column of white marble. There were names carved on it from the First and Second World Wars, names I'd heard before

– *Caron, Didier, Marigny and Paget.* Then with a jolt, as though I'd known him myself, I saw: *1954. Indochine. J-L Aumage.*

Mrs Bell would presumably know that, I reflected on Tuesday as I put some of her clothes out in the shop. She must have been back to Rochemare at least a few times, I thought as I hung up her Pierre Cardin houndstooth suit. As I gave it a brush I wondered what she'd felt when she'd found out.

Next I wanted to put out Mrs Bell's evening wear, but then I remembered that most of it was still at Val's. And I was just wondering when I could go and collect it when the bell over the door rang and two schoolgirls walked in for a lunchtime browse. While they looked through the rails I put a Jean Muir green suede coat of Mrs Bell's on a mannequin. As I buttoned it I glanced up at the last cupcake dress hanging on the wall and wondered who would buy it.

'Excuse me.' I turned round. The two girls were standing at the counter. They were Roxy's age – perhaps a little younger.

'Can I help you?'

'Well . . .' The first girl, who had shoulder-length dark hair and an almost Mediterranean complexion, was holding up a snakeskin wallet that had been in the basket with the other wallets and purses. 'I've just been looking at this.'

'It's from the late sixties,' I explained. 'I think it's £8.'

'Yes. That's what the ticket says. But the thing *is* . . .' She's going to start haggling, I thought wearily. 'It's got this secret compartment.' I looked at her. 'Here –' She pulled back a flap of leather to reveal a concealed zip. 'I don't think you knew that, did you?'

'No, I didn't,' I said quietly. I'd bought the wallets at auction and had just given them a quick wipe before putting them in the basket.

The girl unzipped it. 'Look.' Inside was a wad of bank notes. She handed the wallet to me and I pulled them out.

'Eighty pounds,' I said wonderingly. Into my mind flashed Ginny Jones at Radio London asking me if I'd ever found cash in any of the things I sold. I felt like ringing her to say that I had.

'I thought I should tell you,' the girl said.

I looked at her. 'That's incredibly honest of you.' I separated two of the twenty-pound notes and handed them to her. 'Here.'

The girl blushed. 'I didn't mean . . .'

'I know you didn't, but please – it's the least I can do.'

'Well, thanks,' the girl said happily. She took it. 'Here, Sarah . . .' She offered one of the notes to her friend, a girl of similar height but with short fair hair.

Sarah shook her head. 'You found it, Katie – not me. Anyway, we'd better hurry – we don't have long.'

'Are you looking for anything in particular?' I asked them.

They explained that they were looking for special dresses to wear for a ball in aid of the Teenage Leukaemia Trust.

'It's at the Natural History Museum,' said Katie. So it was the same event that Roxy was going to. 'There'll be a thousand of us there, so we'll all be desperately

242

trying to stand out from the crowd. I'm afraid we don't have a huge budget,' she added apologetically.

'Well . . . just have a good browse. There are some very eye-catching fifties dresses – like this one.' I unhooked a sleeveless glazed cotton dress with a vibrant, semi-abstract print of cubes and circles. 'That's £80.'

'It's very unusual,' Sarah said.

'It's by Horrocks – they made wonderful cotton dresses in the late forties and fifties. This print was designed by Eduardo Paolozzi.' The girls nodded then I saw Katie's eyes stray to the yellow cupcake dress.

'How much is that one?' I told her the price. 'Oh – too expensive. For me, I mean,' she added hastily. 'But I'm sure someone will pay that because it's just . . .' She sighed. 'Fantastic.'

'You'll have to win the lottery,' said Sarah, looking at it. 'Or get yourself a Saturday job that pays better.'

'I wish,' said Katie. 'I only clear £45 a day at Costcutters, so I'd need to work for what . . . two months to buy that dress, by which time the ball would be long over.'

'Well, you've got £40 there,' said Sarah, 'so you've only got to find another £235.' Katie rolled her eyes. 'Try it on,' her friend urged her.

Katie shook her head. 'What's the point?'

'The point is that I think it will suit you.'

'I couldn't afford it, even if it does.'

'Do try it on,' I said. 'Just for fun – plus I love seeing the clothes on my customers.'

Katie looked at the dress again. 'Okay.'

I got it down and hung it in the changing room. Katie went in and emerged a couple of minutes later.

'You look like . . . a sunflower,' said Sarah, smiling.

'It is lovely on you,' I agreed as Katie gazed at herself in the mirror. 'Yellow's hard to carry off, but you've got the warm complexion for it.'

'But you'll need to stuff your bra,' said Sarah judiciously as Katie adjusted the bodice. 'You could get some of those chicken-fillet things.'

Katie turned to her wearily. 'You're talking as though I'm going to be buying this dress – I'm not.'

'Can't your mum help?' Sarah asked.

Katie shook her head. 'She's a bit credit-crunched. Maybe I could get an evening job,' she mused as she put her hands on her waist then turned this way and that, the petticoats rustling.

'You could babysit,' Sarah suggested. 'I get five quid an hour to sit my neighbours' kids. Once I've got them into bed, I do my homework.'

'That's not a bad idea,' Katie mused as she stood on tiptoe looking at herself sideways. 'I could put a card up in the toy shop – or in Costcutters' window come to that. Anyway, it's been great just seeing the dress on.' She gazed at her reflection for a few moments, as if trying to fix in her mind the image of herself looking so lovely. Then, with a regretful sigh, she drew the curtain.

'Where there's a will, there's a way,' Sarah called out cheerfully.

'Yes,' Katie replied. 'But by the time I'd have saved up enough, sod's law someone else would have bought it.' A minute later she came out of the changing room and looked down mournfully at her grey school blazer and skirt. 'I feel like Cinderella after the ball.'

'I'll keep my eyes peeled for a fairy godmother,' said

Sarah. 'How long can you reserve things for?' she asked me.

'Usually not more than a week. I'd love to keep it for longer, but . . .'

'Oh, you can't,' said Katie as she picked up her backpack. 'For all you know, I might never come back for it.' She glanced at her watch. 'It's a quarter to two. We'd better scoot.' She looked at Sarah. 'Miss Doyle goes berserk if we're late, doesn't she? Anyway' – she smiled at me – 'thanks.'

As the girls left, Annie returned. 'They looked nice,' she said.

'They were lovely.' I told Annie about Katie's honesty over the wallet.

'I'm *impressed.*'

'She's fallen for the yellow cupcake,' I explained. 'I'd like to keep it for her in case she saves enough to buy it, but . . .'

'That's a risk,' Annie said judiciously. 'You could lose a sale.'

'True . . . but how did your audition go?' I asked anxiously.

She took off her jacket. 'Hopeless. The world and his wife were there.'

'Well . . . fingers crossed,' I said disingenuously. 'But can't your agent get you more work?'

Annie ran her fingers through her short blonde hair. 'I don't have one. My last agent was useless, so I sacked him, and I can't get a new one because I'm not in anything for them to see. So I just keep sending off my CV and occasionally I get an audition.' She began wiping the counter. 'What I hate about acting is the lack of control.

I can't stand the idea that at my age I'm sitting around waiting for a director to phone me. What I really need is to write my own material.'

'You said you like writing.'

'I do. I'd like to find a story that I could turn into a one-woman show. Then I could write it, act in it and set up the performances – *I'd* be in charge.' Into my mind flashed Mrs Bell's story, but even if I could tell it to Annie, the problem was that the ending was too sad.

I heard my phone bleep and looked at the screen. I felt my face flush with pleasure – it was Miles asking me to the theatre on Saturday. I texted him back then told Annie I was going up to The Paragon.

'Are you seeing Mrs Bell again?'

'I'm just going to have a quick cup of tea with her.'

'She's your new best friend,' said Annie genially. 'I hope I'll have some nice young woman to visit me when I'm old.'

'I hope you don't mind me inviting myself over,' I said to Mrs Bell twenty minutes later.

'Mind?' she repeated as she ushered me inside. 'I'm delighted to see you.'

'Are you okay, Mrs Bell?' She looked thinner than when I'd seen her the week before, her face a little more shrunken.

'I'm . . . fine, thank you. Well, not really fine, of course . . .' Her voice trailed away. 'But I like to sit and read or just look out of the window. I have one or two friends who come. My help, Paola, is here two mornings a week, and my niece arrives on Thursday – she is staying with me for three days. How I wish I'd had children,'

Mrs Bell said as I followed her to the kitchen. 'But I was very unfortunate – the stork refused to visit me. Women today can get help,' she sighed as she opened a cupboard. They can, I reflected, but it doesn't always work – I thought of the woman who'd bought the pink prom dress. 'Sadly, the only thing my ovaries have ever given me is cancer,' Mrs Bell added as she got down the milk jug. 'Awfully mean of them. Now, if you could carry the tray . . .'

'I've just returned from Avignon,' I said as I poured the tea a few minutes later.

Mrs Bell nodded thoughtfully. 'And was it a successful trip?'

'In the sense that I bought some lovely stock, yes.' I handed her her cup. 'I also went to Châteauneuf-du-Pape.' Now I told her about Miles.

She sipped her tea, supporting the cup with both hands. 'That sounds very romantic.'

'Well . . . not in every way.' I mentioned Roxanne's behaviour.

'So you were in Châteauneuf-du-*Papa*.'

I smiled. 'It did feel like that. Roxanne's very demanding, to put it mildly.'

'That will be tricky,' said Mrs Bell judiciously.

'I think it will be.' I thought of Roxy's hostility. 'But Miles seems to . . . like me.'

'He would be quite insane if he didn't.'

'Thanks . . . But the reason why I'm telling you this is that on the way back to Avignon I got lost – and found myself in Rochemare.'

Mrs Bell shifted on her seat. '*Ah*.'

'You didn't tell me the name of your village.'

247

'No. I preferred not to – and there was no need for you to know.'

'I understand. But I recognised it from your description. And I saw this old man sitting at the bar in the square and I even got it into my head that he could be Jean-Luc Aumage –'

'No,' Mrs Bell interjected. She put down her cup. 'No, no.' She was shaking her head. 'Jean-Luc died in Indochina.'

'Then I saw the war memorial.'

'He was killed at the battle of Dien Bien Phu. Apparently while trying to help a Vietnamese woman to safety.' I stared at Mrs Bell. 'It's strange to think of it,' she observed quietly. 'And I have sometimes wondered whether that gallant action of his might perhaps have been prompted by guilt over what he had done a decade before.' She held up her hands. 'Who knows?' Mrs Bell looked towards the window. 'Who knows . . .?' she repeated quietly. Suddenly she pushed herself out of her chair, grimacing slightly as she straightened up. 'Excuse me, Phoebe. There is something I'd like to show you.'

She left the room and crossed the corridor into her bedroom where I heard a drawer being opened. In a minute or two she returned with a large brown envelope, the edges of which were faded to ochre. She sat down, opened it and slid out a large photo, which she looked at, searchingly, for a few seconds before beckoning me to her. I pulled up a chair by her side.

In the black-and-white image were a hundred or so girls and boys, eagerly standing to attention in their rows, or looking bored with their heads cocked to one side, or with their eyes half closed against the sunlight, the older children standing stiffly at the back, the youngest sitting cross-legged in front, the boys' hair rigidly parted, the girls' hair tamed with ribbons and combs.

'This was taken in May 1942,' said Mrs Bell. 'There were around a hundred and twenty of us in the school at that time.'

I scanned the sea of faces. 'And where are you?'

Mrs Bell pointed to the left-hand side of the third row, to a girl with a high forehead and a wide mouth and mid-brown shoulder-length hair that framed her face in soft waves. Then her finger moved to the girl standing on her immediate left – a girl with shiny black hair cut in a bob, high cheekbones, and dark eyes that stared out with a friendly, but somehow watchful gaze. 'And that is Monique.'

'There's a wariness in her expression.'

'Yes. You can see her anxiety – her fear of exposure.' Mrs Bell sighed. 'Poor girl.'

'And where is he?' Mrs Bell now pointed to the boy in the middle of the back row whose head formed the apex of the photo's composition. It was easy to understand Mrs Bell's teenage infatuation with him as I stared at his fine features and wheat-blond hair.

'It's funny,' she murmured, 'but whenever I thought about Jean-Luc after the war, I used to think, bitterly, of how he would no doubt live to a ripe old age and die peacefully in his sleep, surrounded by his children and grandchildren. In fact, Jean-Luc was twenty-six when he was killed, far from home, in the chaos of battle, bravely helping a stranger. The citation – Marcel sent me the cutting – said that he had gone back to help the Vietnamese woman, who survived, and who described him as "a hero". Which to her, at least, he was.'

Mrs Bell lowered the photo. 'I have often wondered why Jean-Luc did what he did to Monique. He was very young, of course – though that is no excuse. He hero-worshipped his father – though unfortunately René Aumage was no hero. And he may have been partly motivated by a sense of personal rejection – Monique had kept her distance from him, with good reason.'

'But Jean-Luc could have had no idea what Monique's true fate was likely to be,' I said quietly.

'No, he could not have known, because no one knew, until afterwards. And those who *did* know and were in a position to tell were simply not believed – people said they must be *mad*. If only . . .' Mrs Bell murmured, shaking her head. 'But the fact remains that Jean-Luc behaved horribly, as so many people did at that time: and many behaved heroically,' she added. 'Like the Antignac family, who it turned out had been sheltering in their home four other children, who all survived the war.' She looked at me. 'There were many brave people like the Antignacs and these are the people I think about.' She slid the photo back into the envelope.

'Mrs Bell,' I said gently, 'I also found Monique's house.' At that she flinched. 'I'm sorry,' I said. 'I didn't mean to upset you. But I recognised it because of the well – and the lion's head over the front door.'

'It is sixty-five years since I last saw that house,' she said quietly. 'I have been back to Rochemare, of course, but I never once returned to Monique's home – I could not bear to. And after my parents died in the 1970s

250

Marcel moved to Lyon and my association with the village ended.'

I stirred my tea. 'It was strange for me, Mrs Bell, because when I was standing there, I saw a movement behind the shutters; it was just a fleeting shadow, but somehow it gave me a . . . shock. It made me feel . . .'

Mrs Bell bristled. 'Feel what?'

I stared at her. 'I'm not quite sure – it was something that I can't explain, except to say that it was as much as I could do not to go up to the front door and knock on it and ask . . .'

'Ask what?' said Mrs Bell sharply. Her tone had taken me aback. 'What could you ask?' she demanded.

'Well . . .'

'What could you possibly find out, Phoebe, that I do not know myself?' Mrs Bell's pale blue eyes were blazing. 'Monique and her family perished in 1943.'

I returned her gaze, struggling to remain calm. 'But do you know that for sure?'

Mrs Bell lowered her cup. I could hear it rattling slightly in the saucer. 'When the war ended, I searched for information about them, dreading what I might find out. I looked for them under both their French and German names through the tracing service of the International Red Cross. The records that they uncovered – and this took more than two years – showed that Monique's mother and brothers were sent to Dachau in June 1943; their names were on the transportation lists. But there is no record of them after that because those who did not survive selection were not registered – and women with young children did not survive that process.' Mrs Bell's voice caught. 'But the Red Cross did find a

251

record there for Monique's father. He was selected for forced labour, but died there six months later. As for Monique . . .' Mrs Bell's mouth was quivering. 'The Red Cross could find no trace of her after the war. They knew that she had spent three months in Drancy before being sent to Auschwitz. Her camp record – the Nazis kept meticulous files – showed that she had arrived there on August 5th, 1943. The fact that she had a record means that she survived selection. But she is believed to have been killed there, or to have died there at some date unknown.'

I felt my pulse quicken. 'But you don't know for *sure* what happened to her.'

Mrs Bell shifted on her seat. 'No. I don't, but –'

'And you haven't searched again since?'

Mrs Bell shook her head. 'I spent three years looking for Monique, and what I found convinced me that she had not survived. I felt that it would be futile and upsetting to seek for her further. I was getting married, and moving to England; I had been given the chance of a fresh start. I decided, ruthlessly perhaps, to draw a line under what had happened: I could not drag it through my life forever, punish myself for*ever* . . .' Mrs Bell's voice caught again. 'Nor did I dare mention it to my husband – I was terrified that I'd see in his eyes a look of disillusionment with me that would have . . . spoilt everything. So I buried the story of Monique – for decades, Phoebe – telling no one in the world about it. Not a soul. Until I met you.'

'But you don't *know* that Monique died in Auschwitz,' I insisted. My heart was thudding in my ribcage.

Mrs Bell stared at me. 'That's true. But if she didn't

die there, the chances are that she died in another concentration camp or in the chaos of January '45 as the Allies closed in and the Nazis forced those inmates who could still stand to march through the snow to other camps inside Germany – less than half of them survived. *So* many people were displaced or killed in those months that thousands upon thousands of deaths went unrecorded, and I believe Monique's to have been one of them.'

'But you don't *know* –' I tried to swallow but my mouth had gone dry. 'And without that certain knowledge you must *surely* sometimes have wondered whether –'

'Phoebe,' said Mrs Bell, her pale blue eyes shimmering, 'Monique has been dead for more than sixty-five years. And her house, like the clothes you sell, went on to have a new life, with new owners. Whatever you felt when you stood outside her house was . . . irrational. Because all you had seen was a glimpse of some person who lives there *now*, not some . . . I don't know . . . "presence" – if that's what you're suggesting – compelling you to – I know not what! Now . . .' Her hand flew to her chest and fluttered there like an injured bird. 'I am tired.'

I stood up. 'And I should get back.' I took the tea tray into the kitchen then returned. 'I'm sorry if I've upset you, Mrs Bell. I didn't mean to.'

She exhaled painfully. 'And I am sorry to have become . . . agitated. I know you mean well, Phoebe, but it is painful for me – especially now, as I face up to the fact that my life will soon end and I will die knowing that I was never able to put right the wrong that I did.'

'You mean the mistake that you made,' I corrected her gently.

'Yes. The mistake – the awful mistake.' Mrs Bell put out her hand to me, and I held it. It felt so small and light. 'But I appreciate the fact that you think about my story.' I felt her fingers close around mine.

'I do. I think about it a lot, Mrs Bell.'

She nodded. 'As I think about yours.'

TEN

On Thursday Val phoned me again about collecting the repairs, so I drove over to Kidbrooke straight after work. As I parked outside her house I desperately hoped that Mags wouldn't be there. I felt embarrassed and ashamed now about the psychic reading. It had all been so absurd and . . . *low.*

As I put my hand to Val's bell I jumped. A fat-bodied spider, of the kind that emerges in the autumn, had spun its web across it. I knocked loudly instead, then, as Val opened the door, I pointed it out to her.

She stared at it. 'Oh, that's *good.* Spiders are lucky – do you know why?'

'No.'

'Because a spider hid the baby Jesus from Herod's soldiers by weaving a web over him. Isn't that incredible? That's why you should never kill a spider,' she added.

'I wouldn't dream of it.'

'Ah . . . that's interesting.' Val was still peering at it.

'It's running *up* its web, which means that you've been on a journey, Phoebe.'

I looked at her in surprise. 'I have actually – I've just been to France.'

'If it had been running *down* its web then that would have meant you were about to *go* on one.'

'Really? You're a mine of information,' I said as I went inside.

'Well, I think it's important to know these things.'

As I followed Val down the hall I detected the scent of Magie Noire with bass notes of nicotine. *Maggie Noire,* I thought dismally.

'Hi, Mags,' I said with a forced smile.

'Hi, sweetheart,' Mags rasped as she sat, filling the armchair in Val's sewing room. She was eating a digestive. 'Shame about the other day. But you should have let me keep trying.' She scraped at the corner of her mouth with a crimson fingernail. 'I think Emma was just about to come through.'

I stared at Mags, suddenly outraged at hearing my best friend referred to in this crass way. 'I don't think so, Maggie,' I said, struggling to keep calm. 'In fact, as you've brought it up, I don't mind telling you that I thought the sitting was a complete waste of time.'

Mags looked at me as though I'd slapped her. Then she pulled a packet of tissues out of her cleavage and removed one. 'The problem is you're not *really* a believer.'

I stared at her as she unfolded the paper hanky. 'That's not true. I *don't* disbelieve the idea that the human soul may continue or that we can even detect the presence of someone who's died. But as you got every single thing about my friend wrong – including her gender – I can't help feeling a bit cynical about your particular abilities.'

Mags blew her nose. 'I was having an off-day,' she sniffed. 'Plus the ether's often a bit murky on Tuesday mornings.'

'Mags really *is* very good, Phoebe,' Val said loyally. 'She put me in touch with my granny the other night – didn't you?' Mags nodded. 'I'd lost her lemon curd recipe so I got her to give it to me again.'

'Eight eggs,' said Mags. 'Not six.'

'That's what I couldn't remember,' said Val. 'Anyway, thanks to Mags, Gran and I had a nice little chat.' I discreetly rolled my eyes. 'In fact, Mags is *so* good that she's been invited to be a guest medium on the *In Spirit* show on ITV 2, haven't you, Mags?' Mags nodded. 'I'm sure she'll bring comfort to lots of viewers. You should watch it, Phoebe,' Val added amiably. 'Every Sunday at two thirty.'

I picked up the case. 'I'll make a note of it,' I said.

'These will look wonderful,' Annie said the next morning as I showed her the garments that Val had mended – Mrs Bell's yellow knife-pleated evening dress, the glorious pink Guy Laroche silk cocoon coat, the Ossie Clark maxi dress and the damson-coloured gabardine suit. I showed her the Missoni rainbow-striped knitted dress that had had moth damage at the hem. 'What a clever repair,' Annie said as she examined it. Val had knitted a piece to cover the hole. 'She must have used tiny needles to match the stitches and the colour is perfect.' Now Annie held up the Chanel Boutique sapphire blue silk faille evening coat with elbow-length sleeves. 'This is gorgeous.

It should go in the window, don't you think? Maybe instead of the Norma Kamali trouser suit,' she mused.

Annie had come in at eight to help me rearrange the stock before the shop opened. We'd put away at least half the clothes, replacing them with garments in the key shades for autumn – midnight blue, tomato red, sea green, deep purple, and gold – jewel tones redolent of the colours seen in Renaissance paintings. Then we'd found clothes that reflected the season's silhouettes – sculpted A-line coats and dresses with stand-away collars and full skirts; architectural leather jackets with exaggerated shoulders and curved sleeves. We'd gone for fabrics that tied in with the seductive fabrics of the moment – brocade, lace, satin and damask, crushed velvet, tartan and tweed.

'Just because we're selling vintage doesn't mean that we can ignore trends in shape and colour,' I'd said as I came down from the stockroom again clutching several outfits.

'In fact it's probably even more important,' Annie had pointed out. 'There's a "statement" feel to this season,' she'd added as I'd handed her a Balmain cherry red dress with a flaring tulip skirt, an Alaia Couture chocolate brown leather suit with a nipped-in waist and huge lapels, and a Courrèges futurist orange crepe dress from the mid sixties. 'Everything's big and opulent,' Annie had gone on. 'Hot, bold colours, structured shapes, stiff fabrics that stand away from the body. You've got all of that here, Phoebe – all we have to do is put it together.'

Annie had put out most of Mrs Bell's evening wear and was now looking at her damson-coloured gabardine two-piece. 'This is lovely, but I think we should update it with a soft wide belt and a fake-fur collar – shall I look something out?'

'Yes. Please.'

As I hung the suit on a rail I imagined Mrs Bell wearing it in the late forties. I thought of the conversation I'd had with her three days before; I reflected again on how hard it must have been for her, in the aftermath of war, trying to find out what had happened to Monique. If, God forbid, there were some comparable situation today, she'd be able to launch an appeal on radio and TV; she could scatter e-mails around the globe or post requests for information on internet message boards or on Facebook, MySpace or YouTube. She could simply put Monique's name into a search engine and see what, if anything, came out of the ether . . .

'Here,' said Annie as she came downstairs with an 'ocelot' collar. I think this will work – and this belt should tone in.' She held it against the jacket. 'It does.'

'Could you put them on the suit,' I asked Annie as I went into the office. 'I just need to . . . check the website.'

'Sure.'

Ever since Mrs Bell had told me her story I'd wondered about searching the net for any possible references to Monique, however unlikely. But what would I do if I did find something? How could I then keep that from Mrs Bell? Given that it would almost certainly be negative, if not devastating, I'd resisted the urge to do it. But since going to Monique's house I'd felt differently. I'd been gripped by the desire to know. And so, prompted by some inner compulsion that I couldn't explain, I sat at the computer and typed Monique's name into Google.

Nothing of any significance came up, just some references to an Avenue Richelieu in Quebec, and to the Cardinal Richelieu Lycée in Paris. I put in the name without the first 'e'. Then I typed in 'Monika Richter', and up came a Californian psychoanalyst, a German paediatrician, and an Australian conservationist, none of whom would be likely to have any connection with their older namesake. I then did the same search spelling Monika with a 'c'. Then I added 'Auschwitz', thinking that there might just be some eye-witness account that mentioned her, out of all the billions of words that had been written about the camp. Now I added 'Mannheim', because I remembered that that was where she had originally come from. But nothing that seemed to relate to Monique/Monika or her family came up – just a few references to an exhibition there by Gerhard Richter.

I stared at the screen. So that was that. As Mrs Bell had said, all I'd seen in Rochemare was the fleeting movement of a living person in a house that had long since shrugged off the memory of its wartime occupants. And I was about to close Internet Explorer when I decided to look at the Red Cross website.

On the Home page it explained that their Tracing Service had been started at the end of the war and that its archive in northern Germany now contained nearly fifty million Nazi documents that related to the camps. Any member of the public could request a search, which would be carried out by the IRC archivists; on average each search took between one and four hours. Given the volume of requests, the enquirer could expect to wait three months 'maximum' for a report.

I clicked on the 'Download Form' box. I was surprised

at how short the form was: it simply asked for the personal details of the person being sought, and the place where they were last known to have been seen. The enquirer had to provide their own personal details and to explain their connection to the person they were seeking. They then had to give the reason for their search. There were two choices for this – 'Documentation for reparations' or 'Desire to know what happened'.

'Desire to know what happened,' I murmured.

I printed off the form then put it in an envelope. I'd take it to Mrs Bell when her niece had left and we'd fill it in together, then I'd e-mail it to the Red Cross. If in their vast repository of information they could find any references to Monique then, I reasoned, there'd at least be the chance that Mrs Bell might finally gain closure on the issue. Three months 'maximum' implied that the report might well come back in less – perhaps in only one month, I reflected, or even a fortnight. I wondered about enclosing a note, explaining that, due to illness, time was short. But then that would be the case with so many enquirers of Mrs Bell's generation, I reflected, the youngest of whom would now be well into their seventies.

'So have you got many internet orders?' I heard Annie call.

'Oh . . .' I forced my thoughts back to the shop, and quickly navigated to the Village Vintage website then opened the mailbox. 'There are . . . three. Someone wants to buy the emerald green Kelly bag, there's interest in the Pucci palazzo pants and . . . hurrah – someone's buying the Madame Grès.'

'That dress you don't want.'

'That's right.' The one that Guy had given me. I came back into the shop and removed it from the rail to pack up and send. 'This woman asked me for the dimensions last week,' I said as I slipped it off its hanger. 'And now she's come back with the money – thank goodness.'

'You're dying to get rid of it, aren't you?'

'I suppose I am.'

'Is that because it was from a boyfriend?'

I looked at Annie. 'Yes.'

'I did guess, but as I didn't know you I wasn't going to ask. Now that I *do* know you, I feel I can be a bit nosey . . .' I smiled. Annie and I did know each other now. I liked her friendly, easy company and her enthusiasm for the shop. 'So was it a bit acrimonious?'

'Well, you could say that.'

'Then selling that dress is totally understandable. If Tim dumped me, I'd probably chuck everything he'd ever given me – except the paintings,' she added, 'just in case they turned out to be worth anything one day.' She put a pair of Bruno Magli scarlet stilettos in the shoe display. 'And how's the sender of the red roses? If you don't mind my asking.'

'He's . . . fine. In fact, I saw him in France.' I explained why.

'That sounds good – and he's obviously nuts about you.'

I smiled. Then as I did up the buttons on a pink cashmere cardigan I told Annie a bit more about him.

'So what's his daughter like?'

I draped several heavy gold-plated chains around the neck of a wooden display head. 'She's sixteen, very pretty – and terribly spoilt.'

'Like so many teenagers,' Annie observed. 'But she won't always be a teenager.'

'True,' I said happily.

'But teenagers *can* be vile.'

Suddenly there was a tap on the glass and there was Katie, in her uniform, waving at us. And teenagers can be lovely, I thought.

I unlocked the door and Katie came in. 'Hi,' she said. Then she glanced anxiously at the yellow prom dress. 'Thank God for that.' She smiled. 'It's still here.'

'It is,' I said. I wasn't going to tell her that someone had tried it on only the day before. It had made them look like a grapefruit. 'Annie, this is Katie.'

'I remember seeing you here a week or two back,' said Annie warmly.

'Katie's interested in the yellow prom dress.'

'I adore it,' she said longingly. 'I'm saving up for it.'

'Dare I ask how it's going?' I said.

'Well, I'm babysitting for two families, so I've now got £120 in the fund. But as the ball's on November 1st I've got my work cut out.'

'Well . . . keep at it. I wish *I* had children – then you could babysit them . . .'

'I was just passing on my way to school and couldn't resist having another peek – can I take a photo of it?'

'Of course.'

Katie held her phone up to the dress and I heard a click. 'There,' she said, looking at it, 'that'll keep me motivated. Anyway, I'd better rush – it's a quarter to nine.' Katie shouldered her school bag and turned to go, then stooped to pick up the newspaper that had just landed on the mat. She handed it to Annie.

'Thanks, sweetheart,' Annie said.

I waved to Katie then began rearranging the evening-wear rail.

'Good God!' I heard Annie exclaim.

She was staring, goggle-eyed at the front of the paper. Then she held it up for me to see.

Covering the top half of the *Black & Green* was a photo of Keith. Above his drawn-looking face was the headline, LOCAL PROPERTY BOSS IN FRAUD PROBE – *EXCLUSIVE*!

Annie read the article out to me. '"Prominent local property developer Keith Brown, Chairman of Phoenix Land, today faces the possibility of a criminal investigation after this newspaper's discovery of evidence implicating him in a massive insurance fraud."' I thought, with a sympathetic pang, of Keith's girlfriend; this would be awful for her. '"Brown started Phoenix Land in 2004,"' Annie read on, '"with the proceeds from a huge insurance payout after his kitchen business had been destroyed by fire two years earlier. Brown's insurers, Star Alliance, disputed his claim that his warehouse had been torched by a disgruntled employee who had subsequently disappeared and could not be traced . . . Refused to pay out,"' I heard her say as I rearranged the dresses. '"Brown started proceedings . . . Star Alliance eventually settled . . . Two million pounds . . ."' I heard Annie gasp and looked at her. '"Now the *Black & Green* has been handed compelling evidence that the blaze was started by Keith Brown *himself* . . ."' Annie stared at me, her eyes like tea-plates, then returned her gaze to the paper. '"Mr Brown declined to answer the questions we put to him last night, but his attempt to get an injunction against the *Black & Green* failed . . ." Well!' she exclaimed with censorious satisfaction. 'It's good to know we weren't too hard on him.' She handed me the paper.

I quickly read through the piece myself, then I remembered Keith's quotes in the *Guardian* about how 'devastated' he'd been as he watched his warehouse burn, and how he had 'vowed to build something worthwhile out of the ashes'. It had all felt a bit phoney, and now I knew why.

'I wonder how the *Black & Green* got the story,' I said to Annie.

'Presumably because the insurers, having been suspicious all along, have just come up with this "compelling evidence", whatever it is.'

'But why would they take it to a local newspaper? Surely they'd go straight to the police.'

'Ah.' Annie clicked her tongue. 'Good point.'

So this must have been the 'difficult' business story that Dan had been working on – the one that Matt had phoned him about when Dan and I were sitting in the Age Exchange.

'I hope the girlfriend isn't going to stand by him,' I heard Annie say. 'Mind you, she can always visit him in prison in her green prom dress, looking like "Bloody Tinker Bell".' She giggled. 'And speaking of prom dresses, Phoebe – have you e-mailed your American dealer yet?'

'No – I need to do that, don't I?' I'd been so preoccupied with Monique that I'd forgotten.

'You do need to,' Annie said. 'The party season's coming up – plus prom dresses are "in" this season according to *Vogue* – the more petticoats the better.'

'I'll e-mail him now.'

I went back to the computer and opened Outlook Express to contact Rick, only to find that he'd got there first. I clicked on his e-mail.

Hi Phoebe – I left a message on your phone the other day to say that I've got six more prom dresses to offer you, all top quality and in perfect condition. I clicked on the photos. They were lovely cupcakes in vibrant shades that would be perfect for the autumn – indigo, vermillion, tangerine, cocoa, deep purple and kingfisher blue. I zoomed in on the images to check whether the net looked faded anywhere, then I clicked back on the text. *Also attached is the jpeg of the purses – sorry, 'bags' – that I mentioned and which I want to include with the dresses, as a job lot . . .*

'Damn,' I murmured. I didn't want them, especially with the pound having fallen so much against the dollar lately; but I realised I might have to buy them in case Rick stopped sending me the things that I did like. 'Let's have a look then,' I said wearily.

The bags had been photographed together on a white sheet and were mostly from the eighties and nineties. They were fairly ordinary, apart from a very handsome leather Gladstone bag probably from the 1940s and an elegant white ostrich-skin envelope clutch from the early seventies.

'How much does he want?' I murmured. *The deal is $800 US, inclusive of shipping.*

I clicked on reply. *Okay, Rick,* I typed. *It's a deal. I'll pay you by Paypal when I get your invoice. Please send everything asap. Cheers, Phoebe.*

'I've just bought six more prom dresses,' I told Annie as I went back into the shop.

She was changing one of the mannequins. 'That's good news – they should be easy to sell.'

'I've also bought twelve bags: most of which I don't want – but I have to have them as they're the quid pro quo.'

'There's not much space up there in the stockroom,' she said as she re-positioned the mannequin's arms.

'I know; so when they arrive I'll just give the non-vintage ones to Oxfam. But now I'm going to post the Madame Grès.'

I went into the office and quickly wrapped the dress up in tissue paper with a white ribbon then put it in a jiffy bag. Then I turned the 'Closed' sign on the door to 'Open'. 'See you later Annie.'

As I left the shop my mother phoned. She'd just got to work. 'I've decided,' she whispered.

'Decided what?' I asked as I turned down Montpelier Vale.

'To forget about all these silly treatments I've been looking into – all this plasma regeneration and fractional resurfacing and radiofrequency rejuvenation nonsense.'

I glanced into the window of the beauty salon. 'That is such good news, Mum.'

'I don't think they're going to make the slightest difference.'

'I'm sure that's right,' I said as I crossed the road.

'And they cost *so* much.'

'They do – it would be a complete waste of money.'

'Exactly. So I've decided I may as well go straight for a facelift.'

I stopped dead. 'Mum . . . *Don't.*'

'I'm going to have a facelift,' she repeated quietly as

267

I stood by the sports and kite shop. 'I'm terribly low and it'll give me a boost. It'll be my sixtieth birthday gift to myself, Phoebe. I've worked all these years,' she added as I walked on. 'So why shouldn't I have a little cosmetic "refreshment" if I want to?'

'No reason, Mum – it's your life. But what if you're not happy with it?' I had visions of my mother's pretty face looking grotesquely stretched or oddly lumpy and bumpy.

'I've done my research,' I heard her say as I passed the toy shop. 'Yesterday I took the day off work and had consultations with three plastic surgeons. I've now decided that Freddie Church is going to wield the scalpel, at his clinic in Maida Vale: it's all booked for November 24th.' I wondered whether Mum had remembered that that was Louis' first birthday. 'And don't try to talk me out of it, darling, because my mind's made up. I've paid my deposit and I'm going ahead with it.'

'Okay.' I sighed as I crossed the road. There was no point in protesting – once Mum had decided on something she stuck to it; plus I had a lot on my mind and lacked the energy for a fight. 'I only hope you don't come to regret it.'

'I won't. But, tell me, how's your new man? Is that still going on?'

'I'm seeing him tomorrow. We're going to the Almeida Theatre.'

'Well, you seem to like him, so please don't do anything silly. I mean, you're *thirty-four* now,' Mum added, as I turned into Blackheath Grove. 'Before you know where you are, you'll be forty-three –'

'Sorry, Mum, I have to go now.' I snapped shut the

268

phone. The Post Office was empty so it only took two minutes to post my parcel. As I walked out again I saw Dan coming towards me, smiling. But then today he had something to smile about.

'I was just looking out of the window and saw you.' He nodded up at his office, above the children's library on our right.

I followed his gaze. 'So that's where you are – very central. Congratulations, by the way – I've just read your scoop.'

'It's not my scoop,' Dan replied judiciously. 'It's Matt's – I just sat in on the talks with the lawyers. But it's a fantastic story for a local paper like ours. We're all a bit cock-a-hoop about it.'

'I'm dying to know who you got it from,' I said. 'Not that you can reveal your sources . . . Can you?' I added hopefully.

Dan smiled then shook his head. ''Fraid not.'

'I feel sorry for his girlfriend though. Plus she'll probably lose her job.'

Dan shrugged. 'She'll get another one – she's very young. I've seen photos of her,' he added. Then he asked me about France, reminding me that I'd said I'd go to the cinema with him again. 'I don't suppose you're free tomorrow night, are you, Phoebe? I know it's short notice, but I've been very preoccupied with the Brown story. We could go and see the new Coen brothers film – or just have dinner somewhere.'

'Well . . .' I looked at him. 'That would have been great. But I'm . . . doing something.'

'Oh.' Dan smiled at me ruefully. 'But then, why wouldn't a girl like you be busy on a Saturday night?'

269

He sighed. 'More fool me. I should have asked you before. So . . . are you seeing someone then, Phoebe?'

'Well . . . I . . . *Dan*,' I said, 'you're discombobulating me again.'

'Oh. Sorry.' He shrugged. 'I don't seem to be able to help it. But, look, did you get the invitation for the eleventh? I sent it to the shop.'

'Yes, I got it yesterday.'

'Well, you said you'd be there so I hope you'll come.'

I looked at Dan. 'Yes. I will.'

This morning I found it hard to concentrate on work because I kept thinking about Miles and about how much I was looking forward to seeing him at the theatre. We were going to see *Waste* by Harley Granville-Barker. In between customers I read a couple of reviews of it online, partly to remind myself of the plot – I saw it years ago – and partly so that I'd be able to impress Miles with my trenchant remarks. But then the shop became very busy, as it always is on Saturdays. I sold Mrs Bell's Guy Laroche cocoon coat – I was almost sorry to see it go – and a Zandra Rhodes apricot silk organza tunic with gold beading at the hem. Then someone asked to try on the yellow prom dress; it would be the third time it had been tried on in a week. As the woman went into the fitting room I glanced anxiously at her figure and realised that it would probably fit her. As I drew the curtain round I prayed that she wouldn't like it. I heard the rustle of the tulle then the sound of the zip being pulled up, followed by a little grunt.

'I *love* it!' I heard her exclaim. The woman opened the curtain again then gazed at herself in the mirror, turning this way and that. 'It's fabulous,' she said as she stood on tiptoe. 'I adore the froth and sparkle of it.' She beamed at me. 'I'll take it!'

My heart sank as I imagined Katie's disappointment. I thought of her taking the photo of the dress, and now I remembered how lovely she had looked in it – ten times more attractive than this woman, who was too old for it, and not slim enough with her fleshy white shoulders and plump arms.

The woman turned to her friend. 'Don't you think it's fab, Sue?'

Sue, who was tall and angular – a Modigliani to her friend's fleshy Rubens – was chewing on her lower lip, making little sucking noises. 'Well . . . to be honest, Jill, sweetheart, I don't. Your skin tone's too pale for it, plus the bodice is tight – look – which makes you bulge at the back, here –' She turned her friend round. Jill could now see that a good half-inch of fat spilled over the stiff-ened panels, like dough.

Sue cocked her head to one side. 'You know those puddings you can get – a frozen lemon that's been stuffed with sorbet that's sort of squishing out of the top of it . . .?'

'Yes?' said Jill.

'Well, you look like one of those.'

I held my breath to see how Jill reacted. She stared at herself then nodded slowly. 'You're right, Sue. Cruel – but right.'

'What are best friends for?' said Sue amiably. She flashed me a guilty smile. 'Sorry – I just lost you a sale.'

'That's okay,' I said delightedly. 'It's got to be perfect, hasn't it? Anyway, I'll be getting some more prom dresses

271

soon, so one of those might be a better fit – they should be here next week.'

'We'll be back.'

Once the women had gone I put the yellow dress on the 'reserved' rail with 'Katie' on it – my nerves wouldn't take any more fittings. Then I brought down a Lanvin Castillo raspberry pink silk evening gown from the mid 1950s and hung it on the wall in its place.

I closed the shop at 5.30 on the dot then sped home to shower and change before rushing up to Islington to meet Miles. As I half ran down Almeida Street I saw him standing outside the theatre, looking out for me. As he saw me he lifted his hand.

'Sorry I'm late,' I said breathlessly. The bell was ringing. 'Is that the five-minute bell?'

'It's the one minute.' He kissed me. 'I was worried that you weren't going to come.'

I slipped my arm through his. 'Of course I was.' I found Miles' anxiety touching and as we went inside I wondered whether it was prompted by the fourteen years between us, or whether he always felt a little insecure when he liked someone, whatever their age.

'It's a good play,' he said an hour or so later as the house lights went up for the interval. We stood up. 'I've seen it before – years ago, at the National. I think it was in '91.'

'It *was*, because I also saw that production – with my school.' I remembered Emma coming back for the second half reeking of gin.

Miles laughed. 'So you would have been Roxy's age; and I'd have been thirty-one – a young man. I'd have fallen in love with you then too.'

I smiled. And now we made our way into the foyer, then drifted towards the bar with everyone else.

'I'll get drinks,' I said. 'What would you like?'

'A glass of Côtes du Rhône, if they have one.'

I looked at the board. 'They do. I think I'll have the Sancerre.' As I stood at the bar, Miles waited a little way behind me. 'Phoebe . . .' I heard him whisper after a few moments. I turned round. He was suddenly looking uncomfortable and his face had reddened. 'I'll see you outside,' he murmured.

'Fine,' I replied, bemused . . .

'Are you okay?' I asked him when I found him a few minutes later standing by the entrance. I handed him his glass of wine. 'I was worried that you might be unwell.'

He shook his head. 'I'm okay. But . . . as you were waiting to be served I spotted some people I wanted to avoid.'

'Really?' My curiosity was aroused. 'Who?' Miles discreetly nodded towards the far end of the foyer at a blonde forty-something woman in a turquoise wrap and a sandy-haired man in a dark coat. 'Who are they?' I asked him quietly.

Miles pursed his mouth. 'Their name's Wycliffe. Their daughter's at Roxy's old school.' He sighed. 'It's just not a great . . . connection.'

'I see,' I said, remembering now that Miles had said that there'd been some 'misunderstanding' at St Mary's. Whatever it was, it still had the power to upset him. Hearing the bell for the second half, we went back to our seats.

Afterwards, while we were waiting to cross the road

to the restaurant opposite the theatre, I saw Mrs Wycliffe give Miles a sideways glance then discreetly tug at her husband's sleeve. As we started dinner I asked Miles what the Wycliffes had done that had so offended him.

'They were awful to Roxy. In fact it was very . . . unpleasant.' As he lifted his glass of water his hand was shaking.

'Why?' I asked. Miles hesitated. 'Didn't the girls get on?'

'Oh they did.' Miles lowered his glass. 'In fact Roxy and Clara had been best friends. Then at the start of the summer term there was . . . a falling out.' I looked at Miles, wondering why this would have upset him quite so much. 'Something of Clara's went missing,' Miles explained. 'A . . . gold bracelet. Clara accused Roxy of having taken it.' Miles pursed his mouth again, the muscles at the side of his mouth flexing.

'Oh . . .'

'But I knew that it couldn't be true. I know Roxanne can be annoying, in the way that teenagers often are, but she would never do anything like *that*.' He ran a finger under his collar. 'Anyway, the school phoned me and said that Clara and her parents were maintaining that Roxy had stolen this wretched bracelet. I was incensed. I said that I would not have my daughter being falsely accused. But the headmistress behaved . . . *outrageously*.' As Miles said that I saw a vein at his left temple jump.

'In what way?'

'In the bias she showed. She refused to accept Roxy's version of events.'

'Which was . . . what?'

Miles sighed. 'As I said, Roxanne and Clara had been very good friends. They constantly borrowed each other's things in the way that girls of that age do. I saw it when Clara stayed with us at Easter,' Miles went on. 'She came down to breakfast one morning dressed entirely in clothes that were Roxy's, with Roxy's jewellery – and vice versa. The girls did it the whole time – they thought it was fun.'

'So . . . you mean that Roxy *had* the bracelet?'

Miles had flushed. 'It turned up in her drawer – but the point is, she hadn't *stolen* it. I mean, why would she need to take anything from *anyone* when she has so much of her own? She explained that Clara had *lent* her the bracelet, that Clara had some of *her* jewellery – which she did – and that they swapped their things all the time. That should have been the *end* of it.' Miles sighed. 'But the Wycliffes were determined to make something of it. They were vile.' He heaved a bitter sigh.

'What did they do?'

Miles drew in his breath then slowly released it. 'They threatened to call the police. So I had no choice but to make a counter threat of my own that I would start libel proceedings against them if they didn't stop defaming my daughter.'

'And the school?'

Miles' mouth had become a straight line. 'They sided with the Wycliffes – no doubt because the man's donating half a million towards their new theatre. It was . . . nauseating. So . . . I took Roxy away. The moment she'd taken her last GCSE, I was waiting there to drive her home. It was *my* decision for her to leave that school.'

Miles had another sip of water. And I was just

wondering what to say when the waiter came to take
our plates. By the time he'd gone and then quickly come
back with our main courses, Miles was less agitated, the
unpleasantness at Roxy's old school receding, then seem-
ingly forgotten. To lift the atmosphere further, I chatted
to him about the play a bit more. Then Miles got the
bill. 'I drove here, by the way,' he said. 'Which means
that I can take you home.'

'Thank you.'

'I can take you home to your home,' Miles said. 'Or,
if you like, to mine.' He looked into my face, seeking
my reaction. 'I can lend you a tee-shirt again,' he added
quietly, 'and I can give you a toothbrush. Roxy has a
hairdryer, if you need one. She's at a party tonight, in
the Cotswolds.' So that explained why he hadn't had
twenty calls from her on his mobile. 'I'm going to collect
her tomorrow afternoon. So I thought that you and I
could spend the morning together, then have lunch
somewhere.' We stood up. 'How does that sound,
Phoebe?'

The maître d' was handing us our coats. 'It sounds
. . . lovely.'

Miles smiled at me. 'Good.'

As we drove through South London with Mozart's
clarinet concerto on the CD player I felt happy to be
going back with Miles. As he pulled up outside his house
I glanced at the front garden, which was prettily land-
scaped with low box hedging enclosed by a wrought-
iron fence. Miles unlocked the door and we stepped into
a wide hallway with high ceilings, panelled walls and
black-and-white marble floor tiles that had been polished
to a watery shine.

As Miles took my coat I glimpsed a large dining room with oxblood walls and a long mahogany table. Now I followed him down the hall to the kitchen with its hand-painted units and granite worktops that glittered darkly under the spotlights that spangled the ceiling. Through the French windows I could just make out an expanse of tree-fringed lawn rolling away into the gloom.

Miles took a bottle of Evian out of the American fridge then we went up the wide staircase to the first floor. His bedroom was decorated in yellow, with a big en-suite bathroom with a free-standing iron bath and a fireplace. I got undressed in here. 'Could I have that toothbrush?' I called out.

Miles came into the bathroom, gave my naked form an appreciative glance, then opened a cupboard in which I could see bottles of shampoo and bubble bath. 'Now where is it?' he murmured. 'Roxy's always looking for things in here . . . Ah – got it.' He handed me a new brush. 'And what about a tee-shirt? I can get you one.' He lifted my hair and kissed the back of my neck, then my shoulder. 'If you think you'll need one.'

I turned to him, and slid my arms round his waist. 'No,' I whispered. 'I won't.'

We woke late. As I glanced at the clock on the bedside table next to me I felt Miles' arms encircle me, cupping my breasts.

'You're lovely, Phoebe,' he murmured. 'I think I'm falling in love with you.' He kissed me then placed my hands above my head, and made love to me again . . .

'You could swim in this bath,' I said a while later as I soaked in it. Miles poured in some more bubble bath then got in with me, lying behind me while I lay against his chest in an island of foam.

After a few minutes he picked up my hand and examined it. 'Your fingertips are wrinkling.' He kissed each one. 'Time to get dry.' We both stepped out then Miles picked up a soft white bath sheet from the bale on the bathroom stool and wrapped it round me. We cleaned our teeth then he took the toothbrush from me and put it in the holder with his. 'Keep it in there,' he said.

'My hair.' I touched it. 'Could I borrow a dryer?'

Miles wrapped a towel round his waist. 'Come with me.'

We crossed the landing, the early autumn sunshine flooding through the floor-to-ceiling sash windows. As I looked up I saw a beautiful portrait of Roxy hanging on the far wall.

'That's Ellen,' Miles explained as we paused in front of it. 'I commissioned it for our engagement. She was twenty-three.'

'Roxy's so like her,' I said. 'Although . . .' I looked at Miles. 'She has your nose – and your chin.' I stroked it with the back of my hand. 'And is this where you lived with Ellen?'

'No.' Miles opened a bedroom door with *Roxanne* on it in pink letters. 'We lived in Fulham, but after she died I wanted to move – I couldn't cope with the constant reminders. And I'd been invited to a dinner party at this house and had loved it; so when it came up for sale not long afterwards the owners offered me first refusal. Now . . .'

Roxy's room was huge, thickly carpeted in white, with a white four-poster crowned with a pink-and-gold

278

damask canopy. There was a white dressing table on which were an array of expensive face creams and body lotions and several different-sized bottles of J'adore. In front of the pink and gold curtained windows was a chaise longue in pale pink brocade and on a low table beside it were perhaps two dozen glossy magazines, their covers gleaming icily.

I noticed a doll's house on a side table – a Georgian townhouse with a gleaming black front door and floor-to-ceiling sash windows. 'It's just like this house,' I said.

'It *is* this house,' Miles explained. 'It's an exact copy of it.' He opened the front and we peered inside. 'Every detail is correct, right down to the chandeliers, the working shutters, and the brass doorknobs.' I gazed at the replica of the claw-footed iron bath in which I'd just soaked. 'I gave it to Roxy for her seventh birthday,' I heard Miles say. 'I thought it would help to make her feel more at home – she still plays with it.' He straightened up. 'Anyway . . . come through here . . .' Now we were in her dressing room. 'This is where she keeps her hairdryer.' He nodded at a white table on which was an arsenal of hairdressing appliances. 'I'll go and make breakfast.'

'I won't be long.'

I sat at Roxy's hairdressing station, with its professional hairdryer and its smoothing irons and curling tongs and carousel of heated rollers, and its paddle brushes, combs and slides. As I quickly blow dried my hair I looked at all the clothes on the rails which ran around the three walls. There must have been a hundred dresses and suits. To my left was a brick red Gucci suede coat that I recognised from last year's spring collection. In front of me I could see a Matthew Williamson satin trouser suit and a Hussein Chalayan cocktail dress. There were four or five skiing outfits and at least eight long dresses bagged up in muslin protectors. Ranged beneath the clothes was a chrome rack on which were around sixty pairs of shoes and boots. Along one wall were a number of sisal baskets containing perhaps three dozen bags.

By my feet was a copy of this month's *Vogue*. I picked it up and it fell open at a fashion spread, half the garments in which had been marked with heart-shaped pink Post-its. A Ralph Lauren baby blue silk ball gown costing £2,100 had a pink heart next to it; as did a Zac Posen one-shouldered black dress. A Roberto Cavalli hot pink mini dress at £1,595 had been similarly earmarked with *Check Sienna Fenwick's not getting this* scribbled on the heart in large, round letters. A Christian Lacroix couture 'stained glass' silk evening gown had also been stickied. It cost £3,600. *By special order only*, Roxy had written. I shook my head as I wondered which of these creations Roxanne was destined to possess.

I turned off the hairdryer, putting it back exactly where I'd found it. As I walked back through her bedroom I paused to shut the front of the doll's house which Miles had left ajar. As I did so I looked inside it again and now noticed in the sitting room two dolls – a daddy doll in a brown suit and next to him on the sofa a little girl doll in a pink-and-white gingham pinafore.

Now I went back to Miles' bedroom, got dressed and made up, retrieved my earrings from the green saucer on the bathroom mantelpiece, then followed the scent of coffee downstairs.

Miles was standing at the breakfast bar with a tray of toast and marmalade.

'The kitchen's lovely,' I said glancing around. 'But it's different from the one in the doll's house.'

Miles depressed the plunger on the cafetiere. 'I had it done up last year – not least because I wanted a professional wine store.' He nodded to my left and I glanced at the store with its two large fridges and its floor-to-ceiling bespoke wooden racks for red wine. He picked up the tray. 'We'll have some Chante le Merle sometime, as you like it.'

On the wall by the French windows was a photo montage with a dozen or so snaps of Roxy skiing, riding, mountain biking and playing tennis. There was a photo of her smiling in front of Table Mountain, and another of her standing on top of Ayers Rock.

'Roxy's incredibly lucky,' I said as I looked at a photo of her fishing from the back of a yacht in what looked like the Caribbean. 'For a girl of her age she's done so much – and, as you said, she *has* so much.'

Miles sighed. 'Probably *too* much.' I didn't reply. 'But Roxy's my only child and she means the world to me – plus she's all I have of Ellen.' His voice had caught. 'I just want her to be as happy as possible.'

'Of course,' I murmured. *Elle est son talon d'Achille.* Is this what Cecile had meant? Simply that Miles spoilt Roxy?

As we stood on the terrace I gazed at the long, wide lawn fringed on both sides by undulating beds of herbaceous plants and shrubs. Miles put the tray on the wrought-iron table. 'You wouldn't get the newspaper, would you? It'll be outside the front door.'

While he poured the coffee I went and picked up *The Sunday Times* and carried it back out to the garden. As we sat having our breakfast in the soft autumn sunshine Miles read the main section while I flicked through Style. Then I unfolded the business section to take out the News Review, and as I did so I saw the heading PHOENIX FALLS. I looked at the half-page article. It had picked up on the *Black & Green* story, repeating the allegation of fraud. Except that there was a photo of Keith Brown's girlfriend, captioned KELLY MARKS: BLEW THE WHISTLE. So *she* was the source?

The article alleged that Brown had once drunkenly bragged to his girlfriend about the way he had planned and carried out the fraud; he'd blamed it on a disgruntled employee who, it turned out, had false I.D, and who had disappeared after the fire, presumably to evade justice. The police had circulated a photo-fit, but the man had never been traced and was still classified as a missing person. Brown, euphoric after securing some huge property deal, had foolishly boasted to Kelly Marks that not only had the man never existed, but he himself had started the blaze. Two weeks ago she had decided 'after searching her conscience' to reveal this to the *Black & Green*. The article had a quote from Matt saying that, although he couldn't comment on his sources, he stood by every word that his newspaper had printed on the matter.

'How extraordinary,' I breathed.

'What is?' I passed Miles the article and he quickly read it. 'I know about this case,' he said. 'A barrister friend defended the insurance company against Brown's claim. He said he never believed Brown's story, but as

282

it wasn't possible to disprove, Star Alliance were forced to pay up. Brown obviously thought he'd got away with it – and then he was careless.'

'It did cross my mind that it might be his girlfriend.' I told Miles about their unhappy visit to Village Vintage. 'But I dismissed the idea – why *would* she shop him, given that he was her employer as well as her boyfriend?'

Miles shrugged. 'Revenge. Brown was probably two-timing her – that's the usual scenario – or he was trying to dump her and she found out. Or maybe he'd promised her a promotion then given it to someone else. Her motive will come out in the wash.'

I suddenly remembered what Kelly Marks had said when she'd paid for the dress:

It's £275. That was the price.

ELEVEN

This morning I called Mrs Bell.

'I would love to see you, Phoebe,' she said, 'but it will not be possible this week.'

'Is your niece still staying with you?'

'No, but my husband's nephew has invited me to stay with him and his family in Dorset. He is collecting me tomorrow and bringing me back on Friday. I need to go now, while I am still well enough to travel . . .'

'Then can I see you after that?'

'Of course. I will not be going anywhere else,' Mrs Bell said. 'So I would be particularly glad of your company if you have a little time.'

I thought of the Red Cross form still in my bag. 'Could I come on Sunday afternoon?'

'I look forward to it: come at four.'

As I put the phone down I looked at Dan's invitation for his party on Saturday. It gave nothing away, being just an *At Home* card with his address and the time. It didn't even mention his shed, which was obviously something much grander, I reflected; perhaps a summer house or one of those offices in the garden. Maybe it was a games room with a massive billiards table or some fruit machines – or an observatory, with a telescope and a sliding roof. Simple curiosity compelled me to go – combined with the fact that I'd come to enjoy Dan's conversation and his *joie de vivre* and his warmth. I also hoped to be able to ask him about the Phoenix Land story. I still wondered why Brown's girlfriend had done what she'd done.

On Monday there was more about it in the press. Kelly Marks had admitted to the *Independent* that she was the source but, when quizzed about her motive, had refused to comment.

'It was the dress,' Annie said as she looked at the *Black & Green*'s latest piece about it on Tuesday morning. She lowered the paper. 'I told you – vintage clothes can be transforming; I reckon the dress made her do it.'

'What? You mean the dress possessed her and "told" her to shop him?'

'No . . . but I think her intense *desire* for it gave her the strength to dump the man – in spectacular fashion.'

On Thursday the *Mail* ran a piece headed TOP MARKS applauding Kelly for exposing Brown, and citing other women who'd shopped their 'dodgy' boyfriends. The *Express* had a piece about arson-linked fraud, pegged to 'Keith Brown's alleged torching of his own warehouse in 2002'.

'How can the newspapers print all this?' I said to Miles that afternoon. He'd popped into the shop on his way back to Camberwell: as there were no customers he'd stayed for a chat. 'Isn't it prejudicial?' I asked him as he sat on the sofa.

'As criminal proceedings haven't started yet, no.' He got out his BlackBerry, put on his spectacles and began thumbing it. 'For the time being, the papers can repeat the allegations about Brown and print anything else they can justify – like the girlfriend's role in revealing his alleged crime. Once he's been charged, they'll have to watch what they say.'

'And why hasn't he been charged yet?'

Miles looked at me over his glasses. 'Because the insurers and the police are probably arguing about who's going to bring the prosecution – a costly business, obviously. Now, can we please talk about more uplifting matters? On Saturday I'd like to go to the Opera House. They're doing *La Bohème* and there are still a few seats in the stalls, but I'll need to book them today. In fact I could call them right now . . . I've just got the number.' Miles began to dial it then looked at me again, perplexed. 'But you don't seem keen.'

'I am – or rather I would be; it sounds wonderful. But . . . I can't.'

Miles' face had fallen. 'Why not?'

'I'm already doing something.'

'Oh.'

'I'm going to a party – just locally. It's very low key.'

'I see . . . And whose party is it?'

'This friend of mine – Dan.'

Miles was staring at me. 'You've mentioned him before.'

'He works for the local paper. It's a long-standing invitation.'

'You'd rather go to that than to *La Bohème* at the Opera House?'

'It's not that, it's simply that I said I *would* go, and I like to keep my word.'

Miles was looking at me searchingly. 'I hope that he's . . . not more than a friend, is he, Phoebe? I know we haven't been together for very long, but I'd rather know if you have any other . . .'

I shook my head. 'Dan's simply a friend.' I smiled. 'A rather eccentric one, actually.'

Miles stood up. 'Well . . . I'm a bit disappointed.'

'I'm sorry – but it's not as though we'd planned anything for Saturday.'

'That's true. But I just assumed . . .' He sighed. 'It's okay.' He picked up his bag. 'I'll get Roxy to come. I'm taking her to buy her ball gown in the afternoon, so accompanying me to the opera can be the quid pro quo.'

I tried to grasp the notion that being taken to the Royal Opera House would be the 'price' Roxanne paid for her father buying her an incredibly expensive dress . . .

'Perhaps we could do something early next week?' I said to Miles as he stood up. 'Would you like to go to the Festival Hall? Say on Tuesday? I'll get tickets.'

This seemed to reassure him. 'That would be lovely.' He kissed me. 'I'll call you tomorrow.'

Saturday was, as usual, a very busy day, and although I was happy to be doing such a good trade I realised that I could barely manage on my own. After lunch, Katie came in. She saw the Lanvin Castillo dress hanging where the yellow cupcake had been and her face fell. For a moment I thought she was going to cry.

287

'It's okay,' I said quickly. 'I've put it on the Reserved rail.'

'Oh, thanks.' She clapped her hand to her chest. 'I've got £160 now, so I'm more than halfway there. I'm on my break from Costcutters so I thought I'd dash up. I don't know why, but that dress has really *got* to me.'

I was hoping to get away on the dot at five thirty, but at five twenty-five a woman came in and tried on about eight garments, including a trouser suit that I had to get off a mannequin out of the window, before rejecting all of them. 'I'm sorry,' she said as she put on her coat. 'I guess I'm just not in the right mood.' By now, at five past six, neither was I.

'No problem,' I said with as much geniality as I could muster. It doesn't do to be irritable if you run a shop. Then I locked up and went home to get ready for Dan's party. He'd written seven thirty on the invitation with a request that we should be there by eight.

It was almost dark when my cab pulled up outside the house – a Victorian villa in a quiet road close to Hither Green station. Dan had made an effort, I reflected as I paid the driver. He'd threaded fairy lights through the trees in the front garden; he'd hired caterers – an aproned waiter opened the door. As I walked in I could hear talking and laughing. It was quite a select gathering, I now realised as I went into the sitting room where there were a dozen or so people. There was Dan, smartly dressed for once in a dark blue silk jacket, chatting to everyone and topping up champagne glasses.

'Have some of these canapés,' I heard him say. 'We won't be eating until a bit later.' So it was a dinner party. '*Phoebe*,' he exclaimed warmly as he saw me. He planted a kiss on my cheek. 'Come and meet everyone.' Dan quickly introduced me to his friends, one of whom was Matt, and Matt's wife Sylvia; there was Ellie, a reporter from the paper, with her boyfriend, Mike; there were a few of Dan's neighbours and, to my surprise, the rather grumpy woman from the Oxfam shop whose name, I now learned, was Joan.

Joan and I chatted for a bit, and I told her that I'd be getting some handbags from the States that I'd probably be bringing in to her. Then I asked her if she ever got any vintage zips – metal ones – as I was running low on them.

'I did see a batch the other day,' she said. 'And a jar of old buttons, now I think about it.'

'Would you keep them for me then?'

''Course I will.' She sipped her champagne. 'Did you enjoy *Anna Karenina*, by the way?'

'It was wonderful.' I replied then wondered how she knew that I'd gone.

Joan took a canapé from a passing tray. 'Dan took me to see *Dr Zhivago*. Beautiful, it was.'

'Oh.' I glanced at Dan: he was full of surprises – rather nice ones, I reflected. 'Well . . . it's a fabulous film.'

'Fabulous,' Joan echoed. She closed her eyes then opened them again. 'It was the first time I'd been to the pictures for five years – *and* he bought me dinner afterwards.'

'Really? How lovely.' I found myself fighting back tears. 'Did you go to Café Rouge?'

'Oh *no*.' Joan looked shocked. 'He took me to The Rivington.'

'Ah.'

I looked at Dan. Now he was chinking the side of his glass and saying that as everyone was here it was time to get down to the main business of the evening, so would we all kindly go outside.

The back garden was a good size – sixty feet or so – and filling the end of it was a large . . . shed. That's all it was – a shed; except that there was a red carpet leading to it and across the door a red rope suspended between two metal posts. On the wall was some sort of plaque, awaiting its official unveiling, judging by the pair of little gold curtains that covered it.

'I don't know what's *in* that shed,' said Ellie as we walked down the carpet towards it, 'but I *don't* think it's a lawn mower.'

'You're right – it isn't,' said Dan. He clapped his hands. 'Well, thanks to everyone for coming here tonight,' he said as we stood outside it. 'I'm now going to ask Joan to do the honours . . .'

Joan stepped forward and took hold of the curtain cord. As Dan gave her the nod, she turned to us. 'It is my great pleasure to open Dan's shed, which I am delighted to re-name . . .' She pulled on the cord.

The Robinson Rio.

'The Robinson Rio,' said Joan, peering at the plaque. She was clearly as mystified as the rest of us.

Dan opened the door then pressed a light switch. 'Come on in.'

'Amazing,' Sylvia murmured as she stepped inside.

'Blimey,' I heard someone say.

A glittering chandelier hung from the ceiling, above twelve red velvet seats arranged in four rows of three on a swirly patterned red-and-gold carpet. A curtained screen filled the end wall; positioned in front of the near wall was a large, old-fashioned projector. On the right-hand wall was a royal blue board with white plastic letters, announcing THIS WEEK'S PROGRAMME: *Camille* and COMING ATTRACTIONS: *A Matter of Life and Death*. On the left-hand wall was a framed vintage cinema poster for *The Third Man*.

'Sit wherever you like,' Dan said as he fiddled with the projector. 'There's underfloor heating, so it's not cold. *Camille*'s only seventy minutes long, but if you'd rather not see it, then just go back to the house and have another drink. We'll be having dinner when the film finishes just after nine.'

We took our seats – I sat with Joan and Ellie. Dan closed the door and dimmed the lights, then we heard the projector whirr into life, then came the hypnotic clicking of the film as it passed over the sprockets. Now the motorised curtains swished aside to reveal the MGM lion, roaring away, then music, and opening credits, and suddenly we were in nineteenth-century Paris.

'That was *wonderful*,' said Joan as the lights went up again. 'It was like being in the *proper* cinema – I used to love that smell of the projector lamp.'

'It was just like old times,' Matt said from behind us.

Joan turned in her seat and looked at him. 'You're much too young to be saying that.'

'I mean that at school Dan ran the film society,' Matt explained. 'Every Tuesday lunchtime he used to show Laurel and Hardy, Harold Lloyd and Tom and Jerry. I'm glad to say his focusing's improved since then.'

'That was on my old Universal,' Dan said. 'This

projector's a Bell and Howell, but I've rigged up some modern amplification – and put in air conditioning. And I had the shed sound-proofed so that the neighbours don't complain.'

'We're not complaining,' said one of his neighbours. 'We're here!'

'But what are you planning to do with the cinema?' I asked Dan as we all walked back to the house.

'I want to run it as a classic film club,' he replied as we stepped up into the big square kitchen-diner where a long pine table had been laid for twelve. 'I'll do a screening every week and people can turn up on a first-come first-served basis, with a discussion afterwards over a drink for anyone who's interested.'

'Sounds wonderful,' said Mike. 'And where are the films?'

'Stored upstairs in a humidity-controlled room. I've collected a couple of hundred over the years from libraries that were closing down and at auction. I'd always wanted to have my own cinema. In fact, the big shed was one of the main attractions of this house when I bought it two years ago.'

'Where did you get the seats?' Joan asked him as Dan pulled out her chair for her.

'I got them five years ago from an Odeon in Essex that was being pulled down. I've been keeping them in storage. Now . . . Ellie, why don't you sit there? Phoebe, you come here, next to Matt and Sylvia.'

As I sat down Matt poured me a glass of wine. 'I recognised you, of course,' he said, 'from the feature we did about you.'

'That was a very helpful piece,' I said as the caterer

set a plate of delicious-looking risotto in front of me. 'Dan did a wonderful job.'

'He seems a bit chaotic but he's a . . . good man. You're a good man, Dan,' Matt declared with a chuckle.

'Thanks, mate!'

'He is a good man,' Sylvia echoed. 'And do you know who you look like, Dan?' she added. 'I've suddenly realised – Michelangelo's David.'

As Dan blew Sylvia a grateful kiss I saw that it was true. *That* was the 'famous person' I'd been struggling to think of.

'You're a dead ringer for him,' Sylvia went on. She cocked her head to one side. 'A cuddly version anyway,' she added with a laugh.

Dan slapped his rugger-player's chest. 'I'd better get myself down to the gym then. Now, who needs a drink?'

I unfurled my napkin then turned back to Matt. 'The *Black & Green*'s doing . . . extremely well.'

'Beyond our wildest dreams,' Matt replied. 'Thanks to one particular story, obviously.'

I picked up my fork. 'Can you talk about that?'

'As it's all been in the public domain, yes: but the interest from the national press has boosted our circulation to sixteen thousand – which means we're starting to make money – with advertising up by thirty per cent. We would have to have spent a hundred grand on PR to achieve the awareness of the paper that this one story's given us.'

'And how did you get the story?' I asked.

Matt sipped his wine. 'Kelly Marks approached us direct. I knew about Brown from my time at the *Guardian*,' he went on. 'There'd been rumours about him for years. Anyway, there he was, just about to float his company, getting his face in the business press as much as possible, when out of the blue this woman phones me, anonymously, saying that she's got a "good story" about Keith Brown and would I be interested?'

'So you *are* interested,' Sylvia continued. She passed me the bowl of salad then nodded at Matt. 'Tell Phoebe what happened.'

He put down his glass. 'So – this was on a Monday, three weeks ago – I invited the woman to come in.' Matt flicked out his napkin. 'She arrived at lunchtime the next day – I realised that she was his girlfriend, because I'd seen photos of her with Brown. When she told me the story I knew that I wanted to run it – but I told her that there was no way I'd be able to do so unless she was prepared to sign a detailed statement saying that it was true. So she said that she would . . .' Matt picked up his fork. 'And at that point I thought I'd better consult Dan.'

I nodded. Then I wondered why he'd had to consult Dan when it wasn't as though Dan was the assistant editor, or even an experienced journalist, come to that. I glanced at Dan. He was chatting to Joan.

'You could hardly not consult Dan,' I heard Sylvia say. 'As he co-owns the paper!'

I looked at Sylvia. 'I thought that Dan worked for Matt. I thought it was Matt's paper and that he'd hired Dan to do the marketing.'

'Dan does do the marketing,' she replied. 'But Matt didn't hire him.' She seemed to find the idea amusing. 'He approached Dan for financial backing. They each put up fifty per cent of the start-up money, which was half a million.'

'I . . . see.'

'So of course Matt had to have Dan's agreement about the story,' Sylvia added. That was why Dan was in on the discussions with the lawyer, I now realised.

'Dan was as excited about it as I was,' Matt continued as he passed Sylvia the parmesan. 'So then it was a question of getting Kelly's signed statement. I told her we don't pay for stories, but she insisted that she didn't want money. She seemed to be on some sort of moral crusade against Brown even though it turned out that she'd known about the fire for more than a year.'

'So something must have happened to make her angry with him,' Sylvia said.

Matt lowered his fork. 'That's what I assumed. Anyway, she came in and we took her statement. But then, when it came to signing it, she suddenly lowered the pen, looked at me, and said she'd changed her mind – she *did* want money.'

'Oh.'

Matt shook his head. 'My heart *sank*. I thought that she was about to ask us for twenty grand and that this had been her plan all along. And it was on the tip of my tongue to tell her that we were going to have to forget the whole thing when she said, "The price is £275." I was amazed. Then she said it again. "I want £275. That's the price." So I looked at Dan, and he shrugged then nodded. So I opened the petty cash, got out £275, put it in an envelope and handed it to her. She looked as happy as if I *had* given her twenty grand. Then she signed the statement.'

'The envelope was pink,' I said. 'Disney Princess.'

Matt looked at me in surprise. 'It was. Our accountant's

little girl had come into the office with him the day before. She'd brought her writing set with her and as that was the first envelope I saw, I used it because I was in a hurry to close the deal. But how do you *know*?'

I explained that Kelly Marks had come into the shop and bought the lime green prom dress that Brown had refused to buy her a fortnight before. Dan had now joined the conversation. 'I told you about that, didn't I, Dan?' I said. 'About Kelly refusing the discount?'

'You did. I couldn't discuss it with you,' he added, 'but I was sitting there, trying to work it out. I thought, okay, the dress cost £275 and she had asked Matt and me for £275, so there's got to be some connection . . . but I didn't know what.'

'I think I know,' Sylvia said. 'She wanted to end the relationship with Brown but found it hard to do, given that he was also her boss.' Sylvia turned to me. 'You said Brown refused to buy her the dress. Did she seem upset?'

'Extremely,' I replied. 'She was in tears.'

'Well, that was probably the last straw.' Sylvia shrugged. 'So she decided to blow the relationship apart by doing something from which there could be no going back. The denial of the dress triggered the act of revenge.'

I loved it. And he knew that . . .

I looked at Sylvia. 'To me that makes sense. I think the £275 was symbolic. It represented the prom dress – and her freedom – *that's* why she didn't want to pay less for it . . .'

Matt was staring at me. 'Are you saying that we got this story because of one of your frocks?'

Once I'd tried it on . . . the dress claimed me.

I realised that Annie had been right. 'I think I *am* saying that, yes.'

Matt lifted his glass. 'Then here's to your vintage clothes, Phoebe.' He shook his head, then laughed. 'My God, that dress must have *got* to her though.'

I nodded. 'Those ones tend to do that,' I said.

On my way to see Mrs Bell the following afternoon in glorious autumn sunshine I thought about Dan. He'd had several opportunities to tell me that he co-owned the *Black & Green*, but hadn't done so. Perhaps he'd thought it might have seemed boastful. Perhaps he gave little thought to it himself. But now I remembered how he'd said that Matt had needed his 'help' in setting up the paper – financial help, evidently. Yet Dan hadn't given the impression of affluence – the opposite almost, with his Oxfam-shop clothes and his slightly shambling appearance. Perhaps he'd borrowed the money, I reflected, or remortgaged. In which case it was surprising that, having invested so much in the paper, he didn't want to work for it long term. As I turned into The Paragon I wondered what he did want to do long term.

I'd stayed at the party until midnight and as I'd picked up my bag I'd seen that I'd had two missed phone calls from Miles. When I'd got home there'd been another two from him on my answerphone. His tone of voice was casual, but it was clear that he hadn't liked not being able to speak to me.

I went up the steps of number 8 and pressed Mrs Bell's buzzer. There was a longer wait than usual, then I heard the intercom crackle.

'Hello, Phoebe.' I pushed on the door and climbed the staircase.

It had been almost two weeks since I'd seen Mrs Bell. The change in her was so marked that I instinctively put my arms round her. She had said that she would feel reasonably well for the first month and then not so well . . . She was clearly now 'not so well'. She was painfully thin, her pale blue eyes seeming bigger now in her shrunken face, her hands fragile looking with their fan of white bones.

'What lovely flowers,' she said as I handed her the anemones I'd brought her. 'I adore their jewel colours – like stained glass.'

'Shall I put them in a vase?'

'Please. And would you make the tea today?'

'Of course.'

We went into the kitchen and I filled the kettle and got down the cups and saucers and set the tray. 'I hope you haven't been on your own all day,' I said as I found a crystal vase and arranged the flowers in it.

'No – the district nurse came this morning. She comes every day now.'

I put three spoons of Assam into the pot. 'And did you enjoy your stay in Dorset?'

'Very much. It was lovely to spend time with James and his wife. They have a view of the sea from their house, so I spent quite a bit of time just sitting by the window, gazing out at it. Would you mind putting the flowers on the hall table for me?' she added. 'I don't trust myself not to drop them.'

I did so, then carried the tray into the sitting room, Mrs Bell walking in front of me, painfully, as though her back ached. When she sat down in her usual place on the brocade chair she didn't cross her legs, as she usually did, with her hands clasped on her knee. She crossed them at the ankles, leaning back, in a posture of fatigue.

'Please excuse the mess,' she said, nodding at the pile of papers on the table. 'I have been throwing away old letters and bills – the debris of my life,' she added as I put the cup of tea into her hands. 'There is so much.' She nodded at the brimming wastepaper basket next to her chair. 'But it will make things easier for James. By the way, when he collected me last week he drove past Montpelier Vale.'

'So you saw the shop?'

'I did – and two of my outfits were in the window! You have put a fur collar on the gabardine suit. It looks very smart.'

'My assistant Annie thought it would be a nice touch for the autumn. I hope it didn't make you sad to see your things there, on show to the world.'

'On the contrary – it made me feel glad. I found myself trying to picture the women who will own them next.'

I smiled. Then Mrs Bell asked me about Miles and I told her about my visit to his house.

'So he spoils his little princess.'

'He does – to an insane degree,' I confided. 'Roxy is *so* indulged.'

'Well . . . it's better than if he were neglectful.' That was true. 'And he seems to be very keen on you, Phoebe.'

'I'm taking it slowly, Mrs Bell – I've only known him six weeks – and he's nearly fifteen years older than me.'

'I see. Well . . . that puts you at an advantage.'

'I suppose so, though I'm not sure I *want* to be at an advantage with anyone.'

'But his age is not important – all that matters is whether you *like* him, and whether he treats you *well*.'

'I do like him – very much. I find him attractive and, yes, he does treat me well – he's certainly very attentive.' Then we moved the conversation on and I found myself telling Mrs Bell about the Robinson Rio.

'Dan sounds like a joyful sort of man.'

'He is. He has *joie de vivre*.'

'That's a lovely characteristic, in anyone. I'm trying to cultivate a little "*joie de mourir*",' she added with a grim smile. 'It's not easy. But at least I have had time to put everything in order . . .' She nodded at the pile of papers. 'And to see my family and say my *adieux*.'

'Perhaps they're only *au revoirs*,' I suggested, not entirely flippantly.

'Who knows?' said Mrs Bell. A sudden silence descended. Now was the moment. I picked up my bag.

Mrs Bell looked crestfallen. 'You're not going, are you, Phoebe?'

'No. I'm not, but . . . there was something I wanted to talk to you about, Mrs Bell. Maybe it's not appropriate now, given that you're not well . . .' I opened my bag. 'Or maybe that fact makes it even more important.'

She put her cup back in its saucer. 'Phoebe, what are you trying to say?'

I took the envelope out of my bag, removed the Red Cross form and put it on my lap, smoothing it where it had creased. I took a deep breath. 'Mrs Bell, I've been looking at the Red Cross website recently. And I think that if you wanted to try again – to try to find out what happened to Monique, I mean – then you probably could.'

'Oh,' she murmured. 'But . . . *how* could I? I did try.'

'Yes – but that was a very long time ago. And in the meantime *so* much information has been added to the archive that the Red Cross has. On their website it tells you all about it, in particular that in 1989 the Soviet Union handed over to the charity a vast cache of Nazi files that they'd had in their possession since the end of the war.' I looked at her. 'Mrs Bell, when you began your search in 1945, all the Red Cross had was a card index. Now they have nearly fifty million documents relating to hundreds of thousands of people who went into concentration camps.'

Mrs Bell sighed. 'I see.'

'You could request a search. It's submitted on the computer.'

She shook her head. 'I don't *have* a computer.'

'No, but I do. All you'd have to do is fill in a form – I have one here . . .' I handed it to Mrs Bell and she lifted it with both hands, closing one eye as she read it. 'I would e-mail it back to them for you, and it would be sent to their archivists at Bad Arolsen in northern Germany. You would hear within a few weeks.'

'As a few weeks are all I have, that would be just as well,' she commented wryly.

'I know that time . . . is not on your side, Mrs Bell. But I thought that if you *could* know what happened, you'd want to. Wouldn't you?' I held my breath.

Mrs Bell lowered the form. 'But *why* would I want to know, Phoebe? Or rather, why would I want to know *now*? Why would I want to request information about Monique only to read, in some official letter, that she had indeed met the dreadful end that I suspect she did meet? Do you think that would *help* me?' Mrs Bell straightened up in her chair, wincing with pain; then her features relaxed. 'Phoebe – I need to be calm now, to face my last days. I need to lay my regrets to rest, not torture myself about them anew.' She lifted the form up then shook her head. 'This would bring me only turmoil. You *must* realise that, Phoebe.'

'I do – and of course I don't *want* to expose you to turmoil, Mrs Bell, or to any unhappiness.' I felt a constriction in my throat. 'I only want to help you.'

Mrs Bell was staring at me. 'You want to help *me*, Phoebe?' she said. 'Are you sure?'

'Yes. Of course I'm sure.' Why was she asking? 'I think *that's* why I found myself in Rochemare – I don't believe it was purely by chance – I feel that I must have been guided there in some way by Fate, Destiny – whatever you want to call it. And ever since that day I've had this feeling about Monique that I've been unable to shake off.' Mrs Bell was staring at me. 'I've had this overwhelming sense, Mrs Bell, – I can't explain why – that she might have survived; that you only thought she had died because, okay, yes, that's how it looked. But perhaps by some miracle your friend actually *didn't* die, she didn't die, she didn't, she didn't . . .' My head sank to my chest. A sob escaped me.

'Phoebe,' I heard Mrs Bell say quietly. I felt a tear seep into my mouth. 'Phoebe, this isn't *about* Monique, is it?' I stared at my skirt. There was a tiny hole in it. 'It's about Emma.' Now I looked at Mrs Bell. Her features were blurred. 'You're trying to restore Monique to life because Emma died,' she whispered.

'Maybe . . . I don't know.' I inhaled with a teary gasp then looked out of the window. 'I only know that I'm just so . . . sad . . . and confused.'

'Phoebe,' said Mrs Bell gently, 'helping me by "proving" that Monique survived won't change what happened to Emma.'

'No,' I croaked. 'Nothing can change that. Nothing can ever, ever, *ever* change that.' My hands sprang to my face.

'My poor girl,' I heard Mrs Bell murmur. 'What can I say? Only that you will simply have to try and live your life without too much regret for something that cannot be put right – something that was, in any case, probably not your fault.'

I swallowed, painfully, then looked at her. 'It's enough that I feel that it *was*. I'll blame myself forever, I'll always be carrying it. I'm going to have to *lug* this through my life.' The very thought of it made me feel tired. I closed my eyes, aware of the soft gasp of the fire and the steady tick of the clock.

'Phoebe.' I heard Mrs Bell sigh. 'You have a lot of life left to live; probably fifty years – maybe more.' I opened my eyes. 'You are going to have to find some way to live it happily. Or as happily as any of us can. Here . . .' She offered me a tissue and I pressed it to my eyes.

'It doesn't seem possible.'

'Not now,' she said quietly. 'But it will.'

'You never got over what happened to you . . .'

'No, I didn't. But I learned to give it its place, so that it didn't overwhelm me. You still feel overwhelmed, Phoebe.'

I nodded, then gazed out of the window. 'I go to my

shop every day, and I help my customers, and I chat to my assistant, Annie; I do everything that needs to be done. In my spare time I get together with friends; I see Miles. I function – I function well, even. But underneath I'm . . . struggling . . .' My voice trailed away.

'This is not surprising, Phoebe, given that what happened to you took place only a few months ago. And I think this is why you have, yes, fixated on Monique. Out of your own sorrow you have become obsessed with her – as though you believe that by restoring Monique to life, you could somehow restore Emma to life too.'

'But I can't.' I wiped my eyes. 'I can't.'

'So . . . no more of this now, Phoebe. Please. For both our sakes – no more.' Now Mrs Bell picked up the Red Cross form, tore it in half then dropped the pieces into the bin.

TWELVE

Mrs Bell was right, I realised afterwards. I sat in my kitchen for over an hour, just staring down at the table, my face resting in my hands. I *had* become obsessed with Monique – it was an obsession fuelled by my grief and guilt. I felt ashamed now to think that I had stirred up such painful emotions in a frail, elderly woman.

I waited a few days, then, feeling chastened, I went to see Mrs Bell again. This time we didn't talk about Monique or Emma; we chatted about day-to-day things: what was in the news, local events – fireworks night was coming up – and programmes that we'd seen on TV.

'Someone bought your blue silk faille coat,' I said as we began to play Scrabble.

'Really? And who was she?'

'A very pretty model, in her late twenties.'

'It will go to some lovely parties then,' said Mrs Bell as she put her letters on her rack.

'I'm sure it will. I told her that it had danced with Sean Connery – she was thrilled.'

'I hope that *you* will keep at least one of my outfits,' Mrs Bell added.

I hadn't thought of this. 'I do love your gabardine suit. It's still in the window. Perhaps I'll keep that – I think it would fit me.'

'I'd like to think of you wearing it. Oh dear,' she said. 'I have six consonants. What can I do? Ah . . .' She placed some letters on the board with a shaking hand. 'There.' She had made the word *thanks*. 'And is romance still blossoming?'

I counted her points. 'With Miles?'

She looked at me. 'Yes. Who did you think I meant?'

'That's thirty-nine – a good score. I see Miles two or three times a week. Here . . .' I got out my camera and showed Mrs Bell a photo of him that I'd taken in his garden.

She nodded approvingly. 'He's a handsome man. I wonder why he has never married again,' she mused.

'I wondered that too.' I said as I rearranged my letters. 'He said that there had been someone he'd liked, about eight years ago; then last Friday we had dinner at the Michelin and he told me why it hadn't worked out with this woman, Eva – it was because she'd wanted to have children.'

Mrs Bell looked as puzzled as I had done. 'Why would that have been a problem?'

I shrugged. 'Miles wasn't sure that he wanted to have any more. He'd thought it might be too difficult for Roxy.'

Mrs Bell brushed a silvery wisp from her eyes. 'It might equally have been a positive thing for her – perhaps the best thing.'

'I sort of said that . . . But Miles said he'd been worried that it could affect Roxy negatively if there were other children clamouring for his attention when she needed it so much. Her mum had died only two years before.'

I glanced down into the garden as I recalled the conversation.

'I'd been agonising about it all,' Miles had said as we'd had our coffee. 'Time was getting on. Eva was thirty-five and we'd been together for over a year.'

'I see,' I said. 'So it had come to the crunch.'

'Yes. Naturally she wanted to know . . . where things were going. And I simply didn't know what to do.' He lowered his cup. 'So I asked Roxy.'

I looked at Miles. 'You asked Roxy what?'

'I asked her if she'd perhaps like to have a little brother or sister one day. And she looked . . . *stricken*, then she burst into tears. I felt that I was betraying her by even contemplating it and so . . .' He shrugged.

'So you broke it off with Eva?'

'I wanted to protect Roxy from further stress.'

I shook my head. 'Poor girl.'

'Yes – she'd been through so much.'

'I meant *Eva*.' I said quietly.

Miles drew in his breath. 'She was very upset. I heard that she quite quickly met someone else and did have children, but I came to feel . . .' He sighed.

'That you'd made a mistake?'

Miles hesitated. 'I'd done what I'd thought was right for my child . . .'

'Poor girl,' Mrs Bell said when I'd finished telling her this.

'You mean Eva?'

'I mean *Roxy* – that her father gave her so much power. It's so bad for a child's character.'

Elle est son talon d'Achille . . . Perhaps *that* was what Cecile had meant. That Miles had deferred to Roxy too much – allowing her to make decisions that he alone should have made.

I put my letters down. *Chance*. 'That's twelve.'

Mrs Bell passed me the bag. 'Of course I feel sorry for his girlfriend too. But what if *you* wanted to have children, Phoebe?' She pursed her lips. 'I hope that Miles would not seek Roxy's opinion again!'

I shook my head. 'He said that that was why he'd told me about it. He wanted me to know that if I *did* want to have a family, he would have no objections. As he pointed out, Roxy's almost grown up.' I took some more letters. 'But it's too early to be thinking about it, let alone talking about it.'

Mrs Bell looked at me. 'Have children, Phoebe – if you can. Not just for the happiness that children bring, but because I imagine that the busyness of family life leaves little time for dwelling on regrets from the past.'

I nodded. 'I can imagine that's true. Well . . . I'm thirty-four so there's still time . . .' As long as I'm not unlucky, I reflected, like the poor woman who'd bought the pink cupcake dress. 'Your turn again, Mrs Bell.'

'I am going to make peace,' she said with a smile. She stared at her letters then put them down. 'P, E, A, C, and E . . .'

'That's . . . ten points.'

'And tell me, is the shop busy?'

'It's becoming very busy now because of the party

season. Christmas will soon be here,' I added, then blushed at my lack of tact.

Mrs Bell smiled bleakly. 'Well, I don't suppose *I'll* be pulling crackers with anyone. But then . . . who knows?' She shrugged. 'Maybe I will.'

On Tuesday a woman in her mid forties brought in some clothes for me to see.

'It's all lingerie,' she explained as we sat in my office. She opened the small leather suitcase. 'It's never been worn.'

Inside the case were beautiful silk satin nightdresses and *peignoirs* with lace edging; there were pretty corsets and suspender belts. There was a rather regal ice-blue silk long slip with a gathered bust and netting at the hem.

'You could wear that one to a party, couldn't you?' the woman said as I held it up.

'You could. These are lovely things.' I ran my hand over a salmon pink quilted satin bed jacket. 'They're from the mid to late 1940s and are all wonderful quality.' I lifted out a tea rose bias-cut silk slip with lace insets, and two peach-coloured satin bras with matching cami-knickers. 'These are from Rigby & Peller – they hadn't been going very long then.' Most of the garments still had their labels attached and were in perfect condition, except for one or two orange marks on a girdle where the metal of the suspender clips had rusted against the fabric. 'So was this someone's trousseau?'

'Not exactly,' the woman replied. 'Because there wasn't a wedding. They belonged to my mother's sister, Lydia. She died this year, at eighty-six. She was a "maiden aunt" of the old school and a very sweet person. She was a primary school teacher,' the woman went on. 'She never took any interest in fashion – she always wore plain, practical clothes. Anyway, a couple of weeks ago I went down to Plymouth to sort out her house. I looked through her wardrobe, taking most of her things to the charity shop. Then I went up into the attic, where I found this case. When I opened it, I was . . . *amazed*. I could hardly believe that these things had belonged to her.'

'You mean because they're so pretty and . . . sexy?' The woman nodded. 'So was your aunt ever engaged?'

'No, she wasn't, sadly.' The woman sighed. 'I knew that she'd had a disappointment,' she went on. 'But I'd forgotten the details, except that the man was American. So I immediately phoned my mum – she's eighty-three – and she told me that Auntie Lydia had fallen for this GI, Walter, who she'd met at a dance at the Drill Hall in Totnes in the spring of '43. There were thousands of GIs down there, training at Slapton Sands and Torcross for the Normandy landings.'

'So . . . was he killed?'

She shook her head. 'He survived. My mother said that he was a handsome man and very nice – she remembered him mending her bicycle for her and bringing them sweets and nylons. He and Lydia saw a lot of each other, and before he went back to the States he came to see her again and told her that he was going to send for her just as soon as he'd "gotten things ready", as he put it. So Walter went back to Michigan, and they wrote, and in each of his letters he said that he was going to come and collect my aunt "soon" but . . .'

'He never did?'

'No. On it went for three years – these newsy letters arriving with photos of himself, and his parents and his two brothers and the family dog. Then in 1948 he wrote to say that he'd got married.'

I lifted out a white satin 'corselette'. 'And your aunt had been collecting all these things during that time?'

'Yes – for the honeymoon that she would never have. My mum said that she and my grandmother had kept telling her to forget about Walter – but Lydia clung to the belief that he would come. She was so heartbroken that she never looked at anyone else – such a waste.'

I nodded. 'And it's sad to look at these lovely things and to think that your aunt never got any . . . pleasure out of them.' It was easy to imagine the reveries and hopes that had fuelled their purchase. 'And she spent a lot of money on them – and all her clothing coupons too, I should think.'

'She must have done.' The woman sighed. 'Anyway – it's a shame for them not to be worn; hopefully someone else will have a bit of . . . passion in them.'

'Well, I'd love to buy them.' I suggested a price. The woman was happy with it, so I wrote her a cheque then took the things up to the stockroom. As they'd never been worn I left them to air in order to eliminate the faint mustiness that clung to them: as I was putting them on hangers I heard the sound of the bell, then a male voice asking Annie for a signature.

'It's a delivery,' I heard her call out. 'Two enormous boxes – it must be the prom dresses. It is,' she added as I came down the stairs. 'The sender is . . . Rick Diaz – New York.'

311

'He's taken long enough,' I said as Annie scored open the first box with a pair of scissors. She lifted the flaps and pulled out the dresses in turn, the tulle petticoats bouncing out, as though spring-loaded. 'They're gorgeous,' Annie said. 'Look how dense the underskirts are – and what fantastic colours!' She held up the vermillion dress. 'This one's so red it's as though it's on fire – and this indigo one is like the night sky in midsummer. These will *sell*, Phoebe. I'd order some more if I were you.'

I picked up the tangerine one and shook out the creases. 'We'll hang four of them on the wall, as before, and put two in the windows – the red one and the cocoa brown.' Then Annie opened the second box, which, as expected, contained the bags.

'I was right,' I said as I quickly looked through them. 'Most of them aren't vintage – in fact they're pretty second rate. That Louis Vuitton Speedy bag's fake, for a start.'

'How can you tell?'

'From the lining – the real deal has a brown cotton canvas lining, not grey; and the number of stitches along the base of the straps is wrong – there should be exactly five. I don't want *that*,' I said discarding a Saks navy shoulder bag from the mid nineties. 'This black Kenneth Cole one's frumpy, and the beading's gone on this one here . . . So no to that, no, no – and no,' I said as I opened a Birkin-style bag with a Loehmann's discount designer store label in it. 'I'm annoyed I've had to buy these,' I added. 'But I guess I have to keep Rick happy otherwise he might not send me the things I do want.'

'This one's nice,' said Annie, pulling out the 1940s leather Gladstone bag. 'And it's in great condition.'

I examined it. 'It is – it's a bit scuffed, but it'll polish up and . . . oh – *this* is the one I liked.' I pulled out the white ostrich-skin envelope clutch. 'It's very elegant. I might even keep it myself.' I picked it up, tucked it under my arm and looked at my reflection. 'Anyway, I'll put them in the stockroom for now.'

'And what about the yellow cupcake?' Annie asked as she began to hang the new prom dresses on padded hangers. 'It's still on the Reserved rail – what's happening with Katie?'

'I haven't seen her for over a fortnight.'

'When's the ball?'

'In ten days, so there's still time . . .'

But another week passed and Katie still hadn't come in or phoned. By the Wednesday before the ball I was thinking that I ought to contact her. As I heaved a large pumpkin into the window – my only concession to Halloween – I realised that I didn't know her phone number or her surname. I left a message on Costcutters' answerphone asking them if they'd ring her on my behalf, but by the Friday I still hadn't heard; so after lunch, I put the dress back on the wall, alongside the tangerine, purple and kingfisher blue cupcakes – the indigo one having sold.

As I fluffed up its skirts I wondered whether Katie had found a cheaper dress that she liked as much; or whether she was no longer going to the ball. Then I thought of the dress that Roxy would be wearing – it was to be the Christian Lacroix 'stained glass' evening gown from this season's collection, costing £3,600, as featured in *Vogue*.

'That is a *staggering* amount of money,' I'd said to

313

Miles as we sat in my kitchen the day after he'd bought it for her. It was the first time he'd been to my house. I'd cooked a couple of filet steaks and he'd brought a bottle of delicious Chante le Merle. I'd had two glasses and was feeling relaxed. 'Three thousand six hundred pounds,' I'd repeated incredulously.

Miles sipped his wine. 'It *is* a lot of money. But what could I say?'

'How about, "It's too expensive"?' I suggested gaily.

Miles shook his head. 'It's not that easy.'

'Isn't it?' I suddenly wondered if Roxy had ever heard the word 'No'.

Miles lowered his fork. 'Roxy had set her heart on that particular dress – and this is her first real charity ball. There's going to be media coverage of it, and she thinks she might be photographed. Plus they're having a Best-Dressed Guest prize, so she's feeling a bit competitive about the whole thing, and so . . .' he sighed, 'I said she could have it.'

'Doesn't she have to *do* anything in return?'

'What – like wash the car or pull up weeds?'

'Yes. That sort of thing – or just work extra hard at school?'

'I don't operate like that,' Miles said. 'Roxy knows how much it cost and she's grateful to me for buying it – I feel that's enough. And the school fees are a lot less now that she's not boarding, so I don't actually begrudge it. And I was prepared to spend quite a lot at Christie's, remember?'

I rolled my eyes. 'How could I forget?' As I gave Miles some salad I thought of the wonderful column of white silk jersey with its chiffon trains and wondered whether I'd ever wear it. 'But don't you want Roxy to feel that

314

she's *earned* the dress – or at least contributed something towards it?'

Miles shrugged again. 'Not particularly. No. What's the point?'

'Well . . . I suppose the point is . . .' I sipped my wine '. . . you're letting everything drop into Roxy's lap – without any effort from her. As though the things she wants are simply hers for the taking.'

Miles was staring at me. 'What the hell do you mean by that?'

I flinched at his tone. 'I meant that . . . children need an incentive. That's all.'

'Oh.' Miles' face had relaxed. 'Yes. Of course . . .' Then I told him about Katie and the yellow prom dress.

He sipped his wine. 'So *that's* what's prompted this lecture, is it?'

'It probably is. I think what Katie's doing is admirable.'

'It *is*. But Roxy's in a different situation. I don't feel guilty about spending this much on her because I . . . *can* and because I give generously to charity, so I'm not entirely selfish in how I spend my money. But it's my right to dispose of what the taxman leaves me in the way I choose – and I choose to spend it largely on my family – and that means Roxy.'

'Well . . .' I shrugged. 'She's your child.'

Miles fiddled with his wine glass. 'She is. And I've parented her alone for ten years – and that's no easy task, and I hate it when other people tell me that I'm getting it wrong.'

So others had noticed Miles' indulgent parenting of Roxy, I reflected as I walked up to the shop on Saturday morning. But then it was impossible not to notice. As I unlocked the door I wondered whether, if Miles and I ever had a baby, he'd be the same with that child too. I wouldn't let him be, I decided. Then I found myself wondering what our family life would be like. Presumably Roxy's attitude towards me would soften over time, and if it didn't . . . She's sixteen, I told myself as I took off my coat. She'll soon be making her own way in the world.

As I turned over the 'Closed' sign I wished I had someone to help me as Saturday is always my busiest day. I'd talked to Annie about it but she said she preferred not to work at weekends as she usually went down to Brighton. I'd dismissed the idea of asking Mum if she'd help out as she's not interested in vintage, plus she works full time and needs to relax.

I had eight customers in the first hour alone. The purple prom dress sold, and a Burberry trench from the menswear rail; then a man came in looking for a present for his wife and ended up buying a few pieces of Aunt Lydia's lingerie. After that there was a lull, so I leaned against the counter and took a moment to enjoy the view of the Heath. There were children cycling and scooting; there were people jogging, pushing prams and flying kites. I gazed at the sky with its cloudscape of massive white cumulus and lowering nimbus, with wisps of cirrus far, far above. As I craned my neck I could see planes glinting in the sun as they stitched their trails across the blue. Lower down, a vast underlit cloud with curiously smooth sides seemed to hover over the Heath like a spaceship. Now I imagined the fireworks that would fill this sky a week hence. I love the Blackheath display and it would be nice to be there with Miles. Suddenly I heard the tinkle of the bell.

It was Katie. She blushed as she came in, then she glanced at the wall and saw the yellow dress hanging there, flanked by the new prom dresses. 'So you've put it back,' she said despondently.

'Yes – I couldn't hold it for any longer.'

'I understand – and I'm *really* sorry.'

'So . . . you don't want it then?'

She sighed with frustration. 'I *do*. But I had my mobile phone stolen last week and Mum said that I'd have to pay for the new one as I'd been careless. Then I had two babysitting bookings cancelled because the wife had forgotten that it was half-term, so they've gone away; and I've been laid off at Costcutters as I was only covering for someone. So I'm afraid I can't buy the dress as I'm £100 short.' She shrugged. 'I'd been putting off telling you because I hoped something would turn up.'

'That's a shame – but what will you wear instead?'

Katie shrugged. 'I don't know. There's a ball dress I've had for ages.' She grimaced. 'It's apple green polyester moiré.'

'Oh. It sounds . . .'

'Hideous? It is – it should have a matching sick bag to go with it. I might run up to Next and get something, but I've left it all a bit late. I'm probably not going to *go* to the ball.' She rolled her eyes. 'It's just . . . too difficult.'

'Is there anything else here, a bit cheaper, that you might like?'

'Well . . . possibly.' Katie riffled through the evening-wear rail, then shook her head. 'I can't see anything.'

'So you've earned £175?' She nodded. I looked at the dress. 'Do you *really* want it?'

Katie gazed at it. 'I adore it. I dream about it. The worst thing about losing my mobile was losing the photo I'd taken of it.'

'That answers my question. Look – you can have it for £175.'

'*Really?*' Happiness had lifted Katie on to her toes. 'But surely you could sell it at full price.'

'I could. But I'd much rather sell it to you – as long as you genuinely want it. That's still quite a bit of money – to most sixteen-year-olds at least – so you've got to be sure.'

'I *am* sure,' Katie said.

'Do you want to ring your mum first?' I nodded at the phone on the counter.

'No. She thinks it's lovely too – I showed her the photo. She said she couldn't buy it for me, but she did give me £30 towards it, which was decent of her.'

'Right.' I took it down. 'It's yours.'

Katie clapped her hands. '*Thanks.*' Then she opened her bag and took out her Maestro card.

'What about shoes?' I asked as she put in her pin code.

'Mum's got a pair of yellow leather sling-backs and I've a necklace made of yellow glass flowers – and I've got some sparkly hair slides.'

'That sounds perfect. Have you got a wrap?'

'I haven't, no.'

'Just a moment.' I went and got a lemony silk organza evening stole with silver threads running through it and held it to the dress. 'This will work – but if you could let me have it back afterwards.'

'Of course I will. Thank you.'

I folded the stole into the bag with the cupcake then handed it to Katie. 'Enjoy the dress – and the ball . . .'

'A scary evening last night for the dinosaurs at London's Natural History Museum,' the Sky News presenter announced the following morning. Miles had the kitchen TV on and we'd been half watching it over breakfast. 'A thousand teenagers descended on the museum for the Butterfly Ball, in aid of the Teenage Leukaemia Trust. The black-tie event was sponsored by Chrysalis, hosted by the ever youthful Ant and Dec, and the revellers, who included Princess Beatrice' – now we saw Princess Beatrice smiling at the camera as she swept into the museum in an orchid pink silk gown – 'enjoyed champagne and canapés, danced to tribute band the Bootleg Beatles, and were entertained by the cast of the stage production of *High School Musical*. iPhones, digital cameras and designer goods were raffled, along with a trip to New York to include tickets to the US premiere of *Quantum of Solace*. A total of £65,000 was raised.'

'I wonder if we'll see Roxy,' Miles said as we stared at the screen.

She was still in bed, recovering. She'd been dropped off by a friend's mother just before one. Miles had waited up, but I'd gone to bed.

'Did you tell Roxy that I'd be here?' I asked Miles as I spread marmalade on my toast. 'You said you would,' I added anxiously.

'I'm afraid I didn't. She was a bit the worse for wear, so she just crashed.'

'I hope she'll be okay about it.'

319

'Oh . . . I'm sure she will.'

Suddenly Roxy appeared in her dove grey cashmere dressing gown and pink bunny slippers. My knees began to tremble so I pressed them against the underside of the table. Then I reminded myself that I was twice her age.

'Hi, sweetheart.' Miles smiled at Roxy, who was looking at me with an expression of insolent, studied puzzlement. 'You remember Phoebe, don't you, darling?'

'Hi, Roxy.' My heart was thudding with apprehension. 'So how was the ball?'

She went over to the fridge. 'All right.'

'I know some kids who went to it,' I said.

'How fascinating,' she replied as she got out the orange juice.

'Were many of your friends there?' Miles asked as he passed her a glass.

'Yeah – a few.' She heaved herself wearily on to a stool at the breakfast bar and poured herself some juice. 'Sienna Fenwick, Lucy Coutts, Ivo Smythson, Izzy Halford, Milo Debenham, Tiggy Thornton . . . oh, and good old Caspar – von Schellenberg, that is, not von Eulenberg.' She yawned, cavernously. 'I met Peaches Geldof in the loo. She's really cool.' Roxy took a piece of toast from the rack.

'And was Clara there?' Miles asked.

Roxy picked up her knife. 'She was. I cut her dead. The bitch,' she added casually as she spread butter on her toast.

Miles sighed. 'But apart from that, you had a wonderful time?'

'Yes. I did – until some idiot ruined my dress.'

320

'Some idiot ruined your dress?' I repeated idiotically.
Roxy gave me a level stare. 'That's what I just said.'

'*Roxanne* . . .' My heart leapt. Miles was about to
rebuke Roxy for her rudeness – and about time. 'That
dress was *so* expensive. You shouldn't have let that
happen, darling.' I felt my spirits sink.

Roxy bristled. 'It wasn't *my* fault. This stupid girl
stepped on it as everyone went upstairs for the judging
of Best-Dressed Guest. Having a rip in the back of my
gown didn't exactly help.'

'I could get that repaired for you,' I said. 'If you show
it to me.'

She shrugged. 'I'll get it sent back to Lacroix.'

'That'll cost a lot. I'd be happy to take it to my seamstress for you – she's brilliant.'

'Can we play tennis, Dad?' Roxy said.

'Or I could even mend it myself – if it's a straightforward matter.'

'I really want to play tennis.' She took another piece
of toast from the rack.

'Have you done your prep?' Miles asked her.

'You know it's been half-term, Dad – I haven't had
any.'

'But I thought you had a geography essay to write.
That one you should have done before half-term started.'

'Oh yes . . .' Roxy tucked a hank of sleep-tousled
blonde hair behind her ear. 'That won't take me long –
maybe you could help me.'

He sighed with an air of exaggerated tolerance. 'All
right – and then we'll play.' He looked at me. 'Why don't
you join us, Phoebe?'

Roxy snapped the toast in half. 'Tennis doesn't work

with three.' I looked at Miles, waiting for him to rebuke Roxy but he didn't. I bit my lip. 'Plus I want to practise my serve, so I need you to hit balls to me, Dad.'

'Phoebe?' said Miles. 'Would you like to play?'

'It's okay,' I said quietly. 'I think I'll get back. I've got lots to do.'

'Are you sure?' Miles said.

'Yes. Thanks.' I picked up my bag. One step at a time. It was enough that Roxy knew I'd stayed in the house . . .

On Monday morning I asked Annie to nip up to the bank to get some cash for the till. She came back holding a copy of the *Evening Standard*. 'Have you seen this?'

In the centre pages was a big spread about the ball with a photo of the Best-Dressed Guest – a girl in a kind of futurist crinoline that she'd made herself, using overlapping circles of silver leather – it was beautiful. There was also a group photo of two boys and two girls, one of whom was Katie. She was quoted as saying that her prom dress came from *Village Vintage, in Blackheath, where you can get glorious vintage dresses at affordable prices.*

'Thank you Katie!'

Annie was smiling. 'It's fantastic PR. So she *did* go to the ball, then.'

'She nearly didn't.' I told Annie what had happened.

'Well, you just got your £100 back, Phoebe – with interest,' she added as she put her jacket in the office. 'Now, is there anything happening today that I need to know about?'

'I'm going to look at a collection of clothes in

Sydenham. The woman's retiring to Spain and is getting rid of most of her stuff. I'll be out for two hours . . .'

In the event it was nearly four hours because I couldn't get Mrs Price – a superannuated sixty-something in animal prints – to stop talking. She gabbled away while she pulled out garment after garment, explaining in minute detail where her first husband had bought her this and her third husband had bought her that and why her second husband hadn't been able to bear seeing her in the other and what a nuisance men were when it came to clothes.

'You should have worn what *you* liked,' I said teasingly.

'If only it had been that easy.' She sighed. 'But now I'm getting divorced again, I *will*.'

I bought ten garments including two very pretty cocktail dresses by Oscar de la Renta and a Nina Ricci ball gown of black silk with white silk roses at the shoulder, and an ivory crepe gown with scalloped edging made by Marc Bohan for Dior. I gave Mrs Price a cheque and arranged to collect the clothes in a week's time.

As I drove back to Blackheath I worried about whether or not I'd have enough space to store them – the stockroom walls had developed a bulge.

'You can get rid of those bags you bought from Rick,' Annie said when I discussed the problem with her.

'That's true.'

I went upstairs and found the box with Rick's bags in it and took out the ten that I didn't want, removing a propelling pencil from the Saks bag and some Neiman Marcus receipts from the fake Louis Vuitton Speedy. I looked inside the Kenneth Cole bag and wasn't sure that

I could even give it to Oxfam because the lining had been badly stained by a leaking pen. I put these bags into three large carriers then looked at the two that I intended to keep.

I took out the Gladstone bag. That could go in the shop straight away. The leather was a lovely cognac colour, a little scratched around the feet, but not too noticeable. I gave it a quick polish then turned to the white ostrich-skin envelope clutch. It had an elegant simplicity and the surface was pristine – it had had very light use. Now I checked that the fastener worked properly, but as I lifted the flap I saw that something was inside the bag – a leaflet, or rather a programme for something. I pulled it out and unfolded it. It was for a recital of chamber music, given on May 15th, 1975, by the Grazioso String Quartet at the Massey Hall in Toronto. So the bag had come originally from Canada: and the reason why it was in such good condition was that it clearly hadn't been used since that night.

The programme was printed very simply in black and white. On the front was an abstract design of the four instruments. On the back was a group photo of the players – three men and one woman, who looked to be in their late thirties to mid forties. I read that they had played Delius and Szymanowksi in the first half of the concert, and after the interval, Mendelssohn and Bruch. There was a paragraph about the group, saying that they'd been playing together since 1954 and that this recital was part of a national tour. Now I turned to the inside back cover where there were biographies of the players. I read their names – Reuben Keller, Jim Cresswell, Hector Levine and Miriam Lipietzka . . .

It was as though the air had been squeezed out of my lungs.

Her name was Miriam. Miriam . . . Lipietzka. It has just come back to me.

Now I was breathing again, fast, as I examined the face that went with this name – she was a dark-haired, slightly severe-looking woman in her mid forties. This concert had taken place in 1975; so she would now be . . . eighty. As I read the biography, the programme shook in my hands.

Miriam Lipietzka (first violin) trained at the Conservatoire of Music in Montreal from 1946–49, where she studied under Joachim Sicotte. She then spent five years with the Montreal Symphony Orchestra before co-founding the Grazioso Quartet with her husband, Hector Levine (cello). Miss Lipietzka gives regular recitals and master classes at the University of Toronto where the Grazioso String Quartet is in residence.

I almost fell down the stairs in my haste.

'Careful,' said Annie. 'Are you okay?' she added as I rushed past her to get to the computer.

'I'm . . . fine. I'm going to be busy for a while.' I closed the door, sat down and typed *Miriam Lipietzka + violin* into Google.

It *must* be her, I thought to myself as it loaded the results. 'Hurry *up*,' I moaned at the screen. Now there were all the references to Miriam Lipietzka, linking her to the Grazioso String Quartet, to reviews of their concerts in Canadian newspapers, to recordings that they'd made, and to names of young violinists that she had taught. But I needed a more detailed biography of her. I clicked on the link to the *Encyclopaedia of Music in Canada*. Up came her page. My eyes devoured the words.

> *Miriam Lipietzka, distinguished violinist, violin teacher and founder of the Grazioso Quartet. Lipietzka was born in the Ukraine on July 18th, 1929 ...*

It *was* her. There could be no doubt.

> *She moved to Paris with her family in 1933. She emigrated to Canada in October 1945, where she was discovered by Joachim Sicotte, whose protégée she became ... scholarship to the Montreal Conservatoire ... five years with the MSO, with whom she went on national and international tours. The performances of Miss Lipietzka's life, however, must surely have been during the war, when, as a girl of thirteen she played in the Auschwitz Women's Orchestra.*

'Oh.'

> *Lipietzka was one of the youngest members of that orchestra, whose forty members included Anita Lasker-Wallfisch and Fania Fénelon, playing under the baton of Gustav Mahler's niece, Alma Rosé.*

So she was the same person, and she was clearly alive, because the entry didn't say otherwise and it had recently been updated. But how could I *contact* her? I looked at the Google results again. The Grazioso Quartet had made a recording of Beethoven's late quartets with the Delos label – perhaps I could find her through that. But when I looked it up I saw that the label had long since folded. So now I clicked on the University of Toronto website then went to their music faculty. I dialled the phone number given on their 'Contact Us' page. It rang five times then picked up.

'Good morning – Faculty of Music, Carol speaking, how may I help you?'

Almost incoherent with apprehension, I explained that I wanted to get in touch with the violinist, Miriam Lipietzka. I said that I knew that she'd taught at the university in the mid seventies, but that I had no other information about her. I hoped that the university would be able to help.

'Well, I'm new here,' Carol said. 'So I'm going to have to make further enquiries about this and get back to you. May I have your number?'

I gave it to her, together with my mobile number. 'When do you think you'll be able to call me?'

'Just as soon as I can.'

As I put down the phone I felt sure that someone there would know Miriam. She was probably just a few phone calls away. She and Monique were probably both in Auschwitz at the same time, I reasoned. They might have been in touch with each other in the camp and after-wards – if there *had* been an afterwards for Monique.

The sense that I was being compelled to find out what had happened to her now returned to me with renewed force. Perhaps what I'd felt *hadn't* been an obsession. Fate had led me down a wrong turning to Rochemare.

Now Fate had again brought me close to Monique, via a concert programme that had lain in a small white handbag for thirty-five years. I couldn't shake off the feeling that I was somehow being guided towards her.

I gave an involuntary shiver.

'Are you all right, Phoebe?' I heard Annie ask. 'You seem a bit . . . het up today. Not your usual calm self.'

'I'm fine, thanks, Annie.' I longed to confide in her. 'I'm . . . fine.' I tried to distract myself by answering enquiries from the website. By now it was 5 p.m. – an hour since I'd spoken to Carol.

Suddenly the bell over the door rang and there was Katie, in her school uniform.

'Great photo of you in the *Standard*,' Annie exclaimed.

'And a terrific plug for the shop,' I added. '*Thank* you.'

'It was the least I could do – plus what I said is true.' Katie opened her rucksack and took out a carrier bag. 'Anyway, I just wanted to return this.' She took out the yellow stole, neatly folded.

'Keep it,' I said, still semi-euphoric with the events of the last hour. 'Enjoy it.'

'Really?' Katie looked at me wonderingly. 'Well . . . thank you – again. I'm going to have to start calling you "fairy godmother",' she added as she put the stole back in her bag.

'So how *was* the ball?' Annie asked.

'It was wonderful. Except for one thing.' Katie grimaced. 'I managed to wreck someone's dress.'

'What happened?' I asked, imagining a jogged elbow and a slew of red wine.

'It wasn't really my fault,' she replied wearily. 'I was going up the stairs and I was right behind this girl – she was wearing this multi-coloured silk gown with these chiffon trains floating off it – it was stunning. Anyway she suddenly stopped *dead* to talk to someone and I must have caught her hem with my foot, because when she moved off again there was this loud rip.'

'Oops!' said Annie.

'I was mortified, but before I could even say "sorry" she'd started yelling at me.' I felt my insides coil. 'She said that her dress was this season's Christian Lacroix and that it had cost her father three and a half grand and that I was going to have to pay to have it fixed – if it *could* be fixed.'

'I'm sure it could be,' I said. I wasn't going to let on that I knew the gown's owner and had in fact seen the damage – Miles had shown it to me – and that I'd been able to repair it myself.

Katie pursed her lips. 'Then she stomped off and I managed to avoid her for the rest of the night. Apart from *that,* it was a fairytale – so thanks, Phoebe. But I'll pop in again sometime – I just love looking at the clothes. Maybe I could help you,' she added.

'What?'

'If you ever need a hand with anything, just call me.' She scribbled her mobile number on a piece of paper and gave it to me.

I smiled. 'I might take you up on that.'

'It's almost five thirty,' said Annie. 'Shall I cash up?'

'Please – and if you could turn over the sign.' The phone was ringing. 'I'll take that call in the office.' I closed the door, then picked up. 'Village Vintage,' I said anxiously.

'This is Carol from the University of Toronto Music Faculty. Is that Phoebe?'

My pulse began to race. 'Yes, it is. Thanks for calling back.'

'I have some information about Ms Lipietzka.' Adrenaline scorched through my veins. 'I'm told that she hasn't worked here since the late 1980s. But there's someone in the department who's in close touch with her – a former pupil of hers, Luke Kramer. However he's on paternity leave right now.'

My heart sank. 'Is he taking any calls?'

'No. He's asked not to be contacted.' I let out a sigh of frustration. 'But if he happens to phone in, I'll tell him about your enquiry. In the meantime, I'm afraid you'll just have to wait. He'll be back on Monday.'

'And there's no one else who . . .?'

'No. I'm sorry. As I say, you'll just have to wait.'

THIRTEEN

As I walked up to Oxfam the next morning with the unwanted bags, I berated myself for not having looked through them straight away. Had I done so I wouldn't have missed Luke Kramer. I wondered how I'd be able to wait for a week.

'Hullo, Phoebe,' said Joan as I pushed on the door. She lowered her copy of the *Black & Green*. 'Have you got some things for us there?'

'Yes – some not particularly wonderful bags.'

'Pre-loved,' she said as I handed them to her in their carriers. 'That's what we're supposed to say here now – not second-hand. Pre-loved.' She rolled her eyes. 'Still, I suppose it's better than "cast-off", isn't it? Do you still want those zips and buttons?'

'Please.'

Joan rummaged under the counter and found them – a dozen metal zips in various colours and a large jar of assorted buttons. At the bottom I could see little aeroplane buttons and teddy bears and ladybirds – they

331

reminded me of the cardigans Mum used to knit for me when I was little.

'You missed a good film on Thursday,' Joan said. 'That's £4.50.' I opened my bag. '*Key Largo*. 1948, Bogart and Bacall – a noirish melodrama in which a returning war veteran fights gangsters on the Florida Keys. We had a good chat about it afterwards with reference of course to *To Have and Have Not*, with its mood of post-war despair. I think Dan was hoping you'd come along,' Joan added as I gave her a ten-pound note.

'I will another time. I've been . . . preoccupied lately.'

'Got a lot on your mind?' I nodded. 'Dan too. The paper's sponsoring the hot-dogs stand at the fireworks on Saturday so he's got to find forty thousand sausages. Will you be going?'

'Yes – I'm looking forward to it.'

Joan had put her *Black & Green* down on the counter. I glanced at it; on the front was a piece about the firework display and at the bottom of page 2 was a boxed piece announcing that the paper's circulation had hit twenty thousand – double what it had been at launch. I was happy to think that I'd played my part in this success, however obliquely; after all, the *Black & Green* had helped me. If it hadn't been for Dan's interview I wouldn't have met Mrs Bell, and I felt that her friendship was taking me somewhere . . . that mattered. I didn't know where. I just felt this constant, inexorable pull.

On Friday evening I went to see her. She looked so frail, and kept her hand protectively over her tummy, which was visibly swollen.

'Have you had a good week, Phoebe?' she asked. Mrs Bell's voice was noticeably weaker now. I gazed down into the garden where the trees were shedding their leaves in slow, diagonal drifts. The weeping willow was yellow and sere.

'It's been an interesting one,' I replied, though I didn't tell her about finding the programme. As Mrs Bell had said, she needed to be calm.

'And are you going to the fireworks?'

'Yes – with Miles. I'm looking forward to it. I hope the noise won't bother you too much.' I added as I poured the tea.

'No. I love to see fireworks. I'll be watching them from my bedroom window.' She sighed. 'I suppose it will be the last time . . .'

Then Mrs Bell seemed suddenly to tire, so now I did most of the chatting. I found myself telling her about Annie, and about her acting, and about how she hoped to write a play of her own to perform. Then I told Mrs Bell about the ball and about Roxy's dress. Mrs Bell's pale blue eyes widened in amazement and she shook her head. Then I told her about Katie stepping on it. Mrs Bell's face creased with horrified laughter, then she winced.

'Don't laugh if it hurts.' I laid my hand on hers.

'That was worth the pain,' she said quietly. 'I have to confess that I'm not terribly enamoured of this girl, from what I know of her so far.'

'Well, Roxy isn't easy – in fact she's bloody difficult,' I suddenly said, happy to vent some of my negative emotion. 'She's *so* rude to me, Mrs Bell. I was at Miles' house again last night and every time I spoke to Roxy,

333

she completely ignored me – and if I spoke to *him* she'd start talking across me, as though I wasn't there.'

Mrs Bell shifted painfully. 'I hope that Miles rebuked her for this . . . impolite behaviour.' I heaved a painful sigh. 'Did he?' she added, peering at me.

'Not really . . . He said it would have led to a row and he hates having rows with Roxy – it upsets him for days.'

'I see.' Mrs Bell folded her hands. 'Then I'm afraid it is you who will be upset.'

I chewed on my lower lip. 'It *is* a bit hard – but I'm sure things with Roxy will improve. After all, she's only sixteen, isn't she – and it's been just her and her dad all this time, so I guess it's bound to be a bit awkward to begin with. Isn't it?'

'I imagine that's just what Miles says.'

'It is, actually.' I heaved a sigh. 'He says that I should feel "compassion" for Roxy.'

'Well . . .' said Mrs Bell quietly. 'Given the way she's been brought up, you probably should.'

On Saturday morning I phoned Miles in between customers to discuss the fireworks. 'The display's at eight, so what time will you get to me?' Through the shop window I could see the barriers being put up and refreshment tents being pitched; in the distance an edifice of planks and old furniture was being raised up for the bonfire.

'We'll come to you at about seven fifteen,' I heard Miles say. So Roxy would be coming. 'Is it okay if Roxy brings her friend Allegra?'

'Of course it is.' In fact, it would make it easier, I

reflected. 'You won't be able to drive,' I added. 'The roads around the Heath will be closed off.'

'I know,' said Miles. 'We'll take the train.'

'I'll make something for us to eat and drink then we'll walk up to the Heath.'

When I got home at the end of the day I found a message from Dad reminding me about Louis' birthday on November 24th. 'I thought we could play with him in Hyde Park and then have lunch somewhere. Just you, me and Louis,' Dad had added tactfully. 'Ruth will be filming in Suffolk that day.'

I turned on Radio 4 for the *Six o'Clock News*. They had yet another report on the banking crisis. Suddenly I heard Guy being introduced. I hit the 'off' button. Hearing him would be like having him in the room.

I put the canapés I'd bought on the way back into a low oven while I got ready. At ten past seven Miles phoned. Allegra couldn't come after all, so Roxy didn't want to come either. 'Which gives *me* a bit of a problem,' he added.

'But why? Roxy's sixteen – if she doesn't want to come, surely she can stay at home for a couple of hours?'

'She says she doesn't want to *be* on her own.'

'Then she has to come to Blackheath with you – because that's where you've arranged to be.'

I heard Miles sigh. 'She's not easy to persuade. I've been trying.'

'Miles, I've been looking forward to this evening.'

'I know . . . Look, I'll make her come with me – we'll see you later.'

By seven forty they still hadn't arrived. So I called Miles and told him that if they hadn't arrived by ten to eight, I'd walk up to Village Vintage and they could meet me there. At five to eight, feeling despondent now, I put on my coat and joined the latecomers hurrying towards the Heath.

As we walked up Tranquil Vale we could see the laser beams raking the sky and the apricot glow of the fire. As I leaned against the shop, the music that had been ringing across the Heath from the fun fair was drowned out by the sound of the vast crowd counting down.

'Four . . . Three . . . Two . . . *One* . . .'

WHOOSH!! BOOM!! KER-*ACK*!!

The rockets exploded against the night like gigantic, incandescent blooms. *Why* did Roxy always have to be such a pain – and why did Miles have to be so weak?

BANG!!! BANG-A-BANG!!! *BANG!!!* As more chrysanthemums flowered and shimmered, I thought of Mrs Bell, watching from her window.

PHUT . . . PHUT . . . PHUT . . . Up went the Roman candles, like distress flares, trailing an iridescence of pink and green.

RACK-A-TACK-A-TACK!! BOOM!!! Silvery fountains cascaded overhead, showering sparkles that turned blue, green and gold.

Suddenly I felt my phone vibrate. I put in my earpiece then covered my other ear with my hand.

'I'm sorry, Phoebe,' I heard Miles say.

I bit my lip. 'I assume you're not coming.'

'Roxy threw a huge strop. I tried to get her to come, but she refused. *Now* she's saying that I can go on my own if I want to, but I guess it's too late.'

ZIP!!! ZIP!!!! WHEEEEEEE . . . Little white rockets

were spiralling in all directions, screaming and whistling. There was an acrid scent in the air.

'It *is* too late,' I said coldly. 'You've missed it.' I shut the phone.

BOOOM!! RACK-A-TACK-A-RACK!!! BOOOO-OOM!!

There was a final supernova explosion; its Technicolor embers trembled then faded: the sky was clear except for drifts of pale smoke.

I didn't just want to turn round and go home, so I crossed the road and plunged into the heaving crowd, passing children waving light sabres and fizzing sparklers.

A few seconds later Miles phoned again. 'I'm sorry about tonight, Phoebe,' I heard him say. 'I didn't mean to disappoint you.'

I shivered in the cold. 'Well, you *did* disappoint me.'

'It was very difficult.'

'Really?' There was the scent of frying onions. To my right I could just see the green-and-black logo of the *Black & Green* emblazoned across a floodlit hospitality tent. 'Anyway, I'm going to go and talk to my friend Dan.' I ended the call then wove through the crowd. If Miles felt he was being punished, then fine.

I felt the phone vibrate again. Reluctantly, I answered. 'Please don't be like this,' Miles said. 'It wasn't my fault. Roxy can be very challenging at times.'

'Challenging?' I fought the urge to tell him how she could more accurately be described.

'Teenagers are extremely egocentric,' Miles added. 'They think the world revolves around them.'

'They're not *all* like that, Miles.' I thought of Katie.

'Roxy should have done what *you* wanted tonight – God knows, you do enough for her. A week ago she was wearing a dress that had cost you three and a half *grand*.'

'Well . . . yes.' I heard him sigh. 'That's true.'

'A dress that I kindly mended for her!'

'Look – I know, and I'm sorry, Phoebe.'

'Anyway, can we please leave it now?' I didn't want to be seen having a row in public. I pressed the 'end call' button then put up my hood against the thickening rain.

As I drew nearer to the huge tent I could see caterers in smart *Green & Black* aprons making hot dogs, aided by Sylvia, Ellie, Matt and Dan, who was squishing on the ketchup. I found myself wondering what colour it looked to him – green, presumably. He saw me, and waved. He looked so big and solid and friendly and comforting that I found myself suddenly aching for one of his hugs. I stood to the side of the queue so that I could chat to him.

Dan peered at me. 'Are you all right, Phoebe?'

'Yes . . . I'm fine.'

He squiggled some more ketchup on to a hot dog then handed it to the next customer. 'You seem . . . upset.'

'Not . . . really.'

'Look, let's go for a drink?' He nodded at the beer tent.

'You're too busy, Dan,' I protested. 'You don't have time.'

'I do for you, Phoebe.' He protested. 'Here, Ellie.' He handed Ellie the ketchup bottle. 'You're on squeezing duty now sweetheart. Come on, Phoebe.'

As Dan untied his apron I could feel my phone vibrate. I put in my earpiece. It was Miles again, sounding despondent. 'Look, I've said how sorry I am, Phoebe, so please don't punish me.'

'I'm not,' I whispered into the mouthpiece as Dan stepped out of the tent. 'I just don't feel like talking to you at the moment so please don't ring again.' I pressed the red button.

Dan had taken me by the hand and was pulling me through the still heaving crowd, to the beer tent. 'What do you feel like?'

'Well . . . a Stella – but look, let *me* get them.' But Dan was already standing at the bar, and now he was coming back with the bottles and by some miracle someone vacated the table nearest us and we were able to sit down.

Dan pulled out his chair and looked at me. 'So . . . what's with you then?'

'Nothing.' I sighed. Dan was looking at me sceptically. 'Okay . . . I was supposed to meet my . . . friend here, with his daughter. I'd been looking forward to it, but then she refused to come so he didn't come either, even though she's sixteen and could have stayed at home.'

'Oh dear – so that's spoiled things then?' I nodded. 'But why wouldn't she come?'

'Because she likes ruining our dates, and her dad gave in to her, because, well, he always gives in to her.'

'I see. So he's a bit . . . chick-pecked, is he?' I smiled bleakly. 'How long have you been seeing this man?'

'A couple of months. I like him – but his daughter . . . She makes things difficult.'

'Ah. Well – that's not easy.'

'No. But there it is.' I glanced at Dan's apron. 'I like the merchandise.'

Dan looked down at it. 'Thanks. I thought this sponsorship deal would help boost our profile further as this is such a big event so I ordered some corporate gear. I've had some *Black & Green* umbrellas made too – I'll give you one.'

'Dan . . .' I sipped my beer. 'You didn't tell me that you *owned* the paper.'

He shrugged. 'I don't own it – just half of it. And why would I tell you?'

'I don't know. Because . . . well, why not?' I lowered my bottle of Stella. 'So do you often buy newspapers?'

He shook his head. 'Never done it before – and I don't suppose I'll ever do it again. It was purely because of my friendship with Matt.'

'But how fantastic that you were able to,' I said, wondering where he'd got the required quarter of a million, but knowing that I could hardly ask.

Dan sipped his beer. 'It was all thanks to my grandmother. She was the one who made it possible.'

'Your grandmother?' I echoed. 'Not the one who left you the pencil sharpener?'

'Yes. That one – Granny Robinson. If it hadn't been for her, I could never have done it; it was quite unexpected, you see what happened was –'

'Oh, I'm sorry, Dan.' My phone was vibrating again, the ringtone barely audible above the noise and chatter. I put in my earpiece then pressed the green button, bracing myself for it being Miles yet again. But the number on the screen wasn't his. It had a North American code.

'Could I speak to Phoebe Swift?' said a male voice.

'Yes. Speaking.'

'This is Luke Kramer from Toronto University.' I felt a rush of adrenaline. 'My colleague Carol says you wanted to talk to me?'

'I did,' I said agitatedly. 'I do. I *do* want to talk to you –' I stood up. 'But I'm out . . . it's very noisy, Mr Kramer – I need to get home. Could you give me ten minutes to run back and then I'll phone you?'

'Sure.'

'That seemed like an important call,' said Dan as I pocketed the phone.

'It is important.' I was suddenly euphoric. 'Really important. In fact it's . . .'

'A matter of life and death?' Dan interjected wryly.

I looked at him. 'You could say that, yes.' I put on my scarf. 'So I'm sorry I've got to go, but thanks for cheering me up.' I hugged him.

For once Dan seemed taken aback. 'Any time. I'll . . . ring you,' he added. 'Shall I?'

'Yes. Do.' I gave him a wave and then left.

I raced back to the house, took the phone to the kitchen table and dialled the number. 'Is that Mr Kramer?' I said breathlessly.

'Hi, Phoebe – yes, this is Luke.'

'Congratulations on the baby, by the way.'

'Thanks. I'm still a little shell-shocked – she's our first. Anyway, I understand from my colleague Carol that you want to be put in touch with Miriam Lipietzka.'

'I do want to. Yes.'

'As I'll be putting this request to Miriam, could I ask why?'

I explained, in broad terms. 'Do you think she'd talk to me?' I added.

There was a pause. 'I don't know. But I'm seeing her tomorrow, so I'll pass on what you've told me. Let me write down the relevant names. So your friend is Mrs Thérèse Bell.'

'Yes. Her maiden name was Laurent.'

'Thérèse . . . Laurent,' he repeated. 'And the friend they had in common was Monique . . . Did you say Richelieu?'

'Yes. Though she was born Monika Richter.'

'Richter . . . So this all relates to what happened during the war?'

'Yes. Monique was also in Auschwitz, from August 1943. I'm trying to find out what happened to her; and when I found Miriam's name in that programme, I thought she might know – or at least know something . . .'

'Well, I'll speak to her about it. But let me say that I've known Miriam for thirty years and she rarely talks about her wartime experiences as the memories are so painful, obviously; plus she may have no idea what happened to this friend . . . Monique.'

'I hear what you say, Luke. But please ask . . .'

'How were the fireworks?' Annie asked me when she arrived for work on Monday. 'I was in Brighton, so I missed them.'

'They were rather disappointing.' I wasn't going to say why.

Annie threw me a curious glance. 'That's a shame.'

Then I drove over to Sydenham to collect the clothes

that I'd bought from the garrulous Mrs Price. As she chatted away to me I could now see that she had unnaturally 'open' eyes and a jawline that was too tight, and hands that were a good ten years older than her face. The idea of Mum looking like this made my heart sink.

As I was driving back at lunchtime my mobile rang so I quickly turned into a side road and parked. When I saw the Toronto code on my phone my stomach tightened.

'Hi, Phoebe,' said Luke. So he'd spoken to her. 'I'm afraid there was a problem yesterday when I went to see Miriam.'

I braced myself. 'Doesn't she want to talk about it?'

'I didn't ask, because when I got there I could see she wasn't well. She gets serious chest infections, especially in the Fall – it's partly a legacy of what she went through. The doctor gave her antibiotics and told her to rest; so I'm afraid I didn't mention your phone call.'

'No – of course.' I felt a stab of disappointment. 'Well, thanks for letting me know. Maybe when she's better . . .?' My voice trailed away.

'Maybe – but for the time being, I feel I should leave it.'

For the time being . . . That could be a week, I reflected as I looked in the driving mirror and drove off, or it could be a month – or never.

When I got back to the shop I was surprised to see Miles there, sitting on the sofa, chatting to Annie, who was smiling at him solicitously as though she'd realised that there'd been a problem between us.

'Phoebe.' Miles stood up. 'I was just hoping you might have time to have a cup of tea with me?'

'Yes . . . Erm . . . let me just put these suitcases in the office, then we'll go to the Moon Daisy Café. I'll be about half an hour, Annie.'

She smiled at us. 'Sure.'

The café was busy, so Miles and I sat at one of the empty tables outside – it was just warm enough in the sunshine and it meant we had privacy.

'I'm sorry about Saturday,' Miles began. He turned up his collar. 'I should have put my foot down with Roxy: I know I give in to her too much. It's not right.'

I looked at him. 'I do find things hard with Roxy. You've seen how hostile her attitude towards me is – and she always finds a way to wreck our dates.'

Miles sighed. 'She regards you as a threat. She's been the centre of my universe for ten years now, so it's understandable in many ways.' He paused while Pippa brought our tea. 'But I had a long talk with her yesterday. I told her how angry I was about Saturday. I told her that she means the world to me and always will, but that I also have to be allowed to be happy. I told her how important you've become to me and that I don't want to be without you.' I was shocked to see that Miles' eyes were suddenly shimmering. 'So . . .' I saw him swallow, then he reached for my hand. 'I'd like to get things back on a happier footing with you, Phoebe. I explained to Roxy that you're my girlfriend, and that means you'll be at the house sometimes and that for my sake she has to be . . . *nice*.'

I felt my resentment suddenly flood away. 'Thank you for saying that, Miles. I . . . do want to get on with Roxy,' I added.

'I know you do. And yes, she can be a bit tricky, but at heart she's a good, decent girl.' Miles laced his fingers through mine. 'So I hope that things feel better to you now, Phoebe – it's very important to me that they do.'

I looked at him. 'They do feel better,' I smiled. 'Much better,' I added quietly.

Miles leaned forward and kissed me. 'Good.'

What Miles had said to Roxy seemed to make a difference. She was no longer actively hostile towards me but behaved as though my presence was a matter of indifference. If I spoke to her she would answer, but she otherwise ignored me. I welcomed this neutrality. It represented progress.

In the meantime I'd heard nothing from Luke. After a week I left a message but he didn't respond. I assumed that Miriam was still unwell or, if she was better, that she'd decided against talking to me. I didn't mention it to Mrs Bell when I went to see her. She was clearly in more pain than before and told me that she was now wearing a morphine patch.

Louis' first birthday was coming up – along with my mother's facelift. I was still worried about it and told her so when she came round for supper on Tuesday.

'I repeat that you are still very attractive and don't need it.' I poured her a glass of wine. 'What if it goes wrong?'

'Freddie Church has done thousands of these . . . procedures,' she said delicately, 'and not a *single* fatality.'

'That's not the most glowing recommendation.'

Mum opened her bag and got out her diary. 'Now, I've put you down as next of kin so you'll need to know where I am. I'll be at the Lexington Clinic in Maida Vale.' She flicked through the pages. 'Here's the number . . . The operation's at four thirty and I have to be there by eleven thirty in the morning for the pre-med. I'll be in for four days, so I hope you'll visit me.'

'Are you telling anyone at work?'

Mum shook her head. 'John thinks I'm going to France for two weeks. And I'm not telling *any* of my friends.' She put her diary back in her bag and snapped it shut. 'It's private.'

'It won't be when they all see that you suddenly look fifteen years younger – or worse, that you look like someone *else*!'

'That's not going to happen. I'm going to look *great*.' Mum pushed at her jawline with her fingers. 'It's just a *tiny* lift. The trick is to have a new hair style to distract attention from it.'

'Maybe that's all you *need* – a new hair style.' And some new make-up, I thought. She was wearing that ghastly coral lipstick again. 'Mum, I have a bad feeling about this – will you *please* cancel it?'

'Phoebe, I've already paid a non-returnable deposit of £4,000 – half the total – so I'm not cancelling anything.'

I woke up on Louis' birthday with a sense of foreboding. I told Annie that I'd be out all day, then I went to get the train to meet Dad. As I trundled round the Circle Line I read the *Independent,* which, I was surprised to see, had a story about its owners, Trinity Mirror, being in negotiations to buy up the *Black & Green.* As I walked up the steps at Notting Hill Gate station I wondered whether this would be a good or bad thing for Dan and Matt.

It was gloriously sunny now and felt surprisingly mild for late November as I walked down Bayswater Road. I'd arranged to meet Dad just before ten at the Orme

Gate entrance to Kensington Gardens. When I got there at five to, I saw him coming along with the buggy. I thought that Louis might wave his arms at me as he usually does, but today he just gave me a shy smile.

'Hallo, birthday boy!' I bent down to stroke his apple cheek. His face felt lovely and warm. 'Is he walking yet?' I asked Dad as we turned into the park.

'Not quite. But he will be soon. He's still in the "Confident Crawlers" group at Gymboree and I don't want to rush things.'

'Of course not.'

'But he's just gone up a level at Monkey Music.'

'That's good.' I held up my carrier bag. 'I've got him a xylophone.'

'Oh, he'll love bashing that.'

Now we could hear the wind chimes floating across the grass from the Princess Diana playground: as we rounded the bend in the path the pirate ship loomed into view, as though it were sailing over the grass.

'The playground looks deserted,' I said.

'That's because it doesn't open until ten. I often come at this time on a Monday morning because it's nice and quiet. Nearly there, Louis,' Dad crooned. 'He's usually straining at his straps by this point – aren't you, sweetie? – but he's a bit tired this morning.'

The superintendent unlocked the gate then Dad took Louis out of the buggy and we put him in one of the swings. He seemed to enjoy just sitting there quietly while we pushed him. At one point he leaned his head against the chain, closing his eyes.

'He does seem tired, Dad.'

'We had a broken night – he was a bit whingey for

some reason – probably because Ruth was away. She's been filming in Suffolk, but she's driving back at lunchtime. Now, let's see if you'll stand, Louis.' Dad lifted him out of the swing and put him down but Louis immediately looked upset and held up his arms to be lifted. So I carried him round the playground, going into the wooden cabins with him and posting him down the slide while Dad caught him. But I kept thinking about Mum. What if she reacted badly to the anaesthetic? I glanced at the clock tower – it was ten forty. By now she'd be halfway there. She'd said that she was treating herself to a taxi all the way from Blackheath.

Dad caught Louis as he slithered down the slide again. 'He does seem sleepy today – don't you, darling?' Dad cuddled him. 'You didn't want to get out of your cot.' Suddenly Louis started to cry. 'Don't cry, sweetie.' Dad stroked his face. 'There's no need to cry.'

'Do you think he's okay?'

Dad felt his head. 'He's just got a bit of a temperature.'

'I noticed that he felt warm when I kissed him.'

'It's half a degree over normal, I'd say, but I think he's fine. Let's put him in the swing again – he loves that.'

So we did, and this seemed to cheer Louis for a moment and he stopped crying and sat there, but listlessly now, closing his eyes again, his legs dangling.

'I'll give him some Calpol,' Dad said. 'Could you lift him out, Phoebe?'

As I did so, Louis' little green coat rode up. My heart lurched. His tummy was scattered with red spots.

'Dad, have you seen this rash?'

'I know – he's had a bit of eczema lately.'

'I don't think this is eczema.' I stroked Louis' skin.

'These spots are flat, like little pinpricks – and his hands are like ice.' I stared at Louis. His cheeks were flushed but there was a bluish tinge to his mouth. 'Dad, I don't think he's very well.'

Dad looked at Louis' front then he took the baby bag off the back of the buggy and got out the Calpol. 'This will help – it's good for lowering a high temperature. Could you hold him, Phoebe?' So we sat at one of the picnic tables and I cuddled Louis while Dad poured the pink medicine into the spoon. Then I inclined Louis' head. '*That's* a good boy,' Dad said as he trickled it in. 'Normally it's a struggle, but he's being so good about it today. Well *done,* little boy . . .' Louis suddenly grimaced, then threw it all up. As Dad wiped him clean I felt Louis' brow. It was burning. He emitted a high-pitched cry.

'Dad, what if this is something serious?'

He flinched. 'We need a glass,' he said quietly. 'Get me a glass, Phoebe.'

I ran up to the café and asked for one but the woman said that glass isn't allowed in the Diana Playground. I began to panic. 'Dad – do you have a glass jar with you?'

He looked at me. 'There's a jar of blueberry pudding in the baby bag. Use that.'

I got it out, ran to the loo, washed out the purple mush and rinsed the glass, tearing off as much of the label as I could with my trembling fingers. When I came out I looked to see if there was anyone who might help us, but the playground was almost deserted apart from a few people at the very far end.

Dad held Louis while I pressed the glass to his tummy.

Louis flinched at its coldness and started screaming now, tears spurting from his eyes.

'How do I do it, Dad?'

'Don't you just press it and see if the spots fade?'

I tried again. 'It's hard to tell whether they're fading or not.' Now Dad was dialling a number on his mobile. 'Who are you calling? Ruth?'

'No. Our GP. *Damn* – it's engaged.'

'There's an NHS helpline – you could get the number from directory enquiries.' Now Louis was half closing his eyes and turning his head as though the sunlight was bothering him. I put the jar to his tummy again, but the glass on the bottom was too thick to see through it clearly; then I saw that Dad was still on the phone.

'*Why* can't they answer?' he moaned. 'Come *on* . . .'

Suddenly my mobile phone rang. I pressed the green button. '*Mum*,' I breathed.

'Darling, I just thought I'd give you a call,' she said quickly. 'I *am* feeling quite nervous actually . . .'

'Mum –'

'I'll soon be arriving at the clinic and I do have a bit of a pit in my stomach about it all, I must say –'

'*Mum!* I'm with Dad and Louis in the Diana Playground. Louis isn't at all well. He's got these spots on his tummy, and he's crying and he's got a high temperature and he's light-intolerant and sleepy and he's been sick and I'm trying to do that glass test, but I don't know how to do it.'

'Press the *side* of the glass to his skin,' she said. 'Are you doing it?'

'Yes, now I am, but I *still* can't see.'

'Try again. But it *must* be the side.'

'The thing is, it's a small jar and some of the label's

still stuck to it – so I can't see if the spots are fading or not and Louis really is quite distressed.' He'd thrown back his head, and was emitting another high, keening cry. 'This has all just blown up in less than an hour.'

'How's your father managing?' Mum asked.

'Not that well, to be honest,' I said quietly.

Dad was still trying to phone the doctor. 'Why don't they *answer*?' I heard him mutter.

'He can't get through to the GP . . .'

'Stop!' I suddenly heard Mum say. What was she talking about? 'And can you pull in on the right – into that car park there?' Now I heard the sound of the cab door being opened, then Mum's footsteps tapping quickly over the concrete path. 'I'm coming, Phoebe,' she said.

'What do you mean?'

'Put the baby in the pushchair, leave the playground *now* and walk back towards Bayswater Road. I'll meet you.'

So I strapped Louis into his buggy and now I was pushing it out of the playground with Dad, and we were walking quickly towards the park gate wondering what was going on and suddenly there was Mum, walking – no, running – towards us. She barely registered Dad as she focused on Louis. 'Give me the jar, Phoebe.'

She pulled up Louis' top then pressed the glass to his tummy. 'It's hard to tell,' she said. 'And sometimes the spots can fade and it can still be meningitis.' She felt his brow. 'He's *so* hot.' She took off his hat and unbuttoned his coat. 'Poor little thing.'

'We'll go to my GP,' Dad said. 'They're in Colville Square.'

'No,' said Mum. 'We'll go straight to Casualty. My taxi's just over there.' We ran to it, and lifted in the buggy. 'Change of plan – to St Mary's, please,' Mum said to the driver as she climbed in. 'The A & E entrance, as fast as possible.'

We were there within five minutes, then we got out, and Mum paid the driver then we ran inside and she spoke to the receptionist and we sat in the Paediatric A & E waiting room with the children with broken arms and cut fingers while Dad did his best to comfort Louis, who was still crying inconsolably; then a nurse came out and quickly examined Louis and took his temperature, and now she was telling us to go straight through and I noticed that she was walking fast. And the doctor who met us in the Triage area said that we couldn't all come in, and he thought that *I* was Louis' mother so I explained that I was his sister, and Dad asked Mum if she'd go in with him. So Mum gave me her overnight bag, and I took it back to the waiting room with Louis' buggy and the xylophone and I waited . . .

I waited for what seemed like an eternity, as I sat on my blue plastic chair listening to the whirr and thump of the cold drinks machine, the low chatter of the other people and the incessant babble of the wall-mounted TV. I glanced at it and saw that the *One o'Clock News* was starting. Louis had been in there for an hour and a half. That meant that he had meningitis. I tried to swallow, but there was a knife in my throat. I looked at his empty buggy and felt my eyes fill. I'd been upset when he was born – I didn't even meet him for the first eight weeks: and now I loved him and he was going to die.

Suddenly I heard a baby screaming. Convinced that

it was Louis, I went up to the reception window and asked the nurse if she knew what was happening. She went away, then returned saying that they were doing further tests on Louis to see whether a lumbar puncture was needed. I had visions of his little body trailing drips and wires. I picked up a magazine and tried to read it, but the words and photos were bending and blurring. Then I looked up and there was Mum walking towards me, looking upset. Please God.

She gave me a watery smile. 'He's okay.' Relief flooded through me. 'It's a viral infection. They blow up very quickly. But they're keeping him in overnight. It's okay, Phoebe.' I saw her swallow then she pulled a pack of tissues out of her pocket and gave me one. 'I'm going to go home now.'

'Does Ruth know?'

'Yes. She'll be here before long.'

I handed Mum her bag. 'So I guess you're not going to Maida Vale,' I said quietly.

She shook her head. 'It's too late. But I'm glad I was here.' She gave me a hug then walked out of the hospital.

A nurse directed me to the children's ward. I went up there in the lift and found Dad on a chair, by the end cot, in which Louis was sitting up, playing with a toy car. He seemed himself again, more or less, apart from a bandage on his hand where they'd had to put in a drip. His colour seemed to have returned to normal except . . .

'What's that?' I said. 'On his face?'

'What's what?' said Dad.

'On his cheek – there?' I peered at Louis and then I realised what it was – the perfect imprint of a coral kiss.

FOURTEEN

It took me a day to get over the trauma of Louis' trip to Casualty. I phoned Mum to see how she was.

'I'm fine,' she said quietly. 'It was rather a . . . strange situation, to put it mildly. How's your dad?'

'Not happy. He's in the dog house with Ruth.'

'Why?'

'She's furious with him for not knowing that you go straight to Casualty if you suspect meningitis.'

'Then she should take more responsibility for Louis herself! Your father is sixty-two,' Mum went on. 'He's doing his best, but his instincts just weren't . . . *right*. Louis needs proper childcare. Your father's not a nanny – he's an archaeologist.'

'True – not that he gets any work. But what's happening about your "procedure", Mum?'

I heard a painful sigh. 'I've just paid the other £4,000.'

'You mean you've spent £8,000 on a facelift that you didn't *have*?'

'Yes – because they'd had to hire the operating theatre

and pay the nurses and the anaesthetist and then there was Freddie Church's fee, so there was no getting out of it. But when I explained what had happened, they kindly said they'd give me a twenty-five per cent discount when I do have it done.'

'And when will that be?'

Mum hesitated. 'I'm not . . . sure.'

Two days after this Miles collected me straight from the shop and drove me back to his house for the evening. As I'd been feeling slightly grubby I had a quick bath then went downstairs and cooked dinner. As we sat down to eat we talked about what had happened to Louis.

'Thank God your mother was so near.'

'Yes. It was . . . lucky.' I hadn't told Miles where she'd been going. 'Her maternal instincts came to the fore.'

'But what a bizarre encounter for your parents.'

'I know. It was the first time they'd seen each other since Dad left. I think it's shaken them both.'

'Well – all's well that ends well.' Miles poured me a glass of white wine. 'And you said you'd been very busy at the shop.'

'It's been frantic – partly because I had a nice mention in the *Evening Standard*.' I decided not to tell Miles that it had come from the girl who'd torn Roxy's dress. 'So that's brought in customers, and I've had Americans coming in to buy things to wear for Thanksgiving.'

'When's that? Tomorrow?'

'Yes. I've had a run on "wiggle" dresses – all very retro.'

'Good.' Miles raised his glass. 'So everything's going well?'

'It seems to be.'

Except that I'd heard nothing further from Luke. As two weeks had now gone by I assumed that Miriam Lipietzka had been told about my request and that her answer, for whatever reason, was no.

After supper Miles and I went into the sitting room to watch TV. As the *Ten o'Clock News* started we heard the front door open – Roxy had been out with a friend. Miles went into the hall to speak to her.

I heard her yawn. 'I'm going to bed.'

'Okay, darling, but don't forget I'm taking you in early tomorrow, because I've got a breakfast meeting. We'll be leaving at seven. Phoebe's going to lock up when she leaves a bit later.'

'Sure. 'Night, Dad.'

'Goodnight, Roxy,' I called out.

'Goodnight.'

Miles and I stayed up for another hour or so, watched half of *Newsnight*, then went to bed, wrapped in each other's arms. I felt comfortable with him now that the problems with Roxy were receding. For the first time I could imagine a shared life.

In the morning I was vaguely aware of Miles moving about in the bedroom. I heard him talking to Roxy on the landing, then there was the scent of toast, and the distant slamming of the front door.

I showered, drying my hair afterwards with a dryer that Miles now kept in his bedroom for my use. Then I went back into the bathroom to do my teeth and make-up. Now I went to the mantelpiece to get my emerald ring which I'd left there the night before. I stared at the green saucer in which I'd placed it. In the saucer were three pairs of Miles' cufflinks, two buttons, and a book of matches, but nothing else . . .

My first reaction was to wonder whether Miles had moved the ring for safe-keeping. I didn't think that he would have done that without telling me, so now I looked along the mantelpiece to see if it had somehow been knocked out of the saucer, but it wasn't anywhere there, or on the floor, every inch of which I now searched. I could feel my breathing speed up as the stress of not being able to find it increased.

I sat on the bathroom chair and went over in my mind what I'd done the previous night. I'd come back to the house with Miles, and because I'd been so busy all day I'd had a quick bath. That's when I'd taken the ring off, and had put it in the green saucer, which is where I always put my jewellery when I stay at Miles' house. I'd decided not to put it back on because I was about to do some cooking. So I'd left it in the saucer and had gone downstairs.

I glanced at my watch – it was a quarter to eight: I'd have to get the train over to Blackheath soon, but by now I was in a panic about my ring. I decided to phone Miles. He'd be in the car, but he had a Bluetooth. 'Miles?' I said when the phone picked up.

'It's Roxanne. Dad asked me to answer as he forgot his earpiece.'

'Could you ask him something for me, please?'

'What?'

'Could you tell him that I left my emerald ring in his bathroom last night, in a saucer on the mantelpiece, and it's not there now so I'm wondering whether he might have moved it.'

'I haven't seen it,' she said.

'Could you ask your dad about it?' I reiterated. My heart was pounding.

'Daddy, Phoebe can't find her emerald ring: she says she left it in your bathroom in the green saucer and thinks you may have moved it.'

'No – of course I didn't,' I heard him say. 'I wouldn't do that.'

'Did you hear that?' Roxy said. 'Dad didn't touch it. No one did. You must have lost it.'

'No, I haven't. It was definitely there, so . . . if he could call me later . . . I . . .'

The line had cut off.

I was so distracted about my ring that I nearly forgot to set the burglar alarm. Then I posted the key back through the door, walked to Denmark Hill, got the train to Blackheath then went straight to the shop.

When Miles phoned me he said he'd help me look for the ring later. He said it must have dropped down some-where – that was the only explanation.

That night I drove over to Camberwell.

'So where did you leave it?' Miles asked as we stood in his bathroom.

'In this saucer, here . . .'

Then it came back to me. I'd been too stressed for it to register, but Roxy had told Miles that I'd left the ring in 'the green saucer'; but I hadn't told her that it was the green one – I'd said 'a' saucer. In fact there were three of them, all different colours. I felt a sick see-saw feeling and had to put my hand to the mantelpiece to steady myself.

'I put it *here*,' I reiterated. 'I had a quick bath then

decided not to put it back on because I was going to be making supper, so then I went downstairs. When I went to put it on this morning it had gone.'

Miles looked at the green saucer. 'Are you *sure* you put it here? Because I don't remember seeing it in here last night when I took off my cufflinks.'

I felt my insides twist. 'I *definitely* put it there – at about six thirty.' An awkward silence enveloped us. 'Miles . . .' My mouth seemed to have dried to the texture of blotting paper. 'Miles . . . I'm sorry, but . . . I can't help wondering . . .'

He stared at me. 'I *know* what you're wondering, and the answer's *no*.'

I felt heat suffuse my face. 'But Roxy was the only other person in the house. Do you think there's any chance she might have picked it up?'

'Why would she?'

'By mistake,' I said desperately. 'Or perhaps just . . . to . . . look at it, and then she forgot to put it back.' I stared at him, my heart pounding. 'Miles, please – could you ask?'

'No. I won't. I heard Roxanne tell you that she hadn't seen your ring and that means she hadn't seen it and that's all there is to it.' Now I told Miles about Roxy seeming to know that the saucer in question was green. 'Well . . .' He threw up his hands. 'She knows there's a green saucer because she comes in here sometimes.'

'But there's also a blue saucer and a red one. *How* did Roxy know that I'd left it in the green saucer without my having told her?'

'Because she knows I keep my cufflinks in the green one, so she must have assumed you'd left it in there –

or maybe it was a simple association because emeralds are green.' He shrugged. 'I really don't know – I only know that Roxy did *not* take your ring.'

My heart was thudding. 'How can you be sure?'

Miles looked at me as though I'd slapped him. 'Because at heart she's a good, decent girl. She would never do anything . . . wrong. I've told you that, Phoebe.'

'Yes, you have – in fact you often say it, Miles. I'm not quite sure why.'

Miles' face had reddened. 'Because it's true – and come on' – he ran his hand through his hair – 'you've seen what Roxy *has*. She doesn't need anything that belongs to anyone else.'

I heaved a frustrated sigh. 'Miles,' I said quietly, 'would you please check her room? *I* can't.'

'Of course you can't! And I won't.'

Tears of frustration sprang to my eyes. 'I just want to have my ring back. And I think Roxy came in here last night and picked it up because there's no *other* explanation. Miles, *please* would you look?'

'No.' I saw the vein at his temple jump. 'And I don't think it's right that you ask.'

'*I* don't think it's right that you refuse! Especially as you know that Roxy went to bed an hour before we did, so she had plenty of time to come in here – and you told me that she *does* come in here . . .'

'Yes, to get bottles of shampoo – not to steal my girl-friend's jewellery.'

'Miles, someone took my ring *out* of that saucer.'

He stared at me. 'You have *no* evidence that it was Roxanne. You've probably just *lost* it – so you're blaming her.'

'I *haven't* lost it.' I could feel my eyes fill. 'I *know* what I did with it. I'm just trying to understand . . .'

'And *I'm* just trying to protect my child from your lies!'

I felt my jaw go slack. 'I am *not* lying,' I said quietly. 'My ring *was* there and by this morning it had gone. You didn't take it – and there was only one other person in this house.'

'I am *not* going to have this!' Miles spat. 'I'm *not* going to have my daughter being accused.' He was so angry that the veins on his neck stood out like wires. 'I wasn't having it *before*, and I'm not having it *now*! That's what you're doing, Phoebe – just like Clara and her ghastly parents.' He ran a finger under his collar. 'They accused her too, with as little justification.'

'Miles . . . that gold bracelet was found in Roxy's *drawer*.'

His eyes blazed. 'And there was a perfectly valid explanation as to why.'

'Really?'

'Yes! Really.'

'Miles,' I forced myself to remain calm. 'We can resolve this while Roxy's out. I accept that she's a very young person, and that she may have been tempted to pick it up and then forgotten to put it back. But will you *please* look in her room.' He walked out of the bathroom. Good, he was going to do it. My heart sank as instead he thundered downstairs. 'I'm so upset,' I said impotently as I trailed after him into the kitchen.

'So am *I* – and you know what?' He opened the door of the wine store. 'Perhaps your ring isn't even lost.' Miles took a bottle off one of the wooden racks.

361

'What do you mean?'

He rummaged in a drawer then found a corkscrew. 'Perhaps you've really got it and you're making this up.'

'But . . . why *would I*?'

'To get back at Roxy, for being a bit tricky with you sometimes?'

I stared at Miles, outraged. 'I'd have to be *insane*. And I don't want to get back at her – I want to get *on* with her. Miles, I believe the ring's in her room, so all you have to do is find it, then we say nothing more about it.'

Miles lips were pursed. 'It *isn't* in Roxy's room, Phoebe, because she doesn't *take* things. My daughter does *not* steal things. She's *not* a thief – I told *them* that, and I'm telling *you*! Roxy is *not* a *thief* – she is not, *not*, NOT –' Suddenly Miles threw down the bottle and it exploded against the limestone floor. I stared at the scattered green shards, at the spreading crimson puddle, and at the pretty blackbird label slashed in half.

Miles was leaning against the counter, his hand to his face. 'Please go now,' he croaked. 'Please would you go, Phoebe – I just can't . . .'

Feeling strangely calm I picked my way around the broken glass, found my coat and scarf then walked out of the house.

I sat in the car for a moment, trying to soothe my shattered nerves before daring to drive. Then, my hands still trembling, I started the ignition. I noticed a little splash of red wine on my cuff.

It's always there with Roxy . . .

There was no other explanation.

Roxy has this sense of . . . not having.

Miles had given her so much; letting it all drop into her lap, yes, as though everything was hers for the taking.

What do you mean by that?

So she felt entitled – entitled to take a friend's bracelet, to be bought dresses costing thousands of pounds, to sit and relax while others toiled, to pocket a valuable ring that she'd found. Why would she hesitate to take something when she'd been denied nothing? But the way Miles had reacted . . . Nothing could have prepared me for it. *Now* I understood.

Elle est son talon d'Achille.

Miles was simply unable to accept that Roxy could do anything wrong.

As I unlocked my front door the waves of delayed shock began to break over me. I sat at the kitchen table and let the sobs come, drawing in my breath in teary gasps. As I pressed a tissue to my eyes, I became aware that people were arriving next door. The couple who lived there seemed to be having some sort of party. Then I remembered that they were from Boston. It must be a Thanksgiving dinner.

I realised that the phone was ringing. I let it go on ringing because I knew it was Miles. He was phoning to say that he was sorry – that he'd behaved horribly and that he'd just looked in Roxy's room and yes, he *had* found the ring and would I please forgive him? The phone was still ringing. I wished it would *stop* – but on it went. I must have left the answerphone off.

I went into the hall and picked up the handset without speaking.

'Hello?' said an elderly female voice.

'Yes?'

'Is that Phoebe Swift?' For a moment I thought it was Mrs Bell. Then I realised that there'd been a North American intonation to the French accent. 'May I speak with Phoebe Swift?' I heard.

'Yes – this is Phoebe. Sorry – who's this?'

'My name is Miriam Lipietzka . . .'

I sank on to the hall chair. 'Miss Lipietzka?' I leaned my head against the wall.

'Luke Kramer told me . . .' I could hear now that she sounded wheezy, her chest rattling a little as she spoke. 'Luke Kramer told me – that you wanted to talk to me.'

'Yes,' I murmured. 'I do – I'd love to talk to you. I'd assumed by now that it wasn't going to happen. I knew you'd been unwell.'

'Oh yes, but I am better now, more or less; and I'm therefore ready, to . . .' She paused, then I heard her sigh. 'Luke explained the nature of your call. I have to say that this is a time of my life that I rarely speak about. But when I heard those names again, *so* familiar to me, I knew that I *must* respond. So I told Luke that I would call you when I felt ready. And I do now feel ready . . .'

'Miss Lipietzka –'

'Please – Miriam.'

'Miriam, I'll ring you back – it's long distance.'

'As I live on a musician's pension, that would be kind.'

I grabbed the pad and took down the number. Then I quickly jotted down a few things that I wanted to ask Miriam, to make sure that I didn't forget. I collected myself for a moment, then dialled her number.

'So . . . you know Thérèse Laurent?' Miriam began.

'I do. She lives near me. She's become a good friend. She moved to London after the war.'

'Ah. Well, I never met her, but I always felt that I knew her because I read about her in the letters that Monique wrote to me from Avignon. She said that she had made friends with a girl called Thérèse and that they had fun together. I remember feeling a little jealous, actually.'

'Thérèse told me that she'd been a little jealous of you because Monique talked about *you* so much.'

'Well, Monique and I had been very close. We met in 1936 when she arrived at our little school in the Rue des Hospitalieres in Le Marais – the Jewish quarter. She had come from Mannheim and spoke barely a word of French so I translated everything for her.'

'And you were from the Ukraine?'

'Yes. From Kiev, but my family moved to Paris to escape Communism when I was four. I remember Monique's parents, Lena and Emil, very well. I can see them now, as though it were yesterday,' she added wonderingly. 'I remember when the twins were born – Monique's mother was ill for a long time afterwards and I recall that Monique, who was then only eight, had to do all the cooking. Her mother used to tell her what to do from her bed.' Miriam paused. 'She could have had no idea then what a gift she was actually imparting to her daughter.' I wondered what Miriam meant by that remark, but didn't feel I could interrupt her. She was going to tell this difficult story in her own way and I would have to quell my impatience.

'Monique's family, like mine, lived on the Rue des Rosiers, so we saw a lot of each other: I was heart-broken when they left for Provence. I remember crying bitterly and I told my parents that we should go there

365

too, but they seemed less anxious about the situation than Monique's parents were. My father still had his job – he was a civil servant in the Ministry of Education. By and large, we had a good life. Then things began to change.' I heard Miriam cough then she paused to drink some water. 'In late 1941 my father was dismissed – they were reducing the number of Jewish people working in government. Then a curfew was imposed. Then on June 7th, 1942 we were told that an edict had been passed requiring all Jews in the Occupied Zone to wear the yellow star. My mother sewed it to the left side of my jacket, as instructed, and I remember that we were stared at in the streets and I hated this. Then on July 15th, 1942 I was standing with my father, looking out of the window when he suddenly said "they're here," and the police came in and took us away . . .'

Now Miriam described being taken to Drancy, where she spent a month before being put on a transport with her parents and her sister, Lilianne. I asked her if she was frightened.

'Not really,' she replied. 'We'd been told we were going to a work camp, and we didn't feel suspicious because we travelled there in a passenger train – not the cattle trucks that they used later. We arrived in Auschwitz after two days. I remember hearing a band playing a lively march by Lehar as we stepped down into this barren land, and we comforted each other, saying how could it be such a bad place if there was music playing? Yet at the same time there was all this electrified barbed wire. An SS officer was in charge. He was sitting on a chair with one foot on a stool, his rifle across his lap; and as people walked past him he indicated with his thumb which way they were to go – whether to the left or to the right. We could not have known that in the movement of that man's thumb lay our destiny. Lilianne was only ten, and a woman told my mother to tie a scarf round her head to make her look older. My mother was puzzled by this advice but did it anyway – and that saved Lilianne's life. Then we were made to put our valuables in large boxes. I had to put in my violin – I didn't understand why; I remember my mother crying as she put in her wedding ring and her gold locket with the photos of her parents. Then we were separated from my father, who was taken to the men's barracks while we went to the women's barracks.' While Miriam had another drink of water I glanced at my notes, hastily scribbled, but legible. I would transcribe them later.

Miriam paused for a moment. 'The next day we were put to work, digging ditches. I dug ditches for three months, at night crawling into my bunk – we were packed in, three across, on these pitifully thin straw mattresses: I used to console myself by "practising" my violin fingering on a phantom fingerboard; then one day I happened to overhear two female guards talking, and one of them mentioned Mozart's first violin concerto, saying how much she loved it. Before I could stop myself, I'd said, "I play that." The woman gave me this piercing look, and I thought she was going to beat me – or worse – for having addressed her without permission. My heart was in my mouth. But then to my amazement her face broke into a delighted smile and she asked me if I could really play it. I said I'd learned it the previous year and had played it in public. So I was sent to see Alma Rosé.'

'So that's when you joined the Women's Orchestra?'

'They called it the *Women's* Orchestra, but we were just girls – mostly teenagers. Alma Rosé found me a violin that had come out of this vast warehouse where all the valuables of everyone who had arrived at the camp were stored before being sent to Germany. The warehouse was known as "Canada" because it was so full of riches.'

'And what of Monique?' I now said.

'Well, this is how I *met* Monique – because the orchestra played at the gate when the work gangs went out in the morning and when they returned in the evening; and we played when the transports arrived, so that, hearing Chopin and Schumann, these exhausted, bewildered people would not realise that they had in fact arrived at the mouth of Hell. And one day in early August 1943, I was playing at the gate when the train arrived and in the crowd of new arrivals I saw Monique.'

'How did you feel?'

'Elated – then terrified that she wouldn't pass selection, but, thank God, she was sent to the right – to the side of the living. Then, a few days later I saw her again. Like everyone else her head had been shaved, and she was very thin. She wasn't wearing the blue-and-white striped garments that most inmates wore. She was wearing a long gold evening dress, which must have come out of "Canada", with a pair of men's shoes that were far too big for her. Perhaps there wasn't a prisoner's uniform available for her, or perhaps it was done for "fun". But there she was in this beautiful satin gown, dragging stones for road construction. And the orchestra was walking past, on our way back to our block, and Monique suddenly looked up and saw me.'

'Were you able to speak to her?'

'No, but I managed to get a message to her and we met by her block three days later. By then she had been given the blue-and-white striped dress that the female prisoners wore with a headscarf and wooden clogs. The musicians got more food than the other inmates so I gave her a piece of bread which she hid under her arm. We talked briefly. She asked me if I had seen her parents and brothers – but I hadn't; she asked me about my family: I told her that my father had died of typhus three months after arriving and that my mother and Lilianne had been transferred to Ravensbruck to work in a munitions factory. I would not see them again until after the war. So it was an immense comfort to know that Monique was there – but at the same time I was very afraid for her, because her life was far harder than mine. The work she did was so arduous, and the food she had was so meagre and so awful. And everyone knew what happened to prisoners who got too weak to work.' I heard Miriam's voice catch. Then she drew in a breath. 'And so . . . I started to save things for Monique. Sometimes a carrot; sometimes a little honey. I remember once bringing her a small potato, and when she saw it she was so happy she cried. Whenever there were new arrivals, Monique would go down to the gate, if she could, because she knew that I would be playing there and it comforted her to be near to her friend.'

I heard Miriam swallow. 'Then . . . I remember in February 1944, I saw Monique standing there – we had just stopped playing – and one of the senior female guards, this . . . *creature*. We called her "the beast".' Miriam paused. 'She . . . went up to Monique and grabbed her by the arm, and demanded to know what she was doing there, "slacking", and she said that she was to come along with her – now! Monique started to cry and over the top of my music I saw her looking towards me, as though I might help,' Miriam's voice caught again. 'But I had to start playing. And as Monique was dragged away we were playing Strauss' "Tritsch-Tratsch" polka – such a lively, charming piece – and I have never played it or been able to listen to it since . . .'

As Miriam continued to talk, I gazed out of the window. Then I glanced at my hand. What was the loss of a ring compared to what I was hearing? Now Miriam's voice was faltering again and I heard a suppressed sob; then she continued her story to its conclusion, and now we were saying goodbye. And as I put down the phone the sound of my neighbours drifted through the wall as they laughed and talked and gave thanks.

'Have you heard from Miles *since* this happened?' Mrs Bell asked me the following Sunday afternoon. I had just finished telling her about what had happened in Camberwell.

'I haven't,' I replied, 'and I don't expect to, unless it's to say that he's found my ring.'

'The poor man,' Mrs Bell murmured. She smoothed the pale green mohair wrap which she always had over her lap now. 'It obviously brought back to him what had happened at his daughter's school.' She looked at me. 'Do you see *any* hope of reconciliation?'

I shook my head. 'He was almost insane with anger. Perhaps if you've been with someone a long time you can withstand the odd cataclysmic row, but I'd only known Miles three months and it shocked me. Plus his whole attitude towards what's happened is . . . wrong.'

'Perhaps Roxy took the ring purely to cause conflict between you and Miles.'

'I thought about that and decided that she would see that as a "bonus". I think she took it because she takes things.'

'But you *must* have it back . . .'

I turned up my hands. 'What can I do? I have no proof that Roxy took it, and even if I did, it would still be . . . horrible. I couldn't face it.'

'But Miles can't just *leave* it like that,' said Mrs Bell. 'He should search for the ring.'

'I don't think he will – because if he did he'd probably find it, and that would destroy his myth about Roxy.'

Mrs Bell was shaking her head. 'This is a very bitter pill for you, Phoebe.'

'It is. But I'm just going to have to try and let it go. At the same time I know that there are far more precious things to lose than a ring, however treasured.'

'What makes you say that? *Phoebe* . . .' Mrs Bell was staring at me. 'There are tears in your eyes.' She reached for my hand. 'Why?'

I heaved a sigh. 'I'm fine . . .' It would be wrong for me to tell Mrs Bell what I knew. I stood up. 'But I need to go now. Is there anything I can do?'

'No.' She glanced at the clock. 'The Macmillan nurse will be coming shortly.' She clasped my hand in both hers. 'I hope that you will be here again soon, Phoebe. I love seeing you.'

I bent down to kiss her. 'I will.'

*　　*　　*

On Monday Annie brought in her copy of the *Guardian* and showed me a short announcement in the Media section about the sale of the *Black & Green* to Trinity Mirror for £1.5 million. 'Do you suppose that's good news for them?' I said.

'It's good news for whoever *owns* the paper,' Annie replied, 'because they'll make money. But it might not be good for the staff because the new management might sack everyone.' I decided to ask Dan about it – perhaps I'd go to his next screening. Annie was taking off her jacket. 'What about Christmas decorations?' she asked. 'It's the first of December, after all.'

I looked at her blankly. I'd been too distracted even to think about it. 'We do need to put some up – but vintage ones.'

'Paperchains,' Annie suggested as she glanced round the shop. 'Silver and gold ones. I can pop into John Lewis when I go to Tottenham Court Road for my audition. We should also get some holly – I'll bring some back from the florists by the station; and we'll need some Christmas lights.'

'My mother's got some lovely old ones,' I said. 'Elegant gold and white angels and stars. I'll ask her if we can borrow them.'

'Of course you can,' Mum said when I phoned her a few minutes later. 'In fact I'll look them out now and bring them over – it's not as though I'm doing much at the moment.' Mum had decided to continue with the charade that she was on holiday.

She arrived an hour later clutching a large cardboard box and we ran the strings of lights along the front of the windows.

'They're lovely,' Annie said as we switched them on.

'They were *my* parents' lights,' Mum explained. 'They bought them when I was a child in the early fifties. They've had new plugs but have otherwise lasted: in fact, they look good for their age.'

'Excuse me for being personal, Mrs Swift,' said Annie, 'but so do you. I know I've only met you a couple of times, but you look amazing at the moment. Have you got a new hair style or something?'

'No.' Mum looked happy but bewildered as she patted her blonde waves. 'It's exactly the same.'

'Well . . .' Annie shrugged. 'You look great.' She went and got her jacket. 'I'd better get going, Phoebe.'

'Sure,' I said. 'What's it for this time?'

'Children's theatre.' She rolled her eyes. '*Llamas in Pajamas.*'

'I told you Annie's an actress, didn't I, Mum?'

'You did.'

'I'm fed up with it though,' Annie said. She picked up her bag. 'I really want to write my own show – I'm researching some stories at the moment.'

I wished I could tell her the story I knew . . .

As Annie left, Mum began to look through the rails. 'These clothes *are* rather lovely. I used to dislike the idea of wearing vintage, didn't I, Phoebe? I was quite dismissive about it.'

'You were. Why don't you try something on?'

Mum smiled. 'All right then. I do like this.' She took the Jacques Fath 1950s coatdress with a pattern of little palm trees off the rail and went into the changing room with it. A minute later she pulled back the calico curtain.

373

'That's lovely on you, Mum. You're slim, so you can wear that fitted look – it's very elegant.'

Mum gazed at her reflection with an air of delighted surprise. 'It does look nice.' She fingered a sleeve. 'And the fabric's so . . . interesting.' She looked at herself again then drew the curtain. 'But I'm not buying anything at the moment. It's been a very expensive few weeks.'

As the shop was quiet Mum stayed for a chat. 'You know, Phoebe,' she said as she sat on the sofa. 'I don't think I'll be going back to Freddie Church.'

I sighed with relief. 'That sounds like a good decision.'

'Even at twenty-five per cent off, it's still £6,000. I *could* afford it, just, but now somehow, it seems such a waste of money.'

'In your case, Mum, it would be, yes.'

Mum looked at me. 'I've come round more to your way of thinking on the subject, Phoebe.'

'Why?' I asked, though I knew.

'It's since last week,' she replied quietly. 'Since meeting Louis.' She shook her head, wonderingly. 'Some of my bitterness and sadness just . . . *went*.'

I leaned against the counter. 'And how did you feel, seeing Dad?'

'Well . . .' Mum sighed. 'I felt all right about that too. Perhaps because I was touched by how much he loves Louis, I couldn't feel angry. Somehow everything looks so much . . . *better* now.' I suddenly saw what Annie had seen – that Mum *did* look different; her features had somehow relaxed and she looked prettier and yes, younger. 'I'd love to see Louis again,' she added softly.

'Well, why shouldn't you? Perhaps you could have lunch with Dad sometimes.'

Mum nodded slowly. 'That's what he said, when I left. Or perhaps I could come along when *you* visit him. We could all take Louis to the park – if Ruth didn't mind.'

'She's so busy with her work, I doubt she'd care. Anyway, she's grateful to you for what you did. Think of that nice letter she sent you.'

'Yes, but that doesn't mean she'd be happy for me to spend time with your dad.'

'I don't know – I think it might be okay.'

'Well . . .' Mum heaved a sigh. 'We'll see. And how's Miles?' I told Mum what had happened. Her face fell. 'My father gave that ring to my mother when I was born; my mother gave it to me when I turned forty, and on your twenty-first birthday, Phoebe, I gave it to you.' Mum was shaking her head. 'That's . . . heartbreaking. Well . . .' She pursed her lips. 'What a misguided man he must be – as a father, at least.'

'I must say he's not doing a great job with Roxy.'

'Is there *any* way you might get the ring back?'

'No – so I'm trying not to think about it.'

Mum was staring out of the window again. 'There's that man,' she said.

'Which man?'

'The big, badly dressed one with the curly hair.' I followed her gaze. Dan was walking along on the other side of the road and now he was crossing over, coming towards us. 'On the other hand, I like curly hair on a man. It's unusual.'

'Yes.' I smiled. 'You've said that before.' Dan pushed on the door of Village Vintage. 'Hi, Dan,' I said. 'This is my mother.'

'Really?' He peered at Mum with a puzzled expression. 'Not your older sister?'

Mum roared with laughter, and suddenly looked luminously beautiful. That was the only facelift she'd needed – a smile.

Now she was getting to her feet. 'I'd better go, Phoebe. I'm meeting Betty from bridge for lunch at twelve thirty. Lovely to see you again, Dan.' She gave us a wave and was gone.

Dan started riffling through the menswear rail.

'Looking for anything in particular?' I asked him with a smile.

'Not really. I just thought I ought to come and spend a bit of money in here as I feel I owe my good fortune to this shop.'

'That might be overstating it a bit, Dan.'

'Not by much.' He pulled out a jacket. '*This* is nice – *great* colour.' He peered at it. 'It's a tasteful pale green, right?'

'No. It's bubblegum pink – Versace.'

'Ah.' He put it back.

'This one would suit you.' I held out a Brooks Brothers cashmere jacket in a dove grey. 'It matches your eyes. And it should be big enough across the chest. It's a 42.'

Dan tried it on then appraised his reflection. 'I'll take it,' he said happily. 'Then I was hoping you'd come and have a celebration lunch with me.'

'Oh I'd love to Dan, but I never close at lunchtime.'

'Well, for once why don't you just do something that you never do? We'll only be an hour – and we can go to Chapters wine bar so that you're nearby.'

I picked up my bag. 'Okay then – as it's quiet. Why

not?' I turned over the 'Open' sign then locked the door.

As Dan and I passed the church he talked about the sale of the *Black & Green*. 'It's fantastic for us,' he said. 'It's what Matt and I hoped for: we wanted the paper to be a success so that it would get bought, and then we'd get our money back, hopefully with interest.'

'Which I presume you have done?'

Dan grinned. 'We've doubled our stake. Neither of us imagined that it would happen so fast, but the Phoenix story put us right on the map.' We went into Chapters All Day Dining and were given a window table. Dan ordered two glasses of champagne.

'What will happen to the paper now?' I asked him.

He picked up the menu. 'Nothing much, because Trinity Mirror want to keep it as it is. Matt will remain editor – he's keeping a small shareholding; then the idea is to start up similar titles in other parts of South London. Everyone's staying – except me.'

'Why? You were enjoying it.'

'I was. But now I'll be able to do what I've always wanted to do.'

'Which is what?'

'Start my own cinema.'

'But you have done.'

'I mean a real one – an independent – showing new releases, of course, but with an equal emphasis on classic films, including unusual ones that are hard to see, like, I don't know, *Peter Ibbetson*, a Gary Cooper film from 1934, or Fassbinder's *The Bitter Tears of Petra von Kant*. It would be like a mini British Film Institute, with talks and discussions.' The waiter brought our champagne.

'And with modern projection, presumably?'

Dan nodded. 'The Bell and Howell's just for fun. I'm going to start looking for premises after Christmas.' We placed our order.

'Good for you, Dan.' I raised my glass. 'Congratulations. You risked a lot.'

'I did – but I knew Matt very well and trusted him to produce a good paper; and then we had that huge stroke of luck. So here's to Village Vintage.' Dan lifted his glass. 'Thank you, Phoebe.'

'Dan . . .' I said after a moment. 'I'm curious about something: on fireworks night you were telling me about your grandmother – that it was thanks to her that you were able to invest in the paper . . .'

'That's right – then you had to leave. Well, I think I told you that in addition to the silver pencil sharpener she left me a hideous painting.'

'Yes.'

'It was this horrible semi-abstract thing that she'd had hanging in her downstairs loo for thirty-five years.'

'You said you felt a bit disappointed.'

'I did. But a few weeks later I took off the brown paper in which it had been wrapped, and taped to the back of it was a letter to me from Granny in which she'd said she knew I'd always hated the picture, but that she thought it "might be worth something". So I took it to Christie's and discovered that it was by Erik Anselm – I hadn't even known that much, as the signature was illegible.'

'I've heard of Erik Anselm,' I said as the waiter brought our plates of fish pie.

'He was a younger contemporary of Rauschenberg

and Twombly. The woman at Christie's got very excited when she saw it and said that Erik Anselm was being rediscovered and that in her view the painting might be worth as much as £300,000 . . .' So that's where the money had come from. 'But it sold for £800,000.'

'Good God. So your grandmother was generous to you after all.'

Dan picked up his fork. 'Extremely generous.'

'Did she collect art?'

'No – she was a midwife. She said the painting had been given to her in the early seventies by a grateful husband after a particularly hazardous birth.'

I raided my glass again. 'Well, here's to Granny Robinson.'

Dan smiled. 'I often drink to her – plus she was lovely. I used some of the money to buy my house,' he went on as we ate our pie. 'Then Matt told me that he was having trouble getting the capital he needed to start the *Black & Green*. I'd told him about my windfall and he asked me if I'd be prepared to invest in the paper, so I had a think then decided to go for it.'

I smiled. 'A good decision.'

Dan nodded. 'It was. Anyway . . . it's so lovely to see you, Phoebe. I've hardly laid eyes on you lately.'

'Well, I've been a bit preoccupied, Dan. But now I'm . . . fine.' I lowered my fork. 'Can I tell you something?' He nodded. 'I like your curly hair.'

'You do?'

'I do. It's unusual.' I glanced at my watch. 'But I must go – my hour's up. Thanks for lunch.'

'It was nice to celebrate with you, Phoebe. Do you fancy a film sometime?'

'Oh yes. Anything good coming on at the Robinson Rio?'

'*A Matter of Life and Death.*'

I looked at Dan. 'That sounds . . . great.'

So on Thursday I drove to Hither Green – and the shed was full, and Dan gave me a short preamble to the film, saying that it was a classic fantasy, romance and courtroom drama all rolled into one in which a World War 2 fighter pilot, cheats death. 'Peter Carter is forced to bail out of his burning plane with no parachute and miraculously survives,' Dan explained, 'only to discover that this is due to a heavenly blunder which is about to be put right. In order to stay alive, so that he can be with the woman he loves, Peter pleads his case at the celestial Court of Appeal. But will he prevail?' Dan went on. 'And is what he sees real or only a hallucination caused by his injuries? You decide.'

He dimmed the lights and the curtains swished open.

Afterwards some of us stayed for supper and chatted about the film, and about the way Powell and Pressburger used both black and white and colour. 'The fact that heaven is monochrome and the earth is Technicolor is meant to affirm the triumph of life over death,' said Dan, 'something a post-war audience would have felt very keenly.'

It had been a lovely evening and I drove home feeling happier than I had done for days.

The next morning Mum dropped in and said that she'd decided to buy the Jacques Fath coatdress after all. 'Betty told me that she and Jim are having a Christmas drinks party on the twentieth, so I'd like a new outfit – a new *old* outfit,' she corrected herself.

'Old's the new new,' said Annie brightly.

Mum got out her credit-card holder, but I couldn't bear the idea of taking money from her. 'It can be an early birthday present,' I said.

Mum shook her head. 'This is your livelihood, Phoebe. You've worked so hard for it, added to which my birthday's not for six weeks.' She got out her Visa card. 'It's £250, isn't it?'

'Okay, but you get twenty per cent off, which makes it £200.'

'That's a bargain.'

'Which reminds me,' said Annie. 'Are we going to have a January sale? People have been asking.'

'I suppose we should,' I replied as I folded Mum's coatdress into a Village Vintage carrier. 'Everyone else does, and it'll be good for moving stock.' I handed Mum her bag.

'We could have a preview evening for it,' Annie suggested. 'Hype it up a bit. I do think we should find ways to promote the shop a bit more,' she added as she tidied the gloves. I was always touched at the thought Annie put into making Village Vintage successful.

'*I* know what you should do,' said Mum. 'You should have a vintage fashion show – with Phoebe giving a short commentary about each outfit; I thought of it when I heard you on the radio. You could talk about the style of each garment, the social context of the era, a bit about the designer – you're very knowledgeable, after all, darling.'

'So I should be, after twelve years at it.' I looked at Mum. 'But I like that idea.'

'You could charge ten pounds a head, to include a

glass of wine,' Annie said, 'with the ticket price redeemable against anything bought in the shop. It would get coverage in the local press. You could have it at Blackheath Halls.'

I thought of the wooden-panelled Great Hall with its barrel-vaulted ceiling and wide stage. 'It's a big venue.'

Annie shrugged. 'I'm sure you could fill it. It would be an opportunity to learn a bit about the history of fashion in a fun way.'

'I'd have to hire models – that would cost.'

'You could get your customers to do it,' Annie suggested. 'They'd probably feel flattered – and it'd be fun. They could wear the things they'd already bought from you as well as current stock.'

I looked at Annie. 'They could.' I had a vision of the four cupcake dresses flouncing down the catwalk. 'And the profits could go to charity.'

'Do it, Phoebe,' Mum said, 'we'll all help you.' Then with a wave at Annie and me she left.

I had started to make notes about it all and had called someone at Blackheath Halls to find out how much it cost to hire the Great Hall when the phone rang.

I picked up. 'Village Vintage?'

'Is that Phoebe?'

'Yes.'

'Phoebe – this is Sue Rix. I'm the Macmillan nurse who looks after Mrs Bell. I'm with her this morning and she asked me to call you . . .'

'Is she all right?' I said quickly.

'Well . . . that's a difficult question to answer. She's extremely agitated. She keeps saying that she wants you to come – right away. I've warned her that you might not be able to.'

I glanced at Annie. 'Actually I have help today, so I can – I'll come up now.' As I picked up my bag I felt a shiver of apprehension. 'I'll be a while, Annie.' She nodded. Then I left the shop and walked up to The Paragon, my heart thudding with anticipation.

When I got there Sue opened the door.

'How is Mrs Bell?' I asked her as I went in.

'Bewildered,' Sue replied. 'And very emotional. It started about an hour ago.'

I went to go into the sitting room, but Sue pointed to the bedroom.

Mrs Bell was lying in bed, her head on the pillow. I hadn't seen her in bed before and although I knew how ill she was, it shocked me to see how thin she was beneath the blankets.

'Phoebe . . . at *last*.' Mrs Bell smiled with relief. In her hand was a sheet of paper – a letter. I stared at it, my pulse racing. 'I need you to read this for me. Sue offered to do so, but it must be no one but you.'

I pulled up a chair. 'Can't you read it then, Mrs Bell? Is it your eyes?'

'No, no – I *can* read it, and I have already done so perhaps twenty times since it arrived a short time ago. But now *you* must read it, Phoebe. *Please* . . .' Mrs Bell handed me the cream-coloured sheet which was closely typed on both sides. It was from an address in Pasadena, California.

Dear Thérèse, I read. *I hope you will excuse this letter from a stranger – although I am not quite a stranger. My name is Lena Sands and I am the daughter of your friend Monique Richelieu . . .*

I glanced at Mrs Bell – her pale blue eyes were shining with tears – then I returned my gaze to the letter.

I know that you and my mother were friends, in Avignon, all those years ago. I know that you knew that she'd been transported, and I know that you searched for her after the war and discovered that she had been in Auschwitz. I also know that you thought she must have died – a fair assumption. The purpose of this letter is to tell you that, as my existence attests, my mother survived.

'You were right,' I heard Mrs Bell murmur. 'You were *right*, Phoebe . . .'

Thérèse, I would like you at last to know what happened to my mother. The reason why I am able to write to you like this is because your friend Phoebe Swift contacted my mother's lifelong friend, Miriam Lipietzka, and Miriam called me earlier today.

'But *how* could you have contacted Miriam?' Mrs Bell asked me. 'How could that be *possible*? I don't understand.' I told Mrs Bell about the concert programme that I'd found in the ostrich-skin bag. She stared at me, her mouth agape. 'Phoebe,' she whispered after a few moments, 'not long ago I told you that I didn't believe in God. I think, now, that I *do*.'
I turned back to the letter.

My mother rarely talked about her time in Avignon – the associations were too painful: but whenever she did have reason to mention it, Thérèse, your name would come up. She spoke of you only with affection. She remembered that you had helped her when she had to hide. She said that you were a good friend to her.

I looked at Mrs Bell. She was shaking her head as she looked towards the window, clearly going over the letter in her own mind. I saw a tear slide down her cheek.

My mother died in 1987, aged fifty-eight. I once told her that I felt she'd been short-changed. She said that, on the contrary, she'd had the most wonderful windfall of forty-three years.

Now I read about the incident that Miriam had recounted to me over the phone, when Monique was dragged away by the female guard.

This woman – she was known as 'the beast' – put my mother on the list for the next 'selection'. But on the appointed day, while my mother was on the back of the truck with the others, waiting to be taken – and I can barely write these words – to the crematorium, she was recognised by the young SS guard who had registered her admission. At that time, hearing that she spoke native German, he had asked her where she came from and she answered, 'Mannheim'. He had smiled and said that he was from Mannheim too, and on those occasions afterwards when he saw my mother he would take a moment to chat to her about the city. When he saw her sitting on the truck that morning he told the

*driver that there had been a mistake and ordered my
mother to get down. She always said to me that that
day – March 1st, 1944 – was her second birthday.*

Lena's letter now described how this SS guard had
had Monique moved to work in the camp kitchen, scrub-
bing floors; this meant that she was working indoors
and, more importantly, was able to eat potato peelings,
a little meat even. She began to gain just enough weight
to survive. After a few weeks of this, the letter went on,
Monique had become a kitchen 'assistant', doing some
cooking, although she said it was difficult as the only
ingredients were potatoes, cabbage, margarine and farina
– sometimes a little salami – and 'coffee' made of ground-
up acorns. She did this work for three months.

*My mother was then assigned, with two other girls,
to cook for some of the female wardens, in their
barracks. Because my mother had had to learn to cook
after her twin brothers were born, she did a very good
job and the wardens enjoyed her potato pancakes and
her sauerkraut and strudel. This success ensured my
mother's survival. She used to say that what her mother
had taught her had saved her life.*

Now I understood Miriam's remark about the true
gift that Monique's mother had imparted to her daughter.
I turned the letter over.

*In the winter of 1944, with the Russians closing in
from the east, Auschwitz was evacuated. Those inmates
who could still stand were forced to march through*

the snow to other camps further inside Germany; these were death marches, and any prisoner who collapsed or stopped to rest was shot. Having walked for ten days, 20,000 prisoners made it to Bergen-Belsen – amongst them my mother. She said that here was hell on earth too, with virtually no food, and with thousands of the inmates suffering from typhus. The Women's Orchestra had also been sent there and so my mother was able to see Miriam. But in April, Bergen-Belsen was liberated. Miriam was reunited with her mother and sister, and not long afterwards they emigrated to Canada where they had family. My mother stayed in a Displaced Persons camp for eight months, waiting for news of her parents and her brothers; she was distraught to be told that they had not survived. But through the Red Cross her father's brother made contact with her and offered her a home with his family in California. So my mother came here, to Pasadena in March 1946.

'You *did* know,' Mrs Bell murmured again. She looked at me. Tears had gathered in her eyes. 'You *did* know, Phoebe. That strange conviction that you had . . . it was right. It was *right*,' she repeated wonderingly.

I turned back to the letter.

Although my mother had a 'normal' existence afterwards, in that she worked, married and had a child, she never 'recovered' from what she'd been through. For years afterwards, apparently, she walked with her eyes cast down. She hated it when someone said 'after you' to her, because in the camp an inmate always had to walk in front of the escorting guard. She would become distressed if she saw striped fabric and would not tolerate any in the house. And she was obsessed with food, forever making cakes which she would give away.

Mom started high school, but had difficulty applying herself to her studies. One day her teacher told her that she wasn't concentrating. My mother retorted that she knew all about 'concentration', and angrily pulled up her sleeve to show the number tattooed on her left forearm. Not long after that she left school, and, although she was clever, she gave up the idea of going to college. She said that all she wanted to do was to feed people. So she got a job with a state-run program for the homeless, and through this she met my father Stan, a baker, who donated bread to the charity's two shelters here in Pasadena. She and Stan gradually fell in love, marrying in 1952 and working together in his bakery: he made the bread, and my mother made cakes, coming to specialise in cupcakes. Their bakery grew into a large concern and in the 1970s it became the Pasadena Cupcake Company, and I've been its CEO for the past few years.

'But I don't understand, Phoebe,' I heard Mrs Bell say. 'I don't understand how you could *know* this and not have *told* me? How could you *sit* with me, Phoebe, a few days ago, and *talk* to me and not *tell* me what you knew?' I glanced at the letter again. Then I read the last paragraph aloud.

When Miriam phoned me today she said that she had already told Phoebe everything. Thérèse, Phoebe felt that you should hear what had happened not from her, but from me, as I am the nearest thing to Monique herself. So she arranged with me that I would write to you, and tell you my mother's story. I am very glad to have had the opportunity to do so.

Yours in friendship,
Lena Sands

I looked at Mrs Bell. 'I'm sorry you had to wait. But it wasn't my story to tell – and I knew that Lena would write immediately.'

Mrs Bell heaved a sigh, then her eyes filled with tears again. 'I'm so happy,' she murmured. 'And so *sad*.'

'Why?' I whispered. 'Because Monique was alive, but you didn't hear from her?' Mrs Bell nodded, then another tear slid down her cheek. 'But Lena says that Monique didn't like talking about Avignon – it's understandable, given what happened there; she probably wanted to draw a veil over that part of her life. Plus she may not have known if *you* had survived the war – or where you were.' Mrs Bell nodded. 'And then you'd moved to London, and she was in America. Today, with modern communications, you'd have found each other again. But in a way you have found each other now.'

Mrs Bell reached for my hand. 'You have done so much for me, Phoebe – more, possibly, than anyone – but I am going to ask you to do one thing more . . . Perhaps you have guessed what it is.'

I nodded then I re-read Lena's PS:

Thérèse, I will be in London in late February. I do hope I may have the chance to see you then as I know that that would have made my mother very happy.

I gave Mrs Bell back the letter, then I went to the wardrobe and took out the blue coat in its protective cover. I turned to her.

'Of course I will,' I said.

FIFTEEN

Christmas had almost arrived. The shop was very busy so I had Katie coming in to help me on Saturdays, and Mum was back at work, feeling happy, and looking forward to seeing Louis again with Dad on Christmas Eve. She decided that she ought to have some sort of party for her birthday on January 10th and joked that she was going to have it on a bus.

I began to plan the fashion show, which was to be held at Blackheath Halls – luckily there'd been a cancellation for the Great Hall on February 1st.

I saw Mrs Bell twice more. The first time she knew I was there, though she was very sleepy with the drugs. The second time, on December 21st, she seemed unaware of my presence. By then she was being given morphine twenty-four hours a day. So I just sat and held her hand and told her how glad I was that I'd known her and that I wouldn't forget her, and that I even felt a bit stronger now when I thought about Emma. At that, I felt a slight pressure from Mrs Bell's fingers. Then I kissed her goodbye. As I walked home in the gathering dusk I looked at the cloud-streaked sky and realised that it was the shortest day and that the light would soon be returning.

As I arrived home my phone rang. It was Sue. 'Phoebe – I'm sorry, but I'm calling to say that Mrs Bell died at ten to four – a few minutes after you'd left.'

'I see.'

'She was very peaceful, as you saw.' I felt my eyes fill. 'She obviously felt very close to you,' I heard Sue add as I sat on the hall chair. 'I assume you must have known her for a long time.'

'No.' I reached into my pocket for a tissue. 'Less than four months. But it feels like a lifetime.'

I waited a few minutes then I phoned Annie, who sounded surprised to be hearing from me on a Sunday evening. 'Are you all right, Phoebe?' she asked.

'I'm fine.' I swallowed. 'But, do you have a few minutes, Annie? Because there's a story I want to tell you . . .'

The next couple of days were busy, then on Christmas Eve the shop went quiet. I watched people walking past the windows laden with bags and I looked across the Heath towards The Paragon and thought about Mrs Bell and about how glad I was that I'd met her. I felt that in helping her I'd perhaps healed some small part of myself.

At five o'clock I was upstairs in the stockroom, sorting things for the sale, putting gloves, hats and belts in boxes – when I heard the door bell ring, then footsteps. I went downstairs, expecting to see a customer in search of a last-minute Christmas present; instead, there was Miles, looking suave in a beige winter coat with a brown velvet collar.

'Hello, Phoebe,' he said quietly.

I stared at him, my heart banging in my ribcage, then I came down the rest of the stairs. 'I was . . . about to close.'

'Well . . . I just . . . wanted to talk to you.' I noticed again the huskiness in Miles' voice that had always tugged at my heartstrings. 'It won't take long.'

I turned the sign to 'Closed', then went behind the counter, pretending that I needed to do something there.

'Have you been well?' I asked him, for want of anything else to say.

'I've been . . . fine,' he replied soberly. 'Quite busy, but . . .' He put his hand into his coat pocket. 'I just wanted to bring you this.' He stepped forward and put a small green box down on the counter. I opened it then shut my eyes with relief. Inside was the emerald ring that had been my grandmother's, then my mother's and then mine, and which might one day, it now occurred to me, be my daughter's, if I was lucky enough to have one. I closed my fingers around it for a moment then slipped it on my right hand. I looked at Miles. 'I'm very happy to have this back.'

'Of course. You must be.' A red stain had crept up his neck. 'I brought it as soon as I could.'

'So you've only just found it?'

He nodded. 'Last night.'

'So . . . where?'

I saw a muscle at the corner of Miles' mouth flex. 'In Roxy's bedside table.' He shook his head. 'She'd left the drawer open, and I caught a glimpse of it.'

I exhaled slowly. 'What did you say?'

'I was livid with her, of course – not just for taking it, but for the lies she told. I said that we were going to get counselling for her about this, because – and this is hard for me to admit – she needs it.' He gave a resigned shrug. 'I suppose I've known that for some time but didn't want to face up to it. But Roxy seems to have this sense of, of not having . . . of . . .'

'Deprivation?'

'Yes. That's it.' He pursed his lips. 'Deprivation.' I resisted the urge to tell Miles that perhaps he should have counselling too. 'Anyway, I'm sorry, Phoebe.' He shook his head. 'I'm sorry in every way, actually, because you meant a lot to me.'

'Well . . . thank you for bringing the ring back. It can't have been easy.'

'No. I . . . Anyway . . .' He heaved a sigh. 'There it is. But I hope you have a happy Christmas.' He gave me a bleak smile.

'Thanks, Miles – I hope you do too.' Now, with nothing left to say to each other, I unlocked the door and Miles left, and I watched him walk down the street until he was quite out of sight. Then I turned the sign to 'Closed' and went back upstairs.

Despite my relief over the ring, the encounter with Miles had left me upset and disturbed. I was moving some dresses from one rail to another and one of the hangers got caught on its neighbour and I was unable to release it; I was tugging at it, trying to unhook it, but I couldn't so I ended up just pulling the garment, a Dior blouse, off the hanger – but so roughly that I ripped the silk. I sank on to the floor and burst into tears. I stayed there for a few minutes, then, as I heard All Saints Church strike six o'clock, I pushed myself to my feet. As I went wearily downstairs my mobile phone rang. It was Dan, which raised my spirits again because the sound of his voice always does. He wanted to know if I'd be interested in going round later for a 'private screening' of a 'particularly seductive' classic.

'Not *Emmanuelle 3*?' I said, suddenly smiling.

'No, but close. It's *Godzilla vs King Kong*. I managed to get a 16mm copy on eBay last week. But I do have *Emmanuelle 3*, if you're interested for another time.'

'Hm – I might be actually.'

'Come round any time from seven – I'll cook a risotto.' I found myself longing to sit with Dan, big and solid and comforting and cheerful, watching a schlocky old classic in his wonderful shed.

Feeling happier now, I got the *Sale!* banners out of their box, ready to plaster over the windows on Boxing Day to announce the first day of the sale on the 27th. Annie was going to be away until early January as she wanted to take advantage of this quiet time of year to write, so I'd got Katie to stand in for her, and then from mid January onwards Katie was going to work for me every Saturday. I got my coat and bag and locked up.

As I walked home, the sharp wind stinging my cheeks, I allowed myself to look forward, if only cautiously, to the New Year. There'd be the sale, then my mother's big birthday, then the fashion show – that was going to take a lot of organising. Later there'd be Emma's anniversary to get through, but I was trying not to think of that now.

I turned up Bennett Street, unlocked my front door

and went inside. I picked the mail off the mat – a few late Christmas cards including one from Daphne; then I went into the kitchen and poured myself a glass of wine. From outside I could hear singing, then the bell rang. I opened the door.

Silent night, Holy night . . .

There were four children, with an adult, collecting for Crisis.

All is calm. All is bright . . .

I put some money in the tin, listened to the end of the carol, then closed the door and went upstairs to get ready to meet Dan. At seven I heard the bell again. I ran down and picked up my purse from the hall table, assuming it to be more carol singers as I wasn't expecting anyone.

As I opened the door I felt as though I'd been plunged into ice-water.

'Hello, Phoebe,' said Guy.

'Can I come in?' he asked after a moment.

'Oh. Yes.' I thought my legs would give way. 'I . . . wasn't expecting you.'

'No. Sorry – I just thought I'd drop by, as I'm on my way to Chislehurst.'

'To see your parents?'

Guy nodded. He was wearing the white skiing jacket that he'd bought in Val d'Isère: I remembered that he'd only chosen it because I'd liked it. 'So you survived the banking crisis?' I said as we went into the kitchen.

'I did.' Guy drew in his breath. 'Just. But . . . can I sit down for a minute or two, Phoebe?'

'Of course,' I said nervously. As he sat at the table I looked at Guy's handsome, open face and his blue eyes, and his short dark hair which was longer than I remembered him wearing it, and visibly greying now at the temples. 'Can I get you anything? A drink? A cup of coffee?'

He shook his head. 'No. Nothing, thanks – I can't stay long.'

I leaned against the worktop, my heart racing. 'So . . . what brings you here?'

'Phoebe,' Guy replied patiently, 'you *know*.'

I gave him a quizzical look. 'I do?'

'Yes. You know that I'm here because for months now I've been trying to talk to you but you've ignored all my letters and e-mails and calls.' He began fiddling with some holly I'd put around the base of a big white candle. 'Your attitude has been completely . . . implacable.' He looked at me. 'I didn't know what to do. I knew that if I tried to arrange a meeting with you, you'd refuse to come.' That was true, I reflected. I would have refused. 'But tonight, knowing that I'd be almost passing your door, I thought I'd just see if you were here . . . because . . .' Guy heaved a painful sigh, '. . . there's this unfinished . . . issue between us, Phoebe.'

'It's finished for me.'

'But it isn't for *me*,' he countered, 'and I'd like to resolve it.'

I felt my breathing increase. 'I'm sorry, Guy, but there's nothing to resolve.'

'There *is*,' he insisted wearily. 'And I need to start the New Year feeling that I've finally laid it to rest.'

I folded my arms. 'Guy – if you didn't like what I said to you nine months ago, then why can't you just . . . forget about it?'

He stared at me. 'Because it's far too serious to *be* forgotten – as you very well know. And as I've tried to live my life decently I can't bear the idea that I would stand accused of something so . . . terrible.' I suddenly realised that I hadn't emptied the dishwasher. 'Phoebe,' I heard Guy say as I turned away from him, 'I need to discuss what happened that night just once – and then never again. That's why I'm here.'

I pulled out two plates. 'But I don't *want* to discuss it. Plus I'm going out soon.'

'Well, would you please hear me out – just for a minute or two.' Guy clasped his hands on the table in front of him. He looked as though he was praying, I reflected, as I put the plates in the cupboard. But I did not want to have this conversation. I felt trapped, and angry. 'First of all I'd like to say that I'm sorry.' I turned and stared at Guy. 'I'm truly sorry if I did or said anything that night that might have contributed, however inadvertently, to what happened to Emma. Please forgive me, Phoebe.' I hadn't expected this. I felt my resentment subside. 'But I need you to acknowledge that the charge *you* levelled at me was completely unfair.'

I took two glass tumblers out of the dishwasher. 'No, I won't – because it was *true*.'

Guy shook his head. 'Phoebe, it was *un*true – and you knew that then just as you know it now.' I put a tumbler on the shelf. 'You were obviously very distressed . . .'

'Yes. I was distraught.' I put the second tumbler on the shelf, so hard that I almost cracked it.

'And when people are in that state they can say terrible things.'

If it weren't for you – she'd still be alive!

'But you blamed *me* for Emma's death, and I've been unable to bear the accusation. It's haunted me, all this time. You said that I'd persuaded you not to go and see Emma.'

Now I faced him. 'You *did* do that! You said that she was that "mad milliner" remember, who "exaggerated" everything.' I took the cutlery basket out of the dishwasher and began flinging the knives into the drawer.

'I *did* say that,' I heard Guy say. 'I was pretty fed up with Emma by then – I don't deny it – and she did make a drama out of everything. But I only said that this was something you needed to bear in mind before rushing round to see her.'

I threw in the spoons and forks. 'Then you said that we should go to the Bluebird, as planned, and have dinner because you'd booked it and didn't want to miss it.'

Guy nodded. 'I admit that I said that too. But I *added* that if you really didn't want to come then I'd cancel the table. I said that it was *your* call.' I stared at Guy, the blood rushing in my ears now, then turned back to the dishwasher and took out a milk jug. 'Phoebe, *you* then said that we *should* go out to dinner. You said that you'd phone Emma again when we got back.'

'No.' I put the jug down on the counter. 'That was *your* suggestion – *your* compromise.'

Guy was shaking his head. 'It was yours.' I felt the familiar sliding sensation. 'I remember being surprised, but I said that Emma was your friend and that I'd go with your judgement on the matter.'

I was suddenly filled with dismay. 'Okay . . .' I *did* say that we should have dinner – but only because I didn't want to disappoint you, and because it was Valentine's Day so it was going to be a bit special.'

'You said we wouldn't be out for long.'

'Well, that's right,' I said. 'And we weren't: then when we got back I *did* phone Emma – I phoned her straight away; and I *was* going to go round to her house then, right *then* –' I stared at Guy. 'But you *dissuaded* me. You said that I was probably over the limit to drive. You were making these drinking-and-driving gestures at me while I was on the phone to her.'

'I *did* do that, yes – because I knew you almost certainly *were* over the limit.'

'Well there you are then!' I slammed shut the dishwasher. 'You *stopped* me from going to see Emma.'

Guy was shaking his head. 'No. Because I *then* said that you should therefore go round to her house in a taxi and that I'd go outside and hail one for you. And I was about to do that, if you remember – I'd even opened the front door . . .' Now I was no longer sliding, but falling, hurtling into a chasm. '. . . when you suddenly said that you weren't going to go after all. You said you'd decided not to.' Guy was staring at me. I tried to swallow but my mouth had dried. 'You said that you thought Emma would be okay until the morning.' At that my legs gave way. I sank on to a chair. 'You said that she'd sounded so tired, and that it would probably be best for her just to have a long sleep.' As I stared at the table, I felt my eyes fill. 'Phoebe,' I heard Guy say quietly, 'I'm sorry to bring all this up again. But having something *so* grave flung at me, without any chance to rebut it, has disturbed my peace of mind all these months. I've been unable to let it go. So I just want – no, *need* you to acknowledge that what you said just wasn't true.'

I looked at Guy – his features had blurred. In my mind's eye I could see the forecourt of the Bluebird Café, and Guy's flat, then the narrow staircase at Emma's house and finally her bedroom door as I pushed on it. I drew in my breath. 'All right then,' I croaked. 'All right,' I reiterated quietly. 'Perhaps . . .' I stared out of the window. 'Perhaps I . . .' I bit my lip.

'Perhaps you didn't remember it quite right,' I heard Guy say softly.

I nodded. 'Perhaps I didn't. You see . . . I was very upset.'

'Yes – so it's understandable that you . . . forgot what really happened.'

I stared at Guy. 'No – it was more than that.' I looked down at the table. 'I couldn't bear the thought of having to blame only *myself*.'

Guy reached for my hand and enclosed it in both his. 'Phoebe – I don't think you *were* to blame. You couldn't have known how ill Emma was. You were simply doing what seemed to be right for your friend. And the doctor told you that it was very unlikely that Emma would have survived even if she had come into hospital the previous night . . .'

I looked at Guy. 'But it's not knowing for *sure*. It's the terrible, tantalising possibility that she *might* have survived if I'd only done things differently.' I covered my face with my hands. 'And how I wish, wish, *wish* that I *had*.'

My head sank to my chest. Then I heard Guy's chair being scraped back and he came and sat next to me. 'Phoebe – you and I were in love,' he whispered.

I nodded.

'But what happened just – smashed everything up. When you phoned me that morning to say that Emma had died I knew then that our relationship wouldn't survive it.'

'No.' I swallowed. 'How could we have been happy after that?'

'I don't think we could. It would always have cast a shadow over our lives. But I couldn't bear to have parted from you on such awful terms.' Guy shrugged. 'But how I wish that it had never happened . . .'

'How I wish that too.' I stared bleakly ahead. 'I wish it with all my heart.' The phone was ringing, forcing me to surface from the fantasy of what might have been. I grabbed a piece of kitchen towel, pressed it to my eyes, then answered.

'Hey – where *are* you?' said Dan. 'The film's about to start and they get shirty with latecomers here.'

'Oh. I will be coming, Dan.' I coughed to cover my tears. 'But a little later, if that's okay.' I sniffed. 'No . . . I'm fine, I think I'm just getting a cold. Yes, I'll definitely be there.' I glanced at Guy. 'But I don't think I can face Godzilla and King Kong.'

'We won't watch it then,' I heard Dan say. 'We don't have to watch anything. We can just listen to music, or play cards. It doesn't matter – just come whenever you can.'

I put the phone back in its cradle.

'Are you with someone now?' Guy asked gently. 'I hope you are,' he added. 'I want you to be happy.'

'Well . . .' I wiped my eyes again. 'I have this . . . friend. That's all he is for now – just a friend, but I like being with him. He's a good person, Guy. Like you.'

Guy inhaled, then slowly let out his breath. 'I'm going to go now, Phoebe. I'm so glad I've seen you.'

I nodded.

I walked him to the front door. 'I wish you a happy Christmas, Phoebe,' said Guy. 'And I hope this year will be a good one.'

'For you too,' I whispered as he hugged me.

Guy held me for another moment, then left.

I spent Christmas Day with Mum, who had at last, I noticed, taken off her wedding ring. She had a copy of the January edition of *Woman & Home* with its 'Ring in the Old' fashion spread, featuring my clothes with a prominent credit, I was glad to see. A few pages further on I saw a photo of Reese Witherspoon at the Emmy awards wearing the midnight blue Balenciaga gown that I'd got at Christie's. So this was the A-Lister who Cindi had bought the dress for. Seeing such a big star in a dress I'd sourced gave me a buzz.

After lunch Dad phoned to say how thrilled Louis was with the Lights'n'Sounds baby walker Mum had given him the day before and with my Thomas the Tank Engine starter set. Dad said he hoped we'd both come and see Louis again soon, and as we watched the *Dr Who* Christmas special Mum did some more to the blue pram coat she's been knitting Louis and which I've given her the aeroplane buttons for.

'Thank God they're getting a nanny for Louis,' she said as she looped the yarn over the needle.

'Yes – and Dad said he's going to do some teaching at the Open University so that's given him a boost.' Mum nodded sympathetically.

On the 27th the sale began and the shop was heaving, and I was able to tell everyone about the vintage fashion show and to ask those customers I had in mind whether they'd be willing to model the clothes. Carla, who'd bought the turquoise cupcake, said she'd love to – she added that it would be the week before her wedding but that it would be fine. Katie said she'd happily model her yellow prom dress. Through Dan I got in touch with Kelly Marks and she said she'd be delighted to wear her 'Tinker Bell' dress, as she called it. Then the woman who'd bought the pink prom dress came in. So I explained that I was putting on a vintage fashion show for charity and asked her if she'd model her pink cupcake dress for it.

Her face lit up. 'I'd love to – what fun. When is it?' I told her. She got out her diary and wrote it down. 'Model . . . happy . . . dress,' she murmured. 'The only thing *is* . . . no, it's okay.' Whatever she had been about to say, she'd clearly thought better of it. 'February 1st will be fine.'

On January 5th I took the morning off to go to Mrs Bell's funeral at the crematorium in Verdant Lane. It was a very small affair: there were two friends of hers from Blackheath, her home-help, Paola, and Mrs Bell's nephew, James, and his wife, Yvonne, both in their late forties.

'Thérèse was quite ready to go,' Yvonne said as we looked at the flowers afterwards by the side of the chapel. She drew her charcoal wrap more closely round her shoulders in the thin wind.

'She did seem contented,' said James. 'When I saw her the last time she told me that she felt quite calm and . . . happy. She used the word "happy".'

Yvonne was examining a spray of irises. 'The card on this one says *With love from Lena*.' She turned to

James. 'I never heard Thérèse mention anyone called Lena – did you, darling?' He shrugged then shook his head.

'*I* heard her mention that name,' I said. 'But I think it was a connection from a long time ago.'

'Phoebe, I've got something for you from my aunt,' said James. He opened his briefcase then handed me a small bag. 'She asked me to give this to you – to remember her by.'

'Thank you.' I took it. 'Not that I'll ever forget her.' I couldn't explain why.

When I got home I opened the bag. Inside, wrapped in newspaper, I found the silver carriage clock and a letter, dated December 10th, written in Mrs Bell's by then very shaky hand.

> *My dear Phoebe,*
> *This clock belonged to my parents. I give it to you not just because it was one of the things I most treasured, but by way of reminding you that its hands are going round, and with them all the hours and days and years of your life. Phoebe, I implore you not to spend too much of the precious time you have left regretting what you did or didn't do, or what might or might not have been. And whenever you do feel sad then I hope you will console yourself by remembering the inestimable good that you did me, your friend,*
> *Thérèse*

I re-set the clock, gently wound it with the little key, then put it in the centre of my sitting-room mantelpiece.

'I will look forward,' I said as it began to tick. 'I will look forward.'

And I did – first of all to my mother's birthday.

She held her party in an upstairs room at Chapters wine bar – a sit-down supper for twenty people. In her short speech Mum said she felt that she'd 'come of age'. All her bridge friends were there, and her boss, John, and a couple of other people from work. Mum had also invited a pleasant man called Hamish whom she said she'd met at Betty and Jim's Christmas party.

'He seemed nice,' I said to her over the phone the next day.

'He's very nice,' Mum agreed. 'He's fifty-eight, divorced with two grown-up sons. The funny thing is that Jim and Betty's party was very crowded, but Hamish started talking to me because of what I was wearing. He said he liked the pattern of little palm trees on my outfit. I told him that it was from my daughter's vintage dress shop. That then led to a longer conversation about fabric because his father worked in the textile industry in Paisley. Then he phoned me the next day to ask me out – we went to a concert at the Barbican. We're going to the Coliseum next week,' she added happily.

In the meantime Katie, her friend Sarah, Annie and I were working flat out on the fashion show. Dan was going to do the lights and sound and had assembled a montage of music that would take us seamlessly from Scott Joplin through to the Sex Pistols. A friend of his was going to build the catwalk.

On the Tuesday afternoon we went to the Great Hall to do the run-through, and Dan brought with him a copy of that day's *Black & Green* in which Ellie had written a preview piece about the show.

There are still a few tickets available for the Passion for Vintage Fashion Show which will take place at Blackheath Halls tonight. Tickets are £10, and will be redeemable against purchases at Village Vintage. All profits will go to Malaria No More, a charity that distributes insecticide-treated nets in sub-Saharan Africa where, sadly, malaria kills 3,000 children every day. These bed nets, which cost £2.50 each, will protect up to two children and their mother. The show's organiser, Phoebe Swift, is hoping to raise enough money for the charity to buy a thousand of them.

During the rehearsal I went backstage to the dressing room where the models were getting ready for the fifties sequence and were all in New Look suits, circle skirts and 'wiggle' dresses. Mum was wearing her coatdress, Katie, Kelly Marks and Carla were in their cupcakes, but Lucy, the owner of the pink one, was beckoning to me. 'I've got a bit of a problem,' she whispered. She turned round and I saw that the top of her dress gaped by a good two inches.

'I'll give you a stole,' I said. 'It's funny,' I added as I looked at her, 'but it fitted you perfectly when you bought it.'

'I know.' Lucy smiled. 'But you see I wasn't pregnant then.'

I looked at her. 'You're . . .?'

She nodded. 'Four months.'

'Oh!' I hugged her. 'That is so . . . *brilliant.*'

Lucy's eyes were shining with tears. 'I can still hardly believe it myself. I couldn't mention it when you first asked me to be a model because I wasn't at the telling stage; but now I've had my first scan, I can talk about it.'

'So it was the happy dress that did it!' I said delightedly.

Lucy laughed. 'I'm not sure – but I'll tell you what I do attribute it to though.' She lowered her voice. 'At the beginning of October my husband went into your shop. He wanted to buy me something to cheer me up, and he saw some lovely lingerie – beautiful slips and cami-knickers and what have you from the 1940s.'

'I remember him buying those,' I said. 'But I didn't know who he was. So they were for you?'

Lucy nodded. 'And not long afterwards . . .' She patted her tummy then giggled.

'Well,' I said. 'That's . . . wonderful.'

So Aunt Lydia's lingerie had been making up for lost time.

Katie was going to wear the Madame Grès dress that I'd bought at Christie's for the 1930s section; Annie, with her slim boyish figure, would be modelling clothes from the twenties and sixties. Four of my regular customers would be wearing the 1940s and 1980s garments. Joan was helping backstage with the changing and accessories and was now hanging the clothes on their respective rails.

After the run-through Annie and Mum put out the glasses for the drinks. As they opened the boxes I overheard Annie telling Mum about her play, which she's almost finished and which is provisionally entitled *The Blue Coat*.

'I hope it ends happily,' I heard Mum say anxiously.

'Don't worry,' Annie replied. 'It does. I'm going to put it on as a lunchtime show at the Age Exchange in May. There's a little fifty-seater theatre there which will be perfect for it.'

'It sounds terrific,' Mum said. 'Perhaps after that you might get it put on at a bigger venue.'

Annie opened a case of wine. 'I'll certainly try, I'm going to invite managers and agents to see it. Chloë Sevigny was in the shop again the other day – she said she'd come along if she's in London then.'

Now Dan and I began to arrange the seating, setting out two hundred red velvet chairs on either side of the catwalk that extended twenty-five feet from the centre of the stage. Then, satisfied that everything was ready, I went and changed into Mrs Bell's damson-coloured suit, which looks as though it was made for me. As I put it on I caught the faint scent of Ma Griffe.

At 6.30 p.m. the doors opened, and an hour later every seat was full. As a hush descended Dan dimmed the lights and gave me the nod. I went up on stage and lifted the mic off its stand, nervously surveying the sea of upturned faces.

'I'm Phoebe Swift,' I began. 'I'd like to welcome you tonight and to thank you all for coming. We're going to enjoy ourselves, look at some beautiful old clothes, and raise money for a very worthwhile cause. I'd also like to say . . .' I felt my fingers tighten around the mic '. . . that this event is dedicated to the memory of my friend, Emma Kitts.' Now the soundtrack started, Dan brought up the lights, and the first models walked out . . .

* * *

It was a day I'd dreaded for so long. Now here it was. No anniversary would be as hard as this one, I realised as I got in the car and drove to Greenwich Cemetery. As I walked down the gravelled path past graves recent and graves so old that you could barely read the names carved on to them, I looked up and saw Daphne and Derek, who appeared calm and composed. Next to them were Emma's uncle and aunt and her two cousins, and Emma's photographer friend Charlie who was chatting quietly to her assistant, Sian, who was clutching a hanky. Finally, there was Father Bernard, who had conducted Emma's funeral.

I hadn't been to the cemetery since that day – I'd been unable to face it – and so this was the first time that I'd seen Emma's headstone. The sight of it gave me a shock – the awful, emphatic, irrefutability of it.

Emma Mandisa Kitts, 1974–2008.
Beloved daughter, forever in our hearts.

Clumps of snowdrops hung their dainty heads at the foot of the grave while crocus spears pushed through the cold ground, unfurling their purple flowers. I'd brought a posy of tulips, daffodils and bluebells, and as I laid it down on the black granite it made me think of Mrs Bell's hatbox. As I straightened up the early spring sunlight stung my eyes.

Father Bernard now said a few words of welcome, then he asked Derek to speak. Derek said that he and Daphne had called Emma 'Mandisa' because that meant 'sweet' in Xhosa and she was a sweet person; he spoke of his hat collection, and of how Emma's fascination with it as a child was what led to her becoming a milliner. Daphne talked of how talented Emma was, of how modest she'd always been, and of how much they missed her. I heard Sian stifle a sob and saw Charlie put his arm round her. Then Father Bernard said a prayer, gave a blessing and it was over. As we all drifted back along the path I wished that the anniversary hadn't fallen on a Sunday – I would have been grateful for the distraction of work. As we reached the cemetery gates, Daphne and Derek invited everyone back to the house.

It was years since I'd been there. In the sitting room I chatted to Sian and Charlie, then to Emma's uncle and aunt; then I went into the kitchen, through the utility room and out into the garden. I stood by the plane tree.

I really fooled you there, didn't I?

'Yes, you really did,' I murmured.

You thought I was dead!

'No. I thought you were sleeping . . .'

Now I looked up and saw Daphne at the kitchen window. She lifted her hand in greeting – then disappeared, and now she was walking across the grass towards me. I noticed how grey her hair had become.

'Phoebe,' she said softly. She reached for my hand. 'I hope you're okay.'

I swallowed. 'I'm . . . fine, thanks, Daphne. I'm . . . well, I keep myself busy.'

She nodded. 'That's a good thing. You've made such a success of the shop – and I saw in the local paper that your fashion show was a great hit.'

'It was. We raised just over three thousand pounds –

enough to buy twelve hundred mosquito nets and so . . . well . . .' I shrugged. 'It's something, isn't it?'

'It is. We're really proud of you, Phoebe,' Daphne said. 'And Emma would have been, too. But I just wanted to tell you that Derek and I recently went through her things.'

I felt my insides coil. 'Then you must have found her diary,' I interjected, anxious to get the awful moment over.

'I did find it,' Daphne said. 'I knew that I should burn it without even opening it – but I couldn't bear to deprive myself of any part of Emma. So I'm afraid I did read it.' I looked at Daphne, searching her face for the resentment that she must surely feel. 'It made me very sad to think that Emma had been so unhappy in the last months of her life.'

'She *was* unhappy,' I agreed quietly. 'And, as you'll now know, it was my fault. I fell in love with someone that Emma liked and she was terribly upset about it and I feel awful at the thought that I caused her any distress whatsoever. I didn't mean to.' My confession over, I braced myself for Daphne's censure.

'Phoebe,' said Daphne. 'In her diary, Emma expressed no anger with you at all: on the contrary; she said you'd done nothing wrong – she said that almost made it worse for her – that she couldn't blame you. She was angry with herself for not being more . . . grown-up, I suppose, about the situation. She admitted that she was unable to conquer her negative feelings, but she acknowledged that she'd get over it in time.'

Time she didn't have. I put my hands in my pockets. 'I wish none of it had ever happened, Daphne.'

Daphne was shaking her head. 'But that's like saying you wish "life" had never happened. This was just life, happening, Phoebe. Don't reproach yourself. You were such a good friend to Emma.'

'No. I wasn't always. You see . . .' I wasn't going to torment Daphne with the thought that I might have saved Emma. 'I feel I let Emma down,' I said quietly. 'I could have done more. That night. I'm . . .'

'Phoebe, none of us knew how ill she was.' Daphne interjected. 'Imagine how *I* feel knowing that I was on holiday, and uncontactable . . .' Tears had pooled in her eyes. 'Emma made an awful . . . mistake. It cost her her life – but we all have to go on. And you must try to be happy now, Phoebe – otherwise two lives will have been spoilt. You'll never forget Emma; she was your best friend and she'll always be a part of who you are, but you must live your life *well*.' I nodded, then reached into my pocket for my hanky. 'Now.' Daphne swallowed. 'I wanted to give you a couple of things of Emma's as a keepsake. Come with me.' I followed Daphne back into the kitchen where she picked up a red box. Inside was the gold Krugerrand. 'Emma's grandparents gave this to her when she was born. I'd like you to have it.'

'Thank you,' I said. 'Emma treasured this, and I will too.'

'Then there's this –' Daphne gave me the ammonite.

I placed it in the palm of my hand. It felt warm. 'I was with Emma when she found this on the beach at Lyme Regis. That's a very happy memory. Thank you, Daphne. But . . .' I gave her a half smile. 'I think I'll go now.'

'But you will keep in touch with Derek and me, won't

you, Phoebe? The door will always be open, so please walk through it sometimes, and let us know how you are.'

Daphne put her arms round me, and I nodded. 'I will.'

A few minutes after I'd got home, Dan called. He asked me about my visit to the cemetery – he knows about Emma now. Then he wondered if I'd look at yet another possible site for his cinema – a Victorian warehouse in Lewisham.

'I've just seen it in the property section of the *Observer*,' he explained. 'Will you come with me while I check out the exterior? Can I pick you up in twenty minutes?'

'Sure.' I welcomed the distraction, apart from anything else.

Dan and I had already looked at a biscuit factory in Charlton, a disused library in Kidbrooke and an old bingo hall in Catford.

'The location's *got* to be right,' he said as we drove up Belmont Hill half an hour later. 'I need to find something in an area where there isn't already a cinema within two miles.'

'And when do you hope to open?'

Dan slowed his black Golf and turned left. 'Ideally I'd like it to be up and running by this time next year.'

'And what will you call it?'

'I was wondering about "Cine Qua Non".'

'Hmm . . . not quite popular enough.'

'All right, then – the Lewisham Lux.'

Dan drove down Roxborough Way then parked outside a brown brick warehouse. He opened the car door. 'This is it.' As I didn't want to follow him over the locked gate in my silk skirt I told him I'd go for a stroll. I walked onto Lewisham High Street, passing Nat West, a curtain shop, Argos and a British Red Cross charity shop. Then I came to Dixons, in the window of which were a number of plasma TV's. As I walked past I suddenly stopped. On the biggest screen was Mags, standing in front of a studio audience, in a scarlet trouser suit and black stilettos. She was holding her fingers to her temples and now she began to pace up and down. As the audio text was on, I could see what she was saying. *'I'm getting a military man. A straight backed sort of fellow. Liked a nice cigar . . .'* She looked up. *Does that mean anything to anyone?* As the audience looked blank I rolled my eyes then was suddenly aware of Dan standing next to me.

'That was quick,' I said, glancing at his lovely profile. 'How was it?'

'Well I liked the look of it so I'll call the agent first thing. The fabric of the building seems fine and the size is perfect.' Now, noticing me staring at Mags he followed my gaze. 'Why are you looking at that, sweetheart?' He peered at the screen. 'Is she a psychic?'

'That's what she says.'

Just think of me as your switchboard operator . . .

I told Dan how I'd met Mags.

'So are you interested in spiritualism then?'

'No. Not really,' I said, as we walked away.

'By the way my mum just phoned,' Dan added as we strolled back to the car, hand in hand. 'She was wondering if we'd like to go over to them for tea next Sunday.'

'Next Sunday?' I echoed. 'I would have loved to, but I can't – there's something I have to do. Something important.'

As we drove away I explained what it was.

'Well . . . that *is* important,' Dan said.

415

EPILOGUE

Sunday 22nd February, 2009

I am walking down Marylebone High Street, not as I so often do, in my dreams but for real, to meet a woman I have never met before. In my hand, is a carrier bag that I clutch as tightly as if it held the crown jewels.

It was my fantasy that I would one day give Monique the coat . . .

I pass the ribbon and trimming shop.

. . . and can you believe, it still is?

When Lena phoned me to say that her hotel was in the heart of Marylebone my heart had lurched. 'I've found a great little café close to the bookshop,' she'd said. 'I thought we might meet there – it's called "Amici's". Would that be all right?' And I was about to say that I'd rather go anywhere else because of the painful associations that that particular café has for me, when I suddenly changed my mind. The last time I'd been there something sad had happened. Now a positive thing would take place there instead . . .

As I push on the door, the owner, Carlo, sees me and gives me a sympathetic wave, and now, I see a slim, smartly dressed woman in her early fifties leave her table and come towards me, smiling tentatively.

'Phoebe?'

'Lena,' I say warmly. As we shake hands I take in the lively expression, high cheekbones, and dark hair. 'You're like your mother.'

She seems astonished. 'But how would you know?'

'You'll see in a moment,' I say. I get the coffees, exchanging a few words with Carlo, then I take them to the table. In her soft Californian accent Lena tells me about her trip to London, to attend the wedding of an old friend the next day at Marylebone Register Office. She says she's looking forward to it, but is very jet-lagged.

Now, with the social pleasantries out of the way we come to the purpose of our meeting. I open the carrier and I hand Lena the coat, the story of which she mostly knows.

She fingers the sky blue cloth, stroking the nap of the wool, the silk lining and the fine hand stitching. 'It's lovely. So Therese's mother made this . . .' She looks at me with a surprised smile. 'She was *good*.'

'She *was* good. It's beautifully made.'

Lena strokes the collar. 'But how amazing to think that Therese *never* gave up on the idea of giving it to Mom.'

I have kept it for sixty-five years, and I will keep it until I die.

'She just wanted to keep her promise to her,' I say. 'And now, in a way, she has.'

417

Lena's face fills with sadness. 'Poor girl, though – not knowing what happened all these years. Never putting it to rest . . . until the end.'

Now as we sip our coffee I tell Lena more about what happened, and about how Therese had been distracted that fatal night by Jean-Luc and how she had never forgiven herself for revealing Monique's hiding place.

'My mother might well have been discovered anyway,' Lena says. She lowers her cup. 'She used to say that it was so hard staying in that barn, in silence and solitude, all day – she used to comfort herself by remembering the songs her mother used to sing to her – that it was almost a relief when she was found. Of course she had no idea what awaited her,' Lena adds darkly.

'She was *so* lucky,' I murmur.

'Yes.' Lena stares at her coffee, lost in her own thoughts for a few seconds. 'My mother's survival was . . . a miracle. Which makes my existence one too – I never forget that. And I often think of that young German officer who saved her that day.'

Now I give Lena the padded envelope. She opens it and takes out the necklace. 'It's lovely,' she says as she holds it to the light. She fingers the pink and bronze glass beads. 'My mother never mentioned this.' She looks at me. 'How does it fit into the story?'

As I explain I imagine Therese desperately searching for the beads amongst the straw. She must have picked up every one. 'I think the clasp is fine,' I say as Lena opens it. 'Therese said she had it re-strung some years ago.' Lena puts the necklace on and the beads glimmer and sparkle against her black sweater. 'And this is the last thing.' I hand her the ochre envelope.

Lena slides out the photo, searches the sea of faces, then her finger goes straight to Monique. She looks at me. 'So that's how you knew what my mom looked like.'

I nod. 'And that's Therese, standing next to her, there.' Now I point to Jean-Luc and Lena's face clouds.

'Mom was very bitter about that boy,' she says. 'She could never get over the fact that he'd been her school mate and had betrayed her.' Now I tell Lena about the good thing that Jean-Luc did a decade later. She shakes her head in wonderment. 'How I wish my mother had known. But she cut off all contact with Rochemare though she said she often dreamed about the house. She would dream that she was running through its rooms, looking for her parents and her brothers, and calling out for someone, anyone, to help her.'

I feel a tiny shiver run through me.

'Well . . .' Lena hugs the coat, then folds it. 'I'll treasure this, Phoebe, and in due course I'll pass it on to my daughter Monica. She's twenty six now – so she was only four when Mom died. She remembers her and she sometimes asks me about her life so this will help her know the story.

I pick up a paper napkin. It has 'Amici's' printed on it. 'There's something else that'll help her know the story,' I say. Now I tell Lena about Annie, and about the play.

Lena's face lights up. 'But that's wonderful. So it's been written by a friend of yours?'

I think of how much I've come to like Annie in the six months since I've known her. 'Yes. She's a good friend.'

'Perhaps I'll come back and see it,' Lena says. 'With Monica – if we can, we will. But for now . . .' She puts the coat and photo carefully into the bag. 'It's been so good to see you Phoebe.' She smiles. 'Thank you.'

'I'm glad I've met you,' I say. We stand up.

'So . . . is there anything else?' Lena says.

'No.' I reply happily. 'There's nothing else.' Then we say our goodbyes, and promise to keep in touch. As I walk away my phone rings. It's Dan.

ACKNOWLEDGEMENTS

I'd like to thank the following people for their help in the planning and writing of this book. For their expertise on vintage clothing, Kerry Taylor of Kerry Taylor Auctions, Sonya Smith-Hughes and Deborah Eastlake of Biba Lives, Claire Stansfield and Stephen Philip of Rellik, Marianne Sundholm of Circa Vintage, Dolly Diamond of Dolly Diamond, and Pauline and Guy Thomas of Fashion Era. For information about Provence I'm grateful to Frank Wiseman, and to Georges Frechet of the Avignon Mediatheque for making available to me research material about Avignon during the war. For educating me about viticulture I'm indebted to the Boiron family of Bosquet des Papes, and to Nathalie Panissieres of Chateau Fines Roches. I'd also like to thank Rich Mead, assistant editor of Metro newspaper, Carole Bronsdon, G.P., Jonathan and Kim Causer, Peter Crawford, Ellen Stead, Louise Clairmonte, yet again, the staff of Blackheath Halls and of the Age Exchange, and Sophia Wallace-Turner for correcting my French. Any mistakes or inaccuracies are my own.

I'm indebted to my brilliant editor, Claire Bord, and for additional editorial input I'm very grateful to Rachel Hore and Anne O'Brien. Huge thanks to my wonderful agent, Clare Conville, to Jake Smith-Bosanquet and all at Conville and Walsh, and to Ailsa Macalister. At HarperCollins I owe a debt of gratitude to Amanda Ridout, Lynne Drew, Fiona McIntosh, Alice Moss, Victoria Hughes-Williams, Leisa Nugent, Lee Motley, Bartley Shaw, Nicole Abel, Wendy Neale and all in sales.

Finally I would like to thank Greg, Alice and Edmund for their love, support and endless patience during the writing of this book.

BIBLIOGRAPHY

The following books provided helpful background during the course of my research:

France: The Dark Years by Julian Jackson; Oxford University Press.

Vichy France and the Jews by Michael R. Marrus & Robert O. Paxton; Stanford University Press.

People in Auschwitz by Hermann Langbein; University of North Carolina Press, with the United States Holocaust Memorial Museum.

Hiding to Survive: Stories of Jewish Children Rescued from the Holocaust by Maxine Rosenberg; Topeka Bindery.

It's Vintage, Darling! by Chrisa Weil; Hodder & Stoughton.

Shopping for Vintage by Funmi Odulate; Quadrille Publishing Ltd.

Alligators, Old Mink & New Money: One Woman's Adventures in Vintage Clothing by Alison Houtte and Melissa Houtte; Orion Books.